DEN OF LIONS

THE FINAL REMNANT
BOOK 2

TERRY JAMES

HEATHER RENAE

Den of Lions
Paperback Edition
Copyright © 2022 Terry James and Heather Renae

CKN Christian Publishing
An Imprint of Wolfpack Publishing
9850 S. Maryland Parkway. Ste A-5 #323
Las Vegas, NV 89183

cknchristianpublishing.com

Paperback ISBN 978-1-63977-246-9
eBook ISBN 978-1-63977-692-4
LCCN 2022948213

DEN OF LIONS

DEN OF LIONS

ONE
BROKEN CHAINS

CADEN COULDN'T FEEL his legs, he had walked for so long. He could feel his feet just fine, though; they were killing him. His boots felt like they were squeezing the life out of his toes as his heel and ankles were being rubbed raw. He knew there were blisters.

It hadn't taken long for Caden to realize he was way in over his head. He had camped before, did a little hiking now and then with Papa, but this? This was on another level. A level he didn't even come close to. He thought he had acclimated to the Middle East's environment pretty well, but he hadn't been outside for days on end. He hadn't felt the wind constantly throwing bits of sand and grit into his face. He hadn't known the sun, relentless and indifferent, could make him wish he could bathe in sunscreen. The ground was nuts too. Uneven, rocky, and as dry as bones, like the two-headed camel bones he passed a few days ago. The flesh had been stripped clean, and the bones sandblasted white from the wind. Caden had stared into the vacant, shadowed eyes of the camels, knowing he could be next. That and the Giants' footprints really kept him on his toes.

Caden walked on, trying hard not to slip on the loose ground of the Sinai Desert as sand blew into his eyes. He wrapped his shemagh closer to his mouth and nose and tried not to think of ice clinking lazily around in a nice cool glass of water. Little droplets of water would drip down the glass and make a cool pool on the counter. It would be clear water, refreshing, and-

Caden shook his head with a curse and bounced his slipping backpack higher onto his shoulders. *Can't think about that,* he thought. *Lil El's waiting for me.* As he walked, the baseball bat hanging from his belt bounced against his leg. He doubted Harel still needed it. He'd 'borrowed' it from one of Elezario's kids before he knew Asher would give him a gun. He almost pitched it, but the familiar feel of the wooden grip was the only thing to seem normal. Besides, bats and the like had always been his weapon of choice.

Caden gritted his teeth as the terrain sloped downward, descending into more flat, rocky, thorny ground. Again. It was like the land just copied and pasted itself over and over. That, or Caden was walking in circles. He checked his compass and map all the time, trying to forget he still wasn't quite sure how to use them. Elezaro had shown him, but that was a month ago.

Not a month, Caden told himself, blinking hard as he tried to think. *It was a few weeks. No, no... One week?*

He had left Jerusalem five days ago. Caden shook his head and sniffed, hoping to find Ellie soon so he wouldn't totally lose his mind. Already, he thought he heard voices when trying to sleep. Sometimes it was Ellie calling for him, his little sister stumbling around in the dark. He'd wake with a start and try to find her. Once, he called her name into the darkness. She never answered.

I'll find her, Caden thought, his eyes narrowing as he

forced himself to ignore the raw dryness of his throat. *She's all I have left.*

Trace would've liked the Sinai Desert. He'd enjoy counting all the scorpions, finding the longest thorn of the day, and how far he could see from hilltops. He'd laugh about something stupid and convince Caden that stupid thing wasn't stupid and worth laughing at. And Caden would laugh and smile. He wouldn't be so alone. The vast wasteland of the desert was a sharp reminder of the wasteland of loneliness and helplessness Caden always felt.

This inner wasteland was where his internal screaming heightened to a shrilled cry that never stopped. He was so used to it; the cry was now white noise in the background of his life. Not anymore. Now, as he physically walked through the same huge expanse of emptiness he felt inside, he couldn't ignore it. He knew when he uncovered Ellie's corpse, the emptiness would consume him. Her bones would be as dry as the camel-Freak's remains, blown clean by the wind-

Caden stopped short, his jaw flexing. *Leave me alone.* He listened, the wind buffeting him as the sand stirred between the rocks. *Doeg?* Caden thought. *I know you're here.*

"Ah, you know my name."

Caden lifted his chin as his heart quickened. *Go find a dog to kick-*

"I've already cornered one."

Caden's eyes narrowed, and he took a sharp breath, forcing himself onward. He looked to the surrounding hilltops of sandy-brown mountains. A white, furry monster with a half-bitten face should stick out like a sore thumb, shouldn't it? The Shade was nowhere to be seen. Caden wasn't surprised. He suspected Doeg had followed him but hadn't heard its commentary until last night. Maybe. Caden didn't know, the Demon could wiggle its way into

Caden's thoughts quite easily, so who knows when Doeg started whispering lies again.

Demons, Caden thought, a chill running through him.

Mama Lo had talked about them a few times. She always sat up straighter, her lips becoming a tight, thin line, and her words were few. "Evil," she'd say. "They torment and can control people who aren't giving God the control." He hated Doeg.

"Good," Caden heard in his thoughts. *"The feeling is mutual."*

Caden shook his head as though that would get Doeg out of his mind. *I'll find Ellie and get out of here,* Caden thought. *We'll go back to Jerusalem-*

"The Mizrahis will all perish."

We'll rest there and figure out our new life-

"Martyred for their useless pursuit of holiness."

We'll start over. Be a family-

"You will die out here. Alone."

I am not alone.

"True. You have me."

Caden scoffed and lifted his chin, anger tightening his chest. *I have the Raw Peace.*

"You have an emotion you fabricated to resemble a supreme being who safeguards you!" Caden's nostrils flared as he thought of The Door he saw open all those months ago, showing him another way of life. A life with total security, warm love, and the highest level of peace he'd ever felt. *"Felt!"* Doeg snapped. *"Feelings do not equate to the truth!"*

Caden's dry mouth twitched into a smile. The Shade always got upset whenever he mentioned Raw Peace. *Probably because it's Yahweh. He can't win against Him-*

"I scarred your hand, didn't I?" Caden glanced down at the side of his hand. Ophir had stitched it the best she could, but a scar had formed. *"I will touch you again."*

Caden's breath quickened as he stared at the serpentine scar. *"Nothing you can do will repel or deter me, human boy."*

Caden looked forward and cleared his throat. *Raw Peace.*

"Boy-"

Raw Peace.

"Do you sense peace? Do you have peace? It is far from you!"

Raw Peace. Raw Peace is Yahweh. Yahweh.

"He isn't listening, GJ."

Caden flinched as the old nickname jabbed his heart. *Don't call me that.*

"If you find Ellie, she will perish under your care, just like Trace."

Caden took in a sharp breath. *Stop it-*

"And Nate. And if you and your siblings hadn't invaded Mama Lo and Papa's life, they would not have been crushed under the weight of childrearing."

I didn't kill them-

"Your mother died of cancer."

Yes!

"Cancer, at least, is what you were told."

I can't cause cancer! She got sick!

"Why did she fall ill?"

I-

"What wore down her body's defenses? What weakened her so? Who ended her life?"

I didn't-

"Their blood is on your hands-"

Caden ripped back his shemagh and screamed into the desert. His cry echoed off the far mountains. He stood, panting, his throat longing for the relief of water. With a curse, Caden wiped his brow and stumbled back, wanting to sleep. To get away. He couldn't live like this. He needed help. He needed someone bigger, stronger to show him how to do this impossible thing called life. But who was there for him? Caden slowly looked up to the clear, blue sky. He waited.

You can prove Yourself anytime now, he thought. A few clouds drifted overhead, but nothing else moved. Caden cursed again and hung his head.

"Did He respond this time?"

Shut up.

"I cannot. I'm enjoying myself far too much-"

"Just shut up!" Caden's shout echoed off the mountains again, and he slumped to the ground in the shade of a rock mound beside a craggy mountain. He stared out across the flat expanse from hill to mountain. There was nothing here. Nothing anywhere. He was alone with a Demon-

"Help me."

Caden yelped and leapt over the boulder, scurrying away from the stranger behind him. He gasped, stood, and scrambled for his gun. He raised it and aimed, holding it with both hands; they always did that in the movies, right? He stared down the sight, which was shaking all over, and he doubted the weapon was a threat in his hands.

On the other side of his gun was a woman. She stiffly stood against the mountain's rocks with her arms raised. Her clothes were thin and worn, and her tanned skin was blistered. Her eyes were red-rimmed and wide, and her lips were cracked like the ground at their feet. Wait; Caden blinked. No, her arms weren't raised. Why did she hold them like that? Caden's mouth opened as he took a step back. She was chained. Her arms and legs were chained to the rocks. How long had she been there?

"Please." Her voice was so weak. The wind washed over her, blowing her long, black hair over her face. She didn't acknowledge it. "Please. Water? Do you have water?" Caden didn't move, refusing to lower the gun. The woman opened her mouth to speak again, but stopped and slumped in her chains, too weak to stand. They rattled as she moved. "Just shoot," she whispered, closing her eyes and laying her head against the rock. "It will be a mercy."

Caden took in a sharp breath. With a muttered curse, he lowered the gun. She didn't seem to notice. He set the gun on the boulder and crossed his arms. He stared at her, suddenly irritated. *I don't have time for this! She needs help, and I've got to go!* He continued staring, and his brow furrowed. *What if she was Ellie? She's someone's sister. Someone's family member. Maybe just a little water and we can go our ways.* He eyed her chains. Her wrists were worn raw, and dried blood lined down her arms.

"Why were you chained?" The woman didn't stir. "Hey! Why were you chained up? Who did that?"

The woman's head slowly turned, and her eyes slid open. "Men," she whispered. "In bright white. They didn't like me." Caden lifted his chin, the description of the king's Sentinels sending a hot anger through his blood. "I don't like the king," the woman said. "I won't kneel to his rule."

Caden's eyes narrowed. "Really." She didn't answer for a moment, and Caden thought she had passed out.

"They wouldn't let me go," she whispered. "Their dogs wouldn't stop barking and barking and barking. I hate being hunted. I'm not an animal. I'm not."

Caden turned away as a hard lump formed in his throat. He felt the same. Officer Nathaniel's dogs barking into the night still haunted his dreams. Once awake, he always thought he smelled gunfire and Trace's blood on the ground. Caden straightened as darkness entered his eyes. "I hate the king too."

The woman finally lifted her head. "Then we're on the same team." Caden didn't answer. "Please," she whispered. "Save me? Don't let me die. Don't let the king win."

Caden turned away and scanned the landscape. With a

heavy sigh, Caden removed his pack and propped it against the boulder. He drew closer to her and saw how many bruises and scrapes marked her body. *They are the real animals,* he thought, knowing Nathaniel would've killed him too.

"Hold still." Caden said as he inspected her chains. They were thick and attached to an eyehook embedded into the rock. He shook his head and rubbed his eyes with his finger and thumb.

"Help me." He faced her and saw the unashamed desperation in her eyes. She was so skinny, so beaten. He doubted she would survive without help.

Without me, Caden thought. *I can't take on a person to care for. I just can't!*

"I'm Eshe. What's your name?"

"I'm Cad-Oliver. Oliver Deker."

"Cadoliver?"

"Just Oliver."

She nodded slowly. "Oliver."

"Right. Um, let me figure this out."

"You won't leave me, Oliver?"

"Um... no, I-Just hold on a sec." Caden ran his fingers through his hair, wishing he had a bolt cutter up his sleeve. He looked down, trying to think, and stopped. He stared at her feet and saw red, worn flesh on both ankles. Beside each were chains, broken and lying on the ground. Caden tilted his head to one side, his heart steadily quickening.

"Um," he stammered. "Eshe? Why, ah... Did you break the chains on your feet?" She didn't answer. Caden looked up. Her eyes weren't desperate anymore. They were cold. Hard. Unfeeling. And she was grinning.

Caden cursed as he reacted without thinking. He threw himself backward and ran. He forgot his pack. He forgot his gun. All he knew was to run. Behind him, a shrill raked his ears, followed by the clink of metal. Caden charged up the hill, his already weary legs suddenly empowered by adrenalin. His breath came in harsh bursts that burned his throat. Another ping of metal heightened his panic. He dared to glance over his shoulder.

Eshe was sprinting after him like an athlete. Chains lay in heaps at the rocks as a few links still clung to one wrist. The other links were snapped in two, broken by sheer strength. Eshe was gaining on him, her eyes focused on him like the sites of a gun. With a gasp, Caden spun and ran, knowing she would catch him.

"Come here, Caden Johnson!" Caden's panic consumed him. He was alone, without his weapon, as a Puppet hunted him down.

TWO
INSIDE OUT

PUPPETS HAD a fun way of not letting anything stop them. They could get locked up, chained down, and watched by dogs, and in the end, there'd be a destroyed cell, broken chain links, and dog body parts scattered everywhere. One of the surest ways to prove someone was a Puppet was by making them break through chains. Only a bullet to the head seemed to stop them. Good thing Caden had a gun. Bad thing he left it behind.

Caden tried to breathe as he sprinted up the hillside, knowing the Puppet was gaining on him. Last he checked, she wasn't interested in slowing down in the slightest. It was like getting chased by Nathaniel's dogs all over again. This *animal*, however, was screaming as she ran, as though forgetting her body needed to breathe. The scream rang in Caden's ears. His heart slammed against his chest. He tried to run faster, but his legs weren't working so well anymore. Something kept getting in the way of his legs. Something hard and wooden. *The bat!* Caden seized it and tried to run while untying it from his belt. It was impossible as his legs kept pumping. His legs were so tired. *He* was so tired-

Something hard and sweaty slammed into him. With a shout, Caden fell, rolling across the rough ground. The scream was so close, like right on top of him. *Oh no,* Caden thought as he tried to crawl away.

Eshe, still screeching like a banshee, straddled Caden and grabbed his shirt. She wrenched him back, her strength catching his breath. With one swift pull, she flipped him onto his back, knocking the wind out of him. Caden gulped in air and raised his arms, panic stripping him of logical thought, so all that remained was instinct.

Eshe drew him closer, her grip as firm as Buck's. No matter how hard Caden struggled, he couldn't get away. He felt overpowered by three grown men, not one half-starved, beaten woman. She didn't even look tired as she planted a knee on his guts and reached for his throat. Her small fingers were firm with strength as they wrapped around his neck.

Caden gulped and seized her wrists, his cries for help cut off instantly. His body shook as he tried to breathe, but nothing came. *Now's Your time!* Caden thought, his legs kicking ruts in the sand. *Now's when You prove Yourself! I'll die! Yahweh! Are You listening? YAHWEH!*

An ear-splitting crack echoed across the mountainside. Eshe's head snapped back as she was thrown to the ground. Caden grabbed his neck and rolled onto a side, gasping and coughing. His heart thudded loudly in his skull, each pound intensifying the pain in his head. Caden groaned and swallowed, making sure everything was still working. How hadn't his esophagus collapsed? What had happened?

I'm alive, Caden thought. *For now.*

He forced himself to move away from Eshe, but all he could manage was a crawl. His entire body shook as adrenaline pumped through him. He looked behind him and stopped short, finding Eshe. With several curses, he turned away with eyes closed tight and gritted teeth. Death was everywhere, and yet, when so blatantly splattered across the ground, it still made him sick. It was obvious she was shot right between the eyes.

He dragged himself to his feet and stumbled back just in time to see Eshe move. Caden reeled, trying not to fall over again. She was taking a deep breath. A very deep breath. No, her back was arching. Caden stopped and blinked, unsure of what he was looking at. Eshe's chest rose, and wispy tendrils of black mist lifted into the air. The blackness curled together, its movements graceful and hypnotic, and it hovered over her body.

A chill pricked Caden's arms. He had seen a Spirit like this before. He had been in the Old City of Jerusalem, and this thing had drifted over the crowd he was in. Glowing, ember eyes opened within the dark cloud and bore into him. Caden's internal screaming shrilled again and sent him into a cold, unfeeling panic. He could do nothing but stare into those eyes.

Is that the wrath of God? He thought.

The hot eyes seemed on fire, a fire like the Raw Peace. No, it was different. It was orange and seething, not light and fierce. It was wrath, but of a different kind. That kind that consumes all it touches. Without a word, the Demon coiled and drifted away. It thinned as it rose higher into the air and disappeared.

Caden stared after it and reminded himself to breathe. He ran his fingers through his hair and realized he was still shaking. He wiped his brow, smearing sweat and the Puppet's blood. He staggered back and tried to tell his nerves to calm so that he could have a millisecond to think!

The grumbling groan of a camel broke through his thoughts. Caden turned and found two strangers drawing closer. He tried to contain his panic and weariness, which was like trying to bail a sinking boat with a thimble. He was sinking and fast. Caden looked around for a weapon and cursed himself for leaving his gun behind. *I've got nothing,* he realized. *They can do anything to me.*

They hadn't shot him, which was a plus. But sometimes, death was better than what some strangers had in mind. Caden straightened his back and tried to look strong as his legs fought to buckle out from under him. *I am big,* he thought, and stopped. *The Raw Peace is big and tough, and fierce. Yahweh, are these good guys?*

One look at them, and Caden knew they were not. They were dressed in black robes and shemaghs that covered all but their eyes. It was their eyes that gave him pause. They were as dark and unfeeling as the mist-Demon lifting from its Puppet. One was returning a rifle to its scabbard as the other intently stared at Caden, scarcely blinking behind spectacles. Caden took in a sharp breath, feeling his chin tremble. He frantically untied his bat, his fingers shaking, and held it. He knew it was little defense. *I'm so tired of being terrified,* he thought, but helpless to know how to change.

They stopped a few paces away, their camels towering over him. Caden waited, his heart still beating just as fast as when the Puppet broke from her chains. *Prove Yourself,* Caden thought as he locked eyes with the one who was studying him.

Caden tried to say *shalom,* but his throat was so hoarse and raw, his voice cracked and choked him. He started coughing and grabbed his throat. He heard movement and forced himself to ignore the raw burning of his throat. One of the strangers, the one staring at him, had gotten off his camel. He stepped toward Caden, who couldn't help but stumble away, the bat raising. *Please, don't,* his mind begged. *I don't have anything for you!*

"*They notice you can see my kind.*" Caden's skin crawled.

Grant had wanted to make him a slave, and Nathaniel wanted to kill him once learning he could see Demons. What would these men want? Servitude and complete obedience from masters no better than Demons. Caden would soon comprehend the helplessness of Puppets-

Not now, Doeg! Caden's mind screamed as he stopped coughing and tried to breathe.

"Now is an excellent time."

The stranger straightened his arm, and Caden recoiled despite himself, knowing a bullet would fly any second. The stranger didn't move. Caden finally looked and, instead of a gun, the stranger extended a canteen. He knew if he accepted the water, he was also acknowledging he was in their debt. *But there's no point in running. They obviously can shoot good enough.* Caden took it and drank; it was the best water he had ever had.

The stranger spoke in Aramaic, which Caden quickly tried to explain he only knew English and enough Hebrew to ask where the bathroom was. They, too, seemed to know enough English to also ask such limited questions. Talking was difficult, Caden's throat still strained with each word, and he would stop to cough and gag.

The men were named Faadi, who had offered the canteen, and Oba, who was the sharpshooter. Caden asked the way to Cairo, and, as he suspected, he was completely lost. They knew the way, or so they said. They wanted Caden to join their mini caravan because, obviously, they were up to something. Why wouldn't they? Caden knew he had nothing to offer but himself.

They probably think I'm a rich American. He swallowed the hard lump in his throat, letting them think that as he communicated, with gestures and short words, he needed to get his backpack. He tied his bat to his belt and didn't tell them about the gun.

As he walked back to the rockface, rubbing his throat,

he heard the two strangers talking quietly. His stomach twisted with each step as he ignored the sinking feeling of dread. *This is stupid*, he thought. *They look just like Grant's men! But I'm lost. I can't be out here anymore by myself.* With a gag and wheezed breath, Caden glanced into the sky. *What are You getting me into, God?* There was no reply.

———

IT WAS Caden's turn to ride the camel. Horses gave him pause back in America, but this was nothing like a horse. Horses didn't sound like they had constant indigestion or have those weird lips that kept moving. Caden didn't care. He wanted to sit and rest, even on a camel's back. Faadi tried to teach him how to lean and hold on when the camel stood, but Caden still fell off the first time. The creature moved with such force when it stood! By the third mount, he didn't fall and settled high onto the saddle. Both Oba and Faadi were laughing at him, but he didn't care.

Just take me to my sister, he thought as he clung to the handle in front of the saddle. Caden still felt like he was about to fall off when the camel started walking. Its tromping, jerky strides took quite a while to get used to. After a bit, Caden permitted himself to relax. He was still shocked that Faadi had offered to let him ride. The man quickly walked beside him, humming softly. Caden glanced at Oba, leading them on. The man didn't know a lick of English, and Caden wasn't sure he liked him. Actually, he wondered if Oba liked anyone. He was missing a few fingers on one hand and had more weapons on him than Faadi. *They're helping me*, Caden reminded himself. *For now.*

As the sandy miles slowly passed, Caden let his thoughts drift. He kept thinking of Jerusalem and the family who'd adopted him. The Mizrahis were different than anything Caden had ever known. They enjoyed one another and were a team. They were loyal to their God. They were loyal to Caden too.

Caden let out a long sigh, regretting, once again, leaving them. Yes, he had to find Lil El, but they were going back to Jerusalem and his new Dad. That wasn't what Elijah said to call him. What was it again? *Abba*, Caden thought. It was such a simple word with more weight than Elijah could understand. After a lifetime of suffering under the hand of a cruel father, Caden needed an abba.

He thought of the Mizrahis, of Hili laughing in the kitchen, and Elezaro playfully taunting the youngsters. Ophir was always there when he needed help, and Asher wanted him back. *My brother*, Caden thought, emotion tightening his chest. His blood brothers were all dead. Now, he had a new one, one who had watched his back and faced Giants with him.

Caden knew he had to be careful though. His blood family was all dead because of him. Apparently, his very presence brought about death and suffering. Perhaps, it was best not to return. He was a bad luck charm. An evil. Only an obscenely self-indulgent, unreliable person would willingly put loved ones in harm's way so recklessly-

Raw Peace, he thought, knowing Doeg's words were overpowering his thoughts. *Raw Peace. Yahweh, please-*

"You worthless creature-"

I need Your peace-

"If He watches, it is to enjoy your suffering."

I need Your words. Why don't You answer?

"He abandons all who are unworthy. There is nothing left of His so-called truth for you."

Caden blinked and tilted his head to one side. *Yes, there is*, he thought, grabbing the pack wrapped around his middle.

"What do you intend?" Caden didn't answer as he unzipped the pack and withdrew a small book. Its black leather sides were worn, and pages so thin a strong wind could tear it apart. *"Focusing on more lies?"*

Caden cleared his throat and opened the book he avoided as a kid, the one who annoyed him most of all. The Bible's small pages flapped in the wind, and he shielded it with his hand. *Can't believe I'm doing this*, he thought.

"Then stop."

He nearly burned the dead weight at the beginning of his journey. Why would he need a Bible? It was a useless book filled with ramblings from old, dead prophets that were probably half out of their minds. Right before tossing it into the flames, one line caught his eye and made him pause. "I will never leave you," the text read. "I will never forsake you." The words were in red. They seemed to catch the fire's light and reminded Caden of the Raw Peace. He had quickly put the book away and hadn't taken it out since. He tried to forget about it, but the daily weight around his waist was enough of a reminder.

It's not like it'll make sense even if I try to read it, he thought.

"How many times did a bullet enter Trace?" Caden froze, the question sending ice through his blood. *"I counted five. And you?"*

Caden cleared his throat and refocused on the small book. If nothing else, reading the Bible seemed to really irritate Doeg. Caden refocused on the mini lines of text. Once again, the Bible was filled with weird concepts Caden tried to wrap his head around and just couldn't.

Some guy named Moses was talking to God. Caden thought he was the same one floating in that basket down the Nile as a baby. Maybe that was another Moses. Anyways, God was sending Moses and his family into the desert. No, wait, it was a lot of people. The Israelites? *That's what Elijah said,* Caden thought, *his ancestors were slaves in Egypt and had to walk through the Sinai Desert to reach Israel.*

So, this was when God sent them out. Yahweh wasn't sure He wanted to go with them, because they were stubborn, He'd just get mad and wipe them out. Moses wanted Him to come. Really, really bad. God, much to Caden's surprise, seemed to change His mind.

"My Presence will go with you," it read, "and I will give you rest."

Caden stopped and stared at the single sentence. God, the creator of all, willing to travel with stubborn, annoying people. Not only that, but give them rest. *Rest like peace. The Raw Peace. And He just gives it away.* Caden watched circling vultures as the wheels of his mind turned. *Does He still do that? And does He want to be with me, or am I also too stubborn?*

"You know the answer to that, boy. You have survived American gangs, hungry Giants, hunting Sentinels, and a brutal father. And still, you refuse to follow Him. You are stubborn. Enough to abandon."

Caden lifted his chin and slowly nodded. *I guess He's let me live through a lot.*

"What do you foresee these men doing to you-"

I should choose to follow Him, Caden thought as he slowly closed the book. *He's keeping me alive. I can't do this on my own-*

"But you have! All this is your strength! Your own might!"

Caden shook his head as he glanced into the sky. *I just need a little push,* he thought. *Something to really make me seal the deal. I don't know.* He looked down, unsure of what he meant. Yahweh knew what he meant. Didn't He? *I mean, He made me. Shouldn't He know me best?*

"He knows the most efficient ways to destroy you from the inside out." Doeg growled.

Doeg, please-

"Why would He treat you any differently than your father?"

Caden took in a sharp breath, trying to calm his nerves. He frowned and sniffed again as he looked around the rocky landscape. *Something's dead-*

"You, with time."

Behind a thicket of thorns, vultures squabbled over the scraps of a poor animal. One of the vultures was squawking at the others, its winy sounds shaping crude words. Caden blinked, identifying Hebrew as the vulture fluffed its feathers and spoke. Though he didn't know much, Caden could make out a bit of the bird's meaning:

"Back legs, back legs. So best! Yum! Yum! Back legs!" Caden shivered, never liking when birds talked. "My back legs. Juicy, nice, meaty. Males are better!"

Caden glanced down at the carcass the vultures fluttered about. It looked attacked not too long ago, the blood still fresh on the ground. The animal had been turned inside out. *Could wolves do that?* Caden thought as his stomach turned. He knew wolves could start eating their prey before they fully died. This didn't look like a carnivore's feast though. This just looked like a killing. A thrashing, reckless killing.

"Yum! Yum! Meat so yum!"

As Caden stared, he noticed the carcass had a shoe on. With a curse, Caden flinched and looked away from the unfortunate human, or what was left of it. Oba let out a fierce laugh and spoke to Faadi, who drew his shemagh over his nose. The wind picked up, and the stench intensified. Caden tried not to gag.

While passing, the vultures scattered, hopping about or darting away with uncertainty. The talking one remained. "Back legs, mine!" The vulture leapt onto the body and eyed it. "Juicy, nice, meaty!" Caden turned away as it started feasting.

"Am, good you with us," Faadi said from beside the camel. He shook his head and removed his glasses to clean them. "We watch you. We help."

"Why would anyone do this?" Caden's voice was still raw but only scratched from time to time.

"Am." Faadi shrugged. "Robbed? Giants hungry. Maybe infidel." Caden stiffened, the small book in his hands suddenly heavy.

"An infidel," Doeg whispered. *"Such as a Christian."* Caden took in slow breaths, trying to stay calm. *"Choose your allegiance accordingly, human boy."*

Caden didn't answer as he quickly put away the Bible and hoped no one saw it. *Raw Peace,* he thought, his stomach tightening further. *Raw Peace!*

"Your so-called Raw Peace may be the very thing that destroys you." Caden didn't have an answer to that.

———

CADEN PROPPED himself against the rockface of a mountain as he sat by the fire. It was morning, and Faadi was roasting two lizards and a scorpion. Caden stared at his breakfast and thought of Ophir's eggs in tomato sauce with fish and bread. He turned away, but his stomach growled. "How much further?" Faadi didn't answer as he turned a lizard over. "Faadi? How much more to Cairo?" He still couldn't believe Ellie went to Cairo right before the Day of Vanishing. What were the odds?

Faadi sniffed and adjusted his glasses. "Not far."

"But how far?" Faadi stared at him and shrugged before diving into Aramaic. Caden sighed and held up a hand, understanding Faadi didn't know enough English to explain. *They're up to something; they have been from the start,*

Caden thought as he tried to act at ease. *I've got to get out of here. Could I sneak off with one of their camels in the night?*

He rubbed the back of his head, knowing Oba wouldn't hesitate shooting him down like the Puppet. Caden rubbed his throat, still having trouble swallowing now and then, he knew bruises had formed. He sighed and warmed his hands over the fire, waiting for Oba to share what he found. He sometimes left before the others awoke and returned with more food. He never said where he found it, and no one asked. It was safer that way.

That morning, he returned with another canteen, a bedroll, and three hardish pieces of flat bread. Caden eyed the valuable belongings and tried to think of another way to escape. It wasn't like they were holding him hostage. On the contrary, he could just walk off right now without them chasing him. But he needed supplies to survive the desert. Supplies he knew they weren't going to give him. The three ate in silence.

"You are an infidel." Caden frowned and continued eating. *"Remember that."*

What are you going on about-

Several camels charged from around the rockface. Caden recoiled as their camels leapt up with a start. Someone was shouting. Lots of people were. Oba drew two guns and aimed. Faadi wasted no time in sprinting away. Caden crawled back, feeling the hard rock butt against him as he shielded his eyes from the kicked-up sand and dust. He coughed and looked up.

We're surrounded, he thought, his guts twisting.

Each of the six riders hefted AK-47s as their faces lay concealed under wraps or shemaghs. One shouted and turned in his saddle high above them. He lowered his gun and fired. Though he was aiming away from them, Caden still flinched with each volley and covered his ears.

Everything was moving too fast, Caden didn't know

what was happening. Their camels were spooked and started running from the gunfire. Faadi, who Caden was sure lay dead in the sand, was walking back with arms raised high. *Am I going to die this time?* Caden wondered. *Wait, I have a gun!*

He reached for it just as hands seized him. "Get off!" He kicked but realized two looters were dragging him into the open. He could do nothing but stumble along to keep up. They stopped him and propped him upright as one held him firm while the other patted him down. They quickly took the bat and found the gun. Caden watched his only defense slip into the belt of a stranger casually smoking a cigarette. His throat bobbed, and he was thrown down and kept on his knees.

Faadi, breathless and pale, was ordered to kneel beside him. Oba came last of all, his brow split and bleeding as three men forced him to obey. Caden stared at the grains of sand between his knees as he tried to catch his breath. Panic, as always, grabbed his throat. He felt his hands starting to shake. *I'm sick of this,* he thought. *I can't take it anymore!*

"I will not free you from terror, human fool," Doeg hissed. *"Remember, your flesh is mine."*

Caden's hands clenched as his heart beat with force. Fear surrounded him, a fear he knew all too well. With a heaved sigh, he straightened his back and looked up. He was sick of fear. Sick of avoiding death. *Just kill me or not,* he thought, facing his captors. *Yahweh's kept me alive so far. Maybe He will again.*

His eyes met with one captor still atop his camel. Caden refused to turn away. The man tilted his head to one side and dismounted as the camel knelt. He approached Caden, his stride unwavering. He was a tall, skinny guy and reminded Caden of Seth. Caden couldn't see his face, for only the stranger's dark eyes were seen beneath his shemagh. He stared down at Caden, his eyes looked amused. Caden's fists became white-knuckled.

The stranger slowly turned to Oba and withdrew a pistol. He pointed it right at Oba's head. Caden stared at the sand again, preparing his ears to ring from the clap of gunfire. Instead, the stranger shouted a question. Oba answered, his gestures aggressive and irritated. The tall stranger stepped to Faadi and placed the gun to his head. He asked the same question and Faadi cowered as he nodded.

I'm next, Caden thought. It was suddenly difficult to breathe. The gun's muzzle was cold metal. Caden would've thought the desert would make it warm, at least. But cold? The stranger asked his question and Caden raised hands.

"I don't speak that. I don't speak that! Please! Wait!" Caden leaned back, wanting to leap up and run away, but he knew they'd shoot him down.

The tall stranger grumbled something and moved closer. "Do you follow Allah?"

The entire world stopped at that moment. Caden felt nothing but the cold metal against his forehead. *This can't be happening-*

"Allah! Do you follow him?"

Caden closed his eyes as the muzzle pressed into his head. "No." he stammered and instantly regretted it.

"Who do you serve?" Caden held his tongue. He remembered the disfigured infidel as vultures picked the body clean. The sharp twang of rot still lingered in his nose. The stranger cocked the gun's hammer, nearly drawing Caden into a ball at his feet. "Answer!" the stranger cried. Sweat dripped down Caden's brow. "Who do you follow?"

Caden gritted his teeth and looked past the gun to the stranger. Their eyes locked again. "I follow Yahweh and

Yeshua and their Raw Peace. I am a Christian." The stranger stared down at him, not moving. Without a word, he smiled, a gleam in his eye. Caden tried not to puke as he closed his eyes and waited for the bullet to make him more vulture food.

THREE
AKAL ESH

YAHWEH, *what's happening?* Caden ignored the bead of sweat that trickled from his brow. He wouldn't be in this mess if not for Yahweh. Didn't He know this was going to happen? If He was so loving, He wouldn't let Caden travel with Faadi and Oba! Caden had asked for protection! But that doesn't mean that's what Yahweh would give. *Ophir said Christians and Yahweh are a team. You're not being a good Teammate!*

Caden held his breath, finally wondering if all his blasphemed views of God had now caught up to him. Maybe God had lured him to be with Faadi just so He could watch Caden's death. *Then why not let the Puppet kill me, and what's taking this guy so long?*

Caden glanced up as his eyes narrowed. The tall, skinny stranger gave a gruff laugh and stepped back. "What's your name?" he asked.

Caden gritted his teeth, images of Nathaniel and his dogs filling his mind. *He'll find me.* He knew Nathaniel told other KUS camps in America about him. Could word reach way out here?

"Caden Johnson?"

Caden's face turned pale. So, it was true. Word had reached the Middle East. Nathaniel was coming. The tall stranger laughed again and turned to the smoking stranger. "Can you believe it?" He said in Hebrew. "Got him!" Caden blinked, it was the first Hebrew phrase he confidently translated. The smoking stranger didn't answer, his half-closed eyes on Caden.

The tall stranger barked orders again and Faadi and Oba were dragged to their feet. One of their camels was returned to them as the looting gang claimed the other. They were given some water and a little food and ordered to go. *But not me,* Caden thought, his chest tightening with dread. He glanced at the tall stranger and saw his gun was still drawn. At least it wasn't pointed at him.

Caden closed his eyes and dipped his head. The nerves in his fingers tingled as he forced himself to face the truth. They were going to kill him. Caden's heart quickened, images of the mangled vulture food sending a shiver down his spine. *Yahweh's presence went with them,* he thought, remembering the verse he read in the Bible. *And He gave them rest. He was with them and gave them rest.*

Caden willed himself to calm, knowing it was his last chance to taste peace before the knives and fists rained down. Before they took everything from him, stripping him down to a begging, weeping, pathetic human. It was inevitable and unavoidable; something as frail as you will bend-

Gave them rest. And was with them, Caden thought, trying to ignore Doeg's words. *He could be with me too. He could give me rest too-*

"Steel yourself." He heard the stranger's footsteps crunch across the sand and rocks as he approached. *"This will be thoroughly entertaining."*

Caden made fists and forced himself to look up. He was alone, Oba and Faadi were a dot far in the distance.

The strangers were picking through the left belongings and securing their newly acquired camel. Caden's hair stood on end, for he was in the center of their group and surrounded. Helplessness was an evil companion Caden was learning how to deal with. The tall stranger, who everyone seemed to listen to, still had his gun in hand. He slowly sat across from Caden and lay his hands on his crossed knees.

"So," he said at last in English. "Caden Johnson." His voice was heavily accented, but Caden was tracking better than when he first arrived in Israel. "The Sinai Peninsula isn't for tourists." Caden didn't answer. The stranger sniffed and pulled his shemagh from his face. He had a sharp nose, angular features, and his beard was dark and thick. His face wasn't shrunken and sickly.

They conquer wherever they go, Caden thought. *They're not without food or water. Do they loot? Or is there a larger camp they all stay at?*

"Why are you here?" Caden lifted his chin. He couldn't tell him about Ellie. No way! Guys like this with his sister… he didn't want to think about it. The stranger's head tilted to one side before shifting his gun closer to Caden.

"I," Caden stammered. "I got lost." Well, that was true. Sort of.

The stranger's brows rose with a grunt. "Lost?"

Caden nodded. "Those guys found me."

"Friends?" Caden scowled. The stranger nodded slowly and withdrew a small rag from his robe. He unfolded it, revealing various small cleaning supplies, and dismembered his gun. Caden watched as he carefully began cleaning each part of his gun. "Where are you from?"

"America-"

"Yes, yes. *Where?*"

"Oregon."

"What brought you out here?"

"A plane."

"Alone?"

"The pilot flew here too." The stranger didn't answer as he continued cleaning. *Why did I just say that?* Caden thought, a lump forming in his throat.

"I can break you."

Oh, God. Caden turned away.

"It would take thirty minutes. Probably less." Caden sucked in a breath, finding it hard to breathe again. "So why not cut this smart-alecky attitude, loosen your own tongue, so I don't have to, and talk? Hum? Torture takes so much effort; just do as you're told."

Caden squeezed his eyes tight and wiped the sweat from his brow. "I came with friends," he said quietly. "They're still in Jerusalem."

"Why?"

"They weren't told to come here."

"Told by who?"

Caden stared at the grains of sand, not knowing how to answer. "By... by Yahweh."

The stranger chuckled, and Caden closed his eyes. "Why aren't you begging? A soft American boy like yourself should be groveling right now. Offering me a deal, telling me about some rich daddy across the ocean."

"I don't have anyone anymore."

"No one to come save you then."

Caden looked away as his hands fisted. "No, I'm all alone. Everyone I care for is dead."

"Hum. Bummer. Tell me about your God."

Caden cursed under his breath and shook his head. "I-" he cleared his throat. Was he really supposed to preach to these guys? Right now? "I don't know, um, He's... this is the End Times and-"

"That's not what I asked."

"I, I don't know. I don't know! I haven't been following Him for long."

"How long?"

Caden cursed again and shrugged. "Like, I became a Christian about ten minutes ago, okey."

The stranger snorted a laugh. "Bad timing, don't you think?" Caden looked away. "Why did you follow that God now? You could've chosen many other religions that wouldn't get you killed."

"It wouldn't be right," Caden mumbled. "The Raw Peace, er-Yahweh wouldn't like that. He's kept me alive, saving me all the time when everyone else just kicks it so, so He has that going for Him. And,"

Caden rubbed the back of his neck and sighed. He closed his eyes and tried to forget he was surrounded by cut-throats who were going to kill him. Maybe this was the only time these people heard about Yeshua. Mama Lo always talked about all the sad people who never, ever hear about God and His love. *Is that why I'm here?* Caden thought. He didn't really care about their souls, but he did care about Yahweh. He didn't want to let Him down.

"I'm a Christian because I suck," Caden said. "I can't live life without God. I've tried. It's too hard. There's too much pain, death, sorrow, and horrible stuff to do it on my own. And I want God's peace. He has a very powerful, very violent peace that I'm searching for. I hope He gives me some. I dunno if He will, but… He did to the Israelites when they were in the Sinai Desert too, so maybe there's some left over for me." Caden didn't move as he waited for the strangers' laughs or cutting words.

"Raw Peace? What is this Raw Peace? Did you make that up?"

"Ah, well, I made the name, but Yahweh actually made it."

"What is it?"

"It's like," Caden paused, trying to put it into words. "Like peace that's too big to be real. It's not from this world, or anything close. But it's also really powerful. And dangerous. It looks like fire. I've seen it fall from the sky and into one of my friends. We thought he died."

The stranger glanced up from his cleaning tools. "You saw the *Akal Esh*?"

"Um-?"

"You saw it? With our eyes, the eyes of the flesh? Not spiritual eyes."

"I-What's *Akal Esh*?"

"Yahweh's Consuming Fire." Caden blinked as the stranger leaned closer. "You saw it, didn't you? Where?"

"At, at the Wailing Wall."

"When?"

"About two weeks ago. Maybe more-"

The stranger sat back and glanced at his companions. Caden turned, realizing everyone had stopped looting and were listening. *What've I done?* Caden thought, his skin crawling. *Did I just lead them to Elijah? I've got to stop talking!* The seated stranger smiled and talked to his companions; his Hebrew far too fast to understand. *How do they know about the Consuming Fire?* Caden thought. *I thought Muslims weren't into that.*

The stranger laughed and began assembling his gun. The looters looked excited. Caden thought he was going to puke. "Come," the stranger said. "You're traveling with us now."

Caden's stomach twisted painfully, and he didn't move. "What do you want with me?"

"Our elders will want to hear of the *Akal Esh* and your friend in Jerusalem."

No, Caden thought, his nostrils flaring. *You cannot make me talk.* He swallowed the hard lump in his throat, knowing that was a lie. He was stronger than he used to be, but not nearly enough compared to these guys. *Yahweh, help me-*

"Get up."

Caden still didn't move. The gun's hammer slid into place with a loud click. Caden flinched with a curse. The stranger chuckled. The smoking looter stepped forward and spoke to the leader, his voice a soft whisper, but his eyes were sharp. The leader sighed and snapped something back. Caden kept staring at the sand as he tried to pick out any words he identified. He found two: "Tell him."

Tell me what?

With a growl, the leader swatted a hand at his companion and motioned to Caden. "You. Look at me." Caden's hands fisted as he slowly lifted his chin. The stranger slid his gun into his belt and extended a hand. "Yohanan Nuri. I am not going to kill you," Caden's brow furrowed as he glanced at Yohanan's hand. "Or harm you. This is the fastest way to find real fellow believers."

Caden's mouth dropped open as he leaned back. "*Fellow* believers? You mean-"

"We also follow Yeshua, Yahweh, and His *Akal Esh*."

Caden's response would've made him not look like a Christian in the slightest. He slowly shook his head. *So, you're on my side? This doesn't make any sense!*

"I'm not trying to scare you." Yohanan said.

Liar. You're having way too much fun!

"I want the truth. Guns have a way of getting the truth faster. My wife keeps telling me to be loving and gentle like Yeshua." Yohanan shrugged. "I haven't found a good time to practice yet." Caden didn't answer as Yohanan slowly lowered his extended hand. "We have food. Shelter. There are many of us, so there is no threat of looters or Giants."

Nathaniel said the same thing, Caden thought.

"And we follow Yahweh, so evil Spirits don't come around. Too much."

Caden blinked and looked up. "Evil Spirits don't go into your camp?"

Yohanan shrugged again. "They're like bugs; they crawl in places they don't belong. Yahweh will squish them. He's good at squishing." Caden frowned but didn't speak. Yohanan stared at him for a long, silent moment and clapped a hand on his leg. "So. Get up? Join us? Or die out here alone? It's your choice."

"I'm not a captive?"

Yohanan barked a laugh as he stood. "If you were my captive, you'd already be beaten and tied to the back of my camel. No, you are a friend of Yahweh's. You're a friend of mine."

Caden took in a slow breath as anger tightened his chest. "Do you make all your friends kneel with guns to their heads?"

Yohanan smiled as he packed away the cleaning supplies. "Choose what you'll do and do it. We leave in a few minutes. Oh, and Caden. You will regret not coming." Caden turned away as a cold thrill rushed through him. Yohanan raised his hands and stepped back. "Not a threat. I swear, I swear! Just facts. Don't get all worked up over facts." Yohanan chuckled again and turned to his camel while barking orders to those around him.

Caden stayed on his knees, too afraid to move. *I can't go,* he thought as his gaze returned to Yohanan. *They obviously want information from me. I won't tell them about Elijah or Ophir. I can't. I won't trust them. I won't be a fool again.*

He had trusted Nathaniel and had paid dearly for it. Actually, Trace had paid dearly. Caden could still hear the baying of dogs sometimes late at night. Still smell the sting of gunpowder and the unblinking stare of his baby brother, another fatality to God's games-

Doeg! Please! Shut up!

"*Beg.*"

Caden cursed under his breath and ran a rough hand over his face. *I can't stay out here alone. Either way, I'm dead-*

"*Correct.*"

I won't survive out here. I'm lost! But I can't go with these guys-

"*What? Your fellow believers?*"

They are not on my side! I can't think that. They are lying. They want to use me to get information. I just, I just need to stay calm. Lie my way out of this. Maybe I can escape and still find Ellie.

He heard Doeg snort a laugh. "*Doubtful.*"

"Caden!" He flinched and cowered in the sand. Yohanan walked over and shook his head. "Stop this. I'm not going to hurt you! Get up! Let's go! We'll reach the camp in time for dinner."

I don't like this, Yahweh. Why aren't You saving me? Caden slowly stood and glanced at Yohanan. *Just give me The Door. Let me walk through it! Let me go home to that place, wherever it is.* With a heaved sigh, Caden gave a small nod.

"About time," Yohanan grumbled. "You'll have to walk. There's no room on the camels." The smoking stranger shouted again and pointed to his own camel. "Or ride Noam's camel. What a servant of Yahweh, eh?" Noam gave Yohanan a sharp glance before telling his camel to kneel.

"Um," Caden muttered. "My gun? I'd like it back." Yohanan stopped and stared at him. Caden crossed his arms and didn't move toward Noam's camel. Yohanan shook his head and motioned to Noam. He approached and handed Caden his gun again. "See? I'm not a bad guy." Yohanan said.

That's what all bad guys say.

"Just know, if you try to shoot one of my men or anyone in our camp, I'll gun you down. Understand?" Caden's answer was tucking his gun into his belt. He turned and mounted Noam's camel without another word. "Fine, Caden Johnson," Yohanan said as he ordered his camel to rise. "Don't trust us yet. I don't blame you. But be sure to get over your fears enough to talk to our leaders about the *Akal Esh* and your friends."

Caden didn't answer as his camel stood. *Yep,* he thought as sweat dripped down his back. *I'll be dead by morning.*

————

CADEN KEPT one hand on his gun as Noam's camel followed Yohanan deeper into the desert. Every lurching step from the camel jarred Caden's already strained nerves further. Couldn't he just tell the camel to run? He could get to Cairo faster that way. Is that what Yahweh wanted all along? For him to get his hands on a camel?

Caden shook his head and wished Yahweh could talk to him. Ophir acted like He used to, but that was before the Day of Vanishing. *Am I just supposed to do this all by faith?* Caden thought. He snorted and cursed; he knew the answer. *Typical,* he thought. *If You're not making someone get swallowed by a big fish or sticking them in a den of lions, You're surrounding them with bad guys. All for faith.*

Mama Lo had said that was all he needed, and it didn't take much either. "Just a pinch." she'd say.

How about a grain, Caden thought as he shifted in the saddle and tried to keep himself calm. How could he stay calm? Yohanan and his friends wanted answers, answers he was unwilling to give. *Raw Peace,* Caden thought, fixing his mind on The Door. *Come on, calm down! Raw Peace!*

They traveled for little less than an hour as the sun sank into the west. Caden saw their camp before reaching it. He turned away and regretted ever coming to Israel. Even if Ellie was still alive, he was no use to her mangled and turned inside out as vultures picked him to bits-

Caden took a breath through gritted teeth. *Raw Peace-*

"You cannot deny your fate."

Raw Peace-

"You are not that much of a fool, GJ."

Raw Peace!

The camp was filled with tents haphazardly thrown together. Blankets and reed mats formed the walls as tents and sticks kept them upright. They were large tents, able to hold many and tall enough for Caden to stand in. Corrals, made of various materials, penned in goats and, a larger section, for camels. Everyone in the camp noticed Caden right away. It was horrible. The children rushed over, saying who-knows-what in whatever language they were speaking. The women clustered about, whispering softly, and the elders hobbled through the sand, just staring. Caden didn't want to get off his camel, he didn't want everyone to see how much he was shaking.

"Come," Yohanan said as the two stepped from their camels. "Dinner should be ready. I'm starved!" He turned and started walking further into the camp and didn't bother to check if Caden followed. Caden knew Noam was right behind him. The guy hadn't strayed from his camel for a second. Any moment now, Caden knew his gun would dig into his back.

"What's wrong?" Noam muttered. "Hungry?"

Yohanan finally realized he wasn't following and raised both hands. "Didn't you hear me? Let's go!"

Caden's heart quickened as he stepped back and glanced at the sandy ground. "I…" he stammered.

"What?"

"You can't make me talk!" Caden closed his eyes and forced himself to breathe.

"Hum?" He heard Yohanan approach and couldn't bring himself to lift his head. "What did you say?"

"You can't," Caden's voice cracked, and he cleared his throat. "You can't make me talk. I'm not telling your people about the Raw Peace."

Yohanan shook his head. "You keep calling it that. It's called the *Akal Esh*-"

"I won't betray my friends!" When Yohanan didn't answer, Caden glanced at him, not knowing what to expect.

"You know," Yohanan muttered, stepping closer with a pointed finger. "You're getting really annoying. I said we follow Yahweh and Yeshua too."

Steel entered Caden's eyes and forced his shoulders back. "Words mean nothing. Actions are what counts-"

"Are you wounded? Beaten? Dead?"

"You put a gun to my head! That's not what I'd call a Christian welcome!"

"Welcome to the End Times!" Caden cursed him; he couldn't help it, it just slipped out. Yohanan tilted his head to one side as he smirked. "Hum, I'm starting to like you. This way. There's someone I want you to meet." Caden didn't move, and Yohanan sighed. "My *wife*. That's who we're seeing. I understand, she can be a force to be reckoned with, but she usually doesn't bite until after befriending someone. Ah," he said as he faced the steady flow of newcomers. "Here she is now. *Neshama*!"

Caden crossed his arms and looked down. *What are You getting me into?* Caden thought. *I just want my sister back. That's it!*

"Relax," Noam said around his cigarette. "She's nice. Good cook." Caden's nostrils flared, and he looked away as a woman joined them.

Yohanan smiled and wrapped his arm around her as he drew close to her ear. "I got you a surprise-"

"Cade!"

Caden's heart leapt. He knew that voice. Turning, he found a short Middle Eastern woman beneath layers of robes, gowns, and a head covering. Her hair, from the little that he could see, was light brown, and her eyes were blue. Though tanned and hardened by the desert, Caden knew who she was. He would recognize his Lil El anywhere.

FOUR
COW ANGEL

CADEN DIDN'T MOVE as he stared at his little sister. She looked so different, so much like someone of the desert! But she was still his Lil El. That same sparkle was in her blue eyes, and her smile still pulled a little more to the left than the right. He wanted to hug her tight, kiss her forehead like he used to, but he couldn't. *They* were watching. These people who wanted answers. They could use her as leverage. He couldn't watch another sibling die-

Ellie leapt forward with a squeal, nearly tripping over her robes, and wrapped her arms around him. Though a short gal, she squeezed all the breath from his lungs. "Cade!" She cried. He could feel his shirt getting wet as her tears of joy fell. "Thank Yahweh! I've prayed for you every day! All the time! Oh! You're here! See?" She faced Yohanan with a sniff. "I told you have faith!" Yohanan nodded with a gentle smile. "And now you're here! We can be a family! Why aren't you hugging back? What's wrong?"

Caden didn't answer as he watched Yohanan out of the corner of his eye. *If they touch her, I'll cave right away,* he thought. *I can't show I care-*

"Cade?"

I can't put her in danger-

"Cade, you're safe here. Cade!" Ellie stepped back and looked him square in the face. Her brows pinched together as she wiped tears from her eyes. "You look like you're about to face Dad. You're safe. These are friends. They won't hurt you."

Caden glanced down at her and didn't know what to do. "I," he stammered. "I can't. They'll-" All he could think of were Nathaniel's dogs and Trace's unblinking stare.

"I told him we're Christians too," Yohanan said. "He won't believe me."

Ellie gasped with a smile. "You're a Christian?" Caden nodded slowly. Ellie laughed and flung herself into his arms again. "You always hated God. I can't believe it! Do you still hate God? I guess you don't. Oh, now you're extra, extra safe with us *and* God!" Ellie stiffened suddenly and pulled back again. "Why don't you believe we're all Christians too?" Caden didn't answer as he gave Yohanan a guarded, quick glance. Ellie's face hardened as she glared at the spindly man. "What did you do?"

Yohanan raised his hands. "Nothing-"

"What did you do?"

"I made sure he was one of us!"

"How? Tell me! Did you do that to him?" She pointed at Caden's neck, and he remembered the bruises the Puppet had left. That terrifying exchange felt like decades ago.

"No!" Yohanan cried. "I just... you know." He crossed his arms. There was a gleam in his eyes.

"Yohanan!" Without warning, Ellie started ranting in perfect Hebrew. Caden blinked and stared down at her, shocked. Yohanan answered, his words loud and gestures animated. She cut him off, continuing in Hebrew. With a scoff and swatting hand, she turned away from him. "He's a horrible person," she grumbled. "I'm sorry he did that. He's your brother-in-law, Yohanan! We're family!"

Yohanan nodded. "Exactly."

Ellie sighed heavily and adjusted her head covering, composing herself. "Caden," she said, firmly grabbing his hand. "Look at me." She acted just like the time she told him about her trip to Egypt. He had disagreed and said it was stupid and dangerous. Her dead-set yet gentle stubbornness had irritated him further. She calmly stood before him now, that same dead-set look in her eyes. "This entire camp is Christians. We left Cairo because there was too much persecution. We couldn't bear it any longer. Other people joined us, some from Jordan or Israel," she motioned to Yohanan, "who were also stuck in Egypt. We guard our own, but you are now one of us. Please. Let us welcome you. At least let *me* welcome you."

Caden didn't answer as he held her hand, his heart beating loudly in his ears. *I can't get you killed. Anyone I cherish becomes a feast for wolves. My failure will snuff out your zeal for that monstrous God and your manic husband. I cannot let down my guard. I cannot be at peace. If you do succumb to their wooing, death will swallow you whole. I will orchestrate it to the last detail-*

Caden closed his eyes slowly and gritted his teeth, Doeg's words straining his already spent resolve. Ellie sighed, and her hand squeezed his gently. "Oh, Cade," she whispered. "What have you gone through?" Caden dipped his head; she was always able to read him too well. "Caden, no one is going to try to kill you. They're not going to tie you up or beat you or anything to cause you harm."

You don't know that, Caden thought.

"They're not going to make you watch as they harm me either." He took in a sharp breath and faced her. He knew his gaze was fierce and unwavering, just like when he'd take the blame for something she did, knowing Dad wouldn't show any mercy. She shook her head and smiled. "Be at peace, dear brother," Ellie whispered as she reached up and gently touched his cheek. "Yahweh brought you here. Trust He knows what He's doing."

You did answer my prayer, Caden thought. *Here she is. Alive and well. You honored my request, even when I still hated You.* Caden's eyes filled with tears as he took in a slow breath. *Thank you, Yahweh.* He stepped forward, drew Ellie into his arms, and held her.

She softly laughed. "I can't believe you're here."

Caden permitted a small smile. "Me either."

"How did you get here? Did you fly or take a boat? Wait, wait, are you hungry? You're so skinny! You must eat! I made enough for some guests. Noam?" She broke off in Hebrew, and the smoking stranger answered with a nod and smile.

"Come." Ellie said as she linked her arm with Caden's. They used to do that all the time; Caden remembered walking to high school art class with her, arm in arm. Yohanan stepped closer, reaching to take her other arm, but she pulled back. "You're in trouble!" He frowned. "Don't come close to us. Now you're in the hole!"

"The hole?"

"You need to gain his trust, but you did the opposite."

"I didn't hurt-"

"Yohanan!"

He smiled and stepped back with his hands raised. "Fine, *neshama-*"

"Don't 'sweetheart' me." Ellie grumbled as she led Caden into the camp.

Caden frowned as he followed her. "I thought that meant 'my soul'?"

"Oh, whatever. English is such a limited language!"

They walked through the camp to a tent close to the

outer edge. Inside, vividly colorful blankets lay all across the floor. Equally as bright pillows lined one wall as a shelf housed simple cooking supplies. The room smelled of rich spices as dinner was already laid out on the floor.

"Please," Ellie said, motioning to one of the pillows. "Grab one. Sit and eat." Noam's wife joined, a dark-brown-haired, willowy Egyptian who nearly stood as tall as Yohanan. Her name was Auset. They all sat together on the floor as Ellie and Auset poured tea and set out the plates. There were no utensils, and Ellie handed Caden flatbread, telling him to pretend it was a spoon. Before eating, they all held hands to bless the food. Caden stared hesitantly at Noam's offered hand, and the Israeli nodded respectfully before withdrawing. No one seemed to mind.

"You'll get used to this," Ellie whispered. "Please relax, you're so wound up."

He was. He couldn't help it. *I did have one of these guys put a gun to my head this morning,* he thought in his defense. Had Noam been the one to pat him down and take his gun? He couldn't remember.

Yohanan said the blessing in Hebrew, and they began to eat. Caden stayed quiet and as small as possible, watching the strangers' every move. He watched Yohanan most of all, convinced Ellie was with him because she needed to survive. Now that Caden was there, she didn't need Yohanan anymore. Yohanan couldn't use her or play games with her, like he had with Caden. As they ate, Caden saw Ellie laugh as Yohanan told a story. She smiled and leaned on him, talking in Hebrew with a bright gleam in her aqua eyes. He stared, remembering she always got that look when talking about ancient Egypt or after taking a walk with Papa.

She's happy here, he realized. *She's at peace. Does she have the Raw Peace?* He was grateful she left him alone; she knew him so well. He needed time to observe, to think, and to ease into this new environment. And to stop thinking of Yohanan as a torturous terrorist. *He did enjoy me on my knees,* Caden thought as anger heated his blood. *He could still be a bad guy.* Caden was starting to doubt it as he watched Yohanan playfully jest with Noam and ask Auset about a blanket she was weaving. There was laughter, acceptance, and life among these people. *Kind of like the Mizrahis,* Caden realized. *It's the Raw Peace. It is here too. Yahweh's here.*

It wasn't until after the meal Caden forced himself to take a deep breath and sit straighter. Ellie instantly noticed and smiled. "Can you tell us anything of your adventures?"

Caden stared at her, Nate's shrunken, starved face and Trace's unblinking stare flashing across his mind's eye. He had to tell her they were the last surviving members of their family. How could he do that? A hard lump formed in his throat, and he tried to speak, but couldn't.

Ellie must've known. Her smile fell as she turned away. With a sharp breath, she lifted her chin and cleared her throat. "I'll go first. But please, please tell me everything after! Alright?"

Caden glanced at Yohanan and sighed. "Sure."

Ellie told him how she landed in Cairo nearly four years ago, two weeks before the Day of Vanishing. She was about to fly home when every Christian disappeared. She was grateful she wasn't on a plane, she was sure they would've crashed into the ocean, but her flight was delayed. There was mayhem, panic, and chaos. Luckily, she had hit it off with one of the tour guides, and he was willing to house her for a few days.

"Long enough to get my bearings," she said. "But it was nuts. I had to get out of Cairo as soon as I could."

She stayed with the tour guide's family until they, too, started falling apart. Food was running out. Looters were everywhere. Everyone was carrying guns. Then, their saviors came, dressed in white. The King's United Society entered and offered order, stability, and a force strong enough to deal with the corrupt.

"We thought they were angels," she said and frowned. "It shows how desperate we were."

The Sentinels resurrected society enough for people to start living again, not just surviving. Cairo started filling with people again, but not just people. Giants made their home in the city too. Ellie had thought the Sentinels would drive them away, but they claimed to welcome any with opened arms. Freaks of Nature started weaseling their way in too. There was order, but it came with false security.

"The ones who knew the Bible started speaking up," Ellie said. "I remember them yelling in the streets, warning anyone who'd listen. They seemed so desperate for us to know their truth."

"How'd you get saved?" Caden asked.

Ellie smiled and glanced at Yohanan, laying a gentle hand on his knee. "Oh, some young, handsome Israeli came over. I had a pest control problem. What was that animal again?"

"A scorpion," Yohanan said. "With wings."

Caden grimaced. "That sounds awful!"

"It was!" Ellie nodded. "I was too afraid to hunt it down, and my roommates wouldn't touch it. But Yohanan didn't mind. He came walking in, stared at the thing, and laughed."

Yohanan shrugged. "It was funny. I felt like all of life had become a huge joke."

"I asked him why he wasn't afraid of it," Ellie said with a smile. "He said he wasn't afraid of anything because of King Yeshua. We talked. He asked me to dinner. And here we are."

Yohanan cocked a brow. "Woah! What an oversimplification, Spiny!" Caden shot him a look.

"What?" Ellie snapped. "That's what happened!"

"You forgot all about your uneducated butt totally confused and leaning on me to understand everything."

"I had only been in Israel for two months! I couldn't know a language by then!"

"Sure, you could."

Ellie huffed and crossed her arms as Yohanan smiled. She muttered Hebrew, and Yohanan raised a hand, sitting back. "Anyway," Ellie sighed, adjusting her head covering. "We met with other believers. It was like church, but not so stuffy and forced and stressful. It was just hanging out with other people who wanted to be with us and help us."

"A big family." Yohanan said.

"Right! That's where we met Noam and Auset. We would all go out and tell others Yeshua was coming soon. Things were going well, until people stopped wanting to listen to us preach." She fell silent, and Yohanan rubbed her back.

Caden stared at his sister and, for the first time, wondered if she'd seen more horrors than he. He swallowed the hard lump in his throat, wanting to fix all the pain he saw in Ellie's eyes. "I'm sorry, El." he whispered. She nodded and ducked her head.

With a forced smile, Ellie wiped her eyes and lifted her chin. "Anyways," she said, taking a deep breath. "We fled shortly after. Only a few of us made it, but... but here we are. Alive. Together. With my brother!" Ellie beamed as she motioned to Caden. He gave a small smile. "Okey, ding!" Ellie said. "Your turn!"

Caden didn't answer as he stared down at his plate. He heard his heart pounding in his ears. Yohanan nearly killed him that morning! Had everyone just forgotten that? With a hissed curse, Caden ran fingers through his hair. Yohanan moved to speak, but Ellie held up a hand, silencing him. Caden sniffed and lifted his chin. He faced Ellie.

Just talk to her, he thought. *I can't just let fear be the boss. I'm the boss! Or... is God the boss now?*

"I'm all that's left of our family."

Why did he start with that? That was terrible! Like, the worst way to tell Ellie everyone was dead! She blinked slowly and nodded. "I figured as much. When I heard America was one of the Dark Lands, I prayed for you all, but..." She sighed and turned away. "I'm just grateful you're here." Caden stared at her, seeing the deep sadness in her eyes. "Can you, I mean... would you be willing to share how they died?"

Caden shifted under the weight of failing his family and turned away. He told her. It was the first time he told anyone about finding Nate starved to death and Trace's blank stare as he lay in his blood. It was freeing, as though he was finally taking off a backpack full of rocks.

"What about Dad?" she whispered, her eyes misty.

"Oh, him? Car accident on the Day of Vanishing."

"Did he become a Christian?" Caden grimaced and shook his head. She seemed sadder about that than losing her brothers.

How Christianly of you, Caden thought, realizing he hadn't considered his dad's salvation at all. He detailed the con he, somehow, pulled off with the Mizrahis and how they got to the Middle East.

"I can see you doing that." Ellie said.

Caden frowned. "What? I'd never done something like that in my life!"

"Oh, please! You were always conning Dad!"

"Huh?"

"To keep us safe, you always were tricking Dad into

thinking one thing or another. You always acted like someone else around him too."

Caden's frown deepened. "I did?"

"You could totally pull off a con." She gave him a thumbs up. "Nice."

"Ah... thanks?"

"Got any enemies?" Yohanan asked.

Caden glanced at him and took in a slow breath. "Yeah. Lots." He told them about Officer Nathaniel wanting him dead, Grant Yarrow wanting to enslave him, and Bobby Rut wanting to eat him. "And one more. He's... he's real different. Followed me from America too."

Noam and Yohanan stiffened. "Do we need to have a lookout?" Noam muttered around his cigarette.

Caden shrugged. "Wouldn't do any good. He's a Demon." The room fell silent as all turned and regarded him. Caden forced himself not to look away as his hair stood on end. *There's no going back now.* "I see them now and then. The Demons. They don't harm me. I hear them, we talk sometimes, but only one's touched me." He held out his hand and traced the pale scar with his finger. "I think, I'm not sure, but I think that Demon was attacked because he touched me." Yohanan tilted his head to one side as Noam took a long drag from the cigarette.

"Am," Auset muttered. "Do you attack Demon?"

"I tried, I couldn't touch it, but something else, something I couldn't see, swooped in and," Caden held up his hands. "I don't know what happened. The next thing I knew, the Demon was in the mud, its side all burnt, and half its face was bit off." Caden waited for them to say he's crazy or find ropes to secure their newfound resource. *Please don't make me a slave,* he thought, unable to keep Grant Yarrow out of his head.

Yohanan nodded slowly. "Cool."

"No." Caden glared at him. "Not cool. I nearly died.

Anyways, the KUS call Demons Heralds. Nathaniel said the Heralds told him to kill us. That's all I know. I still don't understand why that would be enough reason to kill someone."

"Perfect reason," Noam said and breathed out a puff of smoke. Caden shifted with a frown. "Demons can't hurt you, but humans can. They wanted their human pets to kill what they can't. Perfect reason."

Caden stared at him, his mouth slack as he tried to think of something to say. *It couldn't be that easy!*

Noam grinned and removed his cigarette as he pointed at Caden. "You know I'm right."

"Sounds right," Yohanan said. "If I was a Demon, I'd try to kill you too."

Caden ran fingers through his hair and turned away. It made sense. This entire time, Caden thought it was a misunderstanding, or he and Trace had done something horrific by accident. *It's because they aren't permitted to harm me. Is that why you tried to get me to jump off the cliff? You couldn't push me yourself?* Caden straightened as his eyes darted around the tent, seeing if Doeg was close.

"See any?" Yohanan asked as he rubbed Ellie's back. Caden shook his head. "Shame. We could run it off."

"One is around though. All the time. He's followed me into the Sinai Desert too."

Ellie's brow furrowed as Yohanan laughed. "Feisty thing! What's he want?"

"My death. But spiritual death first, he told me. Then physical."

"How nice."

Noam leaned forward, his brows pinched in thought. "Is his face bit? Side burned?" Caden nodded. "Vengeance."

"Yep."

"Hum," Ellie grunted. "You have a lot of enemies."

"Yep."

"Do you know what hurt him?" Yohanan asked. Caden shook his head. "Tell me about what happened."

Caden did, in as much detail as he could. He was shocked they all listened and, most of all, believed what he said. As he shared about the massive gusts of wind and several wings flapping, it all sounded so unreal. *It happened*, he thought. *I know it did.*

"Hum," Yohanan grunted. "Seen any other Spirits that weren't Demons?"

Caden shook his head, then stopped. "Well, one, I think. It was just eyes. Like, lots and lots of eyeballs. They were floating over my bed, just staring. I think Trace saw them too, but he said they had big arms with huge fingers held up, like ready to grab someone, and why are you smiling?"

Yohanan glanced between the three others, a gleam in his eye. "Have you seen any ox tracks around you? Cow hoof prints?"

Caden's face scrunched with confusion. "Ah, no?"

"You sure?"

"Yes. That's the most random-" Caden cut short and blinked. *Ophir,* he thought, remembering back when he was tied to the Mizrahi bed, his broken leg still healing. *She had asked where my cow was. She had seen tracks in the mud!*

"Hoof prints," he muttered with a slow nod. Yohanan's smile grew, and Caden shifted restlessly. "Well? Spit it out."

"Cherub," Yohanan said, lifting his chin. "You've got a Cherub protecting you."

Caden snorted a laugh. "I have a little, chubby toddler flying around with a mini bow and arrow? I don't think so."

"No, the *real* Cherub, how the Bible describes them in Ezekiel."

Caden fell silent as Noam set down his cigarette. "It's a cow angel?" Caden asked.

"Their feet are hooves."

Weird, Caden thought as his brows rose.

"And they have four wings, oh, and four faces too."

"They have what?"

"One's an ox, another's an eagle, am... one's a bear-no a lion. It's a lion. The last one's a human face." Caden shook his head, the visual image getting more and more chaotic. "And," Yohanan leaned forward. "They're covered, I mean covered, in eyeballs. Oh, and they have swords on fire. Your Demon friend's face got bit off, so," he shrugged, "maybe the lion took a chunk out of him. The sword of fire did the rest."

"I," Caden stammered. "I didn't see it. I would've seen *that*."

"The Bible says they move like lightning, so very fast. Too fast to see. Besides, sounds like you were wounded and trying not to die." Caden stared at Yohanan as the Israeli sat back with a smug grin on his face. "Need any other spiritual questions answered?"

Caden didn't answer as he rubbed the back of his neck again, trying to comprehend that Cherubim weren't toddler angels but instead multifaced, eyeballed creatures. *They sound dangerous,* he thought as his hair stood on end. *Is it here right now?* He glanced around but saw nothing.

Caden grabbed his cold cup of tea and sipped, but he didn't taste it. *I don't want to meet that,* he thought. *They sound like monsters from a horror movie! Will it stand over me tonight?* Caden's stomach twisted, and he knew this new thing had stood over him for many, many nights. *Yahweh, keep me safe. I can't handle* another *Spirit tormenting me!* A small hand reached forward and slid into his. Caden blinked, his thoughts shattering, and faced Ellie.

She gave him a soft smile. "I'm glad you're here."

Caden held her hand as his anxious thoughts slowed to a standstill. He was still unable to believe his little sister was right here. *You proved Yourself,* he thought. *And I'm now following You. Your presence came with me out into the desert. You are giving me rest.* Caden closed his eyes and kissed his sister's hand, never wanting that little moment to end.

"You'll have to speak to the elders." Yohanan said.

"Why?" Ellie asked.

"He's seen the *Akal Esh*."

"What? Where? What happened? Was it amazing!" Caden glanced at Ellie and tried to decide which question to answer first.

"He'll tell the elders." Yohanan said.

"I can't go in there though!"

"Sucks for you, Spiny."

"Yohanan-"

"I'm sure he'll tell you about it after. Tomorrow though, Caden. You've got to talk to them."

Caden felt unease creep over his nerves, but he lifted his chin. "And take you all back." Yohanan frowned. "We've got to go to Jerusalem."

"What for? They won't agree."

Caden stared at him and blinked. *What do I do with that?* "Well... that's what my friend said to do, my friend with the *Akal Esh*." The group stared at Caden in confusion, and he swatted a hand. "You'll learn tomorrow with the elders." Yohanan shrugged and sipped his tea.

"They won't do it," Noam muttered. "Too afraid of KUS."

"Well," Caden said with a sigh. "That's what I have to tell them."

"Good luck." Yohanan sniffed and straightened. "I'll stand with you." Caden glanced at him. "We're family." Caden frowned. "You don't believe me?"

Caden's brows rose as he crossed his arms. *Has he really forgotten about this morning?*

"Fine. Maybe this could get me out of the hole, hum?"

Caden didn't answer. *How do I make them all come with me?* He thought. *If no one comes, is that my fault? Will Yahweh say I failed? Why do they need to be in Jerusalem in the first place?*

Caden sighed and ran fingers through his hair. *Now's when I use faith, isn't it?* He cursed under his breath as his stomach knotted with unease. He was new to this Christian faith stuff, and already, it was annoying.

FIVE
THE TURNING DOORKNOB

CADEN SLOWLY ROLLED over with a moan as the camp's bustling noise woke him. He blinked the sleep from his eyes and stared up at the colorfully striped tent ceiling and the ropes and wooden, irregular poles that supported it. The wind gently swayed the tent, and he could hear a camel walking by. He looked around and saw he was the only one in Ellie and Yohanan's tent.

Of course, he's my brother-in-law, Caden thought with a curse as he slowly rose. He rubbed his forehead where Yohanan's gun had pressed, and he tried not to shiver. The stranger had looked so bloodthirsty, so intense. *And now we're related.* Caden took in a breath, hoping Ellie was telling the truth and that she wanted to be married to him. He had seen some of what women did in the name of survival. He would hate for his Lil El to resort to such means.

He slowly shook his head, running fingers through his hair and feeling the bits of sand. He was grateful they gave him a sleeping mat, but he couldn't help but think of before the Day of Vanishing. And showers. And cars instead of camels.

At least I found her, he thought as he stood. He straightened his clothes and rolled up the bedroll. After a stretch, he looked around the tent for something to eat, he noticed the doorknob turned. Caden's eyes narrowed. *Tents don't have-*

Smack in the middle of the tent, an upright rectangle swung wide. No, it was kicked open. The invisible Door burst out of the way, kicking up sand and throwing back the corners of some floor mats. Caden stumbled away, suddenly wide awake. He stared in dumbfounded awe as several things happened at once.

First, he realized it was another Door, just like he saw in Camp Little Rock. Second, it was night beyond The Door. Third, two monsters were crashing through it. One was a Shade, the Demon yowling as blood dripped from its mouth. The clawed monster fell through the door, bald, clawed limbs flailing as its white, furry tail lashed out. Caden leapt from its path and clung to the tent's wall. The Shade regained traction and crouched low, readying to pounce. Caden's heart leapt into his throat as the second monster raced after the Shade.

It was huge, walked upright like a man, and its skin was alive. The skin moved and flickered, the same way fire moves, yet it reflected light like metal. The monster's head had no mouth, and one big, black eye stared straight at the Shade. It had no tail, and instead of claws, its hands were clubs, like medieval maces. As it stepped, its clubbed-looking feet sank deeply into the sand.

It charged the Shade, not hesitating a moment, and didn't look wounded or even tired. The Shade yowled and leapt. The metal monster swung its club-like front leg into the Shade's side, sending it into a crumpled heap. The Shade whined, trying to rise.

Is this a Cherub? Caden thought as the metal monster

advanced. *It's beating this Shade too! But it's not how Yohanan described them.*

Another metal monster stepped from the door. It was a bit smaller than the first, yet its skin was alive and moving too. The smaller monster's single black eye turned and regarded Caden. The eye didn't blink. Caden didn't move, knowing if this thing could wound a Shade, he was toast. The smaller monster nudged the other and nodded its bald head at Caden. The larger one turned, and Caden felt all the blood rush from his face. All strength left him, and he nearly sank to his knees.

The larger monster made a sudden noise. It was loud and forceful, as all breath left it. Caden blinked as his brows knotted. *Was that a laugh?*

The monster held up an undefined stubby arm and a small tail-thing stuck upright suddenly. "One sec…" it said. Now Caden was on his knees, unable to stand any longer.

The large monster turned to the Shade, who had barely managed to drag itself to its feet. The Demon's bared fangs dripped saliva and blood as its fur bristled. The larger monster kicked the Demon's middle, flinging the Shade up into the air. As the Demon flew up, the monster windmilled its club-of-an-arm into the Shade's back. The Shade shot to the ground, sending up sand and dust.

Caden flinched back, gasping, seeing the Shade half buried in the sand. Without showing any exhaustion at all, the large monster stepped back as the second monster's stubby arms shifted. Five small tails uncurled from each stubby end of its arm. Caden blinked, his mind trying to understand any of it. Why did it have tails on its arm-?

Fingers! His brain finally screamed. *Those are fingers, retard!*

The monster bent down and grabbed fistfuls of the

Shade's pelt. The Shade limply hung in the monster's grasp as it stepped toward The Door and flung the Demon through, as though tossing out the trash. The two monsters turned to one another, their huge, black eyes still not blinking once, and spoke to one another. Deep in Caden's subconscious, he wondered how they communicated. They didn't have any mouths. If he'd been paying any attention, he'd realize they were speaking Hebrew. The rest of his brain was trying not to black out as his heart hammered in his ears.

The larger monster turned to Caden and grabbed its head. Without warning, it twisted and yanked its head clean off. Caden gulped, recoiling, and grateful he hadn't had any breakfast. He'd be seeing it again real soon.

"Hey, I know this is a lot." Caden felt like someone was stepping on his chest. He could hardly breathe! He cowered back, unable to bring himself to look. The monster growled under its breath. "Oh, I remember this."

"Scary?" That was a female voice. It was accented. Had Caden heard that voice before?

"I nearly puked." The voices stilled, and Caden tried to think of how to escape. Why hadn't anyone heard the shouting? A Demon getting beat up by two cyclopes should make a lot of noise! "And then I thought we were cyclopes."

"What?"

"Well, you know. The helmets kind of look like one, big eyeball."

"Hum... You were very dehydrated then."

"Thanks."

"Look at you!" The voices finally stopped, and Caden licked his cracked lips.

"Caden?"

He didn't move. *How do they know me? Who are they?*

"Look, man. Just look up. We're not going to hurt

you." Caden tried to breathe and think and not die. "Caden, we're from the other side of The Door." The male voice was speaking again. "And you've seen Dasha before."

"He has?"

"When you're older."

"Oh."

Dasha? Caden slowly looked up, memories of the old woman standing behind Gideon flashed through his mind. He looked at the smaller monster and stared in bewilderment. This monster had also taken off its head, only to show a human head beneath. It was a woman.

As his terror wore away, Caden recognized the moving, hard skin was actually armor. She was covered in it, making her look larger than she truly was. The armor, though bulky and covering every inch of her, had scale-like plates beneath that didn't seem to constrict movement. The armor wasn't really metal. It seemed hard like metal, but it was moving, shifting like water or smoke and flickering with an inner light like a candle. It still kept its shape though. It was confusing.

The woman crossed her arms, her smooth, brunette hair pulled back in a tight bun, and her pale blue eyes stared down at him. She wasn't smiling. A nudge from the larger monster, or armored stranger, drew a halfhearted smile out of her. "Weird how you Americans smile."

"Come on!"

"I don't even know him!"

"Do it, crazy Russian." The woman smiled for real this time, her eyes lighting like a clear morning sky, as she glanced at the larger monster. Caden swallowed the hard lump in his throat and faced the second one, unable to stop thinking of the strength in his fists.

It was a man, his armor the same as hers. As he looked, he realized both had swords strapped to their sides. Why hadn't they used them? *They didn't need to,* he realized. The man was very happy to see him. He was smiling ear to ear. His hair was cropped short, and he had no facial hair, revealing a deep, pale scar indenting his chin. Another scar ran up his right cheek and over his cheekbone. It barely missed his eye and shaved the tip of his eyebrow. Another scar lined beneath his jaw, angling toward his throat. They were deep, old scars and told of a life of raw violence.

Caden leaned back, knowing even without the weird armor, this man could kill him. No, kill was putting it lightly. He could obliterate him. But the man's brown eyes, they weren't dark like the eyes of a murderer. They were calm and peaceful.

The man sniffed and planted his hands on his hips. "Yep," he said at last. "I do have scars. One from her even."

Dasha clicked her tongue and glared at him. "How many times do I say I'm sorry!"

The man beamed and nudged her again. "A few thousand more if you please."

"Insufferable American brat."

"It really hurt!"

"It makes you look manly and brave."

"Oh, please."

Dasha tried not to smile, but Caden could see it in her eyes. He licked his lips again and uncurled himself from the ground as he stood. His shoulders still hunched, but at least he had stopped shaking. "Um," he stammered and cleared his throat. "What, um... I'm Caden Johnson." He dipped his head, wondering if he should kneel.

"Don't kneel, please." the man said, holding out an armored hand.

How does he know what I'm thinking!

"I can't read your mind."

A muscle in Caden's jaw flexed. *He just disproved himself.*

"I, um... I simply remember this. And don't bow because we're just people. Just like you."

Caden didn't answer as he raised a brow. *I am nothing like you.*

"I am Dasha Patrov," the woman said with a sound nod. "This is my husband," she said, motioning to the man. "Caden Johnson."

Caden blinked and looked at the stranger as the man's smile grew. *Do we share the same name?* Caden thought but knew that wasn't right.

"Time travel is a possibility in our era," the man said. "You have, or, more accurately, we both have seen our darling Dasha when she's more mature and seasoned." She gave him a firm glare. "And our grandson."

Caden cocked a brow. "Gideon?"

The man nodded. "Now you get to see her again." Caden stared at the larger man, his head spinning. "I know," the man said. "This is a lot. That's why The King permitted time travel after He came."

Caden blinked again and slowly shook his head. "The king is the Antichrist."

"No, I speak of *The King*. The King of kings, Lord of lords. King Yeshua."

"Ah, so is that," Caden mumbled, pointing through the half-opened Door. "Is that Heaven?"

"No."

I'm so confused.

"It's complicated and not why we're here to see you, Caden."

"You're me." Caden muttered.

The man smiled gently and nodded. "I am you." Caden shook his head and ran fingers through his hair. He moaned and squeezed his eyes shut tight. "Caden, Caden, listen, buddy," the man said, stepping closer. "I have a message from The King. The *true* King. Yeshua. He autho-rized this Door; He wants you to know something." Caden took in a breath and faced his older self. His eyes ping-ponged from one scar to the other, his stomach tightening further and further. "Caden-"

"Is it a good message?" He coughed.

"Don't puke."

Caden groaned again and shook his head. "Why can't I feel the Raw Peace?"

"Hum?"

"The Raw Peace comes through The Door. Why can't I feel it?"

Dasha raised her left brow. "What is he saying?"

"The *Akal Esh*. Um, Caden, we aren't in The King's lands. The outlands do not have His Raw Peace. I'm sorry. You will feel it soon. I promise. But listen now. Are you listening?" Caden forced himself to look up into the scarred face of his future. "King Yeshua wants you to accept the hospitality of the first person who offers it. The first person, understand? No matter who or what they are."

A chill washed over Caden's skin. "What are you leaving out?"

"Everything, honestly." his older self said with a sigh.

"So, tell me."

The man shook his head. "The entire truth is too heavy; such is why Yeshua only gives us bits and pieces sometimes. It's frustrating, but safer that way." Caden's eyes narrowed. Who did this guy think he was? Did he know all that Caden had gone through already? "Yes," the man said. "I remember. And I also remember how grateful I was I didn't know everything."

Caden turned away and crossed his arms. He shook his head and sighed before facing them again. "Anything else?"

"When you see me," Dasha said. "Don't say my name. Makes me want to kill you more."

Caden's eyes widened. "Why would you want to kill me?"

"You shouldn't have told him your name." older Caden said.

"Ah," she waved a hand at him, "it is done."

"And I'll be the one to pay for it." he muttered, idly rubbing the scar on his chin.

She shrugged. "I like that scar. Makes me think of us."

"Makes me think of crazy Russians."

"Whatever, Sammy."

That's a weird nickname, Caden thought as he glanced between the two. His unease slowly quieted. "You two are goofy."

Dasha laughed, and older Caden smiled. "Speak for yourself." older Caden said. "Well, we've got to go. There's more Shades and Fiends to beat."

Caden frowned. "Fiends?"

"Ah, other Demons you'll meet later."

Caden's arms fell at his sides. "Great. I do have questions."

"No." Dasha snapped.

"Quick." older Caden said.

"How did you punch that Demon? I tried before, and it didn't work."

"Demons are spirits," older Caden said. "And this," he held up his armored hand and wiggled his fingers, "is spiritual armor. Next question?"

"Ah… why do we have to go back to Jerusalem?"

"Because!" Older Caden shifted his weight. "You, Yohanan, and other believers have lots of work to do in Jerusalem. There are prophecies to fulfill, planes to catch, and nations to warn. Last question?"

"That's not an answer!"

"Last question!"

Caden cursed under his breath, and Dasha clicked her tongue again. "I'm glad you stopped that."

"How old are you?" Caden asked, facing the man.

Older Caden's brow scrunched as he leaned back and stared into the distance. He glanced at Dasha, who also gave him a blank look. "Honestly," he finally said. "After two cen, you really stop keeping count."

Caden frowned. "Cen? What's that?"

"Centuries." Caden had to pick his jaw up off the floor as older Caden laughed.

Dasha shook her head. "We must go-"

"How is that not Heaven?" Caden demanded, pointing to The Door.

Older Caden shook his head. "I said that was the last question."

"But!"

"Caden, listen." Caden stilled and looked up, finding his older self standing close. Old Caden lay a heavy, firm hand on his shoulder and regarded him for a moment. "You are strong and worthy," he whispered. Caden blinked, caught off guard. "Yahweh has selected you for greatness beyond your wildest dreams." Caden's chest tightened as he tried to speak. No words came.

Behind them, Dasha scoffed. "Put that on a card."

"Yeah," older Caden muttered, stepping back. "Well, that's what I needed to hear right now." Dasha muttered something in Hebrew, and older Caden waved a hand at her. "Hang in there," older Caden called as the two stepped toward The Door. "Say hi to Han for me too."

"Who's that?"

"Oh, you haven't met? That's right, well, um... never mind." Dasha nodded to Caden, and he could've sworn she was smiling that time before she walked through the door. "Remember what I said," older Caden called. He set his helmet back into place and stared at Caden. "Accept hospitality from-"

"-the first person to offer, I know. Thanks for encouraging me."

Older Caden waved a hand. "You'll survive. Obviously." He motioned to himself. "*Shalom*."

Caden smiled and dipped his head. "*Shalom*."

Older Caden nodded and stepped through The Door. Caden watched as The Door swung shut, taking the night and the world beyond with it. It shut with a soft click, and Caden glanced around the now quiet tent. He stared at the mini crater the Shade made when punched to the ground. How was he going to explain that to Ellie? Caden ran fingers through his hair and sat down. He shook his head and forced himself to laugh. What was that verse Mama Lo used to say? The Lord works in mysterious ways?

You're telling me, Caden thought.

SIX
MORE NEW MONSTERS

CADEN HATED PUBLIC SPEAKING. In high school, it was the worst class, next to geometry, and he tried to say he had a sore throat all the time. It worked for the first few classes, but the teacher wasn't a dummy. Every time, Caden's guts knotted themselves until it hurt. He always knew he'd slur his words or say something wrong, or his fly would be unzipped. He would fail. Again. Everyone would laugh. Everyone would call him GJ-

Go away, Doeg! Caden cursed as he looked down and tried to focus.

"That was entirely your own conscious, my boy."

Caden took in a deep breath and glanced around. He sat in a big tent, the four walls being partial reed mats and partial blankets. Vividly colorful blankets lay across the floor between trays of tea, pillows, and old men piled beneath dark robes. Yohanan, Noam, and Caden sat in the back with the other younger men and let the elders conduct their own business first. Their voices were loud and confusing. Caden could pick out a few Hebrew words, and a bit Aramaic, but everyone talked so fast! How could he ever communicate with them?

Just tell them what happened, Caden thought. *Tell them Elijah said to come to Jerusalem. I can't make them come. How they respond is their own fault.* He hoped God felt that way too. He better; Caden had no idea how to persuade these people to do a thing.

After a time, one of the elders, the one who looked the most like wrinkled leather, nodded to Yohanan. Caden guessed he was the leader. Had they called him Abra? Yohanan jumped right up and walked before the gathering as though he'd done it all his life. Caden envied his nonchalant as he bowed to the elders and cleared his throat before diving into more confusing Hebrew. He gestured and turned, facing every listener. He smiled, motioned to Caden, and placed fingers to his head like a gun. The gathering laughed, and Caden realized Yohanan was telling how they met.

Great, Caden thought. *They'll think I'm a coward that nearly peed his pants.* He looked down and wished he could pay Yohanan back somehow. With a grimace, Caden let out a breath and knew there were more important things to focus on. Yohanan's face became serious, and the amusement died down as everyone listened. Noam grunted as he glanced at Caden. Others straightened and also gave Caden quick looks.

"What's he saying now?" Caden hissed to Noam.

"That you're brave," Noam muttered. He sat with his hands limply laying on his crossed legs, his eyes half closed as he casually leaned back. "You're Strong. Not weak. Didn't beg or stand down when you thought we'd kill you." Caden straightened and gave his brother-in-law a quick look. Yohanan finished and stared down at Caden. "He stands by you," Noam translated. "He'll fight beside you."

Caden slowly lifted his chin as he blinked. *Maybe he's not so bad after all.*

Yohanan held out a hand, and Caden made himself stand. He tried not to stumble before the elders, but his legs kept feeling wobbly. Yohanan clapped him on the shoulder and stepped back but continued standing by him. "I'll translate." he whispered.

"Don't they know English?"

"Yeah, but they'd rather be talked to in their own language."

Caden looked out across the odd, foreign faces and didn't have a clue of what to say. "Hi, um," he stammered and felt stupid. "So..."

"The *Akal Esh*." Yohanan whispered.

"Right, um." Caden straightened and tried to think of The Door. What would those people do? Would they stammer or speak boldly? "The *Akal Esh* came down in Jerusalem, at the Wailing Wall." As Yohanan translated, the elders glanced at one another and the younger men gasped and whispered. "It entered my friend, Elijah Mizrahi. He is now filled with Yahweh's Consuming Fire." There was more buzzing excitement as he spoke. "Elijah is the first Witness spoken of in Revelation, um... eleven. He's supposed to tell everyone Yeshua is coming soon and to get ready. Oh, and he breathes fire, so that's cool."

Caden had to pause as the men's voices lifted. Some gestured excitedly while others grimly shook their heads. Caden swallowed the hard lump in his throat; he wasn't sure this was going well. "Um, he said!" They slowly quieted down. "He told me I need to take the people I find out here back to Jerusalem. He said Yahweh orders it." The voices lifted again, some shouting, and a few even stood. Caden tried not to step back as he desperately wanted to know what they were saying.

Don't shoot the messenger, he thought, his nerves tingling with apprehension. Everyone was talking at once, and Caden looked from face to face. Were they angry? They seemed emotional, but he couldn't tell if it was good or bad. He turned to Yohanan and saw his set jaw and shadowed eyes. *Not good,* Caden thought as his heart quickened. *What am I supposed to do? Yahweh? Any ideas?*

Some of the elders motioned to Caden as others nodded and gestured to Yohanan. Someone shouted next to Abra, and the old man lifted his hands, his reedy voice lifting over the crowd. He said something, and Yohanan snorted as he shook his head. "He's questioning who you are," Yohanan hissed to Caden. "Some think you're with the KUS or other anti-Christian groups."

"What? But I-"

"Others just think you're mad."

Caden stammered as he looked across the sea of loud strangers. "Why would I be mad?"

"Seriously? Alone, in the Sinai Desert? And you've got those nice choke bruises on your neck."

"It was a Puppet!"

"And you lived."

"Strangers found me and-this is messed up. I'm a good guy! I'm a Christian too!"

"You're a foreigner."

How do I handle this? Caden thought to Yahweh. *I can't hold them all hostage, make them all go to Jerusalem!*

Yohanan slowly shook his head as he faced his people. With a deep breath, he bellowed Hebrew over the throng, but none quieted. He hissed a curse and tried again, but in English. "Believe Caden Johnson or not!" He cried. The new language caught their attention. "Come or stay! We leave in three days!"

Without another word, Yohanan pushed his way through the crowd and ignored his elders' responses, no matter how loud they were. Caden followed, his head held not as high as he glanced over his shoulder. He burst out of the tent, grateful for the fresh air as the feeling of being trapped evaporated.

"Three days?" Caden asked as he caught up to Yohanan. He nodded. "News to me-"

"Why waste time?"

"I'd like to rest."

"Great. You have three days. Besides, you're not very popular here. Spiny's made many friends. There are concerns if you're really her brother or not."

"I risked my life getting here so many times, I can't even count-"

"People will always question. The facts are you are her brother, and we're leaving soon." Caden sighed heavily and glanced over his shoulder. Some of the younger men were stepping out of the meeting tent and watching them. "We won't go alone," Yohanan said quietly. "I know the boys."

"Boys?"

"The young men. They're restless. They'll come."

Caden faced forward and continued following Yohanan to his tent. *I hope You're happy with that,* he thought to God. *I can't make these people do anything.* With a sigh, Caden ran a hand over his face.

"Relax."

"I am relaxed."

"Sure. You look it."

Caden glared at Yohanan as he grinned. "Spiny is the worst pet name in the entire world."

"Is it now."

"Her name's Ellie."

Yohanan shrugged. "She's little and cute. She likes to be active. She survives in the desert. You know, like an Egyptian Spiny Mouse."

"Shut up."

"It's a real thing. Little desert mouse. Its fur looks like spikes down its spine. I'll point one out when I see one."

"You think mice are cute?"

"Spiny's better than Lil El."

"Thanks."

"Come on, let's get packing."

"You said I could rest a bit!"

Yohanan grinned. "Packing's restful. Get inside and start. These guys look like they have questions." Caden glanced behind them and saw a few young men following. They wouldn't make eye contact, but Caden knew they had been watching. "And tell Spiny what's happening."

"Still a stupid pet name."

"Just do it."

Caden gave a clumsy salute and ducked into the tent. *Looks like the desert's calling me again,* he thought. *Just hope there won't be more Puppets.* He cursed under his breath. *Yahweh, please keep us safe.*

————

THEIR DEPARTURE DIDN'T GO SO well. Most of the community didn't believe anyone should go, and they expressed their opinion very, very loudly. And constantly. Caden's three days of rest were anything but. They were full of packing, planning, bartering, and trying for all it was worth to understand Hebrew. It wasn't working. When there was time, Ellie gave him mini-lessons. It made Caden think of Ophir and want to be back in Jerusalem. Could they all stay in Elezaro's house again? No, there wasn't enough room. It had been Heaven there.

The entire camp had gathered to bid them farewell, or so Caden thought. Instead, everyone who disagreed with the trek shouted their objections one last time. It was horrible, especially when Caden noticed the elderly women who were giving him murderous glares. "What's their problem?" He whispered to Ellie; it was giving him the creeps.

"You're stealing their little boys." she said.

"Am not! There are hardly any kids here!"

"Their sons!" She motioned to the young men loading up their own camels.

"Oh." Caden shuffled his feet and tried not to look at them.

With the young men were a few older, worn-looking men and about three women. Noam and Auset came without complaint or question. The Elders and Yohanan seemed to be struggling over how many supplies the caravan should take. Because they didn't agree on the journey, they didn't want to give up food and water. They especially didn't want to hand over their guns.

Yohanan bartered with them, his demanding, condescending demeanor infuriating them further, until he simply turned his back on them and ordered everyone to load up. Most of the camp's protection comprised of the young men who were leaving. They took their guns, and no one could stop them. Caden felt bad as he watched the camp fade into the distance behind him. With a heaved sigh, he faced forward and tried to sway with the camel's lumbering, thumping steps.

The going was exquisitely fast compared to walking on bleeding, sore feet for hours in the wrong direction. The only downside was Caden's camel could talk. Apparently, Caden was the bottom of the barrel. His camel, who insisted on being called Eleazar, had learned English while transporting tourists. "Your girth is lacking. Are you well?"

Caden glanced at the back of the camel's head as he gripped the saddle, trying not to fall off. "Hum?"

"Your weight is that of a female."

Caden cursed. "Get off my back."

"Off? You are clearly on mine."

"That's not what I meant."

"You humans rarely seem to say what you mean. How ineffective." Caden cursed again and fell silent. "Men shouldn't pout."

"Camels shouldn't talk! Your vocabulary is too-"

"Refined? Educated?"

"Creepy."

"We transported the Union Guild of Literature and Culture every month. Mr. Theodore Denton enjoyed me. He said my gait was smooth and serene."

Caden had no response, he didn't want the camel to know he agreed. "Just," he said and sighed. "Please don't talk a lot. It's really weird."

"Animals with the gift of speech are no longer weird," Eleazar muttered. The camel reared his head back and fixed Caden with one heavily lashed eye. "It is the norm. In fact, I heard a flock of birds yesterday chatting about the weather-"

"Please!" Caden held up a hand. "Please just let me be."

Eleazar's ear flicked, he swung his long neck forward again and kept plodding on. "Still a light human."

Caden sighed heavily. He decided to focus on the positives of traveling with a caravan. Now, he had armed friends, experienced travelers, and someone who knew where Jerusalem was. At least, he hoped Yohanan knew. He seemed a very capable guy. All the young men snapped to attention and listened to him. It was a bit unsettling.

But he's on my side, Caden thought. *For now.* Caden could almost feel the cold muzzle of Yohanan's gun pressed between his eyes again. *Who can predict a sudden, manic decision of violence? It is obvious Yohanan relishes the internal writhing of others. When will he crave your wriggling, like a worm on a-*

Caden cursed, and a muscle in his jaw flexed. *Get out of my head.*

"*Listen to logic-*"

You are death.

"*I am truth.*"

Caden snorted. *Far from it-*

"*What else do you have?*" Caden took in a breath and felt the weight of his weapon bag. His gun was again on his side, alongside the Bible. "*The foolish ravings of a drunken ancient!*" Doeg cried in Caden's mind.

Caden's lips twitched into a smile as he heard the hostility in Doeg's voice. *You really hate this book, don't you?* He reached to remove the Bible.

"*I'll startle your camel. Eleazar will flee, leaving you stranded and helpless.*"

Caden froze, knowing the Shade was capable of anything. With a gruff sniff, he bumped Eleazar with his heel. "Stop-"

"I am not a mule!" The camel snapped. "And it wouldn't kill you to say please!"

"Please."

Eleazar slowed, and Caden quickly slipped from the saddle. He handed the lead rope to Ellie, who was on her own camel. "Peculiar human." Eleazar muttered.

"What are you doing?" Ellie asked.

"My camel's going to spook."

Eleazar's ears flicked back as he walked with stomping force. "I will not!" Ellie's brows rose as Caden started walking beside Eleazar. He unzipped the bag and pulled out the Bible.

"*I only warn once.*" Caden ignored the Demon and leafed through the thin pages.

"Disrespectful," Eleazar muttered. "Of all the great men I've carried, I've never-"

The camel flinched suddenly, lurching toward him. Ellie cried out and seized the lead rope in a firm grip. Caden raced back, Eleazar's hind legs nearly trampling him. Caden jogged a distance away, his heart racing. "Calm down!" He heard Ellie cry. "What's wrong with you!"

"Didn't you see that!" Eleazar demanded, ears drawn back as he tugged at the lead rope.

"Stop that!" Ellie said. "There's nothing there."

"I saw it!"

"Nothing!"

Caden turned away from the two and continued walking a distance away. With a deep breath, he continued looking at the book.

"You dare defy me?"

Caden couldn't ignore the shiver that raced through his body. He cleared his throat and opened the book again.

"Is that a Bible?" He glanced up at Ellie as she gently stroked Eleazar's long nose. The camel breathed heavily, his nostrils puffing with effort. At least he fell in step beside Ellie's camel again.

"Yeah," Caden said. "It was a gift from a good friend."

"Priceless!" She sighed. "Yohanan! Cade has a Bible!"

"A what?" Yohanan called from the front.

"A Bible!"

Yohanan turned in the saddle with a smile. "Read some! Out loud! Spiny, you translate!"

"Oh, no," Caden stammered. "I couldn't-"

"Go to the very end. The very, very end. We'll read what we're all fighting for!"

Caden cursed under his breath, his stomach squeezing itself as all eyes fell on him. "Well..." he stammered.

"Tonight, you will awake with my claws pricking your throat."

Caden froze as the wind rustled the Bible's pages. *"You know I will."*

I'm guarded by a Cherub, Caden thought. *A monster with four faces and a sword of fire. Sounds creepier than you actually. Dare to face that?*

Stiff whiskers brushed Caden's neck as hot breath puffed his cheek. Caden cursed and recoiled, sending a fist into nothing.

"Cade?" He ignored Ellie as his heart was beating in his throat.

"I will toy with you as I did on the cliff face."

"Cade, do you see something?"

"You cannot overcome me."

"Just read the Bible. It'll go away." Caden licked his lips and looked down. He lifted his chin and forced himself to breathe as he turned to the very end of the book.

"Tonight," he heard Doeg in his mind. *"Your flesh-"*

"-is mine." The last two words were audible.

Caden suppressed the panic rising in his chest and finally came to the end of Revelation. "'Look, I am coming soon'," Caden read as loud as he could. He paused. "Who's talking?"

"King Yeshua." Ellie said.

"Okey, um… 'My reward is with me, and I will give to each person according to what they have done.'"

Does that mean I'll get nothing? Or punishment? I got my brothers killed.

"Ah… 'I am the Alpha and the Omega, the First and the Last, the Beginning and the End." The wind blew the pages, and Caden lost his spot. He decided to keep reading right below: "'The Spirit and the bride say, "Come!" And let the one who hears say, "Come!" Let the one who is thirsty come; and let the one who wishes take the free gift of the water of life.'" Caden stared at the final lines of the Bible as Ellie translated for those who didn't understand English.

He's coming, Caden thought. *And He'll give everyone what they deserve. I deserve to eat the dirt. Less than that. Manure. My failures compared to His surpassing greatness will find me wanting. I will be justly rejected and abused. Just another form of a Father who will detest my soul and destroy it.*

Caden started to put the Bible away, but stopped. *I... I didn't think that.* He cursed under his breath and forced himself to study the words and ignore Doeg's constant lies. *Yeshua is coming with His reward. Like, for me too?*

"What have you done worthy of-"

"Shut up!" Caden growled.

"What's wrong?" Caden glanced up, finding Ellie studying him, and turned away.

"See!" Eleazar said. "He sees it too!"

Ellie wouldn't understand. How could she? "Cade?" Ellie said. "I see you." He blinked, knowing that was their code. It was how she said she saw he was struggling even when he was trying so hard to hide it.

With a curse, he ran fingers through his hair. "That Demon whose face is ripped up. He, he just won't leave me alone."

"You hear him? Right now?" Caden nodded. "Good!" Caden glared at her. "Whenever they're angry, something good's happening. Did it really start when you got out the Bible?"

"Yeah."

Ellie smiled. "There you go. Read it more. It's a weapon."

"Asher said that too. The one who gave it to me."

"Well, it is. I know it seems like just an old book, but it's an entire bunker of guns, missiles, nukes, knives, or whatever you want in the Spiritual world."

Caden blinked, remembering his future self and the glowing, ever-moving armor. *Spiritual armor,* he thought.

"Read it more," Ellie said. "Memorize it." She nodded. "You'll see. He won't leave you alone, but he can't control you either. Nothing can now. You belong to Yahweh."

Caden lifted his chin as he looked ahead. *Nothing can now.*

"Foolish she-human!"

"And don't talk back to him either," Ellie continued. "That puts too much focus on a Demon. We just look at Yahweh, and He takes care of the rest."

Caden slowly nodded as he flipped through the small Bible. "So, just ignore him when he talks?"

He could hear Doeg's rasping laugh. *"Impossible. I am inside your mind!"*

"For the most part."

"I will become so unbearable, you cannot ignore me. Do not test me, human!"

Caden felt an icy thrill race through him as he tried ignoring the fanged, clawed Demon breathing down his neck. *I can't do this-*

"As I said."

"Where should I start reading?"

"Waste of time!"

"Try John." Caden nodded and pretended to know where that was. "Go to two-thirds of the way through the book." He found it. "Just ask if you have any questions." Ellie said.

"What's the Word, and why was it with God?" Caden asked.

"The Word is Yeshua."

Caden blinked. "Then why not say that?"

"Because, by Yeshua's word, all things were made. Everything in Heaven and on Earth, what's visible and invisible, and all powers. It's all made *for* Him and is kept alive *by* Him. It all started with His word."

"Oh," Caden said. "Cool." He kept reading but didn't hear it. Not really. Doeg was right; the Demon was so unbearable Caden couldn't ignore him.

"Tonight," Doeg rasped. *"You will see me."*

Caden fought back a shiver as he turned the frail page and surged on. *Please protect me,* Caden prayed. *It's so hard to believe I'm safe when I can't see You! Just let me see something good. Please!*

Doeg laughed, and Caden knew only he could hear it. "I am all there is." Caden closed his eyes as a muscle in his jaw flexed; he hated the Demon's audible voice. With a deep breath, Caden refocused on the Bible and was determined to read as much as he could, even if Doeg's wrath was waiting for him that night.

CADEN LIMPED FROM CAMP. Yohanan, who declared everyone should know how to fight, had started training him. Caden had claimed he learned some maneuvers from Elijah, but Yohanan insisted he knew nothing. As the camp was erected, Caden and Yohanan had sparred a distance from the others. Yohanan was so different than Elijah. Elijah was calm and factual, breaking down all the steps and letting Caden take his time as he learned. Not Yohanan. He thought the best way to learn was to figure it out as you go. Caden only figured out how to get hit, how much it hurt to get kneed in the thigh, and that he really didn't know much defense.

He sighed heavily as his brow pinched. He stared down at a thorny bush and wondered how he could grab some of it for the fire. Yohanan was out of his mind! Caden nudged it with his foot, but the firm plant stayed, its long thorns ready to prick his skin. He glanced over his shoulder and saw the caravan setting up for the night. The sun was setting, and Yohanan had asked him to gather bushes or sticks to make a fire. As if anything grew between the sand and rocks.

"You'll find something," Yohanan had said. "Just look harder!"

Caden cursed as he ran fingers through his hair. He didn't think to pack thick, protective gloves. With a sigh, he looked further down the hill and saw boulders. *Maybe something's growing in there.* He trudged down the hill and listened to his steps crunch across the sand.

He shielded his eyes from the sharp orange glow of the setting sun. The fading light highlighted the sandy browns and yellows of the landscape. He knew that, in a few minutes, the shadows would stretch and take over before expanding into another night. He wrapped his coat tighter around himself, feeling the soft yet chilled wind tug at his clothes. *It's the desert,* Caden thought. *It's not supposed to be cold-*

The wind struck him like a blow to the face. He cowered and yanked the shemagh over his mouth and eyes. Dust flew against him as the wind howled in his ears. There was something else in the wind's roar. Wings flapped like a massive flock of birds descending. Caden gasped as his stomach twisted painfully; he had heard that before.

Caden kept the shemagh over his eyes, as though to hide. His body shook, and his eyes pinched shut. His gasps were loud and sudden as he kept forgetting to breathe. He waited, expecting something to burn him or fangs to rip into his flesh. Hadn't that happened to Doeg?

Nothing happened as the wind died down. Caden whimpered despite himself. With heaved breaths, he dared to open one eye. He slowly turned and faced the newcomer. All color drained from his face.

A monster stood before him. Huge. Powerful. Its massive arms stretched over its head as countless fingers spread wide, ready to strike. Its head was huge, and each side looked different and alive. All over its body were dots that disappeared and reappeared, though stayed stationary. No, they weren't dots. They were eyes.

Caden screamed as he fell face down and curled into a ball, his entire body shaking. He knew two things instantly: First, this monster was a Spirit. Second, there was nothing in the entire world that could stop it from killing him.

SEVEN

IMMORTAL UNTIL YOU DIE

HE WAS BEGGING for his life. It was a distant fact that he didn't have time to consider. He kept thinking of Alex Whitney's shredded body dragged from the back of Grant Yarrow's truck. The blood had pooled beneath him. Caden could still see his pale face; eyes wide open and mouth slack as blood made his teeth look weird.

Caden sucked in air through gritted teeth, every muscle tensing for agonizing pain. He'd seen a body slashed by Demons, but this one apparently liked to burn and had fangs to tear flesh. Caden moaned, unable to feel the jagged rocks digging into his legs and side as he hugged his knees tighter.

Somewhere, in the very back of his mind, he remembered Yohanan talking about Cherubs. The memory was faint and distant and, sadly, unnoticed. All Caden had known were Spirits who only wanted to kill and destroy. Why would this one be any different?

"*Shalom.*"

It spoke! The voice was spoken softly, as though trying to whisper, but it still was so loud. Caden recoiled with a cry and jammed his fingers in his ears.

"Oh," he heard it sigh. "You frightened him."

"They're so easy to frighten."

"He needs to know we're on his team-"

"We agreed I'd do all the talking. He'll calm sooner if only my face speaks."

"Yes, that is what we said."

"Agreed."

"Well, speak then!"

"Hush!" The voices stopped, and Caden could only hear his heart slamming against his chest. "Caden," the first speaker whispered even more gently. It still was loud, but not as much. It was like someone trying to play a tuba quietly. It just can't be done. "Caden, don't fear. Yahweh has lifted the veil so that you can see the one guarding you."

Caden didn't move. How many were there? Was he surrounded? Would they take turns maiming him? If he jumped up now, he could run. He'd escaped Demons before, maybe he could again. *No,* he thought, the single word sending ice into his blood. *You're dead. This one's different. Nothing can stop it.*

The monster fell silent, and he heard its steps crunch the sand. He crawled back as his body shook. He heard its steps stop, and it gave a heavy sigh. "Take your time. I understand we are such a shock to your kind."

What does it want? Caden made fists and continued waiting, not trusting a word it said. The monster waited too, and he heard it shift to and fro, the sand moving beneath it. *It said it was from Yahweh,* he thought, licking his dry lips as he tried to think. *Spirits aren't from God! They're all evil! All want to kill!* But it wasn't killing him or even harming him. Why? What did it want?

Caden cursed through gritted teeth and slowly uncurled himself. He lifted his head and looked up. Though the sky was an umbrae from gray to black and the shadows swept the ground in darkness, the monster shone. Caden squinted his eyes, trying to see past the piercing light.

"Too bright?" A voice asked. "How's this?"

The brilliance dimmed to a shimmering, hot glow. Light like a flame emanated from it and cast shadows all around. It was an inner light that moved and flickered like a living, breathing thing. Even within the countless eyes staring down at him, he saw the living fire. And the eyes were everywhere! All over the monster's arms and neck, even its hands and wings!

Wings, Caden thought as he blinked. *Those are wings.*

At first glance, the massive, spread wings stretching out from the monster looked like arms, and the several fingers were feathers. They were sandy brown feathers with black shafts and white spotted tips. Another set of wings tucked behind the first. Caden finally gathered enough nerves to look at the monster's face. His heart quickened again.

At the forefront, and facing him, was the likeness of a man. His black hair was short, and his skin was tanned. His eyes were slightly slanted, and his face was wide and full. He stared down at Caden and smiled. Caden assumed it was meant to be a calming smile, but nothing this thing could do was calming.

"Do not fear." the human face said again.

"I knew I should've spoken to him first!" It was a squawking voice, and it came from behind the monster. The human face frowned and slowly shook his head.

"He will identify with our human face." another speaker said. Caden blinked hard, and it took him a very long time to grasp that the furry, sandy yellow mass on the monster's right shoulder had spoken. He squinted and found the full mane of a lion as velvety ears swiveled to and fro. He caught sight of whiskers and the profile of a lion. The lion's cat-like eye swiveled in Caden's direction, and they also glowed like a flickering yellow fire.

"Yes," another voice said, this one calm and melodic. "He will relate with our human face. It will reassure him sooner."

Caden grabbed his forehead as he tried to grasp what was happening, for the human nor the lion had spoken. *What's on its other shoulder?* Sticking from the human's left side was a big, pink nose and two pale horns pointing forward and backward. It took a moment for Caden to recognize the cow. But it was bigger than a cow. An ox?

"You, eagle," the oxen continued. "Will not calm him."

Though he couldn't see it, Caden kept hearing the squawking sounds of a bird of prey. "His nation values eagles," the voice squawked again. "He will see-"

The oxen huffed, its wide ear twitching. "He is already terrified. Don't torment him further."

"Fine, fine," the eagle muttered. "You're... you're right."

"Thank you." the human head said as he smiled at Caden again. "Caden." He shrank back again. He could feel the unearthly voice; it was like a strike to the chest with every word. "We are the reason why Doeg cannot kill you. We guard you day and night and heard what Doeg promised tonight. You are valiant for not neglecting the weapons of the Spirit, though faced with such a dog. We have guarded you since the Rapture-"

"-Day of Vanishing." the lion interjected.

"And the Lord of Heaven's Hosts has tasked us with protection until your end."

The monster finally stopped talking, and Caden had a moment to process what was happening. As he lay, curled up, trying to breathe, he felt something. Slowly, he lifted his head and regarded the flickering glow from the monster. Those eyes, every last one of them, shown as though windows to an inner furnace. *There's fire inside of it,* Caden realized. *Fire like-*

"The Consuming Fire?" Caden ducked his head again at the oxen's words. "Oh, dear, I'm sorry. We are a bit scary, aren't we?"

This Spirit has the Consuming Fire, Caden realized as he blinked hard. *The Fire is the Raw Peace. The Raw Peace is Yahweh. So this is, is...* He looked up again and slowly stood. *Angel,* he concluded.

"Cherub, actually." the lion said with a flick of an ear.

The human head's smile broadened, and, with it, each eye narrowed slightly. It took Caden a moment to realize the numerous eyes were also smiling. "I, um..." He tried to speak, but his mouth was completely dry. "Thank you. You saved me."

The heads nodded as a few of the eyes blinked. As he stared, Caden realized the angel wore armor. The armor looked very much like older Caden and Dasha's Spiritual armor yet was different. Though bulky and scaled, never hindering movement, the inner fire was fiercer. Also, the armor's smoke, water-like movements flowed far faster, as though stronger and wilder. Caden realized his brow was damp with sweat. As the sun set, he felt a new heat, one that bathed him in warmth. *Is it coming from the armor?* He blinked, wondering if the Spiritual armor's appearance of fire was an understatement.

Hanging from the Cherub's belt was a sheath. Caden could make out tongues of fire dancing from the sheathed sword's hilt. *The sword is on fire,* he thought. *Even in its cover-thing, it's still burning!*

"You are valuable, Caden," the angel's human face said. "You are needed to bolster our Witnesses and fulfill prophecies."

Caden shook his head as he held up a hand. "Wait, fulfill prophecies?"

"Too much too soon." the oxen whispered.

"Do not dwell on it," the human said. "It will come."

"But," Caden stammered, shaking his head. "I'm barely a Christian. I can't do anything."

"Perfect! Inadequacies are favored above the elite. You know you cannot accomplish anything without the King of Kings. Thus, you will accomplish everything." Caden kept shaking his head, but the Cherub didn't seem to mind. They were probably used to it.

"We are here," the human face said. "To convey a message from Yahweh."

More? Caden thought. *Is it more direction?*

"You, Caden, as with all who place their allegiance in Yahweh's care, are immortal until the moment Yahweh declares you shall die."

Caden blinked and tilted his head to one side. "What?"

"Therefore, if it is not yet your time and a gun is trained on you, it will misfire, the shooter will face calamity, or, if by chance you do die, Yahweh's breath of life will fill you again and raise you up."

Caden stood in stunned silence. "I won't die?" He finally asked.

"You will, but only when Yahweh dictates, no one else." The Cherub's wings unfolded a bit, making the angel look twice as big. "No one."

Not even Doeg, Caden thought as he slowly nodded.

"Whatever you face," the human head said. "Know we are with you. More importantly, Yahweh is watching over you."

Caden grimaced and looked down. *I don't want God watching me! He'll see what I think about. Can't have that. It'll piss Him off. He won't like me. He'll reject me.*

"You should see the look in His eye when He talks about you." The human face chuckled as Caden gave him a startled look.

He talks about me? Why would He?

"It's like how a tender Father brags about their son." Caden frowned as he crossed his arms. "He loves you, Caden." All thoughts stilled. "He suffered and died for you." Caden swallowed the hard lump in his throat as he rubbed his arms. "He would die again if that meant saving you. You matter." Caden opened his mouth to speak but couldn't find the words.

"And," the oxen's face piped up. "Once you come Home, He is very excited to play baseball with you."

"Ah," the human face said and grunted. "*So* excited!"

"I saw Him telling an Elder the other day." the lion muttered.

Caden felt himself weakening. He could feel the Raw Peace pulsing off the Cherub in waves and covering him in a fierce love. At first, the love only felt like wildfire, but now, he knew it was real powerful loyalty and affection. *From God,* Caden thought. *God loves me.* He felt himself sinking to his knees, his mind clear of any other thoughts as this one truth overtook him.

"You will go out and conquer," the human face said. "For Yahweh will safeguard you until your proper and fitting end. Arise. Your sister is worried about you."

Caden didn't answer as he continued kneeling, letting the Raw Peace surround him further. *Let her worry.*

"Now, that's not very nice." the oxen muttered.

"Caden." the human face said in a voice no one in their right mind would disobey. Caden stood and bowed to the monstrous angel.

"Don't bow or pay homage to us," the lion face said. "We are similar to yourself: servants of the Most High."

"It is He you bow to," the human face said. "And He alone."

"Right," Caden muttered. "Sorry."

"You're still learning, child." the oxen said.

"What's your name? Can I, um," Caden stammered. "Can I call for you when I need help?"

The human face frowned sharply. "Never do that! No, no, we are a mere servant! We have no authority or power!" Caden blinked in surprise. "No, direct all your biddings to Yahweh. He will decide to withhold or unleash us."

Caden nodded slowly as he stepped back. "Yes, sir-er, um…"

"Jargalsaikhan."

Caden stared with a blank face. "Um-"

"He won't remember that." the lion said.

"Han," the oxen offered. "He can call us Han."

"Can you remember that?" the eagle squawked.

"I, I can," Caden stammered. "Han. Thank you, Han. Is that a Heaven name or something?"

"Mongolian."

"Weren't they, I don't know, horrible people way back then?"

"Judgmental human." the eagle called.

"Most were," the human face said. "But, as always, anyone, no matter the nationality, can choose the path of Yahweh. Even a surviving, baseball-loving, young American." Caden smiled as the countless eyes creased with amusement.

"Go on now," the eagle said. "Ellie's still worried."

"Goodnight, Caden." the oxen said.

"*Shalom*." the human face said.

"*Shalom*, Han," Caden said with a dip of his head. "Will I see you again?" The human face's smile grew as a low rumble came from the lion.

"Most definitely, dear," the oxen said. "Now, do step back. Wouldn't want to knock you over when we fly off."

Caden leapt back and raced several paces away. Even at a distance, he could see the multi-eyes that glowed with a fire from within. *I want that too,* Caden thought. *Do human's eyes glow in Heaven?* He watched as Han turned around and spread their wings. As Han turned, Caden finally saw the back of Han's human face. It was a large bird of prey. Its feathers were brown, and its yellow beak ended in a black, hooked tip. The two locked eyes with one another.

"Get a good night's sleep," the eagle called. "Things are going to start picking up. Fast." Caden straightened, and the oxen gave the eagle a quick glare.

"Didn't have to say that. He'll worry now."

"It's the truth!" The feathers around the eagle's face fluffed, making it look bigger.

Caden opened his mouth to ask what the eagle meant, but the wings had lifted to fly. With one synchronized beat of the wings, Han shot into the air. A second later, Caden heard the roar of wind, quickly followed by the blast. He was nearly knocked to the ground. He let himself stumble back and found he was sitting in the sand again, completely covered in dust.

He didn't move. The feeling of the Raw Peace faded as Han disappeared into the night, but Caden savored it as long as it lasted. *I'll fulfill prophecies,* he thought as he saw two figures ascend the hill before him. One pointed at him and shouted. It was Ellie. She really did sound worried. *And I'm immortal.* Caden smiled as the final thought kept the Consuming Fire still flickering inside him. *God loves me, and He talks about me. Says good things about me. And He,* Caden looked down, trying to decide if this was real or not. *And God wants to play baseball with me.* Gradually, he chuckled. By the time Ellie and Yohanan reached him, Caden was lounging back, gazing at the stars, and laughing.

———

HAN HAD BEEN RIGHT. Caden didn't know why he had doubted the Spirit. Anyone from Yahweh could be trusted, but still. Caden didn't really know any trustworthy Spirits. Regardless, Doeg, as Han said, didn't touch him that night. Either Han stood guard, or Doeg knew better. *Maybe he left,* Caden thought as he followed Noam's camel across the desert the next day. He frowned and knew it wasn't that easy. Doeg was probably not far away, slinking through the sand, its twisted face doing that creepy smile. Running fingers through his hair, Caden spurred his camel closer to Noam's.

Can't think about that Demon, Caden thought. *I'm protected. I'm immortal.* He half smiled; it sounded ridiculous. But Yahweh said it, so it must be true.

He glanced at his camel and remembered it wasn't Eleazar. That camel had demanded to carry someone else, someone less 'troubled', whatever that meant. With a sigh, Caden turned to Noam. "Are there lions here?" he asked as his camel came in stride beside Noam's.

Noam grunted as he puffed on his cigarette. "There were."

"But there are Bible stories of them."

"Bible wasn't written yesterday. Old book from old times." Noam shook his head as he sat back with eyes half closed.

"Do you think they'll come back?" Noam shrugged, and Caden frowned. "Come on, man. We've still got a lot of traveling to do. Wouldn't hurt to talk a little."

Noam didn't answer as the two continued to sway in time with the camels' steps. "When I have a son," he said suddenly. "I will name him Benaiah." Noam nodded to himself and took another puff from the cigarette.

"Because?" Caden prompted.

"He was a mighty man in the Bible. One of King David's. He went into a pit and killed a lion."

"With what?"

"Not a gun." Caden glared at him. "Fearless man. Think if you did that. Going into a pit to kill a maneater. With ax? Bat? Sword? Spear maybe." Noam grunted again. "Benaiah's a good name."

"Could you do that? Go into a pit with a sword and kill a monster?" Without a word, Noam nodded. "Really?" Caden's brows rose as he tried withholding a skeptical smile.

"Went down into a ravine and killed a Giant."

Caden sat back in his saddle. "How did you-No one can do that! I've seen Giants! *American* Giants! I couldn't imagine what they're like here."

"They eat everything."

"Well, so do ours, but, whatever. How'd you do it?"

Again, Noam shrugged. "Had a gun. Shot right. Won."

"That's it?"

Noam took a long drag and, somehow, relaxed further into his saddle. He finally shook his head. "They died, but-"

"Wait." Caden held up a hand. "There was more than one? How many!"

"Two."

"Who helped you kill them?"

"The gun."

Caden cursed and turned away, suddenly grateful Noam was on his team. "You're a good shot." Noam shrugged. "What happened after they died?"

"They attacked again somehow. Something was fighting us. I couldn't see, just things," he sighed heavily, "things went wrong. Camels ran off. Men got sick. Guns stopped shooting."

Demons, Caden thought as he turned away, his skin crawling.

Noam muttered Hebrew under his breath and grunted. "Don't kill Giants. The fight gets worse."

Caden nodded slowly, the wheels of his mind turning. *Do Demons and Giants have something in common? I bet they're on the same team. I don't remember seeing Demons at House Whitney though. Did I miss them?* Caden shivered, imagining himself walking through the vast mansion with blood-thirsty, invisible monsters watching him. *But Han was with me,* Caden thought, lifting his chin. *Han can stop them and—*

"*Angels can also bleed,*" Doeg whispered inside his thoughts. "*Wings can be dislodged, faces decapitated, eyes gouged out.*"

But you can't do that to Yahweh, Caden thought, a muscle in his jaw flexing. *You can't scare me; He said I'm immortal!* He heard a distant, hoarse laugh.

"*Challenge accepted.*"

"Alright, Caden?"

Caden glanced behind Noam and saw Auset staring at him with a furrowed brow. "Sure," he stammered, adjusting his shemagh around his face. "Just…"

"*You cannot tune me out.*"

Shut up!

"Just thinking. Um… Noam, ah, how'd you learn to shoot like that?"

"Army."

"Can you show me?"

"Yohanan showing you."

"Just hand-to-hand combat. Nothing with a gun." Noam didn't move as he lounged back on his camel. Caden's brows rose. Had Noam heard him?

"Sure," Noam finally said. "Tonight. Once camp's up."

"Alright!" Caden said with a smile as he looked on ahead. "I have a gun, but, well… I don't know how to use it."

"I'll teach. You'll be…"

Noam stopped speaking and Caden glanced at him. Noam sat stiffly upright, his eyes wide as he stared toward the rocky hills before them. Caden turned and saw nothing but the rocky face to their left and the steep hills to their right. Gradually, he found two dots racing over the hill. His eyes narrowed, and it took a moment to realize it was the two scouts who went on ahead. They ran from a ravine where two craggy mountains came together. Several rocky hills rolled from the mountains, some very near to the caravan. Noam muttered more Hebrew and withdrew his gun. He motioned behind him and Auset coaxed her camel closer.

Why would the scouts be returning? Caden thought.

He could hardly hear their distant cries. One was waving his arms as their camels charged. The small caravan slowed, and Yohanan shouted to them in Hebrew. Beyond the rocky hillside, he was answered by the crack of gunfire. One of the scouts crumpled to the camel's saddle and stopped moving. Caden's stomach knotted on itself as the remaining scout screamed something. Dotted figures stepped from hiding along the rockface. Each held a gun and aimed down at the travelers. All color washed from Caden's face.

"Still dare to claim immortality?" Doeg whispered inside his mind.

"Ellie!" Caden gasped as he turned to find his sister. Her camel was behind Auset. Their eyes locked, and he reached for her. The strangers opened fire. Caden's ears instantly became overloaded. He didn't know where all the guns were coming from. Some were in the rocks, but some were close. Was the enemy among them too?

He saw Noam's gun muzzle flash with force. A camel fell over. Someone was screaming. Probably lots of people. Caden wouldn't be surprised if he was one of them too. He didn't have time to care as he ducked low and spurred his camel to Ellie. He stopped when he saw her. She had an AK-47. And she was firing!

But you're, you're my baby sister-

"Run!" Ellie shouted. Caden looked beyond her and saw more hidden invaders stepping from hiding. How many were there? Twenty? Thirty!

We're outnumbered. Outgunned. Cold panic stripped Caden of his senses. He couldn't move and, for a moment, the only thing he heard was his heart thudding in his ears. His wide eyes darted to the enemy charging down the rocky hill. There weren't many of them, and they didn't seem to notice the bullets kicking up dust and rock or the fact they were running too fast and could fall at any second. One did fall but leapt right up and ignored his bleeding forehead.

Puppets, Caden realized, thought breaking through his catatonic state. *But, Ellie, I can't leave-*

She was already racing away with others, charging back the way they came. Caden cursed and followed. His back prickled with panic as he waited for the feeling of a bullet to rip through him. *Raw Peace! Raw Peace!* He thought, gritting his teeth. The smell of gunfire stung his nose as dust and sand made it near impossible to breathe. It felt so familiar, like a reoccurring nightmare!

"Consider yourself immortal now?"

Anger struck Caden's chest, heating his blood, and narrowing his eyes. *Bite me!* He cursed; why had he said that? Doeg could literally kill him with one bite!

"Your watchdog prohibits me from touching you." Caden blinked, astonished the Demon would admit defeat. *"Yet not your camel."*

The animal shuddered suddenly and bellowed, its jerky stride becoming uneven and whip-lashing Caden around. Caden gasped and held on. The camel's head snapped to one side, a bullet cutting through it, silencing its bellowing. Caden felt the saddle drop out from under him. It took him a second to realize the camel had collapsed. He hovered in midair, seeing the quickly passing ground far below him.

"Mortal." Doeg whispered.

Caden fell. He slammed against the camel and rolled, both crashing into the rocky, sandy ground. Caden didn't know what was up or down as sand and blood filled his mouth. He curled into a ball, feeling the camel's great weight continue flying past. He stayed in a ball, sand kicking up from bullets all around, and his body feeling broken into a million pieces.

I'm alive? He blinked, too terrified to know it. He dared to move, he had to. He heard footsteps. Swift, thumping, and several of them. He stiffly looked up and froze. Five soldiers were sprinting toward him. They wore sandy-hued camo, and their holsters and belts were bare of weapons. Looking at their faces, Caden knew two things instantly: One, they were not from the Middle East. Two: their eyes were like animals.

Don't panic! Caden thought as the Puppets descended. Panic found him anyways and gripped him, weakening his body. In a fraction of a moment, Caden debated closing his eyes and giving in. He had found Ellie. She clearly knew how to take care of herself. Why would he have to keep fighting? God was tortured and killed for him. And here he was, considering laying down and giving up. How pathetic! How human.

If God can fight for me, Caden thought. *Then I can learn to fight for Him.*

Adrenaline sent him to his feet, his bleeding shoulder and bruised bones ignored for the moment. Something was stuck on his belt. It was long and annoying and-

Harel's bat! Caden grabbed it, couldn't figure out how to untie it for a second, which was the longest second of

his life, but he got it free. He drew the bat back, made a stance, and swung. He hit something that cracked and thudded to the ground. Caden vaguely registered that something was a human but was too focused on drawing the bat back again.

The next Puppet reached for him, his black mouth open in a baritone scream. Caden swung, breaking the man's outstretched hand. Did that stop the Puppet? Of course not. Caden cursed and leapt back, trying to avoid the man's remaining, grabbing hand and swing at the same time. He missed and nearly fell over his dead camel. He swung up this time, crashing it into the Puppet's jaw, and finally giving him a reason to pause.

Han! Caden's mind screamed. *Where are you? I need-!*

Another Puppet danced in his peripheral vision. Caden spun, windmilling the bat straight into the Puppet's temple. The Puppet dropped, kicking up sand as he rolled. A hand seized him. Caden panted and butted the bat into the woman's stomach, dropping her.

The Puppet he hit in the jaw sprinted toward him. Caden saw him just as he dove. They collided, and Caden flew to the ground, landing with a thud. He gasped, the air knocked out of him, and realized it was still near impossible to breathe. He blinked, finding the Puppet on top of him. The Puppet's jaw was broken, making his bleeding mouth offset and grin even more horrific. Caden started crawling and begging, though both were useless.

"Caden Johnson." the Puppet said. His voice was inhuman, gravelly and animal-like.

Like Doeg, Caden realized.

"You should've jumped from the cliff."

Caden's blood turned to ice. Another Puppet grabbed his ankles. Someone held down his arm. He could hardly move. *You failed me!* Caden thought, hoping God could hear him. *Lying, son of a-!*

A Puppet leapt back and fell headfirst. Another lurched back, dropping. The one on Caden looked up and frowned right before his head snapped back. He thudded to the ground and didn't rise. Caden dragged himself to sit upright and stared. Each of the five Puppets were dead. He blinked, his chest heaving, and tried to believe he was still alive.

The dead Puppets stirred. Caden cried as he crawled away, panting. Their backs arched as darkness lifted from two in smoky tendrils, a Shade stepped from one, and Withers drew out of the others. The Demons glanced down at their dead exteriors before each turning and looking at Caden. All color left his face.

"Get up, you idiot!" Caden turned and saw Yohanan charging on his camel. Behind him, Noam still had his gun leveled to clear the enemy from Caden. "Get up!"

Caden stood to shaky feet and flinched as the enemy soldiers' bullets continued to rain down. Why hadn't they hit him yet? They all couldn't be that bad of an aim. Yohanan hardly slowed his camel as the two seized each other's forearms. Caden felt his arm would dislocate as he was heaved up behind Yohanan. He clung to Yohanan as the camel turned and sped away, following the fleeing caravan. It weaved this way and that, avoiding obstacles in their path. Caden glanced back, expecting to see five angry Demons chasing them. They hadn't moved from their Puppets. Caden gasped, facing forward, remembering Han wouldn't let them touch him. He inspected his body for any wounds. Why wasn't he torn apart?

Where's Ellie? Caden thought as he looked ahead. His eyes widened as his guts coiled, kinked, and knotted. The enemy soldiers had cut off the rest of the caravan. They were trapped. Caden's eyes darted around, but he knew there was nowhere to run. As Yohanan reached the caravan, Caden realized several camels and people were missing. They were the obstacles their camel had avoided. More Puppets in military uniform were charging, behind them, enemy troops shot round after round.

In the chaos, he found Ellie. She hid in the sand behind her dead camel. Her leg was bloody, and a knife was in her hand. She was out of bullets. Caden tried not to close in on himself as Yohanan raced to her. *No,* he thought, emotion tightening his chest. *God, You can't-*

"Oh, indeed, He can," Doeg said, it's voice audible regardless of the cacophony of gunfire. "He just relishes slaughtering your beloved family. Right. Before. Your. Eyes."

Why did You let me find her? Caden thought as the Puppets closed in.

Then, the sky broke.

EIGHT
INVASION

CADEN FELT like he was burning up. It wasn't an outside heat, as though the flames were devouring his clothes and flesh. It was from the inside. He could feel the blaze catch in his heart and stomach, sending the flame through his blood and to the rest of his body. It hurt as he felt it swallow his inner being. But it was like a good hurt, a good pain that brought about healing. Like the pains after surgery; they were needed to be made whole again.

Caden clutched his chest and considered the steadily growing inferno within as he flew through the air. He fell from the camel and summersaulted across the sand and few bodies. He landed with a cry and tried to rake in breath. He coughed and doubled over, telling himself he should be in agony, and something should be broken. He felt nothing but the fierce, raging fire inside him. The fire of God. The *Akal Esh.*

I'm not dying, Caden told himself again. *Oh, I should be dead now. Deader than dead. No one like me should see this much of God!*

The fire inside flared suddenly, stealing his breath as he lay in the sand. Caden slowly opened his eyes and stared at his hand. The knuckles were scraped and bleed-ing, but something lifted from the back of his hand. It was small and bright and waved back and forth. Caden blinked, staring at a small tongue of fire. He felt the heat of the fire, but it didn't burn him. It just stayed, defying reality, defying the evil darkness in the world, and filling a broken, weak human with God's Consuming Fire.

Caden swallowed the hard lump in his throat and watched as the flame grew smaller until it died. He blinked, feeling the raging fire inside also dimming. *Don't go. Don't leave me!* There was no answer as the fire kept diminishing. Caden cursed under his breath and looked to the sky. The clouds overhead spiraled and revealed the path Yahweh's fire had fallen. *Fell into who?* Caden thought as he looked down.

All around him, everyone was lying back, dazed and terrified. No one was shooting. No one was speaking. At the center, the sand had been blasted away, leaving a mini crater. Inside lay a body. *Yohanan!* Caden thought as he dragged himself to his feet. He raced to Yohanan's side and checked his pulse. Caden couldn't find it, and panic quickened his breath.

Out of frustration, Caden pressed his ear against Yohanan's exposed chest. Yahweh's Consuming Fire had burned away the top of Yohanan's clothes, just as with Elijah. *There!* Caden thought, hearing the rhythmic beats of the heart. *I've still got you!* Caden barked a laugh and wiped the sweat from his eyes.

"Yohanan!" Ellie screamed as she fell beside him.

"He's alive," Caden said. "He'll just be asleep now for three days."

She stared at him, mouth slack. "You've seen this before?" Caden nodded. "He can't sleep! How'll we get him out of here? How will *we* get out of here!"

Caden's eyes darted around, and he saw the

surrounding enemy steadily gathering themselves. Some were already standing and muttering together. Others were finding their guns. The Puppets prowled back and forth, watching and waiting.

"No," Ellie whimpered. "Lots of times, Yahweh doesn't do things the same way. He could do something different."

Caden tried to breathe as despair crashed into him. *We're still going to die-*

Yohanan bolted upright with a violent gasp. Ellie screamed as Caden leapt back with fists raised. Coughing, Yohanan grabbed his chest and doubled over. "What happened?" he asked in Hebrew.

"Yahweh," Caden answered in English, drawing closer to him. "He's filled you with the *Akal Esh*."

Yohanan slowly lifted his chin and stared at Caden. "Really?" The enemy soldiers called to one another in their foreign language as most stood. The sound of guns clicking and readying to fire surrounded them. Caden cowered lower and looked to Ellie. "That means I'm a Witness." Yohanan said slowly. "I can't be killed. Well... not now."

I could lay on top of her, Caden thought. *Be a shield-*

"Does that mean I can breathe fire now?" Yohanan asked.

"Yah." Caden muttered, hardly listening.

"Really." Caden glanced at Yohanan. Why was he smiling? Without another word, Yohanan stood and faced the enemy soldiers.

"Wait!" Caden called. "I don't think-"

Yohanan ignored him and stripped off his shredded shirt. Caden cursed as Yohanan took a deep breath. Caden leapt onto Ellie and covered her body with his own. He squeezed his eyes shut and ducked his head.

He heard the fire before he felt it. An explosion roared all around him, forcing the air back like a screaming tempest. Sand was everywhere. Screams lifted. Then the heat. Caden could actually feel the hairs on his arms shrivel to singed stubs. Ellie was screaming. Though the dangerous heat demanded Caden ran, he clung to her and refused to move. The air thickened with the stench of burning hair.

Another bout of fire shook Caden. He held Ellie tighter and tried to breathe the hot, smoky air. He flinched as another explosion shook the ground, and the fire howled overhead. *Raw Peace!* Caden thought. *Raw Peace! Oh, God! Raw Peace!*

At last, the bouts of fire stopped, and the crackling blaze of flames filled Caden's ears. Caden lay there, unwilling to let Ellie rise. "Cade?" He didn't answer, and he wondered if there was any skin still on his back. "Caden, I can't," cough, "I can't breathe!"

Caden eased off her, and the two slowly looked around. They were encircled in fire. The high flames beat wildly and sent dark smoke into the sky. Caden could just make out the black, smoking figures lying in the inferno. He reminded himself to breathe and tried not to pass out.

"Yohanan," Ellie whispered. "Yohanan!" There was no answer. Ellie rose and stepped toward the fire. Caden quickly stood and grabbed her, drawing her back. "I've got to-"

"Don't go in there!"

"Yohanan!"

Caden could feel her shaking in his arms. Actually, they both were shaking. As sweat dripped down his back, Caden saw a shadow in the fire. It was moving. Caden's breath quickened as he drew Ellie behind him. *Doeg can't harm me, but what about Ellie?* He made fists as the figure drew nearer. It was strolling through the fire with slow, calm steps. Caden ignored the panic clenching his throat and willed himself to not leave his sister. The shadow drew closer and stepped from the wall of fire. It was a man. He was shirtless and smiling. He looked like a madman-

"Yohanan!" Ellie cried as she limped from behind Caden. She spread her arms to Yohanan but stopped and shielded her face from the fire's heat. Yohanan drew closer to her and wrapped his arms around her. Caden tried to catch his breath as he watched the pair whisper in Hebrew. He turned away, put his hands on his knees, and threw up. He gasped, staring at the mess, and tried not to collapse. A strong hand lay on his shoulder.

He turned to Yohanan, and the smiling Israeli gave him a curt nod. "You're good."

"No," Caden stammered. "I'm not good!" He shook his head, and Yohanan clapped him on the back.

"Missed a spot," Yohanan muttered as he pointed to vomit on Caden's mouth. "Actually. You're a mess. You're covered in blood."

Caden didn't answer as he stared at the flames. *This isn't real life. Can't... I don't understand.* He put his head in his hands and knelt on the ground, too overwhelmed to speak.

"Come on," Yohanan said. "Let's find the others." Caden didn't rise as the two started walking.

"Cade?" Ellie asked.

"I can't," he muttered through his fingers. "I-"

An arm looped under his and helped him rise. He gasped and found himself clinging to Yohanan. "You can do this," Yohanan whispered. "Yahweh wouldn't let you be here if you couldn't."

Caden shook his head. "This is too much-"

"Course it is. That's why it's happening. When we admit we're weak, He can finally be strong through us."

Wasn't that what Han said?

"Stand up, bro. Let Yahweh do the rest." Caden slowly blinked as he gathered his thoughts. With a small nod, he lifted his chin and, leaning heavily on Yohanan, moved forward.

"What about the fire?" Ellie asked, leaning on his other arm. "We can't all just walk through it."

"Yeah," Caden muttered. "Aren't you burned at all?"

Yohanan shook his head. "I think my clothes had a little trouble." He chuckled. "Maybe I've got to find flammable clothes; shouldn't walk around naked all the time. I think we can get through the fire. Let me see."

Caden limped along as Yohanan drew them to the ring of fire. Caden stared at the lashing flames. The smoke smelled funny. Kind of like a barbecue. He cursed under his breath and refused to look at the charred bodies beneath the blaze. The heat graded Caden's face the closer they drew, and he stopped walking. Without a word, Yohanan lifted a hand, and the flames parted. Caden stared in dumbfounded awe as a safe, sandy walkway opened before them.

"Like parting the Red Sea," Ellie muttered as Yohanan smiled. "How'd you know you could do that?"

Yohanan shrugged. "Worth a shot."

Caden didn't speak as they three walked through the flickering hallway. The fire crackled in his ears, and he covered his mouth and nose from the smell. Ellie did the same, but Yohanan didn't seem to notice. Caden thought their walk through the fire would be a few steps, he hadn't realized the dense wildfire they had been surrounded with. They kept walking and walking, passing blackened bodies as great bouts of smoke filled the sky. Sweat drenched Caden as the heat overwhelmed him. He focused on one step at a time. He thought his adrenaline would last longer, seeing as how he was still walking through fire, but he was wrong.

By the time they finally broke through the heat and blaze, he was shaking uncontrollably. They sat him down on a rock alongside Ellie, who also wasn't doing too good, as the others regrouped. Caden stared at the disaster and scanned the rocky hills. *None of the enemy soldiers survived,* Caden realized. *Not one. Can Elijah do this too?* He blinked slowly and looked at his arms. His knuckles were bleeding, and his forearm got a nasty scrape. Oh, and he was misted in Puppets' blood. *But I'm still alive,* he thought. *Because I'm immortal until Yahweh says it's time. Guess it's not time yet.* Caden sighed heavily and hung his head, his shoulders hunching.

"You nearly cursed God's name." A muscle in Caden's jaw flexed as he crossed his arms, as though shielding himself. *"To curse God's Spirit is an unforgivable sin."*

Caden's closed eyes tightened as he slowly lifted his head. "No," he whispered. "That is a lie." He opened his eyes, and every strained muscle stiffened.

Before him, crouching at his eye level, was Doeg. The Demon's white fur waved in the wind as its gray, icy eyes bore into Caden. Its blood-red mouth stretched to one side, pulled by a scar raking from mouth to cheek, revealing rows of yellowed teeth. Doeg's tail lashed like a cat ready to pounce. Its bald hands kept flexing as though the claws were hungry to slash. Caden sucked in a sharp breath as his chest tightened. He could feel his pulse quickening again, images of Alex Whitney's sliced body flashing through his mind.

"You are a blasphemer. Your sentence is Hell." Doeg's lips drew back, reshaping its face into a wide, wolfish smile. "Therefore, you will spend your eternity with me."

"You lie!"

"Ask your prophet friend. I quote from your filthy book."

"Go away." Caden moaned, running a hand through his sweaty hair. A shadow passed close, and Caden flinched back. Noam stopped walking toward him and raised a hand. He stared down at Caden with one brow arched. Caden cursed under his breath and turned away.

"Ah?" Noam stammered. "What's happening?"

Caden opened his mouth to speak but didn't know what to say. He knew no one saw Doeg. What was the point in telling them more? The hackles along Doeg's neck bristled suddenly as a low caterwaul wined from his throat. Caden flinched back, nearly falling from the rock he sat on.

Footfalls crunched the sand behind him, and he found Yohanan helping him stand again. Caden glanced between the young Witness and the Demon as the two stared one another in the eyes. *Elijah could see him too*, Caden remembered as he got behind Yohanan. The Demon cowered back, crouching low to the ground as its tail flicked violently.

"Don't let this dog steal your victory," Yohanan said over his shoulder. "This *thing* knows it'll lose the war." Doeg snarled, saliva flying. "Would you like to taste Yahweh's wrath early?" Yohanan took in a deep breath. Doeg shrilled and leapt away, sprinting from them on all fours. Caden watched it flee over one hill, then another, until it disappeared.

"What'd that thing say?" Yohanan asked.

Noam shifted his weight. "What's happening?"

"Demon. Caden, actually, don't care what it said. It lied."

Caden shook his head. "But it said I can't be forgiven."

"Lies-"

"I blasphemed the *Akal Esh*, Yahweh's Spirit won't forgive that and-"

"If a Demon speaks, it lies. Even when quoting scripture-"

"Is there an unforgivable sin?"

"Yes, but you are forgiven."

"How do you know?"

"You're alive, aren't you? If Yahweh's *Akal Esh* doesn't want to forgive you, He would've killed you in the fire just now." Caden blinked and looked to the still roaring blaze. Yohanan shook his head and scoffed. "We won big today. Big! Don't let that thing ruin it." He drew to Caden's side and lay a hand on his shoulder. "We've gotta move. The Russians won't like thirty of their soldiers crispified."

"Russians?" Caden muttered.

"Yep. Looks like getting back into Jerusalem won't be easy."

The Russians are invading, Caden thought as he closed his eyes. *But so is Yahweh.* He rubbed his arms, feeling the singed hair scratch his skin. *Yohanan's right, this is a war.*

NINE
DYED MY HAIR BROWN

CADEN WAS SHOCKED, most of their caravan survived. Though almost everyone was wounded, casualties were low. They had to dig some shrapnel from Ellie's leg, which made Caden feel helpless and useless as Yohanan held her and Auset dug. He just limped around, restless and angry he couldn't stop her pain. His own pain stopped him though.

Everyone was surprised he didn't have a broken bone. Getting thrown from two camels in under five minutes should've damaged something. His legs and arms were skinned here and there, the bones bruised, which felt awful, but he still functioned. A straight line cut through the skin of his right shoulder, Auset suspected a bullet had grazed him. His eyebrows were half burnt off, and his back was tender from the fire's blaze. Out of everyone, Yohanan had the least number of injuries. You know, the guy who literally breathed fire, then walked through it?

They did lose five camels and three travelers, a husband, a young woman, and an elderly man. The husband's wife mourned loudly as her friends comforted her. They buried them in the sands, and, to Caden's surprise, the wife praised Yahweh for giving them rest from the broken world. The young woman and elder were buried too, what was left of them. The Puppets had a nasty way of scattering remains, just like dogs. Caden blinked, trying not to think of Nathaniel's dogs running him down or Grant's ripping Don apart. He ran fingers through his hair and shivered.

"What is it?" Ellie, who was sitting on their camel behind him, her slim arms wrapped around his waist. They followed Yohanan as he led them to the edge of the Sinai Desert. Finally, he said they were almost at the border.

Caden shook his head, trying to find the right words. "Everything." he finally managed, unable to voice the truth. He suddenly felt cold, as though swallowed by night, his ears ringing from the bays of dogs, and the metallic smell of gunpowder heavy in the air. And Trace, abandoned, slumped to the ground, still not blinking.

I didn't abandon him! Caden thought.

Ellie sighed and lay her cheek against his back. "Give it to Yahweh." she whispered.

Caden's nose wrinkled as he sniffed gruffly. "Right," he said. "I'll get on that."

"I'm serious."

Caden cursed as he lifted his chin, a shadow darkening his eyes. "How do you even do that? Like, you say you need faith to surrender, but in order to have faith, you need to trust Yahweh for everything and give Him all control, which is surrender. But, you can't surrender without faith first. But you need faith to surrender-"

"You're overthinking it-"

"No, I'm not! It's what the Bible says!"

"Cade-"

"It's always confusing and complicated and too hard to do!"

He felt Ellie nod. "If it wasn't too hard, we wouldn't need His help."

Caden scoffed and shook his head. "Feels like Dad's backward games."

"It's not a game. God's not a manipulator like that."

Caden didn't answer as emotions tightened his chest. He wanted to give it all to God, he really did. But how can the same God command to be holy as He is holy, yet call everyone worms or dust? It was impossible. Like trying to build defenses against deadly forces with only Lincoln logs. *Why didn't You give us better tools?* Caden asked, glancing at the sky. *I want to follow You, but what You want and what You've equipped me with is a huge difference.*

"Cade," Ellie said. "All Yahweh wants is you to trust Him and do what He says. That's it."

"He wants me to do impossible things."

"Then tell Him that, try you're best, and He'll make up the difference. He's got your back. All He needs is someone to just have faith."

"And what is that exactly? Believing He is good all the time or something?"

"It's doing the stupid stuff God tells you to do." Caden's eyes narrowed. "It's jumping when you don't see anything to catch you. It's choosing to forgive when all your heart wants to do is hate."

Forgiveness, Caden thought, completely forgetting that was another impossible Christian quality. Dad came to mind, quickly followed by Nathaniel. *Never,* he thought, a muscle in his jaw flexing. *There are limits to what I can do.*

"Just try surrendering," Ellie said. "And when you're stressed out, that's a red flag you haven't surrendered something to Him."

Caden laughed suddenly and shook his head. "I'm never not stressed."

"It's a sign you're trying to do it all by yourself."

"Come on! Are you stressed? You've got to be."

"When I am, I remember this life isn't my responsibility, I've given myself to Yahweh. He's in charge of me. He's responsible. It's His job to get me out of messes. It's the same for you, and it actually does help."

Caden didn't answer as he debated his sister's sanity. *She didn't panic,* he remembered. *During the attack, she was jumpy, but she wasn't losing it. Is that what it's like living in the Raw Peace?*

"Stressed?" She asked. "Then tell Him what's up and decide to believe He'll handle it, then do the crazy stuff He wants you to do."

"He doesn't talk to Christians anymore, remember?"

"He's creative. He'll tell you somehow, just be looking for it."

Oh, yeah, like how I'm supposed to accept the first person's invitation of hospitality. And I won't like it. Caden looked down as the camel's steps swayed them back and forth. His eyes narrowed as his knuckles whitened. *Why is this so hard?*

"You'll forfeit control, permitting another superior male figure to dominate and control you." A hard lump formed in Caden's throat. He could hear his father's footsteps storming behind him, drawing closer, bringing wrath, mercilessness, and pain. *"You cannot yield to such an unpredictable monster so easily. How foolish are you, GJ?"*

"Think about it," Ellie said. "But not too much. Oh, and don't let your Demon friends share their opinion."

"They're not my friends."

"They are when you listen to them." With a heavy sigh, Caden lifted his chin and tried to figure out what to do.

"By all means, give all that you are to someone who refuses to speak to you. Very trustworthy and safe relationship."

Caden cursed under his breath and rubbed his eyes with a finger and thumb. *I want to.*

"Gullible fool."

But I just can't.

"Very good."

On my own.

"Yes, you are a failure on so many levels-"

Maybe He'll help me.

"Or abandon you to struggle and writhe in your own fears."

Caden swallowed hard and lowered his head, his eyes closing. *When we can't do it, He'll make up the difference.*

"No, He'll disapprove of your efforts and demand more when there is none to give. You have experienced this all your life! Why question the obvious?"

I've just got to choose.

"Choose to trust an invisible, silent, slaughtering monster? Is that what I'm hearing?"

Doeg, when you fight me so hard, I know I'm doing the right thing. Caden listened and smiled as silence followed.

"I will behead your sister before your very eyes." Caden's smile fell as he drew Ellie closer to him. *"No faith or surrender could save her, boy."* Caden's breath quickened as the internal screaming mounted again. He felt himself slipping into the cold, nothingness as Doeg's words overwhelmed him with fears and anxiety and-

Stress. Caden sucked in a shaky breath and dared to look ahead. He half expected to see Doeg's icy eyes staring right back at him. *I'll trust You,* Caden thought. *But I'll still fail You. You've gotta make up the difference and catch me when I fall apart. I'm trying to do the right thing. This is all new and weird, and I don't think I'm doing it right.* He cursed and shook his head. *I don't think I ever will. But, um… I surrender me. Somehow. Um, that's all I've got. So, do the rest. Thanks.*

Caden sat in silence as he waited for something. Would Han appear and encourage him? Would Yahweh actually whisper to him, like He did in the Bible? The camel grumbled as it ambled along, and Ellie wiped her nose on the back of his jacket. Caden sighed heavily and looked down.

I didn't do it right. Something's wrong with me. God's rejection will bring me down to the dust and obliterate my very existence-

Caden cursed through gritted teeth and glared all around. If only he could punch that Demon in the face! *Yahweh was with them and gave them rest,* Caden thought, remembering the verse of what God did while His people were in the Sinai Desert. *He's with me and will give me rest.*

"*Rest when He slaughters you-*"

Raw Peace. He'll give me the Raw Peace right now.

"*Don't be so naive.*"

And He is with me. Right now.

"*Do you see Him? Feel Him? Hear Him?*"

Caden sucked in a deep breath, willing himself to ignore the constant lies poured into his heart from the Demon. *He's with me,* he thought. *And will give me His Raw Peace.* He didn't feel the Raw Peace. He didn't sense Yahweh close either. But that's what Yahweh said He'll do. Life was too crazy to keep questioning everything because, by the time it all made sense, Caden would be dead. He had to just choose to trust, regardless of how he felt, which was easier said than done.

In that moment, he felt like staying in the desert, avoiding the mobs of Sentinels in Jerusalem and more invading Russians. There was the cold fact that some, if not all, the Mizrahis could be dead. Oh, and the border crossing. How would they manage that without visas, papers, or any money for bribes?

Raw Peace, Caden thought as he lifted his chin. *I have it right now, though I don't feel it.* He cursed again, hoping he wasn't living in denial and actually doing the opposite of what God wanted.

"*Yes, denial of reality is the first step of being a true believer.*"

Raw Peace.

———

CADEN HAD to keep reciting 'Raw Peace', for they were drawing closer to the Israeli border. It wasn't the looming border that bothered him, his clothes reeked of fire and singed hair. He hadn't slept the past two nights, whenever he closed his eyes, he could see the roaring blaze nearly muffling the screams. In the center of the chaos stood a shirtless Israeli, taking in another breath without hesitating. Caden had prayed they didn't come across more Russian soldiers. He knew Yohanan would make living candles of them without a second thought.

He could do that to anyone, Caden thought. *Do that to me.*

He blinked slowly as he lurched back and forth on his camel. He couldn't help but watch Yohanan out of the corner of his eye as this so-called prophet led them on. The two camels plotted close together, too close for Caden's liking. At least Ellie was near him. She sat behind Yohanan with her head resting on his back and eyes lightly closed. Over the past two days, Caden had played with the idea of escaping this new, fire-breathing monster and dragging his sister to safety. How safe could she be now as the wife of a Witness?

Caden gritted his teeth and forced himself to turn away. He knew she'd never come. Even if he tied her and forced her to go, she'd come back. He wouldn't ever do that to his Lil El though. He wasn't an animal or did anything unnatural like that. But what if it saved her life? He had fought so hard to find her, and now she's bound for the flames. There was rope in his backpack. He knew how to tie secure knots. It wouldn't be too difficult overpowering her, especially now that she's wounded and-

Caden looked down sharply and made a fist. *Doeg, I swear to God-*

"Bite me."

I will kick you down to Hell.

"I'm dragging you down with me."

That's not how it works.

"Doesn't it, GJ?" Caden whispered a curse and lifted his chin. He gave Yohanan another glanced and sniffed before turning away.

"What are you thinking, bro?" Yohanan's question sent a shiver through Caden.

Can he read minds now too? "Bro?" He asked instead. Yohanan shrugged.

"Spiny said it's a fun way to say brother back in America. And we're brothers, yes?" Caden didn't answer as he glanced at Yohanan. He looked into his eyes, half expecting a flaming glow to flicker from their depths. "Ah," Yohanan groaned. "Knock it off."

"What-"

"You're scared." Caden lifted his chin as his pulse quickened. "Everyone's scared."

"Not me." Ellie shook her head.

Yohanan nodded. "Not me either."

You two are nuts.

"What are you so afraid of, bro?" Caden looked ahead and scratched the back of his neck. Why were his fingertips suddenly cold? "Caden."

Caden stiffened; Yohanan had used the same tone when they first met when Caden wasn't cooperating. Anger rose in Caden, tightening his chest as a muscle in his jaw flexed. "You," he snapped. "I'm afraid of you." Ellie's eyes opened slowly as Yohanan nodded.

"Hum," Yohanan grunted. "Makes sense. I have put a gun to your head."

"No!" Caden scoffed. "You breathe fire, man! You killed, like, thirty people!"

"Twenty-seven."

"Whatever! You did it without touching them! What else can you do, hum? Who else will you kill?" Caden fell silent, seeing the saddened look in Ellie's eyes.

"He has a good point." Caden heard Noam mutter from behind.

"Oh, you too?" Yohanan snapped, glancing back. "Fine. I guess I am a weapon now."

Ellie's eyes narrowed. "But that's not why Yahweh lets you breathe fire."

"Yeah, yeah. Warn Yeshua's coming soon, I know. Turn or burn."

Caden arched a brow at him. "Are *you* going to burn them?"

A small smile twitched Yohanan's mouth. He stayed silent for far too long. "I'll turn 'em or burn 'em. Whatever Yahweh says to do."

That's not comforting, Caden thought, but then he remembered Han. That angel was a four-faced, massive, flaming weapon. Caden had been terrified of him, but the Cherub was on his side. He thought back to his conversation with Elijah about how the Raw Peace brought total safety and, with it, the power and aggression to defend. *Yahweh needs weapons too. And He's picked Han and Yohanan to be just that.*

With a heaved sigh, he glanced at Yohanan. "I'll stop avoiding you."

"About time," Yohanan said. "I like teasing you. Can't tease you if you think I'll fry you any second, bro."

Caden cursed and shook his head. He could feel himself smile. "Whatever, Sparky."

Ellie laughed as Yohanan glanced between them. "That's a dumb nickname." Yohanan grumbled.

Caden grinned. "I like it."

"Don't burn too much," Noam said. "Not in Jerusalem."

Yohanan frowned. "I'll do what Yahweh says."

"It'll get us all killed."

"Then don't be around."

Caden glared at him, his fists white as he gripped the saddle's handle. "It'll kill your wife."

Yohanan stilled as he looked ahead. With a deep breath, he nodded. "Fine. I'll hold back until I really need to let loose."

"Thank you." Caden muttered, feeling himself ease a bit. The conversation continued, and Caden felt himself sitting taller. *My brother-in-law breathes fire,* he thought. *Of course. After the World's Crash, I guess anything's possible.*

His ease waned as civilization burst from the monotony of sand and rocky mountains in the distance. "Taba," Ellie whispered. Caden stared at the approaching city and a great body of water. "And there's the Red Sea."

Caden's eyes narrowed as he shielded his face from the sun. "Isn't that in the Bible?"

"The Israelites crossed it when they went from Egypt into the Sinai Desert."

Caden grunted. "Yahweh moved the water out of the way, right? Maybe He can do that again, help us get through." Noam grunted a curt laugh.

"How are we getting across the border?" Ellie asked.

Caden slowly shook his head as his stomach knotted. "Haven't a clue."

"We'll get through." Yohanan said.

"We need passports," Ellie continued. "Visas. Records of where we're staying, who we're traveling with. Money. Do we have money?"

Caden shrugged. He was trying to act nonchalant for her sake, but he could feel his pulse quickening. There was no way to get through. None. Zero. *But then there's God,* Caden thought with a deep breath.

"Well," he said at last. "Yahweh said to go back to Jerusalem. He'll have to make it happen for it to, you know… happen."

Ellie didn't answer. The caravan fell silent as they

drew closer to Taba. Caden tried to remember how to act in a city as the hub of activity, honking of horns, and occasional cries of people clapped his ears. He could smell exhaust and burnt rubber from the roads mixed with some type of animal droppings.

Then there were the people crawling everywhere. He heard Taba wasn't that big of a place, but it was much bigger than anything in the Sinai Desert. Dogs barked behind him, and he ducked his head despite himself. He gasped, his heart quickening, feeling he was hiding behind a tree again, Nathaniel's dogs baying around him.

"You okey?" Yohanan asked.

A muscle in Caden's jaw flexed as he forced air through his nose. Why was it so hard to breathe here? "Yah. Sure."

They headed toward the border crossing, just as Caden was tricking himself to calm down, he saw something else. Something horrible. Sentinels. "Are you sure we don't have money?" Ellie asked.

Caden didn't answer as he stared fixedly at the several white-cladded men and women. He had forgotten how these murderers in white weakened him with fear. He felt himself crouching low in the saddle and praying Nathaniel's messages hadn't reached this side of the world. If they wanted him dead in America, they'd kill him here too. Just like Trace. And, why not kill Lil El while they're at it? Sounded reasonable.

"No," Noam muttered. "No money. Not enough. Caden?"

"Um," he stammered, dragging himself from the crushing thoughts. "I don't have any."

"Enough shekels for dinner," Yohanan said. "Just enough."

"That's not enough!" Ellie snapped.

Just don't make yourself noticeable, Caden told himself. *Keep a low profile so the Sentinels don't see you.*

"We can't bribe our way through all the checkpoints." Ellie muttered.

Caden blinked and swore he heard her wrong. "All the... there's more than one checkpoint?"

"Uh, yah." Yohanan glanced back at him. "There's a couple. Buckle up."

"Great." His stomach coiled further.

He fell silent until they reached the border. Gates and roped-off areas led to a tall building. The path was long and snaked back and forth but was completely empty. He gave a gruff laugh, seeing no one else was trying to enter Israel. Instead, he stared at the flow of people, all hulling luggage, traveling in the opposite direction. *We're idiots for going back.* Armed Sentinels paced around the newly arriving caravan. Caden tried to ignore the Egyptian flag bouncing in the wind, the yellow eagle moved to make way for the Sovereign Lion. He sucked in a breath, knowing that cursed lion's eyes were watching him.

Noam's camel thumped close, its feet stomping the ground. Caden turned to ask him what was next. As he looked up, he came face to face with a white-cladded Giantess. Caden cursed through gritted teeth as his camel pranced backwards.

"Oh, pardon me!" The Giantess' voice shot hot breath over him. "I don't mean to give you a fright!" Caden lurched forward, trying to steady the camel. His shoulder tingled; the same shoulder Bobby Rut pinched when choosing to eat Caden first. "Let me help, Mr. Whitney." the Giantess said. She held out a hand and gently laid it on the camel's nose.

Though he was on a camel, the Giantess was eye-level with Caden. She looked like an Israeli woman but enlarged by five times over. Her dark hair made her white

Sentinel uniform pop. She had the same massive knife, nearly a sword on her hip alongside a baton. On her thigh was a gun that had been specially made to accommodate her sausage-sized fingers. Caden tried to breathe but found he couldn't. Something was in the way, the same thing that wasn't letting him move.

Fear, he thought. *Again.* He blinked, the panic making life slow down. Over the din of his internal screaming, he heard something. It was a whispered voice. A still, small voice. *Yahweh was with them.* Caden's jaw clenched. *I'm not mine, I'm His. He's responsible for me. I'm... I'm immortal until He says so.*

Air rushed through his nostrils, filling him as heartbeats hammered from inside his ears. With another breath, Caden straightened. He lifted his chin and faced the Giantess. *Now, what did she just call me?* Without another thought, he promptly started cussing her out.

Out of the corner of his eye, he saw Noam duck and direct Auset to pretend they didn't know him. Yohanan gave him a sharp look as Ellie's jaw hit the floor. *Don't eat me, please!* Caden thought as he ignored the sweat dripping down his back. The Giantess blinked down at him. Her gaze darkened for a moment, and he thought it was over. Then, she stepped back and looked away, her mouth sealed shut.

"Do you know what I've been through?" Caden heard himself yelling. Why was he yelling so loud? Did everyone have to hear him? "Go to Mount Sinai, they said! It'll be spiritual, they said! Look at me! Do I look enlightened!" He scoffed and motioned to his various wounds and bandages. "And this was the best they could give me out there. Can you believe it! And you come here, spooking my animal even more! Where's your superior, hum? Where is he!"

"Ah, that's unnecessary, Mr. Whitney." the Giantess

said, raising a hand. Caden tried his best not to smile as his brows drew low and he gave his best Alex Whitney glare. "I'm so very sorry," she continued. "I won't scare your camel again."

"See that you don't."

"We, um, we met, sir. A few years back? Right after the World's Crash, there was a conference at your father's house."

Caden raised his brows, suddenly unsure of his decision to be Alex again. "And? Why should I remember you? You're just another Giant." He noticed Yohanan's eyes were steadily bugging from his head.

"No, sir. I mean, I'm Lieutenant Tamar Katz. You were blond then, sir."

Caden's heart leapt as he touched his brown hair and suddenly remembered his missing molar. The *wrong* molar. *They'll figure it out! Not everyone's as gullible as Amanda Whitney!*

"Well!" he spat, scrambling for an answer. "Do you think I want everyone to know who I am? I've been kidnapped! I wanted to disguise myself. Come on! Use your head!"

"Of course, sir." Caden shook his head as he crossed his arms to hide his shaking hands. "Ah, sir, why didn't we find you sooner?"

Caden scoffed. "I was wondering the same thing!"

Tamar's eyes narrowed. "Has your NIIC been deactivated?"

Caden stared at the Giantess and remembered Nathaniel talking about the new Neurologically Integrated Interdependent System. The neural implants were supposed to help society, including a GPS tracker to find anyone lost. Because they came from the King's United Society, Caden was determined to never get one.

"Haven't had it installed," Caden said. "I don't want a way for someone to look into my head."

"Well," Tamar said, choosing her words. "It is wise, sir. We would've found you-"

"I obviously don't need you. I rescued myself!"

Tamar gave a curt nod and glanced away. "May I offer assistance? Are you entering Israel?"

"No, I'm in line for a burger and fries, extra pickles." Tamar's head tilted to one side as she stepped back again. "Yes," Caden said in the best condescending tone he could muster. He was shocked his voice didn't crack. "And I'm taking a plane the rest of the way. Hate these things!" He nudged the camel with his foot, which gave him a grumbling whine.

"Yes, Mr. Whitney," Tamar said. "Does your uncle know you've been rescued?"

So that's it, he thought. *You think I've just been kidnapped. Did Thomas' promise for reward money reach way out here?*

"Nope," he said. "I'm going to tell the ol' man myself. Wanna see the look on his face!"

Tamar nodded slowly and tried to hide the excitement in her eyes. "Well, sir. I can take your visa and passport now to deal with the checkpoints. You can go and-"

"Yeah, I forgot to grab those when I was getting kidnapped," Caden said. "So, run along now and tell your Sentinel friends the heir to Whitney Wings wants to get to Jerusalem, Israel."

Tamar frowned sharply. "Jerusalem? But, sir, that city is not suitable for you-"

"The *heir* to Whitney Wings wants to go to Jerusalem, so the *heir* to Whitney Wings will go." He cursed and shook his head. "How stupid are you? Do I have to spell out the consequences too?" Tamar shut her mouth and a muscle in her jaw flexed. Caden suspected that muscle was as strong as both his arms put together.

"Of course, sir," she finally said. "I'll-I'll get you through."

"And boarding a plane."

"With a plane." Caden nodded and sat back, as though a king dismissing a peon. Tamar sighed heavily and started to march away. "Oh!" Caden called. "And seats for my friends too."

Tamar turned and glared at the caravan. "Which ones?"

Caden glared back and motioned to them. "All of them. We're having a big party!" Tamar's mouth opened to speak, but Caden pointed at her as steel entered his voice. "And don't give me excuses! I do remember you, Tamar Katz! I remember you wanted to rise up the ranks, be top dog! Get us through and on a plane, and I'll put in a good word to Uncle Tom."

Tamar's mouth closed as she slowly straightened. She lifted her chin and adjusted her uniform. "Yes, sir!" She turned and marched to the first checkpoint. The humans standing guard snapped to attention as she stomped up to them.

Caden waited until she was a distance away before breathing out a held breath. He glanced at Ellie. Her face was pale. Auset hid behind Noam as he and Yohanan stared at Caden in silent awe. Caden quietly chuckled and shifted in the saddle. "Just follow my lead." he whispered.

"How haven't you peed yourself?" Yohanan asked.

"I told you," Caden hissed. "I've faced Giants before."

Noam's brows rose as Yohanan shook his head. "You're crazy, bro."

Caden's answer was a mini smile. *Thanks, God,* he thought. *Maybe that Alex gig wasn't such a bad idea after all.* Within the hour, they all were airborne and headed to Jerusalem.

TEN
ICY, BLUE, SIBERIAN EYES

CADEN STARED down at the clinking chunks of ice in his whiskey. The liquid looked like amber; it kept catching the streetlights and making it glow. Caden couldn't help but stare, knowing that just a few weeks ago, he had been dreaming about ice. It was in water, but he wouldn't have complained with whiskey. He sat in a long shuttle as it drove along Jerusalem's streets. Behind him sat Yohanan and Ellie. Noam and Auset were close, and the few others who'd survived piled in behind. Their belongings were stashed, and the camels were being taken to a stable Tamar recommended. Everything was being charged to Thomas Whitney.

Caden's stomach tried to get all knotted on itself, knowing that would leave a paper trail showing where Caden would go. A trail Bobby Rut would happily find. Who else would be tramping all over the Middle East, spending thousands of someone else's tams?

We're not going all over, Caden reminded himself. *Once we get to our hotel, I'll send Tamar away. We'll go sightseeing tomorrow and fade into the crowds. We'll find the Mizrahis in no time. This will work. It better. God, please. I totally don't know what I'm doing.*

With a calming sigh, Caden lifted his chin and took another sip of whiskey as he glanced out the window. Night had settled, and the city was alive with flashing lights of a world gifted with electricity. *Gifted by the king,* he thought, a corner of his eye twitching. *The Antichrist.*

A massive Israeli flag, illuminated by several huge lights, stood out in the darkness. Caden caught glimmers of the Sovereign Lion, and a muscle in his jaw flexed. He took a longer sip of the whiskey and continued staring at the amber liquid. He watched the ice lazily float, seeing the bubbles trapped beneath them slowly fluttering their way to the surface.

Caden blinked slowly and rubbed his brow as his muddled mind slowly refined to a clear, single train of thought. *Two people.* He blinked again, the ice shaking as the shuttle bounced in potholes. *I killed two people.* He didn't understand why it took him this long to realize it. While under attack from the Russians, Caden had grabbed the bat. He had swung that bat, and now two people were dead. Lieutenant Tamar had given him a new change of clothes. She said his old ones were potent, but he knew the speckled spray of blood across his entire outfit was disquieting to some.

Well, they were just Puppets, he thought. Another bubble darted to the whiskey's surface and floated, reflecting light. With a whispered curse, Caden closed his eyes. He didn't want to become this. He wasn't a killer. He was just a kid trying to survive! Though he'd seen countless corpses since the World's Crash, he hadn't actually killed. Sure, he'd held a gun a few times, even fired it at some nasty people. But killed?

With a bat too, he thought. *The irony is just great.* Batting had always been his favorite. Of course, that's the weapon given to him. Caden found himself watching Yohanan as the Israeli held his sister close. He sat upright, letting Ellie lean against his shoulder and rest. He wiped his nose and sat back, his eyes blinking slowly as sleep settled on him. *He killed twenty-seven,* Caden thought. *I wonder if he'll lose any sleep.* He shook his head, not knowing what was worse, shrugging off death or letting the overwhelming guilt crush him. Caden ran fingers through his hair and sat back, trying to find rest.

Before him, wedged between two seats, Tamar tried to turn and look down at him. She sat hunched, her huge foot tapping restlessly. Caden had tried to ignore her the best he could, telling her the shuttle wasn't the limo he was expecting and other ridiculous Alex-type comments. She had been useful though. Tucked away in Caden's pocket was Alex Whitney's ID. Somehow, the resourceful Giantess had got that for him, so now he was *really* Alex. That, coupled with his fanny pack of weapons, his gun and Bible, made him feel even more at ease.

"Comfortable, Mr. Whitney?"

Caden sighed, trying to think of another Alex remark. "Yes. When you stop talking." He closed his eyes and pretended to sleep. Rest was far from him. All he kept thinking of were those Puppets and how red his bat must be now. "Um," he stammered, not wanting to relive that grueling moment. "How long to the hotel?"

"Soon, Mr. Whitney. Half an hour."

"I need a shower."

"There's a TV there too, Mr. Whitney."

Caden's eyes opened. "Really? They got that all hooked up again too?"

Tamar nodded. "I thought you would approve."

Caden grimaced as he closed his eyes again. "We'll see." As he tried to actually calm his mind and be quiet, he heard something. Soft, whiney music was playing. He sat up and glanced around. "What is that?"

"Oh, this?" Tamar held up a little rectangle. It looked the size of a cracker in her hand. It was glowing light from one side-

That's a smart phone, Caden told himself. "Where's mine?"

Tamar gave him a tight smile that screamed her patient, calm exterior was completely forced. "I'll see what I can do, sir."

"Are you on the phone?"

"I'm on hold."

"Oh." Caden's heart quickened. Out of the corner of his eye, Yohanan shifted to hear them better. "The hotel? Tell them to get only Egyptian cotton towels. Shouldn't be that hard this side of the world."

"Um, no, Mr. Whitney. I'm calling your uncle."

Caden's heart leapt into his throat while his stomach did a backflip. On the outside, he masked his sudden panic by giving a huge, uncovered yawn. "I said I wanted to tell him I'm alive in person. I want to see his face!"

"Yes, Mr. Whitney. I understand, but-"

"Great. Hang up the phone."

Tamar gave that patronizing smile again. "I'm sorry, sir. It's out of the question. If we are to continue charging to Mr. Thomas Whitney's accounts-"

Caden scoffed. "Yes!"

"Then we must inform him as to who is doing so."

No, no, no!

"He'll know it's me. Who else will be doing this? He'll get over it." Tamar's mouth stayed a smile, but her eyes darkened with that same inhumane, hungry look Bobby always gave him. Caden's stomach turned, and he tried to ignore his urge to puke.

"American brat." she muttered in Hebrew. Caden

almost glared at her but remembered Alex didn't know Hebrew. He settled with a confused frown instead. "I'm going to speak with your uncle, sir," Tamar said, her voice friendly but tight. "I've been on hold for hours. Communication from the other side of the world is terrible these days-Oh! Hello? Yes! Lieutenant Tamar Katz."

Caden looked down at his whiskey as the Giantess told one of Thomas Whitney's people what was happening. *They'll know it's me, they've got to. Bobby will come for me.* Without thinking, Caden rubbed the shoulder Bobby pinched. Caden watched another bubble burst on the whiskey's surface and decided to down the entire thing in one go. It tasted awful and he couldn't hold back a grimace. It was worth it.

Well, God, Caden thought, glancing out the window. *I'm all Yours. Get me out of this mess. Or don't. You'll do what needs to be done, and I,* he sighed. *I guess I'll just hang on for dear life.*

As he listened to Tamar detail their itinerary and which hotel they were staying in, Caden noticed a star that was acting funny. It was an odd color, a bit on the orange side, and was moving. Caden's eyes narrowed as he leaned closer to the window. The star was falling. No, it was a comet, it had a tail and everything. A very puffy, smokey tail at that. And what was that? Was someone whistling? It sounded like one of Mama Lo's kettles on the stove, ready to blow. It was getting louder and-

A white and orange flash of light blinded Caden. He recoiled, covering his eyes. The bus bounced sideways. Something struck his chest. He felt himself airborne. Nothing had been there. Nothing but air! *It is the air,* Caden realized. *Shockwave-*

The windows burst as a roaring torrent of wind sent little, jagged shards everywhere. Caden curled into a ball, not even feeling when he struck the ground. His ears were ringing. His back stung. Who was screaming? Was that him? No, a woman. He turned to Ellie but felt the world dart back and forth. He held onto the seat's legs as the shuttle's tires skidded on the road, the driver cursing in Hebrew as he regained control.

Caden gasped, struggling to rise as he finally found Ellie. She was hunched in her seat as Yohanan lay over her. His mouth was open, and Caden could've sworn an ember or two drifted from his lips. *No, no! Don't start burning! Think of everyone else-*

Another blast shook the shuttle, sending people from their seats. Caden tumbled, his forearms bracing himself on the floor and finding the little bits of glass. He yelled through gritted teeth and lurched back, only to hear the squeal of tires before a sudden, metallic crash. He was on his face again. Everyone was screaming. Distant whistling descended, followed by explosive blasts.

Well, Caden thought to God. *This isn't really the rescue I had in mind.* Someone was yelling. Someone he knew.

"Bro!" Yohanan shouted. "We've got to move." He hooked his hands under Caden's arms and dragged him upright. "Can you walk?"

"What happened?"

"Crash." Caden glanced at the front of the shuttle. It looked wrinkled in, like metal fabric. The driver was slumped in his seat. He wasn't moving.

"Got to move." Noam muttered, Auset tucked under his arm. The others of their caravan were regaining their bearings and heading toward the door. Caden turned to Ellie. Her cheek was dotted by small cuts, probably from the glass. Her face was pale as she held Yohanan's arm. Their eyes met. Though shaken and bleeding, he could see the fire in her gaze. They were under attack, she was still limping with her wounded leg, and yet, she wouldn't back down. Caden lifted his chin and took a slow breath.

We are immortal until the moment God calls us home, he

thought. She nodded slowly; she always knew what was on his mind.

Yohanan faced him and he drew Ellie close. He gave Caden a firm, determined look. Caden knew Yohanan would gladly burn down the entire city if it kept his Spiny safe. *I've got to trust him,* Caden thought. *He's crazy, but he's good.* He didn't have a choice.

They filed from the shuttle, and Caden coughed in the dusty air and smell of gas and burnt rubber. They had crashed into cars hit by a missile. Fire leapt about the tangled, metal heap. People were screaming. Someone was still stuck in the car. Others lay on the ground, unable to rise. *Raw Peace,* Caden thought as he stumbled away after Yohanan and Ellie. *I have Raw Peace. Yahweh is with me. He will give me-*

All thought stopped as Caden noticed the sky. It was like nature had turned against them, and stars were hurling themselves down. Missiles fell, some at an angle and some straight down, sending a trail of thick smoke behind as their glowing heads promised destruction. Sirens lifted from everywhere as the missiles shook Jerusalem.

Between the blasts echoing around them and people's screams, Caden could hear the slight whistle of movement above. Planes darted overhead. Swift, uncatchable bodies that sent down the killer stars.

Yohanan cursed as he stared at the descending missiles. "Where's the Iron Dome!" he cried into the sky, referring to the Israeli missile defense system. "What did they do?"

Noam grabbed his shoulder. "Got to move." Yohanan cursed again and led the group through the chaos. They jogged together, bent low to the ground and ready to change direction at any second. They passed cars and buildings on fire and skyscrapers with inner rooms exposed like recklessly gutted kills. People ran in every direction. Many looked wounded, but Caden wondered if it was just the darkness playing tricks on him.

No, he told himself. *Many will die tonight. I might die-*

"Ellie might die."

Caden sucked in a breath through gritted teeth as his eyes became dark slits. "Get away!" Caden hissed.

"Never."

"Doeg! I swear to God, I'll-"

White. Orange. Heat. Splitting thunder. He was flying again. He landed eventually and lay, moaning and holding his arm. His ears rang, and he could only see white spots when he opened his eyes. Did he hit his head? Or did the explosion blind him? No, no he could still see. A portion of a building had fallen. Bits of the wall were still clambering into a pile in the middle of the road. Caden blinked slowly, trying to understand what was happening. He could finally hear something. Someone was knocking on something, over and over really fast. Oh, wait. That was his heartbeats.

Caden tried to suck in a breath. He couldn't do it very well. *Where's Ellie?* Coughing, Caden dragged himself to his feet and squinted through the haze of smoke and dust.

"Ellie?" Caden's breath quickened as he searched the street. "Ellie!" He looked to the pile of rubble and slowly shook his head. *Oh, God, please!* He limp-hopped to the mound and searched in the gloom. "Ellie? El!" Why wasn't anyone answering him? Caden placed both hands on his head as sweat dripped from his brow. *Another dead sibling,* he thought.

The fatality rate was staggeringly against him. It was ironic, sacrificing himself daily for those who couldn't survive his very presence. Who would he slaughter next simply by close proximity? Asher? What of this future wife; was she exempt from his fatal nature? It was pathetic. He was pathetic and could never amount to anything worthy of honor or dependability-

"Doeg!" Caden's cry filled the night.

The Demon chuckled, its claws scraping the cement blocks. "I speak truth."

Ignore him! Caden's hands curled into fists that he dug into his eyes.

"There is no escaping pure truth."

If he speaks, he lies, Caden thought, sharply lifting his head. *Lies!*

"If I lie," Doeg whispered, its breath brushing Caden's ear. "Why do you believe me?"

Caden ducked away, cursing, and ran. He didn't know where he was going. He needed to get away and to find his sister. That and cover. Caden ran low to the ground, finally seeing the explosions again. How had he forgotten? Well, fear your beloved sister is dead is a bit distracting-

She's not dead, Caden told himself. *Yohanan's got her.*

"Right. And flames are a failsafe protection against missiles."

Caden forced himself not to answer. He kept running, his head on a swivel. Dust clouded the air and made it hard to breathe. Strangers rushed everywhere in chaos, a father carrying a bleeding daughter, a mother shouting for her child, a teen darting around, eyes wide and face pale. Caden kept calling for Ellie or Yohanan, but no one answered. Bursts of energy blasted through the streets as more missiles fell. He watched as a building crumbled, muffling several screams. At least it was a few streets away.

Caden was suddenly aware of his loud breathing. His feet crunched through shattered glass, and he found he was alone. *It's quiet,* he thought. *What's happening?* He looked up, seeing glowing missiles falling. Why couldn't he hear them? His hair stood on end; something was wrong. Something beyond his human understanding.

He finally heard it. From the stillness came approaching horse hooves. Goosebumps dotted Caden's arms as his face turned pale. Why was he shaking? It was just a horse! *No*, he told himself. *I've got to hide. Now!* He threw himself behind a crashed car and huddled close to the ground.

The hooves clopped nearer. A shadowed figure came down the street. Caden stared wide-eyed. He forgot to breathe or think. All he could do was watch. An odd horseman rode on an even stranger horse. Even in the darkness, Caden could see the animal's solid muscles ripple with each stride beneath a fiery red coat. It was a huge horse and didn't seem the least bit concerned by the chaos around it.

The rider was equally as musclebound and unfazed. He was Israeli yet dressed in ancient armor. He wore a short robe beneath a metal, scaled coat of mail. A pointed helmet covered his head, leather greaves fitted his legs, and sandals protected his feet. In his hand was an inhumanly massive sword. The rider, warhorse, and sword were covered, from head to hoof, in splattered blood.

Caden's stomach turned as all he could hear was the horse hooves crunching over glass and rubble. He was breathing too loud; he clamped his hand over his mouth. His heartbeat was too loud too! *Don't see me!* His mind begged. *Please, don't see me!* The horseman kept his casual pace and, very slowly, continued down another street.

Caden lay huddled behind the car, listening with all his might. The hooves steadily clopped away, leaving Caden in silence. He gasped, his tense body fully collapsing to the ground as though he had just fought a battle. With ragged breaths, Caden stood and stared down the street the horseman went. He cursed under his breath and ran fingers through his hair. *Who was that? WHAT was that?* It looked human, but Caden knew when he saw a Spirit. Did that horseman mean something-?

Another kettle was whistling. Caden scrambled behind the car again. Fire blinded him. The shockwave tried to rip his clothes from his back. He gasped, falling back and landing on some debris. He lay, his body shaking, and made sure he still had his arms and legs.

"Off! Get off!"

Caden lurched upright and scooted away, realizing the debris was actually a person. She sat up and flicked her brunette hair from her face. Her pale blue eyes fell on him, and he caught himself staring. He had seen her before. She had looked different the last time they met, but it was still her. There was something about her face that was off. Her skin was still pale, but it was more... He didn't know. The young lady scoffed and muttered something, but it wasn't in Hebrew. Was that Russian?

Wrinkles. Caden blinked slowly, his mouth dropping open. *She was wrinkly and older.* A surge of strength rushed through him as he scooted closer to the young lady. "Dasha?" The woman stiffened as every muscle tensed to act. "Dasha Patrov?" Horror flashed across her eyes, and Caden held up a hand with a gentle smile. *Is this seriously happening? Right now?*

"Um..." he muttered, suddenly realizing she had no clue who he was. What was he going to say? That he saw them in the future, and they were married and beating up Demons in souped-up, God-fire armor? He stood and wiped his hands on his pants. *I could just offer her shelter,* he thought. *I'll find the Mizrahis. They'll give us a-*

He was falling again. Where'd the ground go? His backside found it hard, and he gasped, the wind knocked out of him. As he sucked in a breath, a blow to his liver knocked it out again. Caden moaned as he doubled over and held his middle. Another explosion shook the city, followed by a second close by. The shockwaves were forcing his head back and forth and, oh no... that's not it. She was punching him.

Caden raised his hands and caught one of her forearms. Without thinking, he drew back his own fist as he dragged her closer. At the last moment, he remembered something important. This was his future wife. It wasn't good to punch your wife. With a sharp twist, she ripped free from his grasp and leapt.

Oh, God, was all Caden had time to think before she landed on him, her knees nearly collapsing his chest. The wind rushed out of him again, and his head bounced at least twice. Caden tried to breathe and blink through the flashing lights obscuring his vision.

He raised his arms and looked up in time to see something shining in her hands. It was long, narrow, and ended in a sharp point. Caden yelled as Dasha two-handedly drove the knife down. He caught her wrists, and the blade stopped a few inches from his throat.

"Dasha!" He gasped and looked up. Their eyes met. There was nothing but gritty determination in those icy blue, Siberian eyes. Without hesitating, Dasha threw her weight into the knife. Caden yelled through gritted teeth and tasted blood. "Please!" He cried. "We're on the same team! Dasha! I-"

She wasn't going to stop. Caden pushed against her hands as the knife's tip drew closer to his throat.

ELEVEN
THE ITALIAN

THERE'S nothing more infuriating than a smaller, weaker person totally destroying you. Nate had been small, but man did he have a killer punch. Caden remembered trying to help him with his anger, directing him to beat his drums instead of Caden's face. It had worked eventually, and Caden hadn't been able to hit back. He just couldn't. It was his little brother! His hurt, angry, scared little brother, who Caden remembered toddling around as a snot-nosed baby and Mom telling him to make sure Nate didn't suck on sticks or dirt.

It kind of felt the same for Caden as he stared up at Dasha, her knife steadily descending upon him. *But this isn't a punch,* Caden thought. *If she wins, I'll die.* He suddenly regretted not punching her. Dasha, her face impassive and mouth a tight, thin line, only stared at him. Her arms were shaking, but so were his.

"Dasha!" he hissed. "You can't-"

Her eyes narrowed as a shadow crossed her gaze. The knife drew closer. "Don't say what I can't do."

Caden tried to wiggle away and force up her hands, but nothing helped. *What's wrong with me? I'm stronger than this!* But he wasn't. Not after being thrown from a camel twice, getting attacked by Puppets, and running from missiles. His body was more or less spent.

He gasped, his throat bobbing. He didn't even hear the falling missiles or the cries around them. All he knew was his future wife and her blade. Something brushed his chin. No, it burned it. Caden tried to hold back a yell as the knife cut into his chin. He jerked his chin up, effectively exposing his throat. The knife kept slowly digging in. He felt it graze against his jawbone. Through gritted teeth, he screamed and felt blood trickle down his neck.

You can't kill me, he thought. *We're a team! How could this be my wife?* The missiles' descent finally reached his ears. They whizzed by like little darts. There wasn't any explosion, but many zipped passed.

Dasha muttered Russian and rolled, dragging her knife with her. Caden gasped and held his throat. He knew he'd find a gaping hole and blood gushing. Blood slicked his fingers, but his throat was fine. *Where's all the blood coming from-*

He lightly brushed his chin. Flaming pain burst across his face. He moaned as he forced himself onto his side. Each breath hurt. His head was in a daze. Someone was shouting. Lots of voices, but they weren't in Hebrew.

Caden turned and found white Shades swarming through the chaos. They carried guns and shouted to one another in... what was that? Italian? Caden blinked and stared, realizing they didn't have tails and one large eye covering their entire face. *No,* he told himself, holding his head. *Not Shades. Sentinels.*

The king's Sentinels swept the road, leaping over rubble and helping survivors. Three were charging straight for him, their weapons drawn. Caden's eyes widened in horror. *Nathaniel caught me.* He turned to curl into a ball but stopped. Dasha stood over him, her knife poised to strike. In that instant, Caden realized they weren't shooting at him. They were shooting at the crazy Russian.

At my wife.

Without thinking, Caden seized her wrists while sweeping her leg. She dropped like a stone, and he rolled over her, shielding her with his body. The whizz of bullets slammed into the debris around them. "I got you!" Caden heard himself shouting as he held her tight. "I got you!"

He could smell gunpowder and dust. He thought he heard dogs but wasn't sure. *I should've done this for Trace. Maybe-*

The bullets stopped suddenly. Dasha moved, kicking with fists drawn back. Caden recoiled, avoiding each blow, as she leapt up and fled. Caden reached out to her but stopped. He didn't have to chase after her for the future to come true. *I'll run into her again,* he thought. *I hope this isn't what our marriage's like.*

He turned to the Sentinels as one raced to his side and knelt over Caden. Caden recoiled, remembering the last time he was this close to a Sentinel's gun. The Sentinel lay a gentle hand on his shoulder while keeping his gun trained on where Dasha had escaped. "I'll shield you."

Caden stared at him, not moving. *You don't know who I am,* he thought. *The king could want my head, but I'm Alex Whitney right now. Where's that ID Tamar gave me?* He patted his pockets, and his heart slowed once he felt it, knowing he could wear his Alex disguise for a bit longer. *Not too much, I hope.*

The Sentinel at last stood and motioned for Caden to go behind him. He did, fighting the urge to peg the king's soldier with a rock. He breathed out a held breath and looked around, trying to regain his bearings. They were on a city street filled with debris, a crashed car or two, and bits of the asphalt was blown apart, sending jagged crags across the road. People ran toward the Sentinels, many yelling and limping or holding some bleeding part of their body. Caden gently touched his chin again.

"Let it be," the Sentinel said as he backed the two away from Dasha. "Looks like it needs stitches." The roar of an engine cried overhead as something big shot past. Caden ducked low and searched for cover. "It's alright," the Sentinel said, his voice just as calm and steady as before. "Our boys will clean the skies."

Caden glanced at him. "Italians?" The Sentinel nodded. Caden didn't have time to ask questions, or even think of any, as the cacophony of guns and missiles sounded in the dark sky. He saw flashes of orange light illuminating the outline of a jet before it zoomed into blackness.

"I have cover for you and a medic to attend to you," the Sentinel said. "Please, follow me."

Caden shook his head as he stepped back. "I have to find my-"

He snapped his mouth shut. *Alex doesn't have a sister.* He turned away from the Sentinel, his mind spinning. *I'll make up some excuse. I can't let her die!*

"You look pretty banged up." He realized the Sentinel was walking toward him.

He reached out a hand right when Caden moved away. "I'm fine-"

He stumbled, slipping in lose rubble. He steadied just before falling and blinked, realizing the Sentinel was holding one of his arms. "This way now. I will help you."

I didn't ask for your help.

"What's your name?"

Caden blinked, wondering if he should say Oliver Deker, Alex Whitney, or nothing. *But my ID's in Alex's name.* "Alex," he said. "Alex Whitney."

"Whitney?"

Oh great.

"Anthony's boy?"

"Um, yeah."

"You're alive! Word came you've been kidnapped!"

Caden didn't answer as he focused on placing one foot in front of the other. As he looked down, blood continued to drip from his split chin. *How deep did she cut me?* Something flashed high above. Heat and a forceful shockwave roared around them, knocking loose debris from buildings and sending the streets into more chaos. A mushroom cloud spread in the night sky, illuminating a downed plane.

Caden gasped, shielding his eyes from more dust and falling bits, only to find the Sentinel's arms wrapped around him. He nearly shoved the stranger away, the murderer dressed in white like a wicked angel, the ones who slaughtered his brother-

"This way, Mr. Whitney." Caden bit his tongue until it hurt as he leaned on the Sentinel.

More Sentinels had swept the area and were helping others, wounded and disoriented, into cars. As Caden passed them, he noticed their white uniforms were altered. The cuffs on their sleeves were vivid, fiery red. On both shoulders were three, fiery red diamonds grouped together. Caden vaguely wondered what the new uniforms meant, but he didn't care enough to ask. He was still trying not to die.

Caden got into a van, and the Sentinel slid in next to him. Behind them, there was a woman clutching a crying child, a man who was missing an arm, and a little boy just staring into nothing. As the door slammed shut, Caden couldn't help but think of piling into Officer Nathaniel's hummers, heading for "salvation".

Or our execution.

"Where, um," his voice cracked, and he cleared his throat. "Where're we going?"

"A bunker," the Sentinel said, safely placing his gun's butt on the floor and muzzle pointed to the ceiling. "Be still about it though," he continued, motioning to the others, "only *you're* going there."

Caden stiffened. *Nathaniel's there.*

No, no, that was nonsense. He was back in America. He didn't even know where Caden was! But he could. He could find out. Or maybe Grant, his weighted cane ready to strike. Which bone would he crush first? A thumb? Perhaps a toe? Being a crippled slave to a madman would certainly inhibit fulfilling prophecies or whatever blabber that Cherub had said. Speaking of Han, had he abandoned you? Of course. Everyone abandons you in due time; either by their own fruition or untimely death-

Caden gritted his teeth, as though barring Doeg's words into his heart. "Um," he muttered. "Why am I the only one going?"

"Because I'm personally escorting you to safety." the Sentinel said, motioning with a hand.

Caden nearly asked why but remembered Alex wouldn't. He would feel entitled and not be grateful in the slightest. *Screw Alex.* "Why?"

"The king provides for his people. Your uncle is an irreplaceable asset to the king and his New Kingdom. It would be unprofessional and downright wrong to leave you."

Caden turned away; this one sounded so much like Nathaniel too. Did all Sentinels receive training to seem personable and caring before stabbing someone to death? Caden's throat bobbed as Simon's wide-eyed expression of shock and pain flashed through his mind. *I am immortal until Yahweh says so,* he thought. He cursed under his breath and stared out the window.

"Here." The Sentinel tapped his arm and handed him a handkerchief. Caden pressed it against his chin and ignored the flaming pain.

They rode in tense silence, the sky sometimes erupting with orange light and fire as the dog fight above continued. The kid wouldn't stop crying. Caden didn't blame her. Everywhere they went, several roads were nearly destroyed, so they had to turn around many times.

All the while, Caden kept searching for Ellie. *Please don't be dead, please don't be dead.* He looked down and closed his eyes, his inability to save her making him feel helpless. And furious. A muscle in his jaw flexed as he thought of God and the dark games He plays. Of course, He let Caden find his Lil El, only to separate them. It was all a sadistic ploy by the monster deity, hanging His superiority and surpassing authority over everyone's heads and making them fail-

Doeg, Caden thought as calmly as he could. *When Yeshua returns, I will punch you in the face.*

"*If He returns.*"

He is.

"*This isn't the End Times as your foolish prophet friend claims. This is simply life. Cruel, unavoidable life.*"

Caden took in a breath as he lifted his chin. *Yahweh was with them and gave them rest,* he thought. *He is with me and is giving me rest. I don't feel it or see it, but it's here.* He cursed again and rubbed his brow, wincing. He touched his face and found his jaw and cheek were starting to swell. He shook his head, not wanting to see Dasha again for a long time.

The ride continued, stopping at a hospital for most people and a slapped-together shelter set up by the King's United Society. As they filed out, the Sentinel leaned back and unsnapped the helmet strapped beneath his chin. Caden watched out of the corner of his eye as his so-called rescuer revealed himself. He was definitely Italian. Olive skin, defined angular facial features, and waving brown hair. Stubble outlined his sharp jaw. Caden was completely and utterly attracted to women, but he knew a handsome fella when he saw one. He caught himself staring. Even in the dark of night, the Sentinel's hazel eyes seemed to glint with some inner... something.

Peace, Caden thought, noting the Sentinel's loose shoulders and finger tapping on his knee in a rhythm. *He's singing in his head,* Caden realized. The Italian noticed him staring and faced him with a smile. It wasn't a just-mouth smile, but it shone in his eyes and straightened his posture, as though his entire being wanted to smile too. Caden blinked and found himself smiling back. *Stop that!* He told himself and looked away.

"Well, Alex," the Sentinel said. "How are you feeling?" He kept talking with his hands. It was weird.

"Beat up, what do you think?" Caden mumbled.

"Yes, who was that? I couldn't see him."

You didn't see anything then, Caden thought. "No clue," he said. "Just jumped me. Psycho foreigners." *That is the weakest lie you've ever told!* Caden ignored his throat constricting as the Sentinel nodded thoughtfully.

"I assume you get that often. Dangerous people wanting to harm you."

Caden scoffed. "You have no idea. I just nearly escaped these last guys!"

"Yes. I heard about your abduction over the radios. We went out looking."

"Well, you didn't find me. I had to free myself."

"Where are the men who got you?" Caden looked out the window, trying to concoct something clever and believable. He was just too tired for games right now. He needed to sleep. And another shot of whiskey. "I don't want to talk about it." He finally said.

The Sentinel nodded and continued tapping out a beat on his knee. "I respect that." Caden didn't answer. "I'm Luca Battistelli."

Caden frowned and glanced at him. "Batti-what?"

Luca's smile broadened. "Battistelli."

Caden grunted. "Hi." Luca started humming to himself and Caden realized his standard Alex persona wasn't annoying him. He didn't seem offended or bothered at all.

"We'll get you home soon enough, Alex," Luca said. "But I suspect this attack will slow things down-"

The van shook as an explosion lit the night right behind them. Caden's heart quickened, knowing if they were a second or two slower, they would've been hit. "Quite a bit, actually. But salvation comes: the king is coming to Jerusalem."

The news was the last thing Caden wanted to hear. He was so tired, and his everything hurt so much. He didn't notice his grimace until Luca stared at him.

"You don't like the king?"

Well, no going back now.

"Nope. I don't fall for all that love-talk all you Sentinels preach about."

Luca arched a brow. "Preach?"

"You're always talking about the king's love and how anyone is welcome into the New Kingdom." Caden cursed and shook his head. "No one's that stupid. Who does that?"

Luca quietly listened as he nodded. "Are you not familiar with unconditional love?"

Caden crossed his arms, seeing the questions were getting a bit too personal. "I live in the real world. No one can do that. It's just dreams for the foolish, but it's empty in the end."

Luca lifted his chin and sighed heavily. For once, he wasn't smiling. "I'm sorry you never had a good father."

Caden fell still as the small, wounded side of him, who still hated his father, sounded alarms. This stranger was getting too close. This was his pain! His inner world! And Luca wasn't invited. "Whatever," Caden muttered with a gruff sniff. "How do you know my dad?"

"I've been to House Whitney," Luca said. "There was a conference after the Day of Vanishing. We talked."

Caden nodded, hardly listening. "Well," he muttered. "He's dead anyways." *And good riddance.*

"Was he the type to change behind closed doors?"

Caden didn't want to answer, but he felt himself nodding. "He," his voice cracked again, and he looked down. Luca said nothing and waited in patient silence. "He didn't value me much. Didn't think I could become anything-"

Caden snapped his mouth shut, knowing he was being stupid. He was Alex! They were talking about Anthony Whitney, not Caden's dad! Not the one who demanded more without giving a thing. The one who always had a cutting word or soul-crushing jab to say. The one who refused to love and accept Caden for how he was and for who he was.

No one believed me when I finally talked about it, he remembered. His teacher had literally patted him on the back and said things are always hard transitioning to adulthood.

"You must've felt helpless."

Caden kept nodding, and he ducked his head. He held himself back from attacking Dad so many times. No one else was going to take a stand against him, it might as well be him. *But who would protect Nate, make sure Trace got his meds, and listen to El talk about ancient Egypt?*

"Alex, may I tell you something my papà told me?"

Great, Caden thought as he rolled his eyes. Sometimes it was nice pretending to be a rude, self-centered, rich kid. *He's going to tell me to forgive and forget or some other lovey garbage.* He held back from swearing something nasty and faced Luca. Luca looked him right in the eyes and held his gaze. Caden blinked, realizing this stranger could, in that moment, see only one thing: Caden. His pain was the only thing in Luca's world, and it was all he cared about.

"Alex, my papà said to not let a messed-up person's messed-up view mess me up." Caden blinked and looked down. "You were given a fool of a father. A fool cannot love, much less care for a son. He failed you." Caden said nothing as he stiffly sat. "The truth of who you are doesn't change if your papà believed it or not."

Caden forced a smile and lifted his chin. "And who am I? Seriously, we just met!"

Luca lay a hand on Caden's shoulder and grinned. "You are a fighter, a survivor." Caden found himself staring into those hazel eyes. "You have faced odds your father's never even seen, and you overcame them! Come on! You're in Israel, surviving terrorists, kidnappers, and Russians attacking! You are more than capable; you are a conqueror. And I am honored to have found you."

Caden realized he wasn't breathing. He didn't know what God's voice sounded like, but he assumed it was something like this. The feeling of peace Luca's words brought him, to his inner, deep parts, it was something else. Something out of this world.

Do you have the Raw Peace too? Caden blinked as he tried to think, his chest tightening with emotions. This felt more than the Raw Peace, even more than Elijah or Yohanan had. *Are you… are you Yeshua?*

Luca's smile grew as he squeezed Caden's shoulder. He withdrew and glanced out the window. "Ah, we're here."

The van parked, and Caden didn't notice the sliding door grind open. He stared down at the stained handkerchief, trying to understand. *Yeshua said He'd come like a thief in the night so no one would know when He gets here. What if He comes early and saves His people? What if He...* Caden closed his eyes and rubbed his brow. His vision was blurry. Were those tears? *I am a conqueror. God believes in me.* He felt a tear trickle down his cheek as he turned to Luca. He didn't know where Luca was going, but Caden was going to follow him.

Luca was talking to a Sentinel who had opened the van door. The Sentinel was an elderly man who looked very concerned. His uniform was far more decorated than Caden had ever seen. Golden tassels swung from his shoulders as metals colored his chest. They were speaking Italian until Luca waved his hand. "Please, not in front of my guest," he said, motioning to Caden. "English, please. Do be polite."

"Yes, your majesty."

Caden blinked through the haze of revelation and stared at the elderly Sentinel with narrowed eyes. *What did he just call him?*

Luca seemed to notice Caden's confused glance and faced him. "I, um... my name is Luca Battistelli, however, my title is much, much longer." Caden stared at him, and a creeping chill seeped into his bones. "I don't need to bore you with the entire name, but the common folk just sum it up quite neatly." Caden swallowed the hard lump in his throat. "They call me the king."

Caden, again, forgot to breathe. It was like his head had been plunged under cold, black water, and no amount of thrashing was going to save him. He sat, his heart steadily beating faster, as his internal screaming started up again, growing louder and louder until it shook his heart. *I've been talking to the Antichrist,* Caden finally thought.

"I know, I know," Luca said with a sigh. "It's a shock. I'm not in appropriate dress. It's just so hard being in the field with all the bells and whistles, you know?"

Caden didn't answer. *And I just told him I don't like this king. Him! He is the king!*

"Look," Luca said, laying a hand on Caden's shoulder again. "I'm not offended you don't approve of my New Kingdom and acceptance of people. Most have trouble believing me at first. But come now. Dinner should be ready soon, and Dr. Ricci should stitch that chin up." Caden's mouth dropped open as his hands became cold and clammy. "After that," Luca continued, "feel free to stay for as long as you wish."

Caden was just about to say no when he remembered something terrible. The Door. Future Caden and future Dasha. His older self said to accept the hospitality of the first person who offered. *No one else has.* Caden took in a tight breath and turned away.

"Sir," he mumbled. "Majesty, are you offering me your hospitality?"

Oh, God no! No! No! Please! Don't let this be happening!

Luca's hand gently squeezed his shoulder. "Of course, Alex. My home is your home." Caden forced himself not to hyperventilate as he stared up at the Antichrist, the false Yeshua, his host.

TWELVE
NO REST

CADEN COULD USUALLY HOLD down his puke when he got really, really upset. Not this time. He blamed it on the attack and chaos of surviving a kidnapping. Luca said he understood and sincerely looked sorry for him. *It's a lie, it's all a lie. He's a bad guy. The baddest bad guy!*

Caden left his mess on the sidewalk as Luca and his Sentinels ushered him to the massive building they parked in front of. Caden found himself leaning on Luca as he held his side, each breath painful, as more explosions shook the city. He looked up into the chaos of the skies as more and more plains roared overhead. The sounds of the engines had changed as different types of planes shot through the night.

"We are winning," Luca whispered. "Jerusalem will be saved, thank God." Caden gave him a sharp look but said nothing.

They rushed into the building surrounded by palm trees and vivid green grass. Caden thought the rough-cut stone structure was a business or government building, until stepping inside. There were couches, tables, chairs, a vast library, and more wealth than Caden had seen in all of Jerusalem. It was like he was in House Whitney again.

This is his home, Caden thought, his throat slowly tightening. The luxurious place was dark and lit only by a few lanterns and the sudden illumination of explosions outside. Luca ushered Caden and the assisting staff through a complicated system of stairs and elevators until they were, Caden suspected, beneath the mansion.

Caden's chest tightened with dread as they stepped into a long, plain hallway. He couldn't help remembering Bobby Rut dragging him through the Whitney's underground prison. He looked for a two-headed Freak barking on the end of its chain but found none.

"We are going to make it, Alex." Luca whispered.

Caden lifted his chin as a thrill rushed through him. *Did he just pick up on my nervousness?* Caden swallowed the hard lump in his throat and tried to ignore his upset stomach, throbbing face, inflamed side, and who was helping him stand.

They made it to a fortified room fitted with a thick, heavy door and shelves of canned food which lined two walls. Cots were against the other, and Luca eased Caden down onto one. "Where is Dr. Ricci?" Luca asked.

"I'll fetch him, your majesty." a young boy offered and raced through the door.

Majesty, Caden thought as he sat, hunched over, trying not to puke again.

"Rest," Luca said. "You look banged up very bad." Muffled booms shook the room, and all conversation quieted as the naked bulb overhead flickered. The shelves rocked a bit, and a few cans toppled over. "Be at peace, everyone," Luca said calmly. He smiled and lay a hand on one of the Sentinel's shoulders. "Be strong and courageous. Do not be afraid or discouraged. We stand together."

Caden could almost feel the tension in the room lift as everyone eased into cots or helped get others settled. He didn't move, too stunned to do anything. As Dr. Ricci inspected him, Caden numbly stared at the blank wall. *Ellie's dead*, he thought. *And so is Yohanan. Why did God want me to come back here? I killed the second Witness. I've failed God and everyone else. Why didn't rubble crush me instead? Rid the world of my complete incompetence and disappointments, thus eradicating my constant shame-*

Caden closed his eyes as Doeg's rasping laugh echoed in his heart. *Please*, he thought to no one in particular. *Please, leave me alone.*

"Hurting here?" the doctor asked, his voice thick with an Italian accent.

Caden sluggishly nodded. When he opened his eyes, he saw a shadow move across the ceiling. It slithered alone, swift and purposeful, pale green eyes catching the light. Caden watched the Viper as it scuttled to the wall and stopped, a black tongue lashing. Another one uncoiled from the shadows in the far corner. Oh, and another one dropped from the ceiling, landing on a Sentinel who, of course, didn't notice. Caden slowly looked up, and his breath quickened as his eyes darted all across the ceiling. It was alive. The ceiling was alive with slithering, coiling Vipers.

"Relax, relax." Dr. Ricci muttered, and Caden slowly looked down, too tired and overwhelmed by pain and helplessness to react.

Out of the corner of his eye, a Sentinel stood from a cot. He wore a furry coat and had something pointed on his head. Caden's heart leapt into his throat, and he forced himself not to flinch back. It was a Shade, and it calmly walked through the gathering. A maid even stepped out of its way, as though she knew it was there, but Caden doubted it. His fingertips were getting cold as flight or fight sank in. He felt weak and shaky, but knew it was the anxiety icing his blood. He could vaguely hear his internal screaming. It was getting louder, about to swallow him in the black void, and he'd feel nothing but sweet oblivion.

No, Caden thought, forcing himself to take a slow breath. He winced, his side throbbing with each inhale. *No!* he repeated, the pain angering him and giving him strength. *I will not hide from this! You cannot take me!* An elderly man, most likely a gardener, was staring at him. They locked eyes, and the man sniffed, easing back into his cot.

"What happened to your arm hair?" Dr. Ricci muttered. "Burned off?"

The gardener crossed his arms and scratched his head, shifting the skin over his eye slightly, and he quickly moved it back into place. Caden didn't turn away from the Wither as he slowly realized the doctor had spoken. Something about his arms? His arms were fine. It was his side that was killing him.

"Arm up." Caden tried to obey but moaned as pain slammed into his side again. He felt his shirt moving up, and the doctor grunted. "Cracked ribs."

He said more in Italian, and Luca cut him off. "English, please. This is my guest."

"Don't lay down, be sure to cough, and stay moving to prevent any mucus buildup in your lungs."

Caden lowered his arm and gritted his teeth. "Any pain meds?" Dr. Ricci glanced at Luca, and he gave a small nod. The doctor opened his bag and fished out a locked box. Taking the key from around his neck, he opened it and produced one small, red pill. Actually, it was half a pill. Caden stared at the old, Ibuprofen and nearly laughed. *That* was not what he needed.

"Edoardo." Luca muttered. The doctor frowned and produced another pill. This one was intact and white.

Caden paused, not knowing what it was. Alex wouldn't care and just take it. Caden, on the other hand, knew Demons were crawling all over the place. There was no telling what it was.

"A little oxycodone," Dr. Ricci said. "Take it?"

Caden stared at it a moment longer. *Will it make me weaker? I can't be weak right now.* Another Shade strolled into the room, its clawed feet scraping on the concrete floor. "Actually," Caden muttered. "I'm good."

"There's no need to prove yourself, Alex." Luca said.

"Nah," Caden muttered with a smile. "I still feel queasy. Don't want to throw that up; it's obviously rare." Dr. Ricci lifted his chin approvingly and tucked away his prized collection. Caden felt his heart thudding in his throat. His hands itched for the meds getting put away, but he had to be alert. He had to not give anyone, or anything, a chance to overtake him.

"Look up." Dr. Ricci instructed as he pulled a spool of thread and a curved needle from the bag. Caden stared at it warily, his heart quickening, and obeyed. He gritted his teeth as the doctor inspected and cleaned his split chin.

Raw Peace, Caden thought, watching the Vipers crawl over one another overhead. *You've given me your Raw Peace. I have it. I just have to walk in it.*

"Little pressure."

He cursed through gritted teeth as the needle dug in. It was horrible, it felt like his chin was being ripped open all over again. He wondered if torture felt this way. Caden cursed again.

"Hold still." the doctor muttered.

"Hey, Alex," Luca said. "I don't want you kidnapped again. I assume you agree. Once you heal, I'd like to show you defensive maneuvers."

Why does everyone want to teach me how to fight?

"I see there's fight in you. I can direct it, take that

driving force and channel it into effective action. It's also a productive release of anger." Luca nodded, and Caden realized he was trying to distract him from the needle entering his skin every few seconds. "If nothing else, we can spar and get to know one another."

Goodie, Caden thought with dry sarcasm as he squeezed his eyes shut tight.

"Think about it."

Does God want me to know how to fight for some reason? I thought Christians were peaceful people who didn't hurt others. Then again, he did take a bat to a few Puppets. He wouldn't have done that so willingly if Elijah and Yohanan hadn't trained him.

"And you are welcome to stay, Alex," Luca continued. "Stay as long as you need. My people will reach out to House Whitney and inform them you are safe. That may take time, however. Communications are usually down for a time after a raid, especially when trying to reach the other side of the world." Caden glanced at Luca and nodded.

"Still, please!" Dr. Ricci snapped.

Caden sucked in a breath, sending a sharp pain along his cracked ribs, and held still. Maybe this was all part of Yahweh's plan. Maybe he was supposed to be here and learn how to fight. Or maybe Caden had just walked right into the enemy's camp and was expected to stay a long time. *Yahweh was with them and gave them rest,* Caden thought, the only Bible verse he knew circling his mind. *He's with me. He's giving me rest.*

"*This pain will weaken you,*" Doeg's voice whispered in his mind. "*And I will prolong it.*"

Giving me rest.

"*Look around you, boy. You are utterly surrounded by every enemy imaginable.*"

Not Grant or Buck! Not Nathaniel. Doeg didn't answer,

and Caden felt his insides tightening. *Right?* Still, there was silence. *Right!* Caden opened his eyes, and all color drained from his face.

A Shade stood behind the doctor, its white fur pale in the shadowed room. It's side was burned, bald flesh and half its face was bitten away. Doeg and Caden stared at one another, and the Shade's smile twitched with glee, its scar twisting its lips unnaturally.

"This is the enemy's camp," it whispered. "There is no rest."

Caden closed his eyes again, suddenly wishing he took that oxy. His chest tightened with dread as his cold hands began to shake. He wanted to curl into a ball under the cot and wait for Elijah to save him or Han to remember he was supposed to guard Caden. The internal screaming shrilled. Caden's stomach turned, threatening to spill again. From the back of his panicking mind, and above the screaming of his soul, Caden remembered two words.

Raw Peace, he thought, imagining The Door and its security and love and acceptance. *I will be there again. Raw Peace.* It was the only two words he permitted himself to think as the doctor kept digging in his needle, the room shook with each close explosion, and the Demons kept circling.

———

CADEN KEPT his elbow tightly tucked at his side against his throbbing ribs. They were cracked, thanks to his future wife, and each breath sent a dull, throbbing pain all over his side and chest. The lower half of his face felt on fire as his chin's deep cut tried to heal. Dr. Ricci had said the cut had exposed a bit of bone. Caden believed him. His face was all pretty again with black and blue splotches and a split brow. Half of him regretted not punching

Dasha in the face, but the other half figured he'd hear about it the rest of his life. He sure wasn't going to let her forget scarring his face.

Caden tried to ignore his burning chin as he stared at the closed elevator doors and his heart hammered in him. A man stood to his left and a woman to his right. No one was speaking. Caden tried not to grimace too hard, his face was a bruised mess. It had gotten worse over the five days he had rested at Luca's house. No, that wasn't the right way to put it. The Antichrist's mansion. Caden swallowed the hard lump in his throat, trying once again to not panic. It was nearly impossible. He was screwed, and he knew it.

At least Alex wasn't a Christian, Caden had thought. But that also was a threat to him. His pack of weapons had half survived the aerial raid. He had ripped it on something during the panic, and the gun was missing. The Bible, though, had been too big to fall out. *Figures,* Caden thought with dark humor. *God, can't I learn how to have faith an easier way?* He had stashed the worn but intact book deep in the air vent in his room.

His room was spacious and reminded Caden of suites he's seen in movies. The main room was the bedroom, connected to a nice bathroom with a tub and everything. Before a huge window overlooking the stretching city was a small table and two chairs. Beside the closet was a mini fridge and a counter with a coffee maker and mugs. The blankets were fresh, the towels fluffy, and clear water flowed from the faucets. Despite the luxury, Caden had to teach himself to rest. It was nearly impossible, knowing he was living under the enemy's roof.

He even had been given an attendant, a Mr. Roberto Costa. He was a pudgy, balding Italian and was incapable of saying two words without waving his hands around. It was like he was trying to conduct music in his head or swat invisible flies. It drove Caden crazy, and he kept losing track of what Roberto was actually saying and just found himself staring at his waving, pointing, flicking, fisting, shaking hands.

Roberto was helpful though. He had fetched Caden blond hair dye and, surprisingly, believed Caden's claim to be sick of brown hair and needed to see himself in the mirror again. Caden had dyed his hair that night and knew he had to figure out how to keep it dyed blond. He couldn't wait to get out of there!

Roberto would also check on Caden's condition every day and tell him to rest and that the king had everything taken care of. That didn't help Caden to rest one bit. Roberto didn't let people bother Caden, though he heard them pass his door. He heard the feet of maidservants and manservants, which was weird; he thought they stopped having servants a long time ago.

One morning, he was woken up by heavy footfalls. They were too heavy to be real. Caden nearly leapt from his bed to hide behind a huge window's curtain as a Giant lumbered past his room. The only thing that had kept him in bed was the agonizing pain whenever he moved. He was glad no one had been there. Alex was used to Giants, he wouldn't have freaked and hid. Caden had done the mature thing and slid deeper under the covers, trying not to think of Bobby Rut as he scratched his shoulder. After that, Caden had tried to expect Giants. It made it a little better.

Caden kept thinking Luca would stop in and visit, but he never did, much to his relief. He did, however, have constant visitors of the unseen variety. Demons crawled all over the place. They strolled through his room as they went about their day, some fading through the ceiling while others popped up from the floor and darted back down without a word. Most didn't seem to notice him. He knew they did. They had to. Someone like him, a follower of Yahweh, with a massive, four headed angel as a bodyguard, had to turn some heads. He wondered if Han was the reason they left him alone.

Doeg showed up a few times, but it seemed a bit too interested in talking with other Shades and a few Withers to acknowledge Caden. It wasn't right. One building shouldn't have *that* many Demons making themselves at home. *I wonder what the White House was like,* Caden thought.

It had taken Caden two days of resting and constantly telling himself not to panic to regain enough strength to think. It took one day to decide to get out of there. Yesterday, he had come up with a plan. Though it was never stated, he wasn't too sure Luca would let him waltz out of his home.

By day five, Caden had had enough. It was time to leave. Though he was nowhere near recovered from the cracked ribs, he was sure Ophir could take over and help him the rest of the way. If only he could find her.

I just got to get out of here, Caden thought as he glanced up at the elevator digitally counting down as the floors passed beneath them.

The woman beside him, a portly elder wrapped in a hijab, sniffed and glanced down at her purse. "Shouldn't leave," she muttered. "This is fun here." Caden closed his eyes and gritted his teeth until it hurt. He took a shallow breath, and his ribs protested with a stabbing pain.

"No, please try to leave," the man, a slender, tall fellow with no hair, save for his startlingly thick brows. "Your escape plan will work. I promise."

Shut up, Caden wanted to scream, but Ellie said to not acknowledge Demons. The two Withers glanced at one another, and the woman sighed as the man shook it's head.

"Did you hear of the fanatics?" the woman Wither asked suddenly.

"Hum? Oh, the fire-breathers?" A shiver shot through Caden's spine, forcing his hair to stand on end.

"Yes! I heard they consume coals, so a fire is always in their bellies. Very interesting!"

The man Wither nodded. "I heard they cook their victims alive before eating them."

"Like a modern Leviathan." Caden forced himself to breathe as his chest tightened. He winced, the throbbing pain of his ribs catching his breath. "Hum," the woman Wither sighed. "I wonder how long the king will let them live."

The elevator opened with a ding. Caden turned sideways, wincing, and slipped through as soon as he could. His heart slammed against him as his side throbbed with each breath. His entire body hunched, as though every limb and body part were working together to protect his cracked ribs. His breath quickened, though he tried to stop it, as his mind spun on the Demons' words. *Elijah and Yohanan are alive, for now,* he thought, his eyes darting around. *Keep surviving! I'm coming!*

He was walking through a laundry room. Women in aprons and pale uniforms carried out their daily work around him, loading laundry, folding clothes, hauling hampers, and promptly ignoring Caden. He squeezed past a woman pulling a cart of cloth bags, two Vipers tucked amid the load, and bolted to the far door. Someone shouted after him. He wasn't sure if it was the Withers or a real person. It didn't matter.

Caden burst from the door into a long, cement garage and loading bay. He wound past the workers, hauling in food and supplies for the army that lived under the massive roof. He walked toward a truck parked against the far wall as he kept his head down. He felt the truck's keys in his pocket and idly wondered if the cook's produce team would get into trouble for losing it. It wasn't his fault they had let him wander the kitchen, of course, when the head cook had an off day. It wasn't his fault some of the workers didn't pay attention when they went out for a smoke break. It had been like stealing candy from a baby.

Caden tried not to look at anyone as he walked by. He wondered if anyone knew who he was. He received a few glances, but that was expected. It wasn't every day they saw a beaten, hunched-over American kid stumbling around. He kept going. He had to get out of this Demon-infested place. He had to find Ellie and make sure she was alright. He had to get to Elijah and Asher. They needed him somehow. *He* needed them. Caden just wanted to be home-

Someone stepped into his way. Someone pudgy with a shiny, sweaty bald head. "What are you doing down here?" Hands waved back and forth, ending with a finger pointing all around. Caden stopped dead in his tracks and stared at Roberto.

He thought of running but knew he could do nothing in his condition. "You said fresh air is good." *Why did I say that? That was a dumb thing to say!*

Roberto's round face scrunched in on his nose. "Is this a fresh place? Eh? Come on, Mr. Whitney! Look at this! Eh!" More hand waving, as though Caden didn't know where 'this place' meant. "Come on, come on." Roberto muttered, gently taking Caden by the arm. Caden was suddenly reminded of Buck's sausage-sized fingers.

"I can walk by myself." Caden snapped, pulling to rip his arm free. It didn't budge.

"Yeah, yeah, come on." Roberto grumbled, keeping Caden at his side.

Now I'm dead, Caden thought as they walked back to the elevator and stood between the two Withers again.

Caden stopped struggling and held his arm close to his ribs. It was like they were being hit over and over again as waves of pain washed over him. Roberto tapped the button to floor seven and sniffed as he leaned back. Caden, needing to focus on something other than how he felt, watched Roberto out of the corner of his eye. Both Withers had moved behind them and were whispering. As Caden watched, he realized Roberto didn't know they were there.

"He didn't make it far." the man-Wither whispered. The woman giggled.

Caden stared hard at the elevator door as his back tingled, knowing Demons were a step away from touching him. *Leave me alone,* he thought to no one in particular. Either Roberto or the Withers, he didn't care. All of them had to go!

Roberto sniffed again, his thick fingers still fastened around Caden's arm. "You've been kidnapped once," he said suddenly. "Wanna do it again?"

"Are you threatening me?" Caden snapped.

"No."

"Then let go of my arm! Your hand is sweaty." Roberto actually chuckled and uncurled his fingers. Caden stepped back and found himself leaning against the wall. He stared at the floor, gasping, wincing, gasping again, and wincing again.

Roberto grunted and drew closer. "Should not come out, eh. Not good, even for *fresh air.*"

Caden didn't have the strength to answer as Roberto eased him upright and supported him. *God, do something,* Caden thought as the elevator lifted, taking him further away from freedom. *I can't be here! I'm obviously too unstable and freaking out all the time. Save me. Please!* Caden closed his eyes tight, hoping God could hear his cry.

THIRTEEN
A CROWDED CHURCH

CADEN STARED down at his shoe and wondered how he was going to tie it. It was so very far away, and bending over, arching his back to grab the laces, and moving his arms to secure the ends sounded like torture. Though his cracked ribs were healing after laying around for nearly two weeks, he was still afraid to move too much. Dr. Ricci gave him six weeks of recovery, five if he stopped trying to walk around.

Roberto had done his best to help Caden obey, but there were limits to Caden's cooperation. The inside was nice and all, being luxurious and as modern as a place could get these days, but there were fewer Demons outside. The manicured lawn, large trees, and nice benches seemed to detract from the haunted type enough to take the edge off. That or the outdoors was much larger than inside, making it seem like less Demons slithered about.

Whatever the reason, Caden found himself outside again. He thought of trying to escape, but Roberto was nearby-talking to the gardeners. Caden knew he was watching him and had concluded his 'attendant' was actually a babysitter. A big babysitter who, Caden swore, had a gun tucked under his arm.

He had ignored the koi fish lazily swimming circles in the small pond before him, until one leapt from the waters with a splash. Caden blinked as the fish bounced on the pebbles surrounding their manicured home. It's sleek, shiny head shook, black eyes blinking, and it moved away from the water. No, it crawled. Tiny legs shoved it along the ground, like a prehistoric creature back from the past.

I would've thought they'd get all the Freaks out of here, Caden thought as he watched the unnatural animal crawl onto a rock and sit, sunning itself. The koi fish stayed perfectly still, save for the white tongue that lashed from its mouth. Caden scoffed and shook his head. He shifted his weight and glanced down again, still trying to figure out the shoelace dilemma.

"I'll get it." a voice said, and someone stooped before Caden could respond.

"Oh, um… thanks."

"Cracked ribs suck," the man said as he stood up and smiled. "I've had a few myself."

Caden realized who he was speaking to, and his stomach clenched itself. *Don't panic!*

"You're majesty!" He blurted, bowing sharply and nearly crying out as his ribs felt like they cracked all over again.

"Oh, no! Alex! Please, sit down. Rest." Luca motioned to a bench beside them, and he helped Caden over.

Go away! Go away! He thought.

"Thanks." Caden said.

You're evil!

"That's very kind of you." he added quickly, as though hiding his thoughts.

I can't be here anymore. God, get me out of here! Caden bit his tongue and hoped Luca assumed his discomfort was from the ribs, not from Luca himself. *Just calm down, calm down,* Caden told himself as he breathed slow and steady. *You've still got him tricked. He still thinks you're Alex. But you better leave before he finds you out!* Caden's eyes flickered to the several Sentinels guarding the perimeter. Each one carried a gun. Each one looked like one of Nathaniel's murderous followers. Caden wouldn't be surprised if the bottom of their boots were caked in more innocent blood-

"I hear you're recovering well," Luca said, motioning to Caden's face and side. "I guess not as well as I hoped. Your face is much better though."

Caden looked away and tried to think of something to say. He didn't want to say anything. Any wrong move could get him killed. *Shut up!* Caden told his thoughts. *Your fear of doing the wrong thing will get you killed!*

"Don't feel much better." he grumbled, which was true.

"Not sleeping?" Caden shook his head. How could he sleep with clawed Demon feet scraping across the walls and ceilings on their way to who-knows-where. "I'll tell Dr. Ricci. I'm sure he'll have something for you. I need some help at night myself."

"Don't sleep either?"

"Can't stop my thoughts," Luca said as he crossed his arms and leaned back. "I swear, a part of me never sleeps. It's always working on the latest dilemma."

"Like what?" Caden blinked, shocked he'd ask that. What business was that of his? It was probably something top secret and important and nothing that-

"Meetings with the Prime Minister."

Caden frowned. "Why? Is England going to help with the Russians?"

Luca chuckled softly. "Not just England has a Prime Minister."

"Oh. So... why are you meeting with the Israeli Prime Minister?"

"We must make peace," Luca said, his casual demeanor slipping as he looked off into the distance. His face hardened, and his eyes narrowed. "We must make peace at all costs." Caden glanced at him and, for the first time, saw a steadfast resolve he'd only seen in Elijah. "We will have it," Luca whispered. "Soon."

Distant, echoing explosions broke their conversation. Caden turned, but Luca didn't bother. "Are there Russians still here?"

Luca nodded. "That's one of the dilemmas that won't let me sleep. All of Israel's been attacked. Heavily. The air strike a few weeks back was the first, but once we got the Iron Dome up and running again, we're safe."

"What happened to it?"

"Terrorists." Luca shook his head. "They snuck in and sabotaged the system."

"Wouldn't that be hard to do?"

"They're Russians. They like doing the hard things." Another distant yet louder explosion caused a few birds to fly from the trees, chattering in alarm to one another.

"Are we," Caden stammered, "we're safe, right?"

Luca nodded. "Just stay under the Sovereign Lion's Watch." Caden didn't answer, and he felt Luca staring at him. "I heard you tried to leave."

A muscle in Caden's jaw flexed as his eyes narrowed. "Yep." Luca quietly nodded as Caden's heart picked up the pace. His fingertips were suddenly cold.

"This is the safest place to be," Luca said. "Out there are Russian soldiers trying to infiltrate our city, terrorist cells are popping up over the nation, and now there's talk of fire-breathing fanatics."

Caden, again, didn't answer as he tried not to react at the mention of his Abba and brother-in-law. *So, you've heard of them too. Does everyone know about them?* With a sigh, Caden leaned back and crossed his arms. *You're Alex, remember? What would Alex say?*

"I don't like being caged up," he snapped suddenly. "Dad did that. I'm not a kid anymore. I can leave when I want!"

Luca, again, calmly nodded. "Yes, you're not a kid, but you aren't home anymore either."

Caden grumbled something and turned away. Inside, he was trying not to panic. *Am I really arguing with the king?*

"I want you to be safe."

Caden cursed. "I'm not a pet to keep caged. Do you want me to start barking too? I want to go home!"

"I understand," Luca said, laying a hand on Caden's shoulder. "You will return home the moment we receive word. This attack has hindered communications and travel, especially to the other side of the world."

Well, at least that's good news. Caden cursed again with a grimace, trying to hide his relief.

"What would make you feel more at home?"

Caden looked down at his hands and, as quickly as he could, tried to think of an 'Alex' answer while still furthering his escape cause. "A smartphone for starters," he said. Actually, he demanded. "And, and the freedom to go out sometimes. I'll come back!"

Luca nodded quietly as he thought. "Alright," he said at last. "I'll see what I can do."

Really? Caden forced himself not to look shocked or grateful as he didn't answer.

"Have you considered my offer?"

"Hum?"

"To teach you to fight." Caden's eyes widened as he slowly leaned away from Luca. The Italian grinned. "Don't look so nervous! This will be perfect, actually! I'm receiving new recruits in a few weeks, about the time you should be healed up."

Caden's eyes narrowed. "Recruits for what?"

"It's a new program we started a few months ago. The effect has been very positive." Caden could see Luca's excitement as his gestures became more expressive and his smile grew and grew. "It's the Civil Refiners Division. Remember the team that was with me when we saved you? They were Refiners. An elite branch from the Royal Sentinel Brigade."

"I'm not elite," Caden said. "I don't even know the basics."

"That's not what I saw when you were fighting for your life."

Caden's eyes narrowed. "I thought you couldn't see what happened."

"Not much. I did see you. Don't deny you've had some training."

Caden rubbed the back of his neck and turned away. *Well, if you count Elijah and Yohanan's sparring, I guess I've been shown a few things.* Caden's stomach clenched as he thought of his Abba and brother-in-law. You know, the enemy of who he was seated next to? *I can't be here.*

"A little," Caden finally said. "But obviously not enough. I was losing."

"Yes, you definitely need more training." Luca leaned closer. "I'll show you."

Caden found himself shaking his head. "I'm tired these days."

"When you heal."

Caden shrugged. *I won't be here when I heal up.* "I dunno." he muttered.

"Alex," Luca said, dropping his voice. "I'm not looking for talented, exceptional people. If that were the case, I myself wouldn't be a Refiner." Caden arched a brow at him. "Some of my best Refiners are, as society would have said, ill-equipped. Some are nearly blind, and others are amputees. In fact, the officer spearheading the hunt to find the terrorists who disarmed the Iron Dome is disabled. He's quite the determined, effective man. Through all their disqualifying traits, their determination to serve is all I need." Caden said nothing as he kept watching the koi fish sunning itself. Luca shifted and sighed, turning away. "I'll tell you what. I'll inform you when the training starts, and if I don't see you there, then I won't bring this up again. If you do go, no one will be able to kidnap or almost kill you again. Deal?"

"Sure." he muttered, his guts coiled on themselves. He was going to figure out how to get out of here long before then.

"Good!" Luca said with a clap of his hands. "I'll let you know when the program begins again." Caden nodded, not looking at Luca. "And, are you afraid of lions?"

Caden glanced at him with a furrowed brow. "Like, if one's sitting in front of me?"

Luca had a twinkle in his eyes, and he swatted a hand. "Never mind."

"No," Caden said, leaning closer. "What?"

A huge smile filled Luca's face, and Caden could tell he was debating whether to tell him or not. "We found different Freaks of Nature."

"Lions? There're no lions in Israel."

"There are now." Caden's brow furrowed. "Ah, you'll see." Luca said at last.

"Tell me!"

"No, you'll see!" From behind, a Sentinel stepped forward and whispered in Luca's ear. His smile fell as he cleared his throat and stood. "Well," he said, facing Caden. "I have a meeting to get to and more fires to put out." Caden nodded and tried to rise. "Please, just rest," Luca said, holding up a hand. "I want you good and ready to join the Refiners."

Caden scowled. "I'm not *joining* anything."

"Oh, come on, Alex! You will regret not coming!" Caden stared up and him and crossed his arms as Luca chuckled. "Rest, and I will keep in touch on your progress."

Caden nodded as he began to walk away. *Yes, please leave,* Caden thought as feeling gradually returned to his fingertips. *He's a bad guy, a bad, bad guy. Why does he think we're friends? Better friends than enemies.* Caden cursed as he closed his eyes, realizing he had to play the game just a little longer to survive.

"Hey! Luca!" Luca and his Sentinel bodyguard turned. "Um, thanks! Thank you for saving me!" Caden made himself smile as Luca waved. He breathed another sigh of relief as Luca quickly went to his meeting. He sat back and rubbed his eyes with a finger and thumb.

What am I doing here, God? He thought. *I don't want to be in the enemy camp. Again!* He thought of Nathaniel and the sickening panic he felt when fleeing from the camp, Simon's shocked look seared into his retinas. *That won't be me,* Caden swore.

He glanced after Luca as he went inside. Luca was up to something. Many somethings. Meeting with the Prime Minister? Training an elite Sentinel branch? Something with lion Freaks? It didn't make sense, but Caden didn't want to stick around to find out.

———

CADEN FELT LIKE A PRISONER. He was trapped in his room with Roberto as a smiling, joking warden. All the Giants, Sentinels, and Demons kept swarming, surrounding him, waiting to take him out. Caden even felt like a prisoner in his own body. After several weeks, he still couldn't move the way he wanted. His face was much better, but his chin had turned from a massive gash surrounded by dried blood and red flesh to a massive, stitched mess of scabs and stretched skin. He kept reminding himself of Frankenstein.

Once hearing he was better, Luca sent Sentinels to question Caden about his kidnapping. It was the most elaborate lie Caden had come up with so far. He tried to stick to the truth as best he could, stating he was kidnapped by a ruthless, crippled guy and his huge henchmen. He didn't feel comfortable using Grant and Buck's names though. The fact that they were on this side of the world made him uneasy. *But maybe I can send Sentinels to track them down and be rid of them.* He knew Grant couldn't be dealt with so easily.

Caden stuck to his story that his unnamed kidnappers, with the help of James West, grabbed him. His kidnappers wanted to make him a slave and break his bones if he didn't obey. They had come to the Middle East because, Caden suspected, they knew it would be harder for Thomas Whitney to find them. Though that reason was a bit weak, Caden just claimed his kidnappers didn't explain their reasons to him, so how should he know? He said friends had tried to save him once in America. That was his extent of mentioning Trace's crazed driving through Grant's camp. Caden claimed all those friends had come with him but died in the aerial attack. Once the Sentinels left, Caden wrote his entire report out again and memorized it. It was getting harder to separate truth from all the lies.

He tried to find ways to escape House Battistelli, but he wouldn't blow his Alex Whitney cover. It was a useful cover, after all, the name carrying great weight, and he couldn't give that up just because he was impatient. Actually, he stayed not because he was impatient. He just wasn't coming up with clever escape plans.

Luca had followed through and given him a smartphone. The platforms Caden had been used to before the World's Crash were gone. Caden was glad; he had been annoyed with the social media sites. He wasn't too happy when he learned of BiggieFishie, a site anyone could post pictures and videos of useless stuff to bog down everyone's feed. He wondered why they named it BiggieFishie; it sounded just as random a name as the other platforms he remembered from long ago. He made a profile anyways and tried to learn about the outside world. It wasn't until he found a weird room did he have the inspiration he needed to escape.

When feeling better and wandering the specific wings permitted him, Caden found a room where every chair was pointed at a framed, shiny picture. Well, it wasn't a picture, it was solid black, and it was pretty big. Two large boxes were on its right and left, one side covered with a mesh that revealed two dishes resting within. Caden shook his head when he finally figured it out; it was a TV room, and the boxes were speakers.

Caden marched down to the screen and found the remote. He finally remembered how to work the thing and turned it on. He actually jumped when the TV flickered to life. He wondered if this was how the cavemen felt when making fire for the first time.

At first, he sat and stared at the vivid color and pictures in motion and the overwhelming sound. It was beautiful. Then he snapped out of it, remembered he had seen TVs before in his life, and started flipping through the channels. There weren't many, but he finally came across one. It was a local news channel hosted by *The King's Modern Times.* Caden leaned forward as the anchorman stood on the Temple Mount.

Caden could see the Dome of the Rock in the background next to a new, ancient-styled building. It was tall, made of cut stone, and along the flat roof's perimeter were golden points. He saw the top of massive, double doors, also gold, and two detailed golden pillars on either side of that.

The new temple, Caden thought. *They finished it already?*

His attention flickered back to the speaker. He looked familiar. After a moment, Caden recognized Lavi, the journalist who recorded Elijah getting blasted with the *Akal Esh.* He was speaking in Hebrew, a little too quickly, but Caden understood if he squinted enough. Behind Lavi was a buzzing crowd. "More and more are coming and listening," Lavi said in Hebrew. "There is much unrest when listening to his words, but…" Caden couldn't catch some of it, "totally destroyed! All of it! Is it more ravings of a madman, or do we have a modern prophet on our hands? Not just one, but two now!"

Caden blinked and looked to the center of the crowd. Past Lavi's shoulder, and through the throng, was a heavily built man with a thick dark beard and a firm, impassive stare.

"Abba." Caden whispered as he watched Elijah turn and speak to those around him.

You're alive! Caden eased himself off his seat and limped to the screen, desperate for any sign of Ellie and Yohanan. *Is Asher there too?* He looked from pixilated face to pixilated face until the news changed to traffic. Caden cursed and stepped back. He rubbed the back of his neck and stared at his feet. *He said there were two of them now. Is he talking about Yohanan?* Caden's heart quickened, daring to believe, for just one moment, Yohanan was alive. He knew his wild brother-in-law would die before letting anything happen to Ellie. *I've got to get to the Temple Mount. I've got to see my Abba!*

Caden turned on one heel and started marching out the door. He came to a stop and frowned. He was living with the Antichrist. It wouldn't be wise for Luca to know he was close friends with the two Witnesses. *Aren't they enemies?* Caden slowly lifted his chin and realized he would have to be careful. *Why would Luca be watching me? He was busy all yesterday in his office, telling everyone what to do. I bet he doesn't even care about what I do.*

Caden sighed heavily, knowing just that morning, Luca asked how his ribs were feeling over breakfast. He remembered how many were cracked and on which side. Also, the one time Caden wanted to walk outside the mansion's grounds, Luca insisted he take an escort. A burly, quiet guy trailed slowly behind, which creeped Caden out and made the walk miserable. Caden cursed under his breath and wished he had Asher there to help brainstorm ideas.

What about you? he thought, glancing around him. *Any bright ideas, God?* He listened, as he always did, but knew he wouldn't hear anything. He shuffled his feet and shoved his hands in his pockets, trying not to feel abandoned. *I'll hear You someday,* he thought. *Just You wait!*

It took until the next day of playing with ideas for Caden to finally come up with something. He reviewed the plan several times, thought it was sound enough, and decided to do it the next day. His stomach instantly knotted, and he didn't sleep all night. Red-eyed and queasy with nervousness, Caden told Luca he was going out while they had breakfast.

"Good idea," Luca said with a nod. He was sipping a cappuccino and reading some document Caden could've sworn was in some oriental language. "You're looking better and better every day. Where do you plan to visit?"

"Oh," Caden said as he shrugged, shoved food in his mouth, and kept talking. He was sure Alex would do something like that. "Around. There's a market in an old part of the city, I hear. The air raid didn't blast that part up much. Lots of street food."

"The Old City of Jerusalem? Good place. Lots of very ancient sightseeing there too."

Caden stared at Luca as he sipped the coffee and chose his words carefully. "You mean all that Jesus stuff there?"

Luca smiled. "Yes, the Prophet Jesus is said to have walked that way when carrying the cross. They call it the Way of Suffering. Just follow the metal numeric signs. Their convex. Can't miss them."

"Hum, no thanks. Not into religion and all that." He sniffed and shifted in his seat. "What about you?"

"I believe there is a god," Luca said as he turned the document's page. "I believe he is nearer to us now than he has been before."

"Hum, cool."

"And Prophet Jesus was a good Man who knew the truth, unlike most people of His time. His Bible has taught me quite a bit in my own life."

Really? Caden tried to hide his surprise. "Haven't read it. Sounds boring."

"Ah, it can be dry at times, but has some hidden gems."

"So, you don't think Jesus came back from the dead and all that?" Luca sighed and set down the document. "Sorry," Caden said, sitting back. "I'll shut up-"

"No, no, Mandarin is taxing to read. Hum... Jesus' death. Well, the deepest grief can sometimes only be endured by twisting reality. It is a sad state to be, but," he sighed again, "I do fear most of Jesus' followers could not bear their so-called King dying like a common criminal. I don't blame them."

Caden nodded, finding it uncomfortable to listen to the Antichrist talk about Jesus with just a touch of admiration. "Well," he said, standing. "I'm off."

"Let Simon go with you again."

Great! It's cool, it's cool. At least I expected this.

"I can't let anyone try to grab you again. Wouldn't forgive myself."

Caden thought of an Alex protest but thought better than to argue with the Antichrist. "Sure."

"And tell the cook if you'll be home or not tonight."

So you'll know how long I'll be gone, Caden thought and forced himself to smile.

"Sure thing. See yah."

"Have a good day, Alex. Do watch yourself."

"Got it covered." Caden said as he forced himself to stroll from the room instead of sprinting out the door to freedom.

Simon was already waiting for him out front, yet another reminder of Luca's efficient follow-through. They took one of Luca's cars, and Simon drove Caden to the Old City of Jerusalem. Caden stared out the window the entire drive, all the while searching for his Lil El. *Just hang in there,* he told himself. *She's safe. She has to be!*

His unease didn't quit as they passed toppled buildings, blown apart roads, overflowing hospitals, and still smoking houses. Though the city was attacked a little over a week ago, many people continued with business as usual. People were buying and selling, cyclists and taxis zipped around, and they drove past people talking on street corners.

Once they reached the old city, Caden was surprised to find it mostly intact. He slowly made his way through the narrow streets. He asked Simon the time and wished he had come out a little closer to noon. The streets were crowded, but not enough to slip through and escape Simon's watchful eye. *Then go to where there are crowds.* Caden tried to casually, yet quickly, make his way to the Church of the Holy Sepulcher. He passed through the

Jewish Quarter, getting some street food to not look suspicious, and knowingly walked right by the Wailing Wall.

He glanced to the massive courtyard and saw a crowd gathering a distance from the wall. *There he is*, he thought and turned away. *Just act cool. Don't lead him on!* He knew Simon was close behind. He could almost feel his eyes burning into his back. *Try and keep track of me at the church!*

The Church of the Holy Sepulcher was said to be where Yeshua's body had been buried. It was in the Christian Quarter of the old city. It was a beautifully decorated, very ancient church that Ophir had told him about. She had also told him to only go early in the morning to avoid the crowds. Upon arrival, Caden tried to hold back a smile as the crowd of people clogged the church's entrance. Caden took a deep breath, told himself it would be okay to be a human sardine for a time, and made his way into the church.

It was a breathtaking building. Caden wasn't one for architecture, but the ceiling went up and up, golden, decorative chandeliers dangled overhead, and everything had a holy vibe about it. Except the air. It was thick with body heat and smelled like sweat and candle smoke. Caden kept battling claustrophobia as strangers pressed on his shoulders, his back, and he, in turn, pressed onto others. He looked around and saw Simon's big bulk slowing down his progress.

As the bodyguard turned to snap at a passerby who had elbowed him, Caden ducked low and started shoving. It was like trying to swim through hardening concrete. Caden ignored the tongue lashings he received as he plunged onward, desperate to find a way out.

By the time Caden burst from the church, he was dripping in sweat and gasping for air. With a laugh, which was cut short by his cracked ribs, Caden quickly set off to the

Wailing Wall. *I should've brought a disguise!* He thought, remembering the news crew. What if they were there again? *Luca might see me. He'll know where I'm sneaking off to. Maybe I could just borrow something. Just for a little bit.* He'd heard thou shalt not steal, but also heard God was merciful and might let things slide.

A little later, after passing a vendor who wasn't paying attention and a guy snoozing at his table, Caden donned his new hat and sunglasses and stepped onto the Temple Mount. The crowd was still there, their hummed words filling the air. Caden made a beeline to them, but slowed when he saw Lavi again with a professional news camera.

Just keep going. I got this. Raw Peace. He whispered a curse and kept looking for Elijah. As he scanned the crowd, he noticed a tall guy, a little older than him, with dark curly hair. Caden's heart quickened as he smiled. *Asher!* He picked up the pace and shoved his hat down to shield his face better. He dug his hands in his pockets and turned a shoulder to Lavi and his camera crew just in case. *Can't wait to see the look on his-*

Someone firmly grabbed his arm above the elbow. Someone big. He started to struggle but felt something firm press against his back. He had felt it before, and he instantly froze. It was the muzzle of a gun. "Quiet now," the stranger hissed Hebrew in his ear. "Don't make a scene."

"Wait-"

Caden's words cut off as the stranger dragged him away from Asher, who, infuriatingly, hadn't noticed Caden in the slightest.

FOURTEEN
UNDER FIRE

CADEN WAS sick of being dragged around. Buck had yanked him all over like a rag doll, twice, and other goons he had the displeasure of meeting thought they could get away with it too. The truth was, they could. He wasn't really a tough guy, being of average height and build, and he hadn't known how to fight. That was changing and, if Luca's offer was legit, Caden was turning into not-so-helpless anymore. Most of all, he was getting angry. Anger had a funny way of making punches land and weakish people suddenly stronger.

Caden was not going to let his family slip away from him again. He hadn't wanted to leave them in the first place, and now, when he could literally see them, he wasn't going to let anything get in his way. Even a much bigger, armed stranger. Half his brain told him this was stupid, and he shouldn't go head-to-head with someone who felt as strong as Buck.

Caden cursed something very unchristianly and leaned back, turning into the stranger. He stepped between his legs and yanked his arm free while catching the stranger's foot with his own. Caden reached for the gun, preparing to twist it free just like Yohanan showed him. He didn't grab it in time. His head flew to one side as everything went black for a second.

Oh great.

He could see stars and taste blood. He heard his sunglasses fall to the ground and felt the stranger grab his shirt collar as he reeled. Without thinking, Caden drew his knee up into the man's groin. That stopped the stranger, but just long enough to get angry himself. Caden tried to pull away but realized he couldn't. Panic constricted his throat as his heartbeat struck his insides. The stranger yanked him close, and the gun now bore into his stomach.

Caden froze, knowing he could do nothing as he stared inches away from his attacker's face. He blinked, and his constricted throat loosened. His attacker's head tilted to one side, and he slowly smiled.

Caden smiled too and laughed. "Hey, Noam."

Noam released Caden and quickly put away his gun, glancing over his shoulder. Caden snatched up his sunglasses and put them back on. "Nice hair." Noam said in English.

"Thanks," Caden said in Hebrew. "I did it myself."

"I can tell." Noam answered in Hebrew. "You really need to learn how to fight. You're going to get yourself killed."

Caden glared at him. Okay, maybe he wasn't so capable yet. He rubbed his now throbbing jaw and spat the taste of blood from his mouth. His still-healing chin was bleeding a little now too. Great. Caden wiped it away and shot Noam a quick look. Noam grinned as his ridged stance eased back into his standard relaxed, nearly uninterested posture.

"Is Ellie here?" Caden asked. "Yohanan?"

Noam nodded, and Caden's heart leapt as he quickly glanced around. "Not *here*, but with us. They're back at the campus." Caden cocked a brow. "They're safe," Noam whispered. "And unharmed."

Caden nodded slowly as he ran a hand over his face. He stood a moment, letting his tensed body ease after hearing his sister was well. *Thank You,* he thought, glancing at the sky. With a deep breath, Caden straightened and glanced at Asher.

"I'm going to see Asher now," Caden whispered. "Still going to kill me?"

Noam shook his head and motioned to the young man who still, amazingly, hadn't noticed the scuffle at all. Actually, most people hadn't noticed, it had happened so fast. Caden straightened his clothes and shook the final stars from his vision as he walked through the crowd. He smiled with excitement as he neared Asher and took off his sunglasses. He calmly stood shoulder to shoulder with Asher and waited.

Asher stepped back and glared at him, but stopped, his eyes widening. "*Achi!*" Caden smiled, so glad to hear Asher call him brother again. Asher pretty much attacked him, strong arms wrapped around him.

"Shhh!" Caden hissed, glancing around and hiding beneath the shades again. "Keep it down. I'm not here!"

"Yes, you are! Wait. You're speaking Hebrew. And why are you blond again?" Caden calmly pocketed his hands again and faced Elijah, as though listening with the others. Asher arched a brow as he crossed his arms. "Caden?"

"Shhh."

"What are you up to? And what's with the disguise? Are you running from someone? Again?"

"No! I just... I needed to lose a tail." Asher squarely

faced him, his eyes narrowing. "It's nothing. He won't track me down."

"You sure?" Caden opened his mouth to say no but stopped himself. Luca didn't seem the type to let loose ends stay loose. "If you're in trouble, tell me," Asher said, his eyes narrowing. "You're family; we face all this together." Caden turned away as he nodded, unsure of what to say as he felt the loyalty between them. Asher nudged him and glanced around. He muttered something in Hebrew, but Caden didn't catch it. Something about killing?

"What?" Caden asked in English.

"Your chin. That'll be a killer scar."

Caden nodded. "You have no idea." The two stood side by side and watched Elijah as he debated with some very red-faced people. Elijah himself wasn't red-faced. He spoke with his unchanging, impassive stare as he simply told the truth, making his listeners' faces even deeper crimson. "I see your Abba's making friends." he said, continuing in Hebrew again.

Asher nodded. "Wait until you see what we've been up to. You won't believe it."

"Yeah? Well, I know I'll beat you on this one."

"Bring it."

Caden lifted his chin. "How's everyone after the air raid?"

Asher's excitement fell, and he was quiet a bit too long. *Oh no,* Caden's stomach twisted as he realized Ophir wasn't there. *No, no, she can't be gone!* That same panic grabbed his throat again, and he took a deep breath, willing himself to wait for Asher to answer.

"Hili didn't make it," he said, at last, his voice low. "And Ido and Harel."

Caden ducked his head, trying to hide his relief. *Thank You, thank You,* he thought to Yahweh. He didn't realize how much Ophir meant to him until that moment. With a deep breath, he looked up and took in the fact that Elezaro's wife and two of his sons were dead. He nodded slowly, remembering Hili's genuine smile and how Ido had joined Elezaro in confronting Grant. He had helped save Caden.

"How's your uncle?" Asher slowly shook his head. Caden didn't know how to answer, and the two continued watching Elijah.

"Lost the house too." Asher muttered.

Caden frowned. "Ah, my room!"

"You mean the storage room."

"I liked it."

"Found a better home now. Bigger. Enough to house everyone. You too."

"Good! I've been counting on you guys."

Asher arched a brow at him. "You're okey?"

Caden nodded with a smile. "I am now. Things have been... tense."

"Join the club. Have you met Noam?" The larger Israeli strolled beside Caden.

"Yeah," Caden said, rubbing his still throbbing jaw. "We've met."

Asher frowned. "What happened?"

"He has a mean jab."

"Were you sneaking up on me?"

"No." Caden lied.

"There's been a few attacks." Caden stiffened. "We're alright, but... now we have." and he said a Hebrew word Caden hadn't heard before.

"Hum?"

"Precautions." Asher said in English and grimaced.

"Hey, I'm learning!"

"Learn faster!" Caden waved a hand at him. The three

fell silent as they waited for Elijah. Asher groaned and shifted his weight from one foot to the other. "We should just go."

Caden frowned. "I want to see him!"

"He's been at it for hours! Who knows when he'll be done! Come on. He should be done once I give you a tour."

"Of your house?"

"Campus. It's pretty big. Beats just standing here in the sun." Caden reluctantly agreed, and the three made their way through the Old City. Asher bumped Caden's shoulder with his own. "Glad you're not dead."

Caden smirked. "You too." The young men smiled.

———

ASHER HAD BEEN RIGHT, where they now lived was enough room to house a small army. Caden stared as the taxi pulled into the parking lot of an old, run-down university. He glanced around at the stone buildings, overrun grounds, and one blown-apart dorm. Instead of cutting the grass, trails had been weaved through the tall greenery, and the few surviving trees grew with wild, stretching branches. The place wasn't a mess, just not like the Old World.

Caden got the impression the university shut down after the World's Crash and, within the last few months, had been revived. Many people walked between the buildings. Some carried books, others lunches, and some maintenance supplies. They weren't college kids, but all ages. As they got out, Caden noticed several students gave Asher respectful nods. Asher motioned to one and asked where Yohanan and Ellie were.

"Close to the yard, sir."

Caden's eyes narrowed, curious about why a university

would have a yard and why everyone treated Asher like he was royalty. *He's the son of a Witness*, Caden remembered, slowly lifting his chin. He followed Asher through the campus and spotted Ellie long before they reached her. Caden picked up the pace and, in turn, she saw him and came running. That was a good sign, her wounded leg properly healed.

"Cade!" Ellie fell into his arms. "There you are!" He held her close, closing his eyes, grateful to find her in one piece yet again. "Yahweh be praised! We looked everywhere for you! Where did you go?"

"A building nearly crushed me. Then I," he paused, remembering the bloodied horseman casually riding through the chaos, "I got distracted."

"Oh, Cade." Caden pulled her back and looked her up and down. "I'm fine," she said. "Got a few scrapes, but-"

She gasped and lay a hand over her mouth. "What?"

"Woah!" Yohanan said as he joined them. "Nice face!"

"Ah," Caden sighed, lightly touching the stitches keeping his chin together. "It looks better now."

"Oh, that's awful," Ellie muttered behind her hand. "What happened?"

"Ah, ran into someone."

"Someone did that to you?"

"A Russian."

"What'd you do to him?" Yohanan asked, a dark smile stretching his mouth.

"Didn't do anything," Caden said. "My host scared her away-"

"*Her*?" Asher barked.

"Now, listen-" They weren't listening. Yohanan and Asher were too busy doubled over laughing. "It wasn't funny!" Caden snapped, crossing his arms. "She was trying to slit my throat!"

"Bro, you've got to learn how to fight," Yohanan said. "A girl! Ha!"

"Why does everyone keep saying that?" Caden muttered, anger tightening his chest.

"Ophir should look at that." Ellie said, stepping closer to him.

"She's here?" Caden asked.

"She will be tonight," Yohanan said between gasps as he finally stopped laughing. "She's out, helping those who can't get to the hospitals."

Ellie sighed and gradually smiled. "And now you're here. Come! We have much to show you! Yahweh is doing such wonderful things!" Caden followed her, and Yohanan nudged him as he walked by. He was about to say something but stopped, seeing Caden wince.

"My ribs." Caden explained.

Asher shook his head. "She really did you over, didn't she?"

"Shut up."

The three took him all over the campus, it was much bigger than Caden first imagined. There were halls and classrooms and an auditorium and dorms. All of it had been rundown and abandoned, but now, after months of hard work, it had come alive again. Sort of. The rooms and buildings that had no use were still untouched, making the place look half done.

"Who cares." Yohanan said with a shrug.

"Some people do." Ellie had muttered. They weaved their way through paths cut across the tall grassy grounds and passed several people. Lots of people actually, mostly men, but there were a few women between.

"It's like a school," Caden said as they passed a filled picnic table, each person's noses shoved deep into old books. "But," he paused as they turned a corner and stared at the field before them. "Different." This stretch of the grounds had been cut very short, and several people were standing and facing the instructor at the forefront. Each person slowly and deliberately stood from one defensive stance to another, their movements fluid and synchronized.

"That's what you need," Asher said. "Moves."

"Yeah, yeah, I get it." *What's the deal?*

"This is our university," Ellie explained. "We call it Under Fire."

Caden glanced at her with a raised brow. "Wow. What a catchy title. Now I really want to join."

"Shut up and listen," Asher said. "It'll make sense in a sec."

"If you have to explain it, it's not good-"

"Shhh!"

Ellie cleared her throat, ignoring the boy's banter. "Everyone here is a Christian and under Yahweh's *Akal Esh*. Also, they're under man's fire too because, well... it's the End Times. People don't like us."

Caden frowned. "You mean the Antichrist won't like us or *everyone* won't?"

"Everyone."

Caden raised a brow. "I just saw Elijah on TV. That Levi guy didn't trash him."

"That's 'cuz Levi works for us." Yohanan explained.

"We will be hated," Ellie said quietly as Asher nodded. "It's only a matter of time."

Caden fell quiet as the four watched the instructor direct his class. "So," Caden muttered. "What happens here exactly?"

"At Under Fire, we train all who come to ready themselves for the final stages of the End Times." Ellie said.

"Like a Christian prepping school." Yohanan said.

"Or," Asher added, "a bible college, but with a few extra subjects."

"Like self-defense," Yohanan said, motioning before them. "And keeping up on Israeli Defense Training."

"Which includes?" Caden prompted. "I'm not from here, guys."

"Survival techniques," Asher said. "How to navigate, basics in field medicine, keeping the body and mind in shape, and how to respond when under fire, to name a few. See that? That's why we named this place Under Fire."

Caden crossed his arms. "Very clever."

"And other things," Ellie said. "Like what we suspect will come in the next few years based on Biblical prophecies."

Caden raised his chin a bit and nodded slowly. If his Abba and brother-in-law could breathe fire, then they also could read an old book and know the future. *Makes sense,* he thought, trying to convince himself it was real. "The future, hum? What's next on the timeline?"

"Well," Yohanan said, running fingers through his hair. "We know one hundred and forty-four thousand students will come through here."

"That's so… specific." Caden muttered.

"Sometimes the Bible is specific."

"But not other times," Asher grumbled. "Multiheaded dragons and lions given human hearts and standing upright like men isn't specific at all."

Caden glanced at him and turned to Ellie. "What's he talking about?"

"Visions of the future from the Bible," she said. "And those do make sense, they represent the superpowers through time."

Caden saw Asher's face turn sour, and he moved on before he could speak again. "Anyways! How many people have you taught so far?"

"Oh," Yohanan said, staring off. "Like, twenty thousand? Maybe thirty? Ask Elezaro. He's keeping tabs on all that."

"No," Asher said, shaking his head. "He's not doing good."

"Because of..." Yohanan trailed off and nodded.

"Is that how many people are here now?" Caden asked.

"No," Ellie said. "They come and go. There's no real graduation or number of credits to reach. People just come and, when they feel Yahweh leading them on, they go."

"And do what?"

"Preach. Bring people to the Kingdom. That's Yahweh's Kingdom, not this New Kingdom garbage the king talks about."

Asher grimaced as he shook his head. "The enemy's so unoriginal; all he can do is copy Yahweh and tweak it here or there."

"One class everyone has to take," Ellie said, her voice lowering with seriousness. Caden glanced at her and saw her face was ridged as she took a slow breath. "How to die while still honoring Yahweh."

You're kidding, Caden thought, but quickly realized she wasn't. "How, um," his voice cracked, and he swallowed. "How many Christians die in the End Times? Like half or something? I know it's bad, but how bad?"

The three exchanged glances. Yohanan and Asher turned to Ellie and waited for her to answer. "Cade," she said slowly. "Out of us four, maybe one will survive." Caden's mouth dropped open as his hair stood on end. "Maybe."

"But not likely." Asher said.

Yohanan shook his head and gave a rough sniff. "Wouldn't count on it if I was you."

"You'll die too?" Caden asked, turning to Yohanan. "But you breathe fire!"

Yohanan stared back, his demeanor impassive, but Caden could see his eyes. They were hard with dark determination. "The Bible is very clear about what happens to us Witnesses." Caden's insides coiled, suddenly wanting to know what happens while, at the same time, not wanting to face the truth.

"We know we win in the end though!" Ellie said suddenly, clapping her hands and hiding her obvious terror behind a wide smile. "It's almost dinner time. I'm sure Elijah and Ophir would love to see you. Shall we?"

Though unease still twisted Caden's guts, he followed them to dinner. He had so many questions but feared the answers. He glanced at Ellie, watching as she talked about how the Russian attack had added to their numbers. He slowly took in a shaky breath. *I can't watch you die,* he thought. *I can't-*

"This is why your Christian phase is foolhardy," Doeg whispered in his mind. *"It is fatal. Don't you realize I'm trying to save you?"* Caden swallowed the hard lump in his throat and fought the urge to tell Doeg where it could go. *"Are you ready to die for a God who refuses to speak to you?"*

I am immortal until-

"But you will die. It is unavoidable."

Caden lifted his chin as a muscle in his jaw flexed. *Raw Peace,* he thought, cursing under his breath.

The dining room was actually the old cafeteria. The place was filled with people from all walks of life, their voices buzzing together like one big sound. Ellie directed Caden to the sectional trays and they got in line. After getting their food, Yohanan led the three through the cafeteria. As they passed the students, most stopped their conversations or meal and nodded to them, Yohanan and Asher specifically, but Caden caught a few nodding to him. Some even stood out of respect. Yohanan smiled at each, and Asher gave curt nods while Ellie talked to some or laid a hand on their shoulders as she passed.

Yohanan led them up a flight of stairs to an old conference room. It had been converted into a private dining room. As he entered, Caden found a handful of people already seated around the conference table, enjoying their meal. Three women quietly served them as two burly men stood guard. Noam, one of the men, gave Caden a quick nod.

"Hey, Abba," Asher said in Hebrew. "Look who I found."

Something deep inside Caden eased when his eyes fell on Elijah. It was like finally coming home. The large man faced him and stared, saying nothing. Caden set down his tray and removed his hat and glasses. The woman next to Elijah gasped, and Caden realized it was Ophir. "Caden!" She leapt up and rushed around the table. She hugged him, muttering something in English about how much she missed him.

"I missed you too," Caden said in the best Hebrew he could muster. "I've missed you all."

Ophir laughed. "Look at you! That sounded very good!"

Caden smiled and glanced at Elijah. He was actually smiling. Like a big, normal-person smile. Without a word, Elijah stood and walked to Caden's side. They embraced, and Caden felt himself loosen even more. In that moment, he was safe again. His bear-sized, fire-breathing Dad was with him again.

"Hi, Abba." he whispered.

"Hello, son." No one spoke as Elijah continued to hold him.

We're going to make it, Caden thought. *Even if we all do die in the end, Ellie's right. We win.* Elijah pulled him back to arm's length and stared at him. His dark eyes darted to Caden's chin, and his smile fell.

"It's doing better." Caden said.

"What happened?" Ophir asked. "And who stitched that? That's... that's a very good job."

Asher stepped closer, a crooked smile on his face. "A *girl* jumped him."

"She's probably a Russian assassin!" Caden snapped.

Elijah's brow raised, and Noam shook his head. "See?" Noam muttered. "Learn to fight."

"Alright, alright!" Caden said, raising his hands. "Everyone's been saying that!"

Elijah grunted as he walked back to his seat and motioned for everyone to sit too. "Maybe Yahweh's trying to tell you something."

"I guess." Caden scoffed as he sat. He looked around the table and found Auset was one of the servers. They began eating their meal, and Elijah motioned to Caden. "Do you have someone to teach you?"

Luca, Caden thought, and his chest tightened with unease. "No."

"Anyone offer?" Caden's jaw flexed as he sealed his mouth shut. Elijah pointed a fork at him with a knowing smile. "Then learn from them. Yahweh put them in your life to teach you."

Caden stared at Elijah. Such confident words for something he knew nothing about. "You don't understand," he muttered. "I'm not going back there. This person is a *real* bad guy."

"I know."

"No, I don't think you-"

"Caden." Caden glanced at Elijah, who had set down his fork and gave Caden his full attention. "Yahweh has spoken of you. He said he's placed you in the middle of our enemies, as though in the den of lions. This is what He wants."

"What? No! I just escaped!"

"It is what He wants." Caden looked away and shook his head, biting back the curse words bubbling to the surface. "I'm sorry. You must stay there. I long for you to be with us, but Yahweh has spoken."

You're wrong, Caden thought, staring down at his plate. *This is my family! This is where I belong! What good could Alex Whitney do?*

"Who are you staying with?"

Caden set down his spoon and sat back with crossed arms. He glanced at them, and they quieted. Caden shook his head as anger tightened his chest. "My host is Luca Battistelli."

A tense stillness overcame the room as everyone stared at Caden, unable to move. "The king?" Ophir blurted. "You're living with the Antichrist!" Caden slowly nodded. Yohanan rigidly sat, his hands balled into fists on either side of his plate, and Ellie sat back with a hand over her mouth. Asher shook his head as Ophir looked a shade paler. Elijah alone did nothing.

"You knew?" Caden asked. Elijah nodded.

"How did that happen?" Ellie demanded.

Caden told them how he and Luca met and how his Alex Whitney disguise was still keeping him alive. "He's the one who offered to teach me how to fight." he said.

"Perfect!" Yohanan said with a smile. "What better way to learn how to fight than from the enemy!" Caden had a few answers for him but refrained; Elijah was present.

"I know this is hard." Elijah said, sitting back and sipping his drink.

You have no idea.

"But to stay would be disobedience."

Caden did curse as he crossed his arms. With a shake of his head, he shifted in his seat and glared at Elijah. "Why should I go back? What else did Yahweh say?" Elijah set down his cup and regarded Caden with his standard calmness Caden craved, but he didn't answer. Caden's eyes narrowed as he leaned forward. *Out with it!* He wanted to yell, but he held his tongue.

"Yahweh wants you to help us," Elijah said at last, "by being our spy."

FIFTEEN
EMOJI ESPIONAGE

GOD'S *just trying to control me again, twist me into His own creation,* Caden thought. The shock of Elijah telling him to spy on the Antichrist wore off as soon as Caden's rage swept in. He sat back, unable to speak, his face gradually turning crimson. *Who can comprehend or anticipate God's motives? I could be slaughtered. Worse. Tortured! Is God interested in my wellbeing or His own agenda?* Caden's teeth clenched as his eyes narrowed. *God only serves Himself and never considers others. That narcissistic, lying son of a-*

Caden blinked and lifted his chin. *He is with me and is giving me peace. His Raw Peace. Only if I follow His ludicrous, suicidal will and-*

Doeg! I will help God kick you down into Hell! Get out of my thoughts! He could almost hear the Demon laughing, and he glanced around the room.

"Caden?" Ophir whispered, reaching across the table. "Are you alright?"

Caden sat back and ran fingers through his blond hair. "No," he said, at last, shaking his head. The room quieted as Caden gruffly sniffed and faced Elijah. "I can't be your spy. Luca will kill me. I can't-"

Caden snapped his mouth shut and turned away. His heart was pounding, and he shoved back his plate of food. He fought the urge to race out the door and run away. That or curse God and His crazy ideas. *I didn't survive so much to willingly put my hand into a bear trap!*

"This is God's own agenda," Doeg whispered. *"He never considered you-"*

Shut up!

"You are Yahweh's slave," Elijah said, breaking through Caden's racing thoughts. "Choose. Obey or not."

Way to sugarcoat that, Caden thought as he glared at the wall instead of Elijah. "I'm not a slave!" he found himself snapping, Grant Yarrow flashing through his mind, sending a shiver down his spine.

"You are. Either a slave to your flesh and own dark desires or a slave to Yahweh. I'd choose Yahweh; He cares for you and purchased you with His own blood. He has already suffered to bring you life. What more will He do to help you?"

Get me killed, Caden thought. *Or keep me alive somehow. I keep surviving crazy things. And He gave me my Lil El again. And showed me my future wife.* He gently touched the rough scab on his chin and shook his head. *This is nuts.*

"What do you decide?"

Caden's glare finally found Elijah. "I can't just decide *now*."

"Why not?"

"It's complicated!"

Elijah shook his head. "The only complication is who's the real god in your life. Yahweh? Or yourself."

"Get off my back, man," Caden hissed as he turned away. "I'm barely surviving as it is!"

"And you will survive far more, *only* if you follow Yahweh. Now. Choose."

Caden cursed and slammed a fist on the table. "I can't! This is too much!"

"If it's too much, Yahweh wouldn't ask this of you."

"I'm not a spy!"

"What are you afraid of?"

"Dying? Isn't that obvious!"

"What are you afraid-"

"He'll see who I am!" Caden's fist loosened, and he looked down, his chest heaving. "I'm afraid if I try and do a job for Yahweh, He'll finally see who I am and just..." He ran fingers through his hair and sat back. "He'll enjoy watching me squirm as he points out every flaw, every sin, every fraction of a mistake. In front of everyone! And He'll like humiliating me and won't stop. Just won't stop. And I," Caden crossed his arms again and shook his head. "I can't be tormented by Him too." he whispered.

The room was quiet. Caden closed his eyes as anger toward Elijah swelled up inside him. Why hadn't he said all this privately? Instead, Elijah ripped open Caden's insecurities right in front of everyone, even people he didn't know! With a sigh, Caden shifted in his chair. *This is the End Times,* he thought. *There's no time for pleasantries anymore.*

"Cade," Ellie whispered. "Yahweh isn't Dad. I was afraid of Him too at first, but He's not like that. He's kind. Merciful. Patient when we mess up."

Caden crossed arms tightened even more across his chest, as though protecting his heart. *No one's merciful. Not when they really see who I am.*

"You are not a failure."

Caden grimaced and looked at Elijah. "Then what am I?"

"You are more than a conqueror through Yeshua. Your strength is in Yahweh, so there's no reason to fear. You are not alone; Yahweh is with you in the fire and raging waters. He listens when you cry, and He comes to save you, wrapped in darkness, riding on a Cherub, and ordering coals to rain down. You are his chosen inheritance, his final remnant, and you will receive your reward when Yeshua returns. He sees your struggles, Caden, your fight for His truth. He is not ashamed of you. He is delighted in you. I am not making this up; everything I've just said is Scripture."

Caden's eyes narrowed. "Wait, He said that? About me?"

"You, me, and everyone. It is all in the Bible. *Neshama*, don't we have a list of that somewhere?"

"Yeah, I think we do," Ophir muttered. "I'll get it before you go."

Caden tried not to glare at her. It didn't work. *I haven't decided yet*, he thought. *You can't make me go back!* Emotion tightened Caden's chest as he stared down at his cold food. He just wanted to be home! To be with his family! Not to run around and play Alex Whitney while lying to the most dangerous person in history. It was stupid. More than stupid, it was insanity. *Why does Yahweh keep wanting me to do things that'll get me killed?*

Caden cursed under his breath and closed his eyes. He remembered feeling this way when choosing to walk into the Sinai Desert. *But I wouldn't have found Lil El if I hadn't gone*, he thought. *Or united the two Witnesses. That's big, I guess.* Caden lifted his head as his eyes narrowed. *Real big, actually.* What had Han said? That Caden was needed to fulfill prophecies? Caden shifted as he rubbed his forehead with his palm; he found it was sweating.

Though he hated to admit it, Elijah was right. It wasn't a complicated decision. Either Caden chose to follow Yahweh, even if it was a bad idea, or Caden chose the safe way. The safe way would keep him alive and free from the threat of torture and imprisonment. *Is that true though?*

Caden blinked as he glanced around the table, looking at each fellow believer. *Most of us will die,* he thought. *Probably all of us. But I don't want to be a pawn in God's war. I long to be free from the oppression of condemnation. I cannot serve a god who only finds fault. He will critique and judge and condemn until there's nothing left of you. Nothing left to kick but a battered body, choking on your own blood–*

Caden closed his eyes as his chin slowly lowered to his chest. The corner of his mouth twitched as Doeg's words faded to silence. *I must choose.*

"*I foresee the future.*" Caden's nose wrinkled in disgust as his shoulders bunched, as though readying to attack. "*You will fail,*" Doeg continued whispering into his mind. "*And encircled by adversaries, as though in a den of starved lions. Hope will abandon you.*"

I just got to choose which god to serve.

"*And your so-called God of mercy will watch as they torture you–*"

And choose to stick with it–

"*–to death.*"

–no matter what.

Stiff whiskers brushed his cheek. "Are you acquainted with a blood eagle?"

Caden gasped and recoiled, Doeg's audible voice always shaking him to the core. He sat back, arms raised in defense, and found nothing beside him but a startled Asher. Caden cursed and ignored everyone asking if he was alright. Running a rough hand over his face, Caden straightened himself and held his fists on the table. His fingers strained as his knuckles slowly turned white.

I am not a god, he thought. *I am not worth living for. And… and dying for.* With a slow breath, Caden lifted his chin and squarely faced Elijah. *But Yahweh is.* "How can I be a spy?" Elijah took another long drink before nodding and giving a small, short-lived smile.

AFTER DINNER, which Caden finally forced himself to eat once Ophir and Ellie nagged him to, he followed Elijah into one of the old study rooms. It was small and private with a few chairs and a table. Noam was stationed at the door, and one of the strangers joined them. He was a large, sharp-featured man who sat as though a board was stuffed down the back of his shirt. When they shook hands, Caden nearly stepped back as the stranger's gaze studied every inch of him. Caden cleared his throat and tried to figure out what this guy was looking for.

"You're young," the stranger said. "But you're all we got, so you'll do."

Elijah refused to give Caden his name. In fact, Elijah refused to show or tell Caden anything else about Under Fire. "You're a spy," he explained. "If you get captured, the enemy could make you talk."

"They will," Caden found himself saying. "Let's be honest; I'm not a soldier."

The stranger breathed out heavily through his nose as he glanced at Elijah. "Why are we relying on this boy?" he said in Hebrew. "He will get us all killed!"

Caden's eyes narrowed as he took a step closer. "Because I'm who Yahweh's picked," he answered in Hebrew. "So, help me or leave."

The man straightened, and Caden had the funny feeling he was thinking of all the ways to make Caden eat his words. It was all Caden could do but stand down. He'd made his choice. He was a spy now. Half his brain screamed, he had no idea what that meant, and he really was going to get everyone killed. He'd killed his brothers. Why not an entire university of several thousand fellow believers? Don't omit his sister either.

By the time Elijah told them to sit, Caden's stomach

was twisting, and his heart picked up the pace again. Caden wiped a hand across his sweaty face, and his eyes narrowed as the stranger started talking. Whoever he was, he knew how to work among the enemy. The three stayed in that room long into the night. Several things were concluded. The unanimous consensus was that Caden hadn't the foggiest clue what he was getting himself into.

The stranger tried to talk Elijah out of encouraging the assignment, but Elijah refused to budge. "Yahweh has spoken."

Caden didn't get it. He hadn't gone to spy school. He didn't know how to communicate in clear yet sneaky ways. He obviously didn't know how to defend himself, and if he got caught, he'd break and tell the enemy everything. Caden's hands stayed in fists during the entire talk. He kept trying to listen while holding down his puke. He wished he hadn't eaten. He wanted to keep thinking he was in over his head and should just quit now, but he chose to remember he was immortal.

Until Yahweh says it's time to die, I won't die. I just won't. No one else chooses that. Only Him. Besides, this is kind of like getting into House Whitney. Except there are no Giants to eat me. Now there's just one guy.

"The Antichrist." A muscle in Caden's jaw flexed as he ran a hand over his face again.

In that brief meeting, the stranger tried to educate Caden on the nuances of espionage. He must always be Alex Whitney, no matter what, because he must assume he's always being watched. Trust no one. Be prepared to kill to maintain his cover. Caden's fists became slick when that was brought up. *I could do that,* he told himself, but he felt his heart quicken. Why was he still lying to himself?

The stranger had a plan for how Caden could send messages. Something about how he tied his shoelaces or how he folded up a newspaper. Caden grimaced and shook his head. "This is Alex Whitney," he said. "He doesn't read newspapers. He's on BiggieFishy."

The stranger's head tilted to one side. "BiggieFishy?"

"It's like the old Facebook or Instagram or... a platform to post stuff. We could make a code. Alex would post things about himself all the time. I could always include a specific emoji when there's a message."

"House Whitney will see your posts. They'll know you're a fake."

Caden shook his head. "America's still a Dark Land. They're too interested in getting lightbulbs working again to notice some rich kid trying to get viral posts."

The stranger's cutting stare didn't relax in the slightest as he slowly nodded. "Good plan." That was the extent of his positive feedback. They made a crude emoji cipher before Caden had to cut their meeting short. He didn't want to cause any suspicion and had to get back to Luca. Besides, he had work to do.

———

CADEN RUBBED his eyes as he yawned and stumbled his way through the empty cafeteria. The stranger had at last left, and Elijah walked beside him. "What time is it?" Elijah shrugged. It was too quiet, and Caden knew most people were fast asleep. His shoulders sagged as he thought of Ellie. He wanted to say goodbye. *I'll see her again.*

They heard soft feet across the floor, and Caden looked up, hoping for Ellie. Ophir came from the shadows, and Caden smiled, a bit disappointed, but not much. She quietly walked between the two and linked both their arms. "And how's the scheming going?"

"Good," Caden said. "We have a plan. A very weak plan, but we have one."

"It's not weak." Elijah muttered.

Caden shrugged. "I just hope it won't get me killed."

Ophir nodded. "I pray so. I don't want my little Caden Giant food again." She leaned over and gently kissed him on the cheek. Caden gave a small smile, suddenly reminded of Mama Lo. He turned away, not knowing what to say.

"I'm proud of you," Elijah said. Caden kept looking ahead but smiled again. "I knew you'd follow Yahweh and become a Christian. What convinced you?"

Caden snorted a quick laugh and shook his head. "Yohanan. That guy is crazy."

"Yes!" Ophir said. "His ideas are very odd. But he is a good young man." Elijah arched a brow at Caden.

"He attacked the people I was traveling with in the desert." Caden explained. "Well, not attacked. Felt like it though. He made us kneel and put a gun to all our heads," Ophir gasped, "and he asked if we followed Allah."

"And *that's* when you chose to be a Christian?" Ophir blurted. Caden nodded. "I don't think Yohanan is the crazy one. Most wouldn't do that."

Caden nodded as they showed him the way out. "Yeah, well, most people don't do half the stuff we find normal. Freaks. Talking animals. Giants. Power-hungry kings. Attacking Russians!" Caden shook his head. "Feels like I'm stuck in a nightmare sometimes." Elijah nodded quietly. As they neared the glass doors, Caden saw the shadowed form of Asher leaning against a lamp post.

"How are you holding up?" Elijah muttered. "I'd imagined Demons behind every corner in the king's house."

"Yes," Ophir said, concern widening her eyes. "I can't even imagine."

Caden lifted his chin as he felt unease press on his chest. He swallowed the hard lump in his throat, finally facing the fact that he was going back. Back to the enemy. "You have no idea."

Ophir clicked her tongue and placed a hand over her mouth. "Is there anyone good there? Any Christian or, or even a decent person?"

Caden stared at her a moment, choosing his words carefully. "It's the Antichrist's home," he said at last. "It's a very dark place." Ophir shook her head and looked nearly about to cry. *I've upset her,* Caden thought, wishing he hadn't said anything.

"Well," Ophir said at last. "There's one good thing there. You." Caden slid a hand into his pocket and glanced at his feet. "And because you're there, Yahweh's there. He said to never leave or reject you so, so He's there too. In all that darkness and ickiness."

Caden nodded slowly. Elijah lay a firm hand on his shoulder. "Believe Yahweh is supporting you."

"And His angels."

"Seen them?"

Caden nodded. "I wish I always saw him. He's so freaky and huge! He has four heads."

"Hum. Cherub."

"Yeah! Turns out, they're not fat, little toddlers."

Elijah chuckled as Ophir smiled. "No. No they are not."

Caden looked at the man who'd saved his life in more ways than he'll ever know. *I can't stay,* he reminded himself. *There's spying to do.* "Good to see you, Abba. If you need anything, just let me know."

"We do. Not yet, but soon." Caden straightened as he stepped forward. "We need to start shipping graduates out. The job of the Witnesses and their followers are to tell everyone Yeshua is returning. Israel and some of the surrounding countries are being reached, but this is a small part of the world."

Caden blinked, seeing where this was going. "You want me to use Whitney Wings to get your people all over the world." Elijah nodded. Caden shuffled his feet as he thought. "How many?"

"Right now, a little under ten thousand." Caden's brows rose. "The Bible states there'll be one hundred and forty-four thousand."

Caden grinned suddenly and laughed. "Right! Oh man! How am I..." He put his hands on his head and stepped back.

"Several thousand will stay in the Middle East," Elijah said. "But about one hundred thousand should fly elsewhere."

Caden laughed again. He had to. This was nuts! "Okey, well... That's so many people!" he said at last. "I'll... I'll come up with something. One hundred thousand people!"

"Preferably sent for reasons other than missions."

"Of course," Caden said and scoffed. "Right, well... Yahweh will have to make it happen."

Elijah nodded. "He's the only one who *can* make anything happen. Not you. Remember that."

Caden nodded as he rubbed his tired eyes with a finger and thumb. "Not me." he whispered and glanced at Elijah.

"You should go. Can't keep the Antichrist waiting." Caden gave a humorless laugh, and the two embraced. Elijah clapped Caden on the back as he stepped away. He turned to Ophir, and they hugged too.

"*Shalom.*" Elijah said with a curt nod.

"*Shalom.*" Caden forced himself to turn away from the couple and walk from the place he wanted to call home. *Come on, come on. I'm not god. Do what Yahweh says!*

Asher straightened as he approached, and the two walked side by side without speaking. They walked through the campus and under the ill-lit lamps. Most of the bulbs weren't there, but there was enough light to not stumble too bad. As they neared the entrance, Asher sniffed. "So, a girl, huh?"

"Shut up." Caden snapped.

Asher grinned. "I expect you to learn from our Luca friend and figure out how to defend yourself. There are a lot of girls out in the world-"

Caden turned and slugged him in the arm. Asher recoiled, grabbing his arm, and Caden smiled as they continued walking. "Seriously though," Asher said. "I'm going to spar with you when I see you again. You better beat me."

"Count on it. I still haven't paid you back for making my face black and blue."

"Hey, that was your bright idea."

"It worked though."

"Sort of. But you forgot what Alex called his golden tooth."

"What idiot names a tooth?"

"An idiot. Remember?"

"Remember what?"

"The name of the tooth!"

"No!" Asher grumbled, and they continued winding through the campus. Caden sighed, and his eyes narrowed. He glanced around, making extra sure they were alone, and stepped a bit closer to Asher. "Keep an eye on Yohanan." Asher shot him a look. "We were attacked by Russians in the desert."

"Yeah, heard on the news they did that a lot."

"Why?"

"They didn't want anyone to see them closing in on Jerusalem. If someone did, they'd just take them out. You're lucky to have survived."

"Yeah, well, Yohanan killed them. All of them. Burned them alive."

Asher nodded slowly. "He told me."

Caden waited for him to continue, but when Asher didn't, he scowled. "That doesn't bother you?"

Asher shrugged. "You were all going to die. He saved your life."

"But! But isn't that very unchristianly? Shouldn't we be turning the other cheek and all that? Not massacring soldiers with Yahweh's *Akal Esh*?"

"There's a time for peace and a time for war."

"Is that an Israeli saying?"

"Bible verse."

Caden fell quiet as they neared the university's entrance. "Yohanan's just unpredictable." Again, Asher simply nodded. Caden cursed under his breath and ran a hand over his face. "Look," he said, stopping. "I just, I don't want my sister to get hurt. I can't protect her anymore. I've tried all my life, and I just can't right now!"

"Don't tell me you feel like a failure."

Caden cursed again and stepped back. "How can I not! I'm her older brother! It's my job to protect her!"

"I was an older brother too," Asher said quietly. "My only sister's dead. Am I a failure?"

Caden turned away and shook his head. "Never mind."

He started walking to the street, but Asher held up a hand. "That's never been your job."

"Yes, it is!"

"Shut up for once!" Caden gritted his teeth and forced his fists not to launch into Asher's face. "You didn't swear before Yahweh and man to protect her. Yohanan did. It's his job. *He's* the one who'll stand before Yahweh in the end. *He's* the only one Yahweh will ask if he protected her or not. Not you. If you want to protect someone, get your own wife." Caden scoffed and, without thinking, lightly touched the healing slice in his chin.

"Let her go," Asher said quietly. "And he's unpredictable, but he's reliable in his devotion to Ellie. It's obvious. And! He breathes fire! How much more protection can you get!"

Caden's bunched shoulders slowly loosened as he gruffly sniffed and turned away. "I guess."

"I guess? Please!" Asher nudged him, and the two kept walking to the street. They passed under the arching entrance to the campus and stood under a lamp as the cars buzzed past and people honked and shouted at one another.

"Thanks." Caden whispered as the two waited for a cab. Asher nodded, and the two fell silent. Caden finally saw a cab and hailed it. As it slowed down, he turned at Asher. "Random question, in the Bible, is there a creepy guy on a horse? Looks like a soldier? Big sword?"

"Was his horse red?"

Caden's eyes narrowed. "Yeah."

Asher shook his head as he whistled. "Man, you see the weirdest things. That's one of the Four Horsemen of the Apocalypse."

"There's four?"

"That one represents war. Makes sense; Russia's attacking."

"What are the other ones?"

"The first one's conquest, the Antichrist. The next one's war, which we're in now. The third is famine." A hard lump formed in Caden's throat, remembering Nate. "And the last is death."

Caden blinked slowly, trying to ignore the unease tightening his chest. "Great." His voice squeaked, and he cleared his throat as he stepped toward the taxi. "Add it to the list of impossible things we're going to face."

"Hey," Asher called, stepping back. "We win."

Caden nodded, letting that fact sink in. "We win."

"Don't forget. Nothing can steal that from us. Nothing."

Their eyes met, and Caden lifted his chin, wishing Asher could come with him. Why did he have to be alone, surrounded by the enemy? *Yahweh's the boss,* he told himself and stepped into the cab. He waved to Asher before he turned and went back into the school. Caden sighed and closed his eyes, letting his head rest against his chest for a moment. *We win,* he repeated. *I can't live with them now, but I will. Someday in Heaven, we will all be a family. For now, I'm Alex Whitney.*

He waited for his stomach to coil or the internal screaming to rise from his heart, but they didn't. Caden lifted his chin and smugly smiled. *I'm turning into Abba, scarred up warrior for God,* he thought. *Awesome-*

The cab's door opened. Someone slid in, scooting right next to him. Caden leaned back and turned, opening his mouth to demand they leave. Something sharp dug into the small of his back. Caden instantly leaned forward, but a hand seized his arm, keeping him in place.

"Darling! You're leaving without me?" It was a woman. She had an accent. A Russian accent.

Caden turned and found Dasha. She nestled against him but left enough space so that the knife had room to penetrate. Probably the same knife that marked his chin. She smiled at him, but her blue eyes were cold and hard. She had a sharp-featured face, but it suited her. Her skin looked soft and pale, and the light was highlighting her hair as if she was on a stage. He hadn't noticed before, but she was stunning.

Caden actually found himself smiling back. It was a real smile that didn't make any sense. *There you are.* His heartbeat had quickened. He didn't know if it was from the knife poking his back or the fact this Russian assassin chick would become his wife.

Dasha's left brow arched sharply, obviously not expecting his response. "Give the driver our address, dear. Let's go!"

Caden stared down at her and quietly chuckled. *I guess I won't be as alone as I thought.* Dasha's arched brow rose a bit higher, and the knife started to hurt.

"Easy." he whispered, his stupid smile finally gone. Man, he was dumb sometimes. Caden turned to the driver and cleared his throat. "House Battistelli."

The man gave the two a sharp look but said nothing as the taxi sped onto the road. Caden tried to look relaxed as Dasha's knife kept boring into his back. He breathed out slowly, idly hoping his future wife wouldn't try to kill him again.

SIXTEEN
KISSING: A LEGIT PLAN

FUTURE CADEN HAD a lot of scars. Younger Caden had only seen his face, so he could only imagine what the rest of him looked like. *Does he have a puncture wound at the small of his back?* Caden rapped his fingers on his knee to keep himself distracted from Dasha's knife. It was really starting to hurt! She obviously didn't like him staring at her the way he did. He should've known better.

"I was thinking." Dasha said, flashing him another fake smile. They were kind of creepy. No one should be able to make such a beautiful smile while stabbing someone in the back.

She's not stabbing me, Caden corrected himself. *Well, not yet.*

"Maybe we should go to a quiet room tonight. Get to know one another? Alone." She leaned closer, and Caden could smell her. There was some girly soap-stuff mixed with sweat. "Smile," she whispered, the knife giving a small yet noticeable twist.

Caden instantly smiled. "That sounds great," he said and turned to the driver. "Hey, turn on the radio, would yah? Need some privacy back here." The driver gave them another judgmental glance and muttered something about the recklessness of youth in Hebrew but obeyed. Caden looked back at Dasha and maintained his relaxed smile. In truth, he was wondering which organ the knife would puncture first.

"You don't need the knife," he whispered. "I'm not going to hurt you."

"Oh," she sighed and laughed as though he had told a joke. "I don't know about that."

Caden tilted his head to one side, telling himself not to headbutt her and take the knife. "I could've punched you last time. You saw. I didn't." Her left brow twitched as she continued fake-creepy-smiling. "Now, lose the knife." Dasha didn't move, her gaze unwavering.

Caden stared back, realizing the kidneys were at the receiving end of her blade. *Can't die right away from a stabbing there,* he thought. *Right? They do have a lot of blood though. Oh, I really don't want to headbutt her.*

Dasha withdrew the knife and discreetly tucked it down her sleeve. If Caden hadn't been watching, he wouldn't have noticed where she concealed the weapon, her movements were too fluid and precise. He cursed under his breath and rubbed the small of his back. He checked his fingers, half expecting there to be blood.

Dasha clicked her tongue and flicked back her hair before leaning close again. "You would know if I stabbed," she whispered. "There's lots of blood."

"I know." Caden rubbed his healing chin. She glanced at it, and her lips twitched into a short-lived smile. Caden glared at her. She eased against him, looking as though they'd been an item for years. She seemed to be at ease, like they'd just went on a date or something.

She's good, Caden thought. He sighed and placed his hands on his knees. He didn't know what to do with them. He wanted to make fists, just in case, but that seemed too hostile. He could cross his arms, but his cracked ribs made that uncomfortable. Maybe go along with it and wrap an arm around her? No, no, that was stupid. He'd expose his ribs and guts by doing that. He had to be careful, she was still a crazy Russian, after all.

"You are a hard one to keep track of." she said, her tone playful and light, but her eyes. Those eyes felt absolutely nothing.

Caden glanced down at her, not sure what to say. She nudged him slightly, her brow pointing up a bit more, and he made his own empty smile. "Keeps you guessing."

She sighed and shook her head. "Oh, I don't need to guess anymore. I know you." Caden's smile faltered. "I've been watching."

What is this? Is she really an assassin? He briefly thought of Nathaniel. Could he have sent someone? This far? *No,* Caden thought. *Stop thinking of that guy. He and his dogs are nowhere near here.*

"What's your name?"

Caden scoffed. "Thought you knew me." She stared at him in silence, and he refused to break the stillness as he chose his words carefully. He had several names to tell her, but which one should she know? Oliver Deker was a nobody, Caden Johnson was hunted in America, and Alex Whitney was dead. Could he trust her with his real name?

She's a crazy Russian, he reminded himself. *She'll stab me in the back without losing sleep. She almost just did.*

"Alex Whitney." he said at last.

That eyebrow arched again, and he flashed her a wide, toothy smile. "Your *real* name."

"No can do. Just call me Alex for now."

She continued staring at him, her expression not changing in the slightest. Her only response was her index finger tapping once on her knee. "I've heard of Alex Whitney. Whitney Wings?" Caden nodded. Dasha's eyes narrowed as she studied him. "Why pretend to be Alex Whitney?"

"Why not tell me why you're in my taxi? With a knife, I might add. That wasn't very comfortable."

"Wasn't meant to be comfortable."

Caden sighed. "Why're you here?"

"Same as you. Mission."

Caden grunted, trying his best to look uninterested in what she meant. "Is that so? Some Russian incognito stuff? Jumping random guys? Scarring up faces?"

"I want into the KUS Headquarters."

"Okey," Caden said slowly. "Why?"

"Because I do."

"Hum… well, I want a world with no Freaks, but we all can't get what we-"

"I want to help you." Caden quieted and stared at her. She didn't move as her fake smile finally fell, and he saw the obstinate determination beneath.

"You," Caden shook his head slowly, "you don't even know what I'm doing."

"You're a fake, pretending to be Alex Whitney for money or power. I don't care which."

Caden sat back and ran a hand over his face. "So, you're after money or power?"

Dasha didn't answer. She just kept staring at him, playing with a long strand of brunette hair. *I shouldn't trust her,* Caden thought and cursed again, turning away. *Of course, I shouldn't trust her, idiot! I don't even know her! Just treat her like a threat. Well… I guess she is a threat. A real big one.*

Caden felt the cut's scab uncomfortably pull the skin around his jaw. "I can't let you help," Caden said at last. "I need someone I can trust. You know, someone who doesn't try to slit my throat. And someone who'll tell me who they are."

"You know my name."

"That doesn't tell me who you are."

Dasha's head tilted to one side as her lips thinned. "How do you know my name?"

Caden grinned and ran fingers through his hair. "Honestly, if I told you, you'd never believe me." Dasha said nothing. Caden sighed and shifted his weight. He saw her reach for the concealed blade again, and he raised a defensive hand. She froze, sitting back. "Like that," he said. "Just that, right there. I can't work around that. I have too much danger as it is. I need someone I can trust."

"You need someone who knows what they are doing."

Caden's brows pinched, shadowing his eyes. "Excuse me?"

"Oh, come now, darling. You cannot think you are a professional con? After three escape attempts, you think you would get out." Caden's hands slowly balled into fists on his knees. Dasha's eyes flashed with amusement. "I said I've been watching you. I know you. You do not know what you are doing. Always jumpy. Always hesitant. Like a lost puppy." Caden lifted his chin as his jaw flexed. "What do you say in America? Ah... you're just winging it."

Oh, she's real good, Caden thought as he refused to answer.

Dasha slowly nodded. "You need help."

"I don't need help."

"You do. I'm trained. By the best."

I have no doubt. "Is that so?"

"I found you again, while still under attack. Followed you for five days or so. And, someone who can fight-"

"Alright! Alright!" Caden snapped, not wanting another person to tell him to man up. "I get it."

"Good," Dasha said with an air of finality. "We'll go."

"What?" Caden asked. "That's not what I was saying-"

"You will anyway so cut to it and say yes."

"Dasha-"

She was holding the knife again. For the life of him, Caden didn't know how she had grabbed it so fast. He tensed and looked at her, glad his hands were ready to throw fists, and waited. When she spoke, he could hardly hear it. He could, however, hear her unwavering severity. "Never say my name. Never."

Caden leaned away and ignored his quickly beating heart. "What do I call you then?"

"Nina Morozov."

"Nina. It's a pleasure to meet you." Dasha's eyes narrowed as she slowly withdrew her knife. *See?* He thought. *You don't know me. Gotta throw you a few curveballs.*

She lifted her chin and laughed for the driver's sake, but her eyes were cold and calculating. "Relax," she said. "You look tense." Caden made himself smile, it was becoming a real pain, and he forced his fingers to uncurl.

"This is the plan," Dasha said quietly. "You and I go in. We say we are old friends from school-"

"No." Dasha's counterfeit smile twitched. "That's not what Alex would do."

"He's uneducated?"

"No, but-"

"Then stick to the plan."

Caden's eyes flashed as he stared down at her. *I don't have time for this.* "Listen," he hissed. "We're doing this *my* way. You want in? Then stop talking." He didn't wait for her to respond. "I went to the Church of the Holy Sepulcher, got lost-"

"Why?"

"Why what?"

"Why go there?"

"I saw you go in."

Dasha clicked her tongue. "Oldest trick in the book."

"I know-"

"Outdated."

"But true. I followed you in, lost my bodyguard-"

"Why have a bodyguard?"

"Because I really did. His name is Simon. I had to lose him and knew the church would be crowded by afternoon." Dasha slowly nodded, that left eyebrow raised slightly. "Anyway, saw you, spent the day wandering through the Old City of Jerusalem. Saw some cool stuff, and I invited you to my place after dinner."

"Which is his majesty's mansion." Caden nodded. "How did you get yourself into there?"

Caden waved a hand. "Long story. The point is, no more knives poking me. We hooked up."

Her brow arched up suddenly. "Hook up?"

"You know. We, just..." Caden stared at her and sighed. "We're dating." Dasha's pointer finger rapped on her knee again. Her cheek moved as she gritted her teeth. Caden stared at her and found himself smiling. "Come on. It'll work." Dasha didn't answer as she quietly thought. Caden's hair slowly stood on end as he tried to remember which sleeve hid her knife.

"Fine." she said at last. Caden couldn't withhold a beaming smile, and Dasha sighed, muttering something in Russian. She smoothed back her hair and sat back, deep in thought.

Caden watched her out of the corner of his eye. Something occurred to him. They had a problem. A fixable one, but a problem. It was a problem he felt so lucky to be stuck in. Caden paused, making extra, extra sure they really had to fix it now, before speaking up.

"Look, um," he stammered. How was he going to say this? "So, we need to kiss."

The only way he knew Dasha heard him was her brow tugged up again. "No."

Caden glared at her. "You wanna wait until we're in

front of the king, surrounded by his Sentinels? We've got to be convincing. Have chemistry and all that."

"All that?"

Caden cursed under his breath and rubbed the back of his neck. "I think it's a good idea."

Dasha rolled her eyes and eased into her seat, relaxed and, obviously, unwilling to move. *This is a legit plan,* Caden thought, trying his best to be logical and think of the mission and not her moist, red lips, slender neck, pale blue eyes, and-

Caden gave his head a quick shake, wondering if Dasha would become a huge distraction instead of an asset. He crossed his arms and stared out the window. *Worth a shot-*

She was close again. Her hands cupped his cheeks, turning him to face her. It took Caden a second to realize her lips were against his. She kissed again, harder and deeper, her hand now on the back of his neck, drawing him closer. He couldn't breathe. He couldn't think. And it was over.

Dasha sat back, her expression just as impassive as before, beside that left brow. It seemed to like arching in a judgmental air as she watched Caden catch his breath. Her mouth slowly opened as her eyes narrowed. "You've kissed before, yes?"

"Yeah," Caden said, running fingers through his hair. "Lots of times."

Dasha kept staring at him and slowly nodded. "Winging it." she muttered and turned away.

Caden didn't care as she moved further back. He tried to hide his smile, but it was impossible. *Nice plan, God,* Caden thought. *Very smooth.* Maybe spying wasn't such a bad idea after all.

———

AFTER A BIT OF SILENCE, Caden and Dasha finally got to work. The rest of the cab ride to House Battistelli, they made their backstory. Dasha had obviously used her Nina alias before and had a complete history and paperwork to prove it. At least Caden had his Alex Whitney ID. She didn't seem too impressed with that, but nothing seemed to impress her. Or bother her. Or phase her at all. Even when gunfire shot through the night close to their taxi, she hardly acknowledged the commotion.

I wonder what her story is, Caden thought as they pulled up to the well-lit and heavily guarded mansion. He glanced at the massive Israeli flag on the entrance's flag-pole lit by floodlamps. The Sovereign Lion's unnatural eyes fixed on him. A corner of his eye twitched, and he looked away. *We win,* he thought, remembering Asher's words. *We win.* He cursed under his breath.

At night, the Sentinels' white uniforms made them look too much like Shades. They went through the check-points, Caden's fake ID letting them breeze on by, and they made it home. *It's not home,* Caden thought. *It's the enemy camp.* When they walked through the doors, they followed their plan and were laughing, arm and arm, and waking in not-so-straight patterns.

Roberto rushed in as they headed toward Caden's room. "Where were you, young man!" He waved his arms around, swatting invisible flies.

"Out." Caden said with a dopey grin. He stumbled against Dasha, and she giggled as she steadied him.

Roberto's brows rose as he muttered Italian and ran a handkerchief over his shiny, sweaty head. "You were to stay with Simon. He was watching you!"

"Don't need a babysitter!"

Roberto grunted and glanced at Dasha. "And who are you?"

"She's with me." Caden said, drawing her closer. It felt

kind of weird holding a stranger that close, but if he was honest, it was kind of fun.

"Hi." Dasha sighed, waving with wiggling fingers. Roberto lumbered over and pulled her away from Caden. "Hey!"

"Arms out."

Caden's inebriated-relaxed state stiffened as he remembered Dasha's knife. *He'll find it. They'll think she's trying to use me to get in here.* A sudden wave of adrenaline surged through him. He made fists. He moved to act. Dasha, on the other hand, rolled her eyes and huffed as Roberto patted her down. Caden watched, ridged and ready, until he realized no knife was found.

"Dude," Caden said, forcing himself to grin and step closer. "That's my job."

Roberto shot him a look and sniffed, a bead of sweat trickling from his shiny head. He checked her ID and asked her a few questions, which she answered in a disinterested, air-headed sort of way. She said she was a foreign exchange student and couldn't believe her Mother Russia was bombing little ol' Jerusalem. It worked, to Caden's shock, and they quickly headed to Caden's room.

"Master Whitney," Roberto called after them. "His majesty invites you to the KUS Headquarters tomorrow. He says you'd know why."

Caden lifted his chin and glanced back at the Italian. *So, that's what You want, God? Luca to train me how to fight. Shouldn't I be turning the other cheek?*

"Seven o'clock," Roberto continued. "Sharp."

A muscle in Caden's jaw flexed, and he gave a curt nod. "I'll be there."

"Master Whitney. His majesty never invites. He orders." Their eyes met. "Don't waste his good favor."

Caden felt his heart quickening, and he wanted to run out the door, screaming he wasn't Alex and this wasn't where he belonged. Instead, he smiled and pointed a finger a Roberto. "Thanks, big fella. Come on, babe!"

Caden felt like he was detaching from himself. His body was relaxed as he smiled and laughed with Dasha, but inside, his real self was trying not to have an anxiety attack. The two walked arm in arm, smiling and whispering until they entered his room. Once the door shut, Dasha gave him a sharp shove and walked to the bed.

Caden watched her out of the corner of his eye and shook his head. *She really has been trained for this,* he thought. *She should give me pointers.* Dasha started tossing blankets off the bed.

"What're you doing?" Caden asked.

She answered by throwing a pillow at him. "You, on the floor." Caden grimaced and glanced at the mound of blankets. "I can take care of myself," she continued. "Don't rescue me."

"Hum?"

"When Roberto searched me, you almost struck him."

"I didn't."

"You were going to." Caden rubbed the back of his neck and turned away. He almost said 'sorry' but realized that was stupid. Why apologize for nearly rescuing someone? "Last thing, Alex, or whatever your real name is. If I wake and find you standing over me, I'll cut off your head." Caden laughed but fell quiet when he saw the look in her eye. "And," she said, her voice just as casual as before, "after a bit of screaming, I'll cut off the head on your shoulders."

Caden stepped back and placed the pillow over his midsection as though it was a shield. "Yes, ma'am." he said and quickly snatched up the bedding. He shook his head and went to the far wall to make his bed. *God, I sure hope You know what You're doing.*

———

CADEN SAT SLUMPED in Luca's armored car, his head butted against the tinted window. His eyes were half closed, and he tried not to fall asleep. He figured Alex was the party type and wouldn't get a goodnight's rest if he brought someone like Dasha home. So, he made himself stay up as he mentally reviewed the emoji key he'd use when communicating with Elijah and... and that other guy. He wished he knew his name.

They're afraid I'll talk, Caden thought.

It kind of hurt his feelings; he wasn't going to betray Elijah! Didn't they know how loyal he was to the Mizrahis? Then again, he'd never been questioned before. Some of the Sentinels looked like inner-city thugs, all cleaned up and in uniform. Super unnerving. That's why Caden was willingly going to walk into the hub of the Royal Sentinel Brigade. The hub of everything within the King's United Society actually. Caden closed his eyes, feeling the cool window pressed on his brow. How he wanted to sleep it all away-

"Do you have a NIIC?"

Caden slowly lifted his head and glanced at Luca, who was seated beside him. He shook his head. "Haven't had the chance. I've been, you know, a hostage for a while."

"You're not anymore."

"Yeah, well..." Caden trailed off. He was not getting a NIIC. Just the thought of some KUS tec surgically inserted into his brain made him sick. Who would do that?

"Well," Luca said as he skimmed through the papers in his hands. "If you want one, just let me know. They're becoming popular. Parents want it for their kids if they ever get lost or, kidnapped," he motioned to Caden. "We would've found you if you had a NIIC."

"I don't like other people in my head."

Luca grinned as he sat back and waved a hand. "It's not like that. No one is in your head."

"But it keeps track of me. Didn't I hear there'll be one in the hand too?"

"Yes," Luca said, perking up. "That's being developed right now. Think of it as a wallet you can never lose."

Caden grunted and turned away. "I'll stick with my wallet for now. I'll think about it though."

Never. They rode in silence as Luca placed the papers back into a file and handed it to an assistant seated behind them. *I wonder what that was,* Caden thought. *Should I start asking more questions?*

"Who's that girl you brought home last night?"

Oh no. Caden made himself beam as he sat right up. "Did you see that? Man! She's something else, isn't she?"

Luca nodded patiently. "Who is she?"

"Nina."

"Nina what?"

Caden shrugged and grimaced. "How should I know?"

"She's Russian."

"Yeah!" Caden blinked, pretending he finally understood what Luca meant. "Right! Russian! We're under attack by them, aren't we? Hum... she's cool though. She's a foreign exchange student." Luca nodded slowly as he glanced out the window. Caden's heart quickened, and he let a little of his worry show through. "Um... that's alright, right? I mean, she's cool."

Luca glanced back at Caden and for one second, Caden thought he'd lost her. "Alright," Luca said with a dismissive wave. "Just be careful."

Caden said some juvenile joke, but inside, he was trying to stay calm. *We can do this,* he told himself. *God brought us together. We're a team, even though she threatened to kill me. Again.* He ran fingers through his hair and forced himself to look ahead. *Just focus on right now. What am I doing right now? How can I survive?* He blinked, remembering God and all that Biblical, sacrificial stuff he was supposed to do now as a Christian. *And how can I help God's people right now?*

His wondering gaze fixated on a tall, modern-looking building that, surprisingly, hadn't been touched by the air raids. His guts coiled as his hair stood on end. Even at this distance, he could see the Israeli flag and the Sovereign Lion watching. KUS Headquarters.

I'm entering the den of lions, Caden thought, hoping he wasn't going to get eaten alive.

SEVENTEEN

THERE ARE THREE OF THEM

CADEN TRIED to walk like the cool, new kid in school as he followed Luca into KUS Headquarters. He was Alex Whitney. He was supposed to get the best, be with the best people, have privileged opportunities, and, through it all, not bat an eye or give one thank you. Well, maybe to a king, he'll say thank you. That was Alex Whitney.

Caden Johnson was trying not to puke again as his stomach wound on itself. Somewhere in his subconscious, he thought to ask Dasha how she stays so calm, but most of him was trying not to panic. There were even more Sentinels here. And Giants. And dogs. He could hear them barking and straining on their chains. He tried not to think of gunpowder, Trace's blank stare, and Nathaniel shouting into the night. He could still hear Nathaniel's voice echoing off the nearby mountains. He sounded so official, so unmoved when saying the Heralds decreed he must die.

They're not Heralds, Caden thought. *They're Demons. You're taking orders from Demons!*

If he thought Luca's mansion was swarming, it was nothing compared to here. Apparently, Demons have headquarters too. A lump formed in Caden's throat as a Viper dropped from the ceiling. He tried to casually step over it while brushing shoulders with who he could've sworn was a Wither. The Sentinels' white uniforms started blurring together with the Shades' white fur. Several of the staff adjusted the skin on their arms or face, like someone trying on new clothes and making them fit just right. Vipers slinked between, up the walls, over furniture, and riding on nearly half the people's shoulders.

Raw Peace, Caden thought. *Raw Peace. Raw-*

Dad. Dad was there. He was standing across the room, just staring. He had that dark, detached look in his eye. The I'll-beat-the-obedience-into-you look. Caden flinched and stopped dead in his tracks. Luca turned with narrowed eyes, stopping the entire parade of attendance and bodyguards. "You okey?"

Caden sucked in a breath, clawed through the panic, reminded himself he's seeing invisible bad guys, and doubled over in a huge sneeze. He wiped his nose, and they kept going. Caden gave the Wither one final glance. The Wither continued the paralyzing glare, making Caden question if it really was Dad or not. Caden blinked and ran a hand over his face, realizing Luca had been talking.

"...where we'll train and practice out in the open." Luca motioned to massive windows which showed a training yard. There were targets, tumbling mats, an obstacle, and a platform. "You're not ready for that quite yet."

Caden's eyes narrowed. "Try me." he heard himself say and instantly regretted it.

Luca laughed and flashed him a wide, surprised smile. "I intend to."

Great.

Caden followed Luca into a glass elevator. As they traveled up, Luca pointed out in broad gestures the classrooms, the offices, which floor was responsible for which department, and which ones were classified. Caden nodded and listened, startlingly reminded of Under Fire. *Both sides are gearing up,* he thought. *The Spirits know what's coming; they're getting their humans ready.*

As they rose higher and higher, Caden saw the far wall had several nation's flags on display. "What's that for?"

"Ah, that," Luca said with pride. "That is every nation who has joined the New Kingdom. We are up to sixty-three zones now. And counting."

Sixty-three, Caden thought. *Wasn't it like twenty-nine a year ago? They move fast!*

"Nice!" He made himself say and felt like he'd be sick. "Who spreads the word around about your New Kingdom? Or do they all just come to you?"

"A little of both. We send out allies as humanitarians who are willing to find those still struggling to survive in this broken world. They offer medical aid, educational programs, safety, and a host of other needs the majority of the world lacks. So far, we've only been able to reach this side of the world. I hope that will change soon."

Caden nodded slowly as he tried to decide which information was useful and which was garbage. "Neat."

The elevator opened, and Caden followed Luca down more halls. The place reeked of advanced security, both physical and spiritual. There were Demons everywhere. Caden wondered if they even knew he could see them; most didn't acknowledge him at all. *They have to know,* he thought. *They're not dumb, and I'm obviously freaking out.* Not obviously enough, Luca wasn't noticing a thing.

They finally entered a room covered with tumbling mats. Two swords decorated the far wall as a punching bag, gloves, water, and other supplies neatly lined a shelf. On the mats were about fifteen guys around Caden's age. As Luca entered, each one jumped to their feet and bowed low at the waist. Together, they said, "Your majesty!"

Luca greeted them with a kind smile and, laying hands on the young men he passed, said, "Good morning! I'm honored to be your instructor today. Please welcome our newcomer, Alex Whitney." Caden felt his heart quicken as he faced the strangers. Most were Israeli, but a handful were European and from abroad. They said welcome, but their eyes told a different story.

They're jealous, he thought. *I'm the foreigner here, and I'm walking in with the king. They want to beat me into my place.* Caden lifted his chin and held his hands behind his back. He nodded once and didn't speak. *Let them try.*

He felt his stomach coiling again, but that was normal. Either the internal screaming wasn't shrilling in that moment or, more likely, he'd gotten too used to it to notice. He took off his shoes and stood on the mat among them. None of them moved for him, and he tried his best not to care. *Don't back down,* Caden told himself. *You're used to this; Dad taught you well. You can beat this! As long as they don't realize who you are. Then you can't beat this. They'll beat you. Into pulp. Nice, red, stringy-*

Caden blinked and looked down. He saw short white hairs tickling his toes. His stomach figured out how to fold itself in half. *Doeg,* Caden thought. *He's here.* If he looked up, he knew he'd see the Shade standing on the ceiling, icy eyes watching expectantly. How was he supposed to learn how to fight, while spying at the same time, with a scar-faced Demon grinning at him?

Raw Peace, Caden thought, followed by a few colorful curses. With a deep breath, Caden lifted his chin and refused to look at the ceiling. He was aware of his heart, it was beating hard enough to feel in his throat, and his hands were getting a bit cold. But he was still there. Still standing, legs shoulder width apart, arms crossed, chin up. He wasn't going anywhere.

"Alright, everyone," Luca said as he clapped his hands, as though they weren't already giving him their full attention. "This is day one of a twelve-week training to enter the honored Royal Sentinel Brigade. But you have chosen to take it a step further. You've decided not to just settle for the white uniform, symbolizing the pure loyalty within the New Kingdom and our United Society. You've chosen this," Luca motioned to his bodyguard, who lifted his wrist. A stripe of fire red circled both wrists. On his shoulders were three diamonds grouped together, reminding Caden of a geometric campfire. "You've chosen the life of a Refiner."

What've I gotten myself into? Caden thought, his eyes blinking.

"To dive into society and improve people's quality of life via offering protection, by encouraging and strengthening our allies' loyalties, and, when needed, filtering through those who are not."

Does he expect me to do that too?

"I respect you all for making that sacrificial choice. Forget any limitations you think you have. Some of my best Refiners are disabled or lame. Your weaknesses I will turn to strengths. The end of you is the beginning of me. Let us begin."

Caden forced himself to breathe steadily and tried to pretend he was alone with Elijah, learning how to spar. *I've killed Puppets*, he told himself. *I can fight enough.*

"Today." Luca continued as he pointed to Caden.

Oh no.

"A foreigner has joined. Come, Alex. Let us see what you're made of."

What? God! Do something! Han!

Nothing stepped in to help him, and Caden found the

entire group watching. Now his heart was really having trouble keeping pace. He clenched his teeth until they hurt as the group spread out and sat along the perimeter of the floor mats. Caden stood alone at its center and faced the king. Luca gave him a smile as he casually walked forward. "I'm going to test your skills."

Caden didn't answer, realizing he was getting a chance to strike the Antichrist. Luca's pace didn't slow as he approached, but his smile vanished. Focused calm came over him. Caden watched as he made fists. Panic tightened Caden's throat. For a moment, he heard it scream for him to run, to stop pretending, to just throw in the towel. But that's not what Yahweh wanted. So that's not what Caden was going to do.

Without another thought, Caden dropped into a stance and raised his fists. *He's bigger than I am,* Caden thought. *Heavier. Taller. He'll beat me.* Luca advanced, a twinkle in his eyes. *But he doesn't know me. He thinks I'm just a weak, rich kid. But I'm not Alex.*

Without slackening his pace, Luca attacked. Caden dodged his fists and stepped in close, punching between Luca's blows. It wasn't until he noticed blood on his fist did he realize he'd made contact. Luca took one step back, his head lowering as blood dripped from his nose. Caden froze. He just punched Luca Battistelli, the king of the only trace of civilization. Was he allowed to do that? Of course not! He was a *king*! The Refiner bodyguard stiffened as well as the recruits. Luca lifted his chin and regarded Caden. He smiled, but his eyes were dark.

Caden cursed, nearly loosening his fists and raising his hands. *No going back now–*

He squared up, fists clenched, just as Luca pounced. In the back of Caden's mind, he remembered to tuck his chin, so his face wasn't as much of a target, and keep his elbows close to his sides to protect his stomach and guts.

That was the last thought he had. The next thoughts were about the ceiling and why it was spinning. Had he fallen, and was that sweat or blood trickling down his brow?

A face came into view. It was a calm face, focused, but unbothered. His nose was bleeding. And he wasn't done. Caden tried to scramble away as Luca straddled him, squeezing Caden's middle with his legs. Caden seized Luca's collar and the back of his neck, trying to yank him closer. Asher had said that once, if taken down, try to get the person too close to punch. Caden didn't move fast enough. A punch to the kidneys knocked the wind out of him. As Caden tried to gasp and not panic, hands wrapped around his throat.

He knows I'm a fake! Caden's mind screamed as Luca squeezed. He grabbed Luca's wrists and bucked, but Luca didn't budge. *He'll kill me,* Caden thought. *This is-*

Something crawled across the ceiling. Something white and furry. Doeg craned its neck back and grinned down at Caden. Its tail whipped, as though longing to join the killing. *"Didn't I tell you, boy?"* Doeg asked in Caden's mind. *"I will be the last thing you will ever see."* Caden fought for breath, but none came. His face felt like a swelled balloon, and his throat felt ready to collapse. *"I win. I always win-"*

No! Caden bared his teeth as he kicked. *No! I am immortal until God says so! You don't decide that! No one does!* Caden felt his body weakening. He tried to pry Luca's fingers loose but only felt them dig in deeper. *I am immortal,* Caden thought desperately, as though that would give him air. *And I will win!* His kicks slowed, and his lips were turning purple.

Without a word, Luca sat back and stood, stepping away. Caden sucked in air and rolled on his side, holding his throat as he rasped for breath. The room was silent. Caden coughed and wheezed, his throat feeling scraped raw with each intake. *Get up,* he told himself. *I know what being choked is like. Get over it! They can't win. I win!*

His legs moved. He heaved himself to his feet. Holding his throat and an elbow protectively tucked against his throbbing side, no doubt from his barely healed ribs, Caden faced Luca again. Blinking away the blood from his split brow, Caden squared up. Luca's eyes widened as Caden raised his fists and waited.

"Mr. Whitney," Luca said in a calm, casual voice. He wasn't even breathing hard. "You impress me. Please sit." Caden, dripping with sweat and still gasping for breath, lowered his fists and stumbled to the others. This time, they made room for him. "Moshe, get him a towel." The young man next to Caden leapt up and obeyed.

Caden noticed Moshe watching his every move with wide eyes. He coughed again and wiped his split brow. "Did I break your nose?" His voice was hoarse and strained. He winced and nearly gagged again.

"No." Luca said.

"Darn."

Luca chuckled. "Who's next?" No one moved, and he had to select someone. He proceeded to thrash everyone and didn't look tired until the very end.

Caden also noticed no one else got the strangle treat-ment. *Why was he extra hard on me?* He scanned the room and realized he was the only westerner. He, on the other hand, had zero official training. *He's testing me,* Caden thought. *He's making me stronger.* He grimaced and rubbed his throat again. He knew there'd be bruises by morning.

Luca waited until everyone was exhausted and about ready to collapse, either from exhaustion or from well-placed blows. No one was seriously hurt, just enough to feel it. The only blow Luca received had been from Caden, but that was just a bloody nose. He did look sweaty and needing a little break by the end. He told everyone to sit again and make the circle tighter. He stood at the center and slowly turned, facing each recruit at a time.

"You've all done very well," he said. "Do not lose heart by today's, how shall I say? Intensity." Caden held back a smart remark as he rubbed his throat again. "We are all allies, like a family. A devoted, loving father permits his children to feel pain in order to excel. I expect greatness from you." Caden blinked and found Luca staring at him. "I have plans for you, plans for you to prosper as Refiners. I don't want to harm you. I want to give you a future and hope so that you can share it with others. You are conquerors. No," he raised a hand, "*more* than conquerors, but only through me."

Luca pointed to his chest. "My name will be above every other name. There will come a day that at the very mention of my name, every knee will bow, and every language will declare I am king. And you," Luca spread his arms, motioning to them all. "You are my new creation. Let me shape you like a potter shapes clay. I am creating you for good works, which have been prepared before-hand. How, may you ask?" Luca smiled, a sparkle alive in his eyes. "I will teach you. More specifically, my own mentor and loyal ally will teach you. Please, welcome my friend, Hugh Wiltshire."

The door opened, and even before Caden could turn his head, he knew something was wrong. Doeg, who still was on the ceiling, had its ears upright and forward, and its tail flicked casually back and forth. Caden heard it give a low, throaty trill. *He looks like a cat excited about something.* Caden made a fist and steeled himself before turning. Nothing would've prepared him for what entered.

At first, he thought the building was on fire, there was so much smoke. But smoke didn't move like that, and it was too dark to be normal smoke. Actually, it was black. The blackness spilled into the room but didn't drift upwards or dissipate as smoke does. It maintained its shape, wafting this way and that, curling and folding on itself like a writhing, living thing.

Caden froze, flight or fight filling him with adrenaline. His senses hyper-focused as his arms felt weak, and all he knew was that moment. Somewhere, the internal screaming shrilled. He had seen this before. The last time it had lifted from the Puppets he killed. It was a Demon, that black, haunting, mist-like Demon with glowing eyes-

There they were. Caden's hair stood on end as a pair of red, ember coals blinked from the gloom. The glowing eyes glanced around and were engulfed in the darkness again, only to reappear on the opposite side. Caden wanted to run. He felt his legs bunching for action, his breath quickening to take in enough oxygen to outrun the Demon. Behind his internal screaming, in a far back corner of his mind, Caden remembered something.

No one else saw Demons, just lucky ol' him. Alex Whitney didn't see Demons. He was undercover. He was Alex Whitney. He didn't see anything. Caden glanced down and raked in a shaky breath. He was going to fail. There was no way he was capable to accomplish *anything* with Shades breathing down his neck and this *thing* floating about and-

We win, Caden thought, his eyes slowly closing. When he lifted his chin and regarded the new Demon, his face was chiseled in stone. Unmovable. Unfazed.

From the depths of the darkness, Caden saw a pair of legs appear. They strolled forward, and the figure of a man came together. He was a middle-aged man, balding, and wore a pair of glasses. "Hello, gentlemen." Now that accent, Caden knew. British. Or UK or something. Some-place over there. The stranger smiled and came to the center of the circle and bowed low to Luca. As he moved, the darkness lazily floated behind him.

"Your majesty." he said, and the two shook hands.

"Hugh, old friend. Thank you for coming all this way. I apologize for not meeting you at the airport. I wanted to-"

Caden's attention snapped back to the darkness. There was movement. The eyes reappeared with their bright, dying fire glow before blinking out again.

"Nonsense, sire," Hugh said. "It is an honor you summoned me. What a fine new batch of Refiners you have! I see you're welcoming them properly." Another pair of eyes blinked from the gloom. Caden whispered a curse and forced himself to look away.

Luca chuckled and laid a hand on Hugh's shoulder. "Listen to this man," he said, turning to the recruits. "I can train your body and mind, but Hugh will train your heart and Spirit." Caden tried not to flinch. "That is where the true battle lies." Luca motioned to the recruits as he stepped away from Hugh.

Hugh bowed again and sighed, holding his hands behind his back, as he faced the ring of listeners. "Gentlemen," he said. "My name is Hugh Wiltshire. It is my pleasure to teach you an invaluable art, granting you access to the most advanced, formidable weaponry known to man. The ancients saw the value of this art, yet, it has only been with the aid of our loyal king that we can now channel this force."

There's three of them, Caden thought, a bead of sweat trickling down his back. He counted again to make sure. Yep, the darkness had three sets of red glowing eyes like angry coals. The eyes lazily weaved and drifted about the darkness, like snakes winding on themselves over and over. Caden's jaw clenched as he felt his heart quicken.

"Come, gentlemen," Hugh whispered, drawing back Caden's attention. "Come closer." Caden swallowed hard, ignoring his twisting guts, as the recruits scooted nearer. Closer to the three dark Demons.

Are these the Fiends older me talked about?

"Hum, yes," Hugh whispered with a smile. "Are you aware we are members of a vast, united society? An intricate network of allies that extends beyond the tangible and into the ethereal? You are. They chose you before the foundations of the world were laid. Every road you have trod has led to here. Now. They long to make known the mysteries of our gracious king's bidding in accordance with their good pleasure. This will be put into effect when the times reach their fulfillment—to bring unity to all things, both the tangible and the ethereal, under our king's rule. Gentlemen, the time is here, and the time is now. Now is when true allies of the King's United Society will serve our king, not only with their actions, but their Spirits as well."

Caden breathed out slowly as his hands became fists on his knees. He knew they were shaking. He hoped his face wasn't white. "Gentlemen," Hugh said. "I am your advocate and helper. Listen with an open mind and heart, and I promise you on the Sovereign Lion's mane, you will fully know why Refiners are the elect." Hugh paused as he slowly turned to each of the recruits. It was like he was waiting for the right moment to give the punchline. Caden focused on staying still and ignoring his internal screaming as more sweat dripped down his back.

"Gentlemen," Hugh said. "Refiners' greatest arsenal are the Heralds."

EIGHTEEN

HELL'S LIQUID FIRE

CADEN WAS SHOCKED he wasn't running. Somehow, for some reason, maybe it was Yahweh, he still sat on the tumbling mat as Hugh grinned and the three Fiends drifted about in their inky black mass. *This is the lion's den,* Caden reminded himself. *Don't be surprised when you find lions. Even though lions rip and tear. They can lick the flesh off bones. Those monsters will lick my Spirit from my body. Can Spirits be tortured? Maimed? Crippled? Only a fool would assume otherwise. Are you a fool, Caden?*

Caden lifted his chin and ignored his internal screaming, sweaty brow, and shaking hands. This was where Yahweh had placed him. This was where he was supposed to be. *Regardless of how I feel.*

"But where is the supposed peace that passes all understanding?" Caden's fists clenched. "This feels leagues away from peace-"

Shut up, I'm trying to listen.

Caden shifted and settled in, his hands loosening. He leaned forward and focused all he had on Hugh. Didn't Yahweh work in mysterious ways? More like suicidal ways. Whatever. This is what Caden was given; a lesson from someone who treated Demons like pets. *It's probably the other way around*, Caden thought as he watched one Fiend's glowing eyes hover close to Hugh's face.

The old man didn't notice as he pushed up his glasses. "Who has heard of our Heralds?" A few hands raised. "Hum, good. Some call them Spirits or Haunts, Ghouls, and the ignorant few stoop low enough to call them Demons." Caden suppressed a grimace. "We do not use such archaic, negative connotations here. The Heralds are invisible, immortal messengers who exist on the other side of reality we cannot see. Does that mean they aren't real?"

He shook his head. "Let us use an analogy, or a parable as it has been said, to illustrate this point. Visualize fish in the sea." As he spoke, the Fiends started moving throughout the room. Caden forced his gaze to stay fixed on Hugh as one Fiend drifted overhead, the second floated to the right of the circle, and the third to the left. They stopped by each recruit, their glowing, hot eyes searching.

"In the sea," Hugh continued, "the fish's entire world is water, fellow fish, and algae. Nothing further exists. However, when salmon return from spawning in the rivers in the mainland, their world is questioned. Salmon return, speaking of creatures living *outside* of the water. First, the sea creatures doubt there is an *outside* the water, but salmon insist there is.

"The salmon share of a massive fish which moves upright on two, long fins. They don't have scales, and algae grows on the tops of their heads. They swim quickly on land, their two fins moving beneath them, but in the water, they are clumsy and slow. These massive fish make loud, terrible sounds, like a whale, but even louder. They are odd, terrifying fish. Are you understanding this parable?" A few of the students slowly nodded as Caden's eyes thoughtfully narrowed.

"You are the fish in the sea. All you know is what is around you. However, there is a world far beyond this." Hugh waved his hands around. "A salmon has no words to describe a human. We are terrifying, odd creatures. Most fish may not believe in our existence, but we exist regardless. It is the same with Heralds."

Caden's head tilted to one side as he listened. *Kind of like angels too. Maybe it will be good to listen to this.*

"Heralds live *outside* our dimension. Their rules of nature, and yes, there are rules, are different than our own. Now, think with me of this: if a salmon sees an automobile, what would he see? A magical creature that lets the upright fish inside its belly, only to let them out again after swimming swiftly down long, narrow strips of black rock. We know there is no magic in a car. It is simply science and mechanics, but on a level mere salmon cannot fathom. Again, it is the same with Heralds."

And angels, Caden substituted.

"They utilize means beyond our understanding. To them, it is simple science and mechanics, but to us, it is magic. Gentlemen, there is no magic here. No magic in the fact that I know young Ally Asim and his wife are living in their car." A young man across the circle stiffened, his eyes darkening with suspicion to hide his sudden fear. "You hope becoming a Refiner will give you and your growing family the stability you need." Asim blinked and sat back. "Hum, I see," Hugh sighed. "I am sorry, I thought you knew. Congratulations." Asim lowered his head, his eyes darting right and left as he slowly grasped that he was a soon-to-be father.

"It is not magic that I know Ally Ruth is here to defend the defenseless, knowing herself the helplessness felt when assaulted and trapped." A young woman's shoulders became ridged as she regarded Hugh with a cold, guarded expression. Hugh bowed to her. "Madam, I honor you for letting such traumatic circumstances redefine you as a warrior, not a victim.

"And you, Ally Moshe." The young man beside Caden stiffened. "It is not magic that I know you don't have enough money for the laundromat to clean your little brother's blood from your clothes." Caden cursed under his breath as Moshe lifted his chin, a muscle in his jaw flexing. "There was nothing you could do to save him, son," Hugh said. "And, I swear to you, the Russian responsible for bombing your apartment was killed. He burned in agony, trapped in his cockpit, as he crashed." Moshe nodded, obviously pleased.

What does he know about me? Caden thought, his hair slowly standing on end.

"This magic," Hugh said, "is the Heralds' hand in my life. I have committed my every breath to the king first and the Heralds second. I have sought them out and reached out to find them, though they are not far away from anyone of us. Within the Heralds, I live and move and have my being. I presented my entire self as a living sacrifice, which is how I serve our king. I will not adhere to the practices of the old ways before the Day of Vanishing. I let the Heralds transform me by renewing my mind. They test me so that I may discern more clearly what they and our kings' wills are, their good and acceptable and perfect wills. And that is what I will instruct you in today. Today, you will become living sacrifices, ready to live and die for our king and his Heralds."

Caden glanced at Luca who was quietly standing against the far wall, arms loosely crossed. *This sounds awfully familiar,* Caden thought. *But backwards. It's kind of like asking the Antichrist into your heart instead of Yeshua. Oh, this is bad. God, please protect me. These Fiends will see I'm Yours! Please. They'll kill me. They'll tell Hugh who I am and my intent. They'll question me, and when I don't comply, they-*

Caden gritted his teeth and lifted his chin as Doeg swiped its tail. *"When you pray, you become prey. We sense your homage. It sweetens your blood."*

Touch me. That worked so well for you last time. Caden blinked, astonished at his own thoughts.

"Gentlemen," Hugh said as he continued turning, giving each his attention in turn. "Follow me on a mental journey. Relax. Let your mind drift."

"What did you say to me?"

Caden heard Doeg's claws scrape the ceiling overhead. Little tuffs of white hair drifted down before his nose and landed on the mat. Caden forced his breath to be slow and steady. Hugh pushed up his glasses again as a Fiend slowly circled his head, engulfing his face in darkness until it dissipated.

"Imagine with me a door. It could be of any craftsmanship." The Fiends kept curling through the recruits. Caden kept his gaze fixated on the floor before him, sweat dripping from his brow. "This door is the door to your home," Hugh continued. "Your inner self. Your very soul."

"You are outnumbered, human," Doeg growled in Caden's mind. *"Look around you!"* The black, smoke-like masses wisped about the circle, the glowing red eyes studying.

"The door is shut," Hugh said softly. "And you sit on the other side. Waiting. You hear feet approach and know something outside of this realm has come."

"My cousins are talented," Doeg whispered. Caden blinked slowly, his middle clenching with dread. *"They are weaponized with projectiles of liquid fire. No, not lava, as your feeble human mind would conceive. I said liquid fire. It is an efficient substance, dripping and running on all and searing the very flesh from bones. Or the soul from a body."* Caden forced in a breath; it was getting harder to breathe.

"You walk to the door," Hugh said. "And open it. Who do you find?" Not a sound filled the room. Sweat dripped off Caden's nose as two Fiends steadily closed in. "Heralds," Hugh whispered. "They come. Please, be hospitable and let them in."

Raw Peace, Caden thought. *You are with me and You give me peace. You are with me-*

Icy cold touched his skin. Blackness swarmed before him, surrounding two glowing, red eyes. They were definitely like coals; Caden literally felt heat on his face. The eyes had no pupils and rarely blinked. Caden held his breath, staring fixedly at the floor, praying it would keep moving as it had done with everyone else.

Doeg was right: Pray and become prey.

The Fiend's casual, smoke-like movements stilled. The eyes stared down at Caden, unmoving. Caden's nostrils flared as his face heated under that gaze. *I am immortal until Yahweh says so,* he thought. *You cannot touch me!* Without a sound, the Fiend moved back, drawing the other two's attention. Each pair of red eyes burned into Caden. He felt it on his face, his left shoulder, and his right side. He knew, if they stared long enough, his clothes would start to smoke.

"Let them in," Hugh was saying. "Let all of them in. They will guide you into all truth. They will go before you and follow you, and you will hear a voice from behind saying, 'this is the way, walk in it'. Trust them. Let them in."

Fierce anger struck Caden's chest. He recognized some of Hugh's words. He was quoting Scripture. He, infected with Demons nearly to the level of a Puppet, leading susceptible minds into evil darkness, dared to quote Scripture? Didn't he know who God was? Didn't he fear God at all?

"Let them in." Hugh repeated.

Never. Caden lifted his gaze from the floor and squarely

faced the Fiend. *I am Yahweh's. I will always be Yahweh's.* A muscle in Caden's jaw flexed as he refused to turn away.

The mass of swirling darkness blinked once and shifted. The smoke drew together, forming a transparent, black head. A long, animal-like snout formed beneath the eyes, fitted with pointed, dark fangs. Spikes grew from the top of the head, the points ending in tendrils of darkness. Two long, humanoid arms extended, shaping into overly sized hands. Each finger, as long as Caden's forearm, flexed eagerly, like a predator readying to strike.

Caden felt weak and dizzy. It was all he could do but sit there and stare. He forgot about Hugh. He forgot about Luca. He just stared at the monster ready to kill him. *God*, Caden's sludgy thoughts finally formed. *I need You. Now.*

The Fiend's mouth opened, revealing rows of teeth as it drooled. Caden blinked. No, that wasn't drool. It was white hot and edged in bright orange. It trickled between the Demon's fangs, and a drop fell to the floor mat. The mat hissed instantly, sending up a strand of smoke as a little melted crater formed.

"Liquid fire." Caden could hear the pleasure in Doeg's voice. *"Enjoy this prequel to the fires of Hell."*

Caden's legs bunched to run. The Fiend's head drew back as the chasm of its throat glowed brighter. Caden's breath quickened. A mass of orange-white, hot fire flowed into the Fiend's mouth. Caden's eyes widened, his body tensed to act. *Be still.* The thought cut through his internal screaming.

Be still and know that I am God. Wasn't that a verse somewhere? Caden sucked a breath through gritted teeth. The Demon's spiked head lunged forward. The liquid fire shot out, like a flaming arrow or dart. *Be still!* Caden didn't move. The liquid fire hardly arched as it shot directly at

Caden's heart. He couldn't withhold a cry as he cowered back, bracing for overwhelming pain.

The liquid fire splashed right and left. Caden flinched, gasping, but felt nothing. He slowly looked up. Something was between him and the Fiend. The liquid fire dripped off the barrier and onto the floor, burning the mat more. Caden heaved in a breath and stared, finding feathers inches from his face. The liquid fire just dripped off, as though it were water, and the feathers weren't even smoking. Caden blinked and looked up. Standing over him, with cloven feet spread for action, were several wings, each blinking with countless eyes.

Han. Caden nearly started laughing as tears welled in his eyes. He drew himself up off the floor and groaned, hugging himself.

"This boy is Yahweh's." Caden flinched again, Han's voice so unbelievably loud. "You will not touch him." That was the human-head talking.

"Or our Lord's glory will slice through your darkness." the lion-head snarled.

"And don't mention him to Hugh," the oxen-head demanded. "Or to anyone."

"Now beat it!" Squawked the eagle-head.

The Fiend's translucent head cocked to one side as its eyes narrowed on Caden. Again, Caden felt the heat of its gaze on his face. Without a word, the Fiend melted back into an undefined, smoky shape and drew behind Hugh. The two other Fiends followed. Caden ran a hand over his face as he looked down. His hands were shaking. He wouldn't be surprised if, when he stood, he'd find a puddle of pee.

"Well done," the oxen-head said as Han shifted. Han's many eyes turned to Caden and softly stared down at him as two of his wings overshadowed Caden. It was like he was under a living, blinking shield. "Yahweh sees your faithfulness. Stand strong. Be at peace."

A hand rested on Caden's shoulder. It was a huge hand from an all-powerful being. Caden stiffened with a gasp, not with fear, but with shock. His shock eased as something flowed from Han's hand down into Caden and filled his entire body. It was warm, gentle, and steadfast.

Peace, Caden thought, his head dropping against his chest. *Raw Peace.* A tear fell from his eye. *Thank You, God.* He sat, eyes lightly closed, as his heart slowed and the tremor in his hands ebbed away. He savored the Raw Peace and was able, for just a moment, to forget the surrounding enemies and four Demons wanting his suffering. In that moment, he was home.

———

CADEN TRIED to stand upright as Luca and he rode the elevator. He was about ready to collapse. His body was spent, and he was just sick of being threatened, by a strangling Antichrist and liquid-fire-breathing Demons. When the Fiend had attacked, Caden flinched back, and the mat burned a bit, everyone noticed. How could they not? Caden was scrambling for a believable lie when Hugh started clapping. He encouraged Caden and used him as an example of how to effectively commune with Heralds. Caden hadn't said a word as he tried to catch his breath.

Caden cursed as he rubbed his throat again and tried to swallow. It was still difficult and reminded him of the Puppet who almost killed him back in the Sinai Desert. *This has been quite a day.* And it was just the morning.

He noticed Luca watching him out of the corner of his eye. "Can I ask you something?" Caden rasped.

"Of course."

"Are you a psychopath?" Luca chuckled. "Seriously, I thought you were going to kill me!"

"No," Luca said, simply shaking his head. "Just testing you."

Caden cursed again and glared at him. "Did I pass?"

Luca didn't answer for a moment, choosing his words carefully. "Not yet. But close." Caden shook his head and rubbed his throat again. After a moment of silence, Luca's head tilted to one side, and he squarely faced Caden. Caden glanced at him, a terrified thrill rushing through him.

"Grab my throat," Luca said. Caden didn't move. Luca lifted his chin and motioned to his neck. "Both hands." Caden whispered a curse as he slowly turned. He didn't move. How could he, with Luca's huge bodyguard standing beside him? "Alex," Luca said calmly. "Obey your king."

You are not my king! Caden thought, anger tightening his chest. *Yeshua is King!*

That was enough for Caden. He lunged forward, both arms outstretched. His fingers latched onto Luca's neck, his thumbs feeling his esophagus bow and arteries pulse as he squeezed. Then his hands were sliding beyond Luca's neck. Why was he tilting forward? Before he could react, Caden felt Luca's knee slamming into his guts. Caden doubled over, nearly falling, as Luca steadied him.

"You're alright," Luca said calmly. "Stand up. I barely kneed you." Caden sucked in a breath and shoved him away with a hissed curse. The elevator dinged, and the door opened. Without even looking, Luca held up a hand, and the newcomers instantly stepped back. The doors shut again. "Come." Luca said, motioning to Caden.

Fighting down every urge to flee, Caden obeyed. Luca broke down the maneuvers he just used and showed Caden how to defend against a double-handed chokehold.

"Just two moves," Luca said. "You can conquer this. Now, we'll try again slowly." Caden battled down his panic as Luca's hands wrapped around his throat again. "I will be gentle. Now, what do you do?"

They ran through the move several times, each time Caden's fear giving way to aggressive anger. The anger took over, and Caden didn't realize how hard he kneed Luca until his bodyguard moved in. Caden retreated, and Luca held up a hand, grunting as he stiffly stood upright. "Good," he wheezed, hand on his middle. "Very good. Remind me later, but I'll show you how to get out from under someone. Very good." Luca sniffed, straightened his clothes, and pushed a button to open the door.

Caden, breathing heavily again, turned away and ran the moves over in his mind. As the two made their way through headquarters, Caden couldn't help but smile. Yahweh had very weird ideas on how to prepare someone for their future. *Whatever,* Caden thought. *At least I'm not a slave like Joseph or getting swallowed by a fish like Jonah.* Now, that would suck.

He glanced around and realized they hadn't gone down, as he suspected, but up. "Where're we going?"

"Short detour. We'll go down for lunch soon." Caden fell quiet as he followed. After a moment of silence, Luca leaned closer to him. "I wanted to find your limit. The moment you break is the moment I can truly shape you into something remarkable."

The hairs on the back of Caden's neck stood on end. "You want to break me?"

"The end of you is the beginning of me. I see your full potential. You're a fighter, but undirected. I want to harness that drive, make you unstoppable."

Caden rubbed the back of his neck as he stared at the ground. He didn't know what to say. A part of him was thrilled the Antichrist saw him as a pet project, someone to

help and underestimate. The other half of him was abso-
lutely freaking out, repeating over and over that the
Antichrist wanted to break him. *God knew this would happen,*
Caden thought. *He's okey with it, so I am too.*

He took in a slow breath and nodded. "Thanks."

"You're weak." Caden gave him a sharp look, and
Luca grinned, holding up a hand. "Not your willpower,
you simply need to use the gym at home. Ask Roberto to
show you where it is. Every morning before training. The
will to fight with no power behind it is wasted resolve.
Strengthen yourself as I train you and Hugh directs your
Spirit." Caden couldn't hold back his discomfort at Hugh's
name. Luca grunted and held up a finger. "I know the
Heralds are unnerving at first. I remember myself how
shaken I was after my first encounter."

The understatement of the century.

"It will take time but let them guide you. They see the
future-"

They lose.

"-they know what's best for you. Trust in them with all
you are. Don't lean on your own understanding. The goal
is that in all your ways acknowledge them, and they will
pave a straight path for your life." Caden made himself
nod thoughtfully as his stomach turned even more. Were
those Bible verses again? This was getting out of hand.

The two fell silent, and Caden noticed this floor was a
lot nicer than the others. The flag they passed wasn't an
Israeli flag. Instead, it was a pure white banner with a
Sovereign Lion in shimmering gold. Even when displayed
so beautifully, the lion's haunting eyes followed Caden.
There were far more Sentinels on this floor than staff.
Like, a lot more. For every human, there were two
Demons too. Caden had to make himself try not to step
over and between them, knowing that most humans didn't

see them and would see his bobbing and weaving as strange.

Han's with me, Caden remembered. *More importantly, so is God-*

A Fiend's inky cloud drifted across the ceiling. Caden let out his held breath and told himself to keep going as the red eyes followed him. *Yahweh is with me and is giving me peace.* For once, Caden's heart quickened, but not as fast as other times. The internal screaming was more like a pathetic whine. Caden lifted his chin and pressed on as more flags with more Sovereign Lions passed. *Totally a den of lions.*

They entered a vaulted ceilinged room and, with one glance, Caden got the layout. Ten Sentinels stood throughout the perimeter, armed to the teeth. Maps of Israel and the world spread across the wall. One map showed the world with several arrows pointing away from Israel and landing in nearly every still inhabited country. A serious-looking Refiner stood at attention beside Hugh, who sat on an expensive-looking couch and smoked a cigar. No wait, those were the Fiends swirling around his head instead of smoke. He was actually sipping some tea, his pinky up and everything.

"Wait here." Luca said, motioning to a cushy-looking chair across the room. Caden plopped down and got out his smartphone. He started flipping through BiggieFishy, pretending to ignore everyone while listening as closely as he could.

"*Shalom*, Ally Rapham," Luca said to the Refiner, who saluted. "How's Ally Gefen and the children?" He was speaking in Hebrew, and Caden was discreetly pleased he understood every word.

"All is well, your majesty." Rapham answered in Hebrew as he gave Caden a sharp look. Luca nodded and turned to Caden with a smile. "Do you understand Hebrew?" he asked in Hebrew.

Caden snapped his head up, a blank look on his face. "Talking to me?"

Luca's charming smile grew. "Because, if you do, I will gut you." Caden's heart leapt into his throat. "I detest lying lips."

"Ah," Caden managed to stammer. "I don't know what you're saying. English please?"

Luca looked away, still smiling. "My apologies, Alex," he said in English. "You should really learn Hebrew. It's all around you now, shouldn't be too hard."

"Yeah, well," Caden muttered, settling deeper into the chair. "I'd rather focus on training instead of learning how to ask where the bathroom is." Luca waved a hand at him and returned his attention to the Refiner. Caden sniffed and refocused on the phone as he tried desperately to control his fast-racing heart. *Just stay calm, keep cool.* Internally, he cursed up a storm as his hair stood on end.

"Your majesty," Hugh said, also in Hebrew. "Who is he?"

"Nephew of Thomas Whitney of Whitney Wings."

"Hum," Hugh grunted, staring at Caden. "There's something about him... the Heralds are very... hum, I'm not sure. Their hand is heavy on him. He may make a perfect Zealot."

Rapham frowned. "I will not fight alongside Puppets." Caden fought to keep his face emotionless as his heart quickened.

"Ah," Hugh sighed. "They are not *Puppets.* I thought you were above such narrow-minded ideals. No, Zealots and, well... other *new* soldiers are the way of the future."

Luca straightened, and the two men fell silent. "Enough of the future. We have trouble today. Were more terrorist cells discovered?" he asked in Hebrew.

"Three, your majesty." Rapham said.

"Hum." Luca nodded to himself. "That officer is making a name for himself."

"Lieutenant," Rapham said. "He's been promoted."

"I admire that man," Luca said. "We need more like him."

Rapham shifted his weight, glancing at Luca. "More disabled soldiers, sire?"

Luca lifted his chin as Hugh stifled a smile. "He's uncovered five cells so far, despite his inabilities. I would choose your words carefully, Ally Refiner Rapham. He's proven his questioning tactics are nearly comparable to your own." Rapham turned away with his lips pressed tight together.

Taking a deep breath and standing taller, Luca motioned to Rapham. "What do you have for me?"

Rapham cleared his throat and stepped toward his king. "They are growing in numbers."

"How many?"

"Currently, seven thousand."

"And how many have graduated?" Caden cocked his head to one side.

"We can't be sure. We speculate thirty-five thousand now." Luca shook his head as Hugh clicked his tongue and continued sipping his tea.

"So, expect more." Hugh muttered. Luca quietly rubbed his nose and muttered something in Italian.

Who're they talking about? Caden wondered as he continued scrolling passed images of slowly restoring neighborhoods, someone with their dog, and a pretty sunset.

"What is their cause?" Hugh asked.

Rapham glanced at Luca and paused. "We believe," he paused again, "we believe some sort of uprising. Anti-kingdom activity."

Luca cocked a brow and raised his hands. "You *believe?*"

"We don't know, your majesty." Rapham everted his gaze and cleared his throat. "We do know it is said the two leaders can breathe fire."

A shot of hot aggression struck Caden's chest as his finger froze in mid-scroll. He blinked once, his mind rushing a thousand miles an hour, and forced himself to relax, act like he's just wasting time on his phone. He listened with everything he had.

"Fire, hum?" Hugh asked, sipping his tea. "There have been far more peculiar happenings since the Day of Vanishing."

Luca hardly responded as he thoughtfully drummed a finger on his chin. "Did we gather more intel about the leaders?"

"One's fifty-one," Rapham said. "Former construction worker here in Jerusalem. The other's just a kid, early twenties, and was a student in Egypt, though both are Israeli. Neither are trained, experienced, or capable."

Hugh snorted. "Obviously, they are. Look at them! Several thousand have flocked to their cause!" The room fell silent as Luca crossed his arms and started pacing the room. Caden could hear his heart pounding.

"Anti-kingdom," Luca muttered. "After all the peace and prosperity I've given to the world. After all my sacrifices." He shook his head and ran a hand over his face. He sighed and stared at the floor. He suddenly looked so tired and, genuinely, sad.

"Send in a spy, one of the rabbis." he said, standing straight again and squarely facing Rapham. "Have them enroll this week and get close to the leaders. I want to know what they like for lunch, how often they blow their nose, and who's in their family tree."

Caden's stomach clenched, imagining Ellie and the

obvious target Yohanan put on her back the moment he became a Witness. Anger against his brother-in-law rose instantly. He sniffed and scrolled through the BiggieFishie feed with a bit more force than necessary. *Knock it off*, he told himself. *I don't have time to be petty.*

"Gather more intel. Learn who our enemies are. Then," Luca paused and nodded thoughtfully. "Then we strike."

Rapham bowed his head and stepped back. "Your majesty." He marched away. As he passed Caden, he gave him a glance. It was so quick, but Caden didn't miss the murderous warning in his eyes. Caden found himself glaring back and turning away, realizing he wasn't breathing.

"Let's go." Luca said.

Caden just about rose, but realized Luca was still speaking in Hebrew. *More tests.* He continued ignoring him until Luca was standing before him. "Ready?" Caden asked with a smile.

Luca nodded. He smiled too, but his eyes were distant. "Come," he said absently, returning to English. "I'm ready for lunch."

"Sounds good." Caden hopped up and waved to Hugh. "Thank you for class, Mr. Wiltshire!" He smiled. The man raised his teacup as his face became covered by the choking cloud of Fiends.

Caden fell in step behind Luca and lifted his chin. Still surrounded by Sentinels and the Sovereign Lion's Watch, he made a post on BiggieFishie. He attached a picture he'd taken another day, one of him smiling in front of the million-dollar view from his room. The text was something stupid about how epic Jerusalem was and how lame Russia was for attacking. After the text, he left a series of emojis, as he always did, but these ones were specific.

Thumbs up. Closed eyes, smiley face.

I have information. He couldn't withhold a smile as he slid the phone into his pocket and glanced at the king. *You really shouldn't trust me,* he thought. *Your spy won't find a thing at Under Fire.* He wondered if Yohanan would use the rat for target practice. Either way, it was the first moment Caden felt like an actual, semi-capable spy.

NINETEEN
DATE NIGHT

THE REST of the day was equally exhausting. After lunch at KUS Headquarters, Luca assigned the Refiner recruits to a Giant who gave them a tour. Caden tried his best to remember Alex was accustomed to man-eaters, but his arm where Bobby Rut had pinched him kept tingling. It was like the Giant's fingers were still there, feeling Caden's flesh as he tried not to drool.

The Giant giving the tour wore the largest Sentinel uniform Caden had ever seen. He actually had a gun on his hip. It was more like a cannon with a handle. There was also a sword which, to the Giant, appeared like a normal dagger. *He's not going to eat me,* Caden reminded himself nearly a dozen times.

The headquarters was a solid place. He didn't know much, but he knew a fortress when he saw one. It was like a modern castle protecting the world's king. Halfway through the tour, screaming came from outside. Each scream was short-lived but kept on coming.

"Ah," the Giant said, laying a huge hand on his muscle-bound middle. "They found more terrorists. Shall we?" Caden's dread twisted his guts further as they neared the courtyard. Stepping out into the light of day, Caden saw a small army of Sentinels surrounding chained, kneeling men. Several were Israeli, but most weren't. They looked European.

Russians, Caden thought, a lump forming in his throat. The air smelled like raw meat.

"This is the king's justice," the Giant said with a sweep of his arm, nearly the length of Caden's body. "Justice and virtue are the foundation of his kingdom."

Caden felt cold as he stared, unable to pull his eyes away. He had seen death. There were bodies all over the place in America. The only few deaths he'd witnessed were quick, and he got out of there even quicker. Even Yohanan burning the attacking Russians had shielded him from the gore of death. He saw it now. It was all around him.

The platform he had seen earlier had three chopping blocks. A Sentinel stood by each and hefted heavy axes. Their white uniforms weren't so white anymore. The terrorists were forced to kneel and, in no particular order, be beheaded. Caden understood the drain before the platform now. A few junior Sentinels were busily disposing of the bodies as others ushered the next three terrorists onto the platform.

"The king, may he live forever, doesn't want any who choose wicked ways to die," the Giant continued, his voice pelting the air over their heads. "He wants all to choose the way of life in his New Kingdom. But. He doesn't hesitate to kill those who are obstinate in their wickedness."

Caden's vision was getting a bit fuzzy, and he realized he wasn't breathing. He finally made himself look away and saw others in the group were also having trouble. He couldn't get the images of the kneeling terrorists out of his head. The Giant had explained they were Russian allies who smuggled the enemy into the country. He detailed all the people that died while on their mission and how much suffering they caused.

Regardless, Caden had to get out of there. He couldn't stand the smell. He felt it seeped into his clothes, even walking to his bedroom in Luca's house, he thought he could still smell it. With a muttered curse, Caden finally made it to his room and shut the door. Sweet silence surrounded him. No one was talking about killing terrorists. No Sentinels watched his every move. And no Antichrists grabbed his throat.

I survived today, Caden thought, feeling his entire body aching from Luca's blows. His brain felt like mush from Hugh and the Giant's lessons. Caden leaned against the door and closed his eyes. He needed to sleep. He had to do it all over again tomorrow-

"You're a Christian." Caden took in a breath as his eyes flashed open. He turned to the small coffee table before the huge window. Someone was sitting there. Someone beautiful and fierce. Dasha tilted her head to one side as she pointed a finger at him. "Don't lie." Caden regarded her, unsure of how to answer. He was so tired. "I met your friends at Under Fire."

How did she know? His eyes narrowed as his arms crossed.

Dasha eyed his ridged posture, and her left brow lifted a bit. "Your taxi left the university? Remember?" He didn't move. Dasha shook her head as her eyes widened. "You look terrible."

"What's Under Fire?" He motioned to the room around them and his ear. "There are no bugs," she said with a wave of her hand. "I checked." She leaned back and nudged the chair beside her. Caden stumbled to it and collapsed, hearing the chair creek as he landed. He half shut his eyes and leaned his head back. He could feel Dasha's eyes on him.

"Very foolish, American brat," she muttered. "Your throat's showing. I nearly sliced it the other day."

Caden grunted and folded his hands across his chest. "Nearly." The two sat in silence as the city's light sparkled beneath them. The muffled crack of gunfire lifted, but neither stirred.

"So?" Dasha suddenly demanded.

"Hum?"

"Are you Christian?"

Caden didn't move as he thought a moment. *I need her,* he thought. *God put her here to help me.* He sniffed. "Yep."

"Another foolish thing. The only god is the king."

Caden nodded slowly. "King Yeshua." Dasha snorted. "What else did you learn?" Caden asked as he sat up and rubbed his shoulder. He didn't know what happened, but since that morning, it was tight and very unhappy.

Dasha flicked her hair as she dunked her teabag in the amber liquid. "You Christians are on a suicide mission. Foolish. All of you. Taking anyone in, teaching them from old books-"

"It's not just an old book."

"I'm talking." Caden smiled as he raised a hand. "And expecting everyone to live and die willingly for an Israeli who died hundreds of years ago. Foolish."

"Yeah, you've said that. I meant more like what did you find out about *me.*"

Dasha casually sipped her tea, but her brow arched up. It was kind of cute. "I learned you are foolish, Christian boy."

"Ah," Caden said with a nod. "Well, coming from a crazy Russian, that's not too bad. And, it looks like you still don't know my real name."

Dasha glanced at him, her mouth a tight thin line and her eyes as cold as ever. They were such a pale blue Caden had never seen before. "I'll call you Sammy." Caden blinked, remembering older Dasha calling his older self that. He suppressed a smile and nodded. Without a word, Dasha stood, shoved in her chair, and walked behind Caden. "Face forward."

Caden frowned as he turned around. "What are you-?"

"Forward!"

Caden didn't move. "Going to stab me in the back now, crazy Russian?"

"If I wanted you dead, I'd have done it last night when you wouldn't stop snoring!"

"I don't snore!"

"Oh, do you sleep with a chainsaw then? Turn around!"

Caden reluctantly obeyed and felt her grab his shoulders. "Hey, easy! What-?" He stopped talking as Dasha began messaging his sore muscles. His eyes closed as he leaned back, the tension leaving him more and more. Dasha said nothing as she continued easing his shoulders, neck, and arms. Caden was just about to fall asleep on the table when she spoke.

"I should've known you're foolish enough to be Christian," she muttered. "Anyone who saves the one trying to kill them is just..." Her voice trailed away, and Caden opened his eyes.

I did save her, didn't I? He remembered during the aerial attack, Sentinels had shot at Dasha. Rolling on her and shielding her with his body had felt natural, like that's just what a man's supposed to do. "Just what?" he prompted.

Dasha didn't answer as she tilted his head down and messaged the back of his neck. "Why?" she whispered. "You shouldn't have done that."

"You would've died."

"I was trying to kill you."

Caden didn't answer. What could he say? She was already calling him foolish; he couldn't tell her about future Dasha and future Caden roughing up Demons together. "I just had to," he sighed, "it just felt right."

"Cheesiest answer, Sammy." Dasha said as she shoved the back of his head and marched back to her chair. She gulped down her tea as Caden eased into his chair with a sigh.

"I'll tell you," he mumbled, trying not to fall asleep then and there. "Sometime. Why're you asking this? I thought you'd ask how I know your name."

He heard Dasha kick her feet up on the table and lean back. "There's no point asking questions when you won't answer."

Caden grinned. "See? I know you're a crazy Russian, but at least you're a smart one too."

"*I'm* not the dumb blond, as you Americans say."

"I'm not blond. It's fake."

"Hum. Why?"

"Alex has blond hair. Gonna tell me why anyone who knows your real name should die?"

"Wanna almost die again?"

Caden chuckled as the two fell silent. After some time, he shifted in his chair. "Wanna go on a date?"

"No."

"Wanna go on a date as a cover to exchange information?"

"Yes. Know how to do that without dying?"

"Hey, you're the one with all the training."

"I'm not getting in the crosshairs!"

"Thought you wanted to help."

"*Help* and *crosshairs* are different."

"How's tomorrow sound?"

"Sammy-"

"I'll be in the crosshairs. Don't worry, just tell me what to do."

"I'll try to pencil you in."

"It's a date then." He couldn't withhold his grin and, even with his eyes closed, could feel her glare try to burn a hole straight through him.

"Is this how you get all your girls?"

"Just the Russian assassin-types." Caden thought she gave a smart remark, but he had already fallen asleep.

THEIR DATE HAD GONE SURPRISINGLY well. Caden couldn't remember the last time he had a date. Maybe in high school before the Day of Vanishing? He couldn't really do that sort of thing while protecting his siblings from Dad and trying to survive Mama Lo and Papa's health declining. That had been a dark time.

But not now. Not deep in the Middle East, enemies on every side, while Freaks and Giants freely roamed and Caden learned how to spy from a smoking hot Russian. In their room, she told him the science of exchanging information while undercover, her expression firm and voice filled with steel. This was serious business, and Caden agreed, but it was so hard to listen as she stood there, hand on a hip, wearing a slim black dress.

She snapped her fingers in front of his eyes. "Are you listening?"

"Be aware the enemy may try to confuse, especially in the areas of intelligence cycle security and its subdiscipline counterintelligence, I heard. What'd you do, memorize the handbook or something?" Dasha fixed him a killer glare and muttered something Russian before marching out the door.

On the way to the restaurant, they took a picture, posing close together as couples do, and posted to Biggie-Fishie about date night and where they were going. *There*, Caden thought, knowing the moment he posted, Elijah

and his boys would see. *Man, this spy stuff is kind of working!*
He tried to hide how shocked he was, but he knew
she saw.

The restaurant was the nicest Caden had ever been in.
He was impressed they were able to keep such refinery,
even after the World's Crash. "All praise to the king," his
waiter had said. "He brings peace and prosperity wherever he goes. May his Sovereign Lion always watch."

Caden enjoyed his meal. Sure, he was still in character
as Alex and on the lookout for Luca's minions, but he was
also chatting with a mysterious gal who was helping him
infiltrate Yahweh's enemies. It was fun. It was exciting! A
waitress walked past, her tray of blue steak leaving a
bloody smell behind her. Caden grimaced and shifted in
his seat, images of beheaded terrorists filling his mind like
a sharp slap to the face.

And we could die at any second, he thought darkly.

As they talked, the busboy discreetly walked through
the gathering, clearing dishes as quietly as possible.
Caden's heart nearly leapt from his chest when he finally
recognized Asher. *Why is he here? He's a huge target! Luca
would string him up and make Elijah dance!* He fought back his
anger and gave a tight smile to Dasha as she talked about
her pedicure the other day. *Stupid. We need to figure this out
better!*

He noticed Asher drawing nearer the more dinner they
ate. Caden scooted back his plate and snapped his fingers
at Asher. "Boy! Come clear this mess!" Asher rushed over
and started taking his plate away.

"Babe," Dasha said. "Give him a tip."

"Why?"

"It's nice!"

"It's *my* money!"

"Babe!" Caden cursed and offhandedly held Asher
several shekels, the notes tightly folded together. "Here,

boy," Caden said. "Go get yourself something nice." Asher dipped his head and hurriedly cleared the dishes away. Caden sniffed and sipped his wine but didn't taste it. Was that it? It seemed too simple. Too quick. Earlier that night, Caden had written a coded phrase onto one of the notes: *"KUS spy. New student. This week. Rabbi."*

They had stayed for dessert and another glass of wine, which was making staying on guard difficult. They returned home, arm in arm, whispering close together with Dasha giggling and Caden's hand resting on the small of her back. Okay, he was still having a little fun. Her smile fell instantly when their room's door shut, and she quickly went to take a shower.

Caden plopped into a chair and sighed. *That went well,* he thought, a bit proud of himself.

―――――

THE WEEKS ROLLED BY, each the same as the last. Every day, at an ungodly early hour, Caden would workout then eat before Luca and he went to KUS Headquarters. At first, Caden dragged his feet getting to headquarters hours before the other Refiner recruits. His attitude changed when Luca's head of security, secretary, and bodyguard started recognizing and nodding to him, even when Luca wasn't there. Even Hugh Wiltshire and he chatted now and then. He seemed like a great guy, except for the Demons swarming around his head. They never drew too close to Caden, but he found one managed to drift behind him every time, encircling him. The Fiends never shaped into their clawed, horned forms, but those ember eyes always followed him. He nearly puked the first time, but it was shocking what becomes normal after a while.

And Demons were normal in KUS Headquarters. Caden stopped trying to keep track of how many Vipers clung to people, curbing their behavior toward darkness. Withers were as abundant as Sentinels, always adjusting the skin they wore. Sometimes, he'd see Dad storming through the hallways, which gave him pause, but he knew who it really was.

Caden didn't realize how familiar Demons had become to him until, one day, he had to walk between three Shades to keep pace with Luca. Each was within arm's reach of him, and their cold, hateful eyes followed him. He didn't even bother giving them a glance, and his stomach didn't even twitch. He remembered back in America, a year ago, when he first started being around Shades. They had surrounded him in the convenience store in that little abandoned town. Nockville? Something like that. He'd ran for his life, and he hadn't even seen them.

Guess I'm getting stronger, he thought.

He was, in every way. Luca's training drove his body to the limits. Hugh's exercises, which usually disturbed Caden, drove him closer to Yahweh instead of the darkness. At night, he'd read a few pages of the Bible. It felt like reading from a textbook and was often really boring, which made him feel bad for Yeshua. When reading about Yeshua's life, it sounded like Yeshua went through a lot of bad times to save Caden and everyone else, but it was hard to read about it.

Maybe it would've been different if the Holy Spirit were here to talk to me about it, Caden thought. It helped when he read it aloud, but Dasha didn't appreciate it too much.

"Stop trying to convert me!" she snapped one night from the bathroom as she got ready for bed.

"Reading out loud helps me understand it better."

"Oh, is that one of your tricks they teach you in your Christian school?" Caden had glared at the pages and tried to read quieter. "Someone might hear you too." Caden didn't answer, he had seen dozens of Demons cringe as he read from the Scriptures. That was one cool part of reading the Bible. They'd stop what they were doing, stare in startled bewilderment at Caden, and dart away. Some got flustered and snarled, fur bristling, or threatened a few things. Caden ignored them. He was reading about the real King.

"This is important," he told Dasha. "Spiritual armor."

She scoffed, stepping from the bathroom. A toothbrush was in her mouth, and her hair was pulled back in an uneven bun. "I don't need that."

Caden shrugged as he turned the page. "Then you'll go to Hell."

"*You* go to Hell!"

"I'm just saying." She spat out the toothpaste and ranted for a bit in Russian. Caden was very glad he had no clue what she said. After she calmed down and washed her face, she marched to bed and plopped down. "They think we're making out, not reading books."

"You'd rather do that?"

Dasha glared at him. "Read the Bible."

Caden chuckled and kept reading just loud enough for her to hear. It took a while, but she stopped complaining. He could've sworn she was listening. In time, he started listening better too. Yeah, it was boring at first, and always stayed a little textbook-like, but this was King Yeshua's life. This is what He did for Caden, and for everyone.

Whenever Caden got to the part about Yeshua dying on the cross, he had to pause. No one had died for him before, let alone a God. It was crazy. Yeshua was crazy! But He had done it. Caden was startled to realize he wanted to meet Yeshua. Never thought that would happen. *Maybe we could play baseball,* Caden thought. *Is that holy enough for You? Probably not. It would be cool though.*

Through all this, Caden felt the most value he gained was being a fly on the wall in Luca's world. Rapham never hid his distrust of Caden. No words were exchanged, but the Refiner was able to threaten prolonged agony with just a quick glance. Caden made sure to avoid him. Luca, on the other hand, didn't seem threatened by Caden in the slightest. Caden was shocked at how often Luca took him into his inner office and spoke Hebrew to his staff. Sometimes he spoke Italian, but mostly Hebrew.

By eavesdropping, and assuming a few details, Caden learned Luca's rabbi spy had failed. Either Yohanan had fried him, or what was more likely, the rabbi just stopped being a spy.

He became a Christian, Caden realized and tried to hide a smile as Rapham and Luca brainstormed another way to infiltrate Under Fire. Caden's suspicions were confirmed when he happened to pass headquarters' courtyard during another round of executions and noticed a rabbi among the Russians and few Israelis. He stopped and stared, knowing this was the former spy. He was a Christian, at least. While all the other terrorists cursed, shook, shouted, begged, and bargained, he alone was quiet. He didn't seem bothered at all as he knelt and placed his neck on the chopping block.

Caden had to look away, his heart racing and fingertips getting cold. *He wasn't a terrorist,* he thought. *He did betray Luca though. But still… he wasn't a terrorist!* To make matters worse, Luca had a media team covering the executions and airing it on TV. It was on nearly every news channel. They were always short, little clips, not revealing too much but enough to get the idea, as the anchorman always praised the king for capturing more enemies and keeping the world safe and at peace. *Peace,* Caden scoffed. *They don't even know what peace really is.*

The repetition of the days was interrupted when Caden followed Luca and Rapham through the higher levels of headquarters. He was scrolling through Biggie-

Fishie again, as was his pastime, while intently listening to their Hebrew. They were talking about the Russians' attack across Israel and which enemy forces were being crushed. It sounded like a slaughter.

"We are driving them back," Rapham said. "Our allies have suffered great losses though."

"This is war." Luca said.

"China was invaded after us. The UK is half on fire. A third of Italy have become refugees with nowhere to go."

At the mention of Italy, Luca fell quiet. "How far are we from launching Kingdom's Peace?" Caden blinked, remembering they had mentioned that before. What had it been again?

"Yosef's dead, your majesty."

"What?"

"Died in a shooting last week."

"Why wasn't I informed?"

"Your majesty, you were." Luca groaned as they passed a detachment of Sentinels. A few Shades were in the ranks, and a Sentinel or two looked like their faces were on wrong.

It's a humanitarian project, Caden remembered suddenly, ignoring the Withers. *Of course, the Antichrist would do one of those.*

"Who else could head up the operation?" Luca asked.

Rapham was quiet. "Everyone capable had been assigned to the war, giving relief to the front lines."

Luca muttered Italian and shook his head. "Keep looking. If we can't find someone who qualifies or is experienced, we must assign someone loyal to the New Kingdom. And who has attention to detail. And a drive to work and achieve. And a calling to the truth." Luca muttered something again and ran his fingers through his hair. The two fell quiet as they reached the elevators. Luca kept looking through his stack of papers. His page-turning became a bit more aggressive with each page.

He's real upset, Caden thought, his hair standing on end. With more muttered Italian, Luca turned away from the document and sighed. One paper drifted to the floor and Caden stooped to grab it. Luca held out his hand, but Caden froze, his eyes fixed on the page. There was a picture of the world and several arrows pointed away from Israel to various countries. Though he couldn't read Hebrew, he could guess what it detailed.

Kingdom's Peace. He realized the same image, far bigger, was in Luca's inner office. As he stared, an idea sprung to life without warning. It was a hair-brained idea, but most of Yahweh's ideas seemed to go in that direction. Swallowing the hard lump in Caden's throat, he handed the map back to Luca.

"What's that?" He asked in English.

"Just a humanitarian project."

"Oh, nice! Those really work. I saw some back in America. *I* didn't need help, but those others sure did. When's that starting up?"

Luca didn't answer as he handed the papers to Rapham and sighed. "Not anytime soon. Our head processer just died."

"How?"

"Shot to death, no doubt by anti-kingdom terrorists."

Caden forced back a grimace, wondering if Luca suspected Under Fire for the shooting. *That's ridiculous!* He fell silent, the hair-brained idea taking over his thoughts again. His chest tightened with unease, and he knew he had to just spit it out before his stomach coiled too much and he couldn't move. "What's the job?"

"Oh, just filtering through the volunteers. Most are genuine, but some have ulterior motives. Especially now if someone wants to get to another country quick."

Like a bunch of Christians wanting to get shipped all over the world and tell people about Yeshua coming back soon.

"Do you have someone to organize the flights too? They're flying right, no boats or anything?"

Luca finally turned and stared at Caden. "Speak what's on your mind."

Here we go.

Caden took a deep breath. "I could fill that role."

Luca's eyes narrowed as Rapham laughed. "Do you know anything about humanitarian work?"

You just said they don't have to have experience, Caden thought. "I know what I needed when I was captured, in a foreign country, running for my life. Isn't that who humanitarians help?" Luca didn't answer as Rapham shook his head.

"Don't give man's work to a child." Rapham said in Hebrew.

"Besides," Caden continued, trying to ignore Rapham. "You know I learn quick, and you keep saying you want to unlock my full potential. So, give me something of value to do." Caden stepped closer and knew what he had to say. It was disgusting and went against everything he stood for, but it had to be done.

"I just want to serve you," he said. "I believe in the New Kingdom and the protection under the Sovereign Lion's Watch. I believe in *you*." Luca continued staring at Caden, and his chin slowly lifted. "Please," Caden said. "My king. Let me share with others what you have shared with me."

"Which is?"

"Peace. Purpose. A cause to live for that's bigger than myself. A reason to fight." Luca's brows knit together with thought as Caden held his gaze. "Besides," he added. "You'll use Whitney Wings to ship everyone out, right?" Luca nodded. "I can help there too, a lot more than anyone else. I'm the only Whitney on this side of the world, after all."

Rapham shook his head and started to say something, but Luca held up his hand. "Are you certain, Alex? This will be unlike anything you've done before."

All of this is unlike what I've done before, Caden thought as he grinned. "I just want to serve."

Luca stared at him a moment longer and turned away. "I will think on it." he said.

Caden's smile grew, and he turned back to his phone, his heart hammering in his chest. *Please say yes,* he thought. *How else can I send nearly a hundred thousand Christians all over?* They said nothing as they rode the elevator down. Caden could see Rapham had plenty he wanted to say, but wisely bit his tongue. Caden felt his killer stare stab into him more than once. *Don't look at him! Don't look!* He felt he'd burst into flames under that stare. *Does he have a Fiend in him or something?*

Before the elevator doors opened, Luca turned to Rapham. He lowered his voice, but Caden barely caught his Hebrew words. "How many more human hearts did we receive?" Caden nearly dropped his phone.

"Fifty-seven."

Luca nodded and took a slow breath, his chest puffing. "Splendid."

Rapham turned away and sniffed gruffly. "Your majesty," he said, equally as quiet. "Are you certain this is wise? Freaks are not known for their military abilities." Caden stopped breathing.

"They aren't Freaks, Rapham," Luca said, laying a hand on his shoulder. "They are the new soldier."

Caden's eyes widened as he struggled to keep calm. He forced himself to keep scrolling through the phone's feed, but his face felt different. He wouldn't be surprised if it was pale. *What does that mean?* He tried not to shiver as the elevator opened and they followed Luca to their next agenda.

As they walked, Caden glanced at a flag. The Sovereign Lion stared back at him, never blinking, always watching. Caden suddenly thought of something Elijah had said, something about the enemy being prowling lions, looking for someone to devour. *Who'll you devour next?*

The Sovereign Lion kept silent. Caden glanced around to the dozens and dozens of Sentinels and wondered if each white-cladded human would be replaced by armed Freaks. His hair stood on end. *Raw Peace,* he thought and reminded himself Han was close, and Yahweh was with him. And so were the Demons. Oh, and the Antichrist too, and soon, Freaks.

TWENTY

THIS SUCKS BAD

CADEN WALKED arm-in-arm with Dasha down a busy market street. Even though gunfire and the occasional explosion pelted above the street's bustle, commerce continued as usual. More members of the Israeli Defense Force walked the streets, hand on their weapons and head on a swivel. Now and then, the roads were pelted with small craters, but people just walked around them. Everyone moved quickly as though on a mission, wanting to find their wares and get home.

People passed on every side as venders squished against the surrounding buildings, shouting their wares. The most random array of merchandise was laid out before them; wine bottles lined in a row next to a shop of herbs and flowers. Potent spices piled high in baskets were beside a fruit vender. Fish and other meats sizzled on huge grills across from clothes strung on lines between bowls of jewelry. Mothers quickly walked with their children, plastic bags crinkling as they swung from their arms, and bikers walked their bikes through the throng. It was loud. It was tight. It was hot. It was perfect for meeting with Caden's handler.

It better not be Asher, Caden thought. It was, and Caden was instantly angry. The tall, well-built Israeli was looking over peppers and tomatoes.

"Oh, these look nice." Dasha said and dragged him over beside Asher. The three completely ignored one another as Dasha talked on and on about random stuff Caden knew she cared little about. He was grateful she didn't blab like this when she was just being herself. "I mean, just look at this place!" She turned all around, smiling ear to ear. "It's perfect!"

Perfect... Caden blinked, slowly pushing aside his anger and remembering that meant something. *Right! The coast is clear!*

"Babe, get some tomatoes, some real good ones," Dasha said, scooting closer to him. "I'll make us something tonight, but right now, there's a dress that's calling for me." She gave him a peck on the cheek and strolled to a shop across the road a few paces away. Caden turned back to the tomatoes and knew she was standing lookout to watch his back. A muscle flexed along his jaw as he stepped closer to Asher.

"Having fun?" Asher muttered.

"Stop coming to meet me."

"Nice to see you too."

"Send someone less important."

"We're all important-"

"Wrong. If Luca had you, he'd make our Abba do whatever he wants."

"You're surrounded by the lions," Asher muttered. "Maybe *you* shouldn't be in so deep."

"Asher-"

"What do you have for me?"

Caden cursed under his breath and told himself to calm down. He selected a few tomatoes as he told Asher about the humanitarian workforce Luca was organizing and how Caden could get Under Fire graduates sent across the world. The day before, Luca had agreed Caden could take the position. Caden didn't have to fake his excitement for that.

"Do you pick the humanitarians or something?" Asher asked.

"I will. I'll be interviewing them and helping organize flights."

"That's odd."

"Luca's orders. He's getting suspicious."

Asher raised a brow as he put another pepper in his bag. "Are you blown?"

"Don't worry about me. Have your people start volunteering. They'll be going all over the world, like we wanted."

"You're the only interviewer?"

"One of ten. Pray they all come to me. If not, Yahweh can figure it out; it's His mission anyways. I'll tell you what we're looking for too. Watch BiggieFishie posts."

"How'll you know who's from Under Fire?"

"Their shoes." Asher fell silent as he shuffled a step away and pretended to inspect something. "The top laces cross like usual, but the bottom two just go straight across." Caden grabbed another tomato as Asher took way to long finding his wallet.

"That's weak." Asher finally whispered.

"Do it."

"Whose bright idea was that?"

"Her's."

"And she is?"

"One of us."

"Christian?"

"Not yet."

"Then, how is she one of us?"

"She is, alright."

"Trust her?"

"Yes." Caden blinked, stunned he said that so quickly. Asher found his wallet and slowly took out shekels. "Questions?" Caden muttered.

"How are you holding up?"

"Doesn't matter."

Asher actually huffed a gruff laugh. "You look horrible. Your chin's messed up. You're all black and blue. You're buffer though." Caden didn't answer. "Ellie's fine," Asher continued. "Misses you. You should come and-"

"No." Caden didn't mean to snap at him but couldn't help it. "I," he rubbed the back of his neck. "I can't let my guard down. I can't relax. Things are heating up." Asher paid the vender and stepped back. "Get ready to move Under Fire," Caden said as they passed. "Luca will probably attack. I'll let you know when I know more."

Asher took out a handkerchief and blew his nose. "We win, *achi*." he whispered.

Caden suddenly felt they were standing shoulder to shoulder again and facing House Whitney Giants with just a shoe and a spear. "We win, *achi*." he whispered, standing straighter. Without another word, Asher walked through the crowd and was gone. Caden continued looking through tomatoes, but he hardly felt the vegetables in his hands. Homesickness struck his chest. He took a sharp breath and rigidly paid for the tomatoes.

He marched back to Dasha and tried to go along with the tourist-like vibes he thought Alex would do about now. Instead, all he could think of was his Abba and *achi*, his brother-in-law, and beloved sister, all somewhere else. He just wanted to be home. *Someday,* he told himself. *Someday we'll all be home with King Yeshua. But today is another battle.*

CADEN WAS SEEING DOUBLE. He yawned and rubbed his eyes, tempted to lay his head down and catch a few winks. He flexed his hand, which had stopped cramping and was now stuck in a clenched, tight-fingered position. The pen slipped from his grasp, and he didn't bother grabbing it again. Moshe, who sat right next to him, chuckled. "Not an office guy?"

"And you are?" Moshe scoffed, rubbing his own sore wrist.

Luca had cleared out nearly the entire first floor of KUS Headquarters for Kingdom's Peace. Caden, Moshe, and eight others were responsible for talking to each volunteer and, as Luca said, organizing the sheep from the goats. "The goats are bad" he had to clarify, seeing Caden's confusion.

"Oh. Alright. Why goats?"

"They don't obey very well."

Of course.

Caden and the other interviewers had gone through an entire week learning the specifics of what Luca classified as a righteous humanitarian ally. It was lengthy, but understandable. Trustworthy, loyal to the New Kingdom, willing to die for the king, a heart for those in need, and a passion to see the king's peace taken throughout the world. Caden couldn't help but marvel at how similar it all sounded to Under Fire's motives too. There were those slight differences though, one said the king was the modern savior of a broken world, and the other knew the King as Yahweh's one and only Son.

After training, and Luca himself pretending to be a volunteer and listening to how each interviewer asked questions, they were ready to begin. They had to wear Refiner uniforms, which meant Caden had to ignore half his brain screaming at him not to dress like the ones who slaughtered his brother. Technically, common Sentinels had shot Trace, but the Refiner uniform still made Caden feel like a traitor. He tried not to think of Trace or what he'd think seeing Caden sitting there, working for the Antichrist, dressed in their white, pure lies.

I'm working for Yahweh, he told himself. *This is what He wants, so just shut up and do it.*

On top of that, Sentinels stood guard between new Israeli flags, the Sovereign Lion watching all. Between all the enemy eyes was Rapham. Caden watched his every move out of the corner of his eye. He kept pacing behind the five tables set up around the room, sitting two interviewers each, and monitoring progress.

No, Caden realized. *He's looking for people not loyal to Luca, who's just trying to get in and cause trouble. He'll get them. Man, he's like a panther ready to pounce.* Every time he drew close, Caden's hair stood on end and his throat felt constricted.

Especially when someone from Under Fire came. He saw at least three within the first half hour. Each wore some type of laced shoe, some sneakers, boots, even a pair of sandals, and each had the unique lace crossing. It did seem a bit weak, but it was working. Only five had made it to Caden's seat, but he saw everyone was given clearance to continue being processed. His unease calmed a bit, seeing, very slowly, they were winning. Somehow, he kept it together, even with Rapham watching, and kept asking the same several questions to the flow of people. And there were a lot of people.

It was late in the afternoon, and volunteers for Kingdom's Peace had started coming in early that morning. There were far more than Caden thought. Though the Russian's attack was gradually getting pushed back, the city, and most of Israel, was still recovering. And yet, with houses blown this way and that and bombers in the streets, people were still volunteering for humanitarian work. He mentioned it to Moshe when there was, finally, a lull in volunteers.

"Ah, yes," Moshe said. "My faith in humanity is slowly restoring."

Caden frowned as he nodded. "Hum."

Moshe groaned as he sat back and rubbed his chin. "You disagree?"

"I just…" Caden fell quiet. He couldn't stop thinking about Trace and Nathaniel. He swore he heard dogs barking somewhere in the building. He shook his head and shifted, not wanting to give himself away.

"Ah," Moshe sighed. "That sucks bad." Caden glanced at him, and Moshe nodded. "I get that."

Caden's eyes narrowed to a cold glare. "I didn't even tell you anything."

"Ah," Moshe shrugged. "I know that pain. It's deep. I have it too. Or I did."

Caden turned away, cursing under his breath. Was he that easy to read? No, he couldn't be. If he was, he'd be dead long ago! *It's the suit,* he thought. *It's shaking me up too much.* Caden took in a sharp breath and sat back. The two fell silent for a time.

"Just don't let it take over." Moshe said.

"Hum?"

"The pain. Don't let it make you a monster. It's crazy how that can happen." Caden slowly nodded and pictured Nathaniel's face. It wasn't how Caden remembered it, but black and blue and nearly falling apart as he screamed and-

Caden closed his eyes, knowing Yahweh wouldn't want him to think of such things. *But the wicked should die. Nathaniel should die!*

"The pain just takes over," Moshe said. "All you feel is just," he made a fist on the table, "hot. Like, like-"

"Like a bloodthirsty wolf wanting to rip something apart."

"Yeah! It sucks bad. But, that's life."

"Yep." Caden felt his heart quicken. He crossed his arms and felt his nails digging into his palms. This wasn't what he should be thinking about; he had to focus! He couldn't stop thinking about Nathaniel. About Trace, staring wide-eyed, as his blood discolored the leaves around him.

"I had a, a friend," Caden muttered. "He was murdered in front of me."

Moshe cursed and shook his head. "Older or younger?"

"Younger."

"That's worse. You feel responsible and all that."

"I do!"

"Ah, sucks bad."

Caden swallowed the hard lump in his throat as his hands itched to feel Nathaniel's throat. Thanks to Luca, Caden knew a few more ways to kill someone than he had a year ago. He also didn't have to pretend people were just baseballs to hit anymore too. *If only I could go back,* he thought. *I'd string him up and-*

He made himself stop there, his heart beating with force. Heavy footsteps fell behind them and a shiver ran up Caden's spine, knowing Rapham was getting close. Somehow, both young men got even quieter as the Refiner sauntered behind them. Caden could almost feel Rapham's gaze leaping from the pages before them to the back of his head. *He doesn't see I'm a spy,* Caden thought, but felt himself bracing anyways. It wasn't until Rapham walked past did Moshe clear his throat and Caden let out a breath. They glanced at each other, both trying to mask their unease.

"Heard he was a guerrilla in Africa when the king found him." Moshe muttered, and Caden's brows rose.

"That makes sense. He's a creepy guy."

"Heard he was given the lead Russians who disarmed the Iron Dome. He and another Refiner." Caden glanced at Moshe. "Heard there was nothing left to bury."

Caden cursed, drawing his crossed arms tighter across his chest. "That's a waste," he whispered. "They probably knew something important."

"Ah, he got all that info first." Moshe sniffed gruffly and lifted his chin. "Serves them right. Everyone needs to stop attacking us."

"Which Refiner helped him?"

"Ah… I don't know his name. A lieutenant."

Him again, Caden thought, remembering Luca mentioning the capable Refiner to Rapham. *Must be quite a guy.* He didn't answer as he thought of Rapham. He, thankfully, had never spoken to the man directly. He wasn't surprised he interrogated prisoners and squeezed until nothing was left. The Sentinels dipped their heads to him. *Why's he loyal to Luca?* Caden thought. *Maybe he's not. Maybe Luca's holding something over him. Whatever. He does Luca's dirty work. Can't be the 'king' of peace with bloody hands. I'm totally surrounded, aren't I?*

Caden closed his eyes and rubbed the back of his head. A story Mama Lo told them came to mind, something about a Christian guy who wouldn't obey the king. He got thrown into a den of lions too. David? Daniel? Something like that. *What had happened to him?* Caden blinked as he thought, trying to draw up the countless stories Mama Lo wouldn't stop telling them. Now, he was grateful.

Yahweh shut the lion's mouths, Caden remembered. *Well, I see the lions. Can You shut their mouths too?*

"Temani was ten," Moshe said and sniffed roughly.

Caden shifted and gave him a quick look. "We played soccer on the street in front of our home."

"Yeah?" Caden said as Moshe cracked his knuckles. "Brother?"

Moshe nodded and Caden cursed. "Our apartment collapsed. He didn't-" Moshe trailed off and turned away.

Caden nodded as he also looked the other way. *That's right,* he thought. *Hugh mentioned that during the creepy, Demon lesson. So, he was right about that.* The two fell quiet again as their arms crossed and fists clenched. Their jaws were set as both remembered screams and cries from memories they longed to forget. *Sucks bad,* Caden thought. *I like this guy. He seems real.* They said nothing until another volunteer headed their way. They both straightened and leaned forward, ready to get to work again.

"Hey, um," Caden muttered before the volunteer sat. "Wanna spar after this?"

"Only if you want to limp tomorrow."

"Bring it."

"I swear, I'm more wolf than you."

Caden glared at him and saw the mischievous gleam in his eyes. "You're going to eat your words. And my fists." Both grinned and snapped into kind, loyal ally-moods as the volunteer sat. She was pretty and young and, when her legs crossed, Caden noticed her flats had laces. *Crisscross, crisscross, and straight across,* Caden thought, and he gave her a big smile.

———

CADEN YAWNED as he grabbed his bag, waved goodnight to Moshe, and left the showers. They had gone straight to sparring once the last volunteer had been interviewed. Moshe hadn't been kidding, he had tried to make Caden limp until the next day. There had been a few close calls where Caden was actually grateful Luca was so hard on him. *Maybe this'll be good for something,* he thought. *Will things get worse around here? Will the war come to me?* Of course, it would. He'd be stupid to think otherwise.

He'd overheard Luca on the phone that morning. He had been speaking Italian, but Caden knew when he said 'Mizrahi'. It had been like an ice bath to Caden, and he instantly hoped he was doing enough to save his friends and family. *They're not my responsibility,* he had told himself. *God's taking care of them. Besides, most of us Christians die before Yeshua comes back anyways.* That left his chest tight and his heart pounding.

Caden shook his head as he stumbled through headquarters. He had called one of Luca's several drivers to take him home and was looking forward to the couch, pillows, and soft blankets. *And Dasha.* He blinked and frowned, realizing he wanted to see her. He didn't really have a reason, he just liked being with her. He actually caught her smiling at him the other day. He didn't even remember what she had been talking about, that smile was far too distracting.

Caden grinned to himself as he reached for the door and ignored the Sentinels standing watch all around. *I'm glad she tried to kill me,* he thought. *Well, not that part.* His chin was finally one piece again, but it was still tender. On the bright side, it taught him to tuck his chin while sparring. *Maybe I should tell her my real name sometime soon. I like how she calls me Sammy though.*

"Alex Whitney!"

Caden's heart sank as the voice filled the huge room. He withheld a curse and glanced over his shoulder. A junior Sentinel quickly walked across the hall, his face stern and urgent. "What?"

"You've been summoned to join his majesty."

Caden sighed, his hand, still resting on the door's handle, dropped to his side. "Doing what?"

"Please, sir, follow me."

Caden stared at him, his fatigue battling with the alarms going off in his head. "Where are we going?"

"Sir." The junior Sentinel motioned back into KUS Headquarters, and Caden sighed.

He slowly followed, feeling his feet were heavier than before. He followed the Sentinel to Luca's floor. As the elevator doors opened with a ding, Caden took in a breath and mentally donned his spiritual armor. He wished he had the fiery, swirling armor his future self wore, but he knew Bible verses and faith would do for now. *I guess that's all God knows I need.*

The doors opened and three Vipers crawled in. One Wither shed a skin, tossing the loose flesh on the ground and standing there like a shriveled, undefined corpse. A few Shades stood in the corner, their long tails flicking as they whispered together. *We win*, Caden reminded himself as they continued to Luca's office.

Several people were seated around Luca's desk. Caden quickly glanced over them and found most were bodyguards or Sentinels. A few looked like military types, their posture at full attention and attitude disciplined. Rapham stood among them, but there was an obvious gap between him and the others. A woman in a business dress stood close to the bodyguards, her glasses slipping from her nose as she wrote on a clipboard. An inky cloud indicated Hugh, who stood calmly chatting with an attendant, both oblivious to the Fiend's glowing eyes.

At the center was Luca and three older men in expensive-looking suits. They were talking in Hebrew very quickly and excitedly, Caden could hardly translate it. "Over three hundred… transplanted through the last six months... seventy-three percent success rate... stand up, like men."

Caden stood at a distance and waited. He couldn't help noticing a few Shades had joined. Oh, and a handful of Vipers; their slithering made the walls and ceiling look alive. *And those guards are Withers,* Caden thought, noticing one man's eye dropping a bit too much. The Demons clustered together and whispered, their heads lowered, and their mouths curled back into smiles. He blinked, realizing the Demons were waiting too. Caden lifted his chin as a shiver ran down his spine. *What's going on?* He shuffled his feet, telling himself not to run.

"Ah! There he is!" Caden's gaze darted to Luca, who resorted back to English, as he waved him over. "Come! Meet our distinguished guests!"

Smile, Caden told himself as he walked over, nearly stepping over a Viper and around a Shade.

"This is Ally Alex Whitney," Luca said as the guards parted for Caden. He felt his heart quickening as the gap instantly closed behind him. He was trapped. "He's been training with our new Refiners."

"Refiners, eh?" one of the older men asked in English as he studied Caden. "Are you related to the Whitneys in America?"

Caden nodded. "My uncle is Thomas Whitney."

Luca cleared his throat and stepped closer to Caden. "Lad, this is Prime Minister Isaac Lapid."

Caden's eyes widened as he stepped back and quickly dipped his head. "Sir! I had no idea! Um-Prime Minister."

The older man nodded, his dark eyes still scrutinizing. "Is he the reason why your Kingdom's Peace volunteers are flying out a few weeks before schedule?" Caden blinked and glanced at Luca; he hadn't known.

"The name Whitney has weight and power," Luca said. "Especially under the Sovereign Lion's Watch."

"Impressive," Isaac muttered. "Someone so young with such sway. Is that wise, my king?"

A coldness settled across Caden as he fought to keep his face impassive. *My king,* he thought. *The Prime Minister just called the Antichrist my king. This is bad.*

"Young Alex has excelled in whatever field I've placed him in." Luca lay a hand on Caden's shoulder and smiled. "He is one of the best recruits, and I know his potential will complement the power House Whitney has." Caden looked down, not knowing what to do. A part of him swelled with pride, his teacher had full faith in him, while the other half wanted to shove the Antichrist's hand off his shoulder.

"That's why I've summoned him," Luca continued. "I want the honest opinion of our New Kingdom's youth."

Isaac's brows rose. "I assume he knows nothing."

Luca shook his head. "He is as oblivious as civilians will be in two weeks." Isaac chuckled as the two older men shook their heads. Caden noticed the lone woman shot him a pitied look. *Oh, God, help me. What's Luca doing?* His throat bobbed, easily remembering Luca's hands squeezing the life out of him all in the name of testing his limits.

It's probably another test, he told himself as his heart quickened and his hands tingled with the urge to fight. *Don't show any fear.* He squared his shoulders and lifted his chin, his face washing off emotion as he glanced at Luca. They stared at one another, and Caden could see the glimmer in Luca's eyes. Caden's stomach twisted with dread.

Isaac grunted. "Have you broken this one yet?" he asked. A shadow darkened Caden's stare.

"No," Luca said quietly as his smile grew. "He was brought overseas by kidnappers after all."

"Interesting. Well, gentlemen? Your majesty?"

"Yes." Luca said, finally turning away from Caden. He led them from his office. Caden fell in step behind the Prime Minister and his men, but felt the bodyguards close around him. They wouldn't let him leave their circle of protection. *Or captivity,* he thought, seeing Sentinels walking among them. Or were those Shades?

They went down an elevator longer than Caden thought possible. He glanced up, seeing the numbers going down and down, and suddenly were negative numbers. A muscle in his jaw flexed as he tried to prepare himself. For what? *Could be anything.*

Nothing could've prepared him for what was waiting.

TWENTY-ONE
BECOMING FLESH

AFTER ALL CADEN had been through, he realized no one had put a bag over his head. He hadn't thought much of it, but now, trying to breathe while the dark fabric kept sticking to his lips and hid every trace of light, he wished it had happened before. If he was familiar with it, the bag wouldn't freak him out so much.

Knock it off, he told himself as someone held his arm and pulled him around. *They're not going to kill you. They don't know you're a Christian. Oh, God, help them not to know. Is this where Rapham questions people?*

They were walking down a long hallway. He could hear their dozens of shoes clicking along the smooth tile. The place smelt like earth and was a bit cold, like a basement. There were several security checkpoints, and he could hear the clink of Sentinel armor and weapons. There were a few dogs even. That was nice. It nearly sent Caden over the edge, and he had to keep telling himself Nathaniel wasn't down here.

Luca just said I wasn't ready to see where we are, Caden told himself. *I'm not ready. Not ready for any of this!*

They entered a room with machines humming and the

sharp smell of rubbing alcohol and... what was that other smell? Kind of like rot or something. Blood. Caden's throat bobbed as they kept moving. Luca and Isaac were talking with a squeaky-voiced, jumpy guy that talked so fast Caden wondered when was the last time he'd spoken to anyone. They kept talking about surgery, something with the chest... open heart surgery with volunteers? No, not volunteers. Something else. Something unconventional, as Isaac had said.

"I understand," Luca had said in Hebrew. "But think of the force behind this new breed of soldier! Nothing would stop us!"

That really helped Caden calm down too. It wasn't until they finally stopped did the bag come off Caden's head. They were in a small, featureless room. There were no chairs or tables. Only one door and a huge window. Caden blinked in the light and leaned back, feeling like a hostage. "Alright, Alex?" Luca asked.

Isaac grunted. "He's already afraid."

"I've been kidnapped, Prime Minister," Caden said, trying not to cop an attitude and failing miserably. "This is way too similar to that horrible experience."

That's not how you speak to a government guy! Caden turned away under Isaac's dark glare and fell quiet.

Isaac glanced at Luca. "He shouldn't be here." he muttered in Hebrew.

"I need his opinion," Luca said and stepped toward the window. "Alex, stand by me." Caden forced himself to obey, his skin crawling with dread. "All I need from you, Alex, is to watch. Watch and tell me what you think."

Caden nodded and faced the window, realizing it was a two-way mirror. Beyond was a large room with floodlights hanging overhead and a drain in the center of the floor. The room was a contrast of sudden white light and dark shadows, but Caden could see the drain was surrounded by dark liquid. All these facts flew through Caden's mind as his gaze fixated on the individuals standing under the lights. Two men, legs spread shoulder's width apart and head on a swivel, wore Sentinel armor and a dagger was on their sides. They firmly grasped a heavy machine gun as the belt of ammo coiled at their feet.

Caden blinked, staring at the gun, and knew no normal man could hold such a huge gun without support. *Those aren't men,* he realized. *They're Giants.* The Giants slowly turned in a circle, staring at each wall. Caden's eyes narrowed, and he noticed doors were in all four walls.

"I'm very eager to see your new soldier, your majesty." Isaac was saying in Hebrew.

"I'm eager to hear your feedback." Luca said.

"I must ask, however, are the new soldiers about to die? Two armed Giants against four soldiers who, as I understand, have just recovered from surgery, sounds like a disaster." Luca didn't answer. "Have you heard of anyone facing *two* Giants and living?"

Luca took in a breath and lifted his chin. "These aren't normal soldiers. These are *my* soldiers."

Isaac turned away and nodded. "Well, the people's moral needs to lift, and once they see your creations, they cannot withhold their loyalty."

"Yes," Luca said, his gaze fixated on the Giants. "They are fearfully and wonderfully made. The people will see my workmanship is marvelous. All who receive my creation receive me. To those who believe in my name, I will give the right to be my allies in this growing New Kingdom."

Hugh nodded as he closed his eyes and lay a hand on his chest. "Let it be so." he muttered.

The Demons who had followed them were nodding and chatting excitedly together. Caden forced his breathing to be steady as his guts coiled on themselves.

Without another word, Luca raised a hand. In the room beyond, Caden saw each of the four doors swing open. The Giants widened their stance and hunched low as the great guns came up. They turned back-to-back; eyes dark with murder.

From each of the doors walked a... a something. Caden blinked several times, his brain desperate to understand. He couldn't. It wasn't right. *That's a Freak,* he finally came up with. *But it walks like a person.*

Four beasts stepped into the room. They were tall, and each step showed rippling muscle beneath sandy fur. Their feet were huge paws, each with dark claws. Their hands were paws too, sort of. No, they had fingers. Fingers? Something like fingers but clawed too. They walked with their backs stooped and round ears directed at the Giants. Long, furry snake-things hung behind them, waving back and forth. They were fuzzy at the ends and never held still... tails, that was a type of tail. One of the beasts had far more fur than the others, a huge, russet mess all bunched around its head, under its chin, and laying across its shoulders. Each walked on their hind legs.

Without pausing, they started circling the Giants. One pulled back its lips, showing a great, red mouth and fangs longer than Caden's fingers. The fur stood up on the backs of their necks, and the tails whipped about even more. Caden felt himself stepping away from the glass. His mouth was open as his eyes bugged from his head.

The Giants stopped and stared at the monsters. Even at a distance, Caden saw all color leave the Giants' faces as one shook his head. Caden's breath quickened as the beasts' muscles bunched for action. Their red mouths opened wide, and a deafening roar made Caden flinch back with fists raised. He didn't even feel himself slam into the person behind him. He blinked slowly, finally grasping what he was seeing.

Lions, he thought. *Those Freaks are lions that walk like men. What has Luca done?*

Without warning, the Giants opened fire. It was like thunder and lightning were trapped in the room. Each cacophony shook Caden to the core. The person he slammed into nudged him away, sending him closer to the glass again. Caden nearly sent a fist into their face but stopped just in time. *Raw Peace,* he thought, staring at the mere glass separating him from flying bullets.

Sparks flew as one of the lights was shot down. Shadowed bodies leapt across the fire blasting from the guns. Abruptly, one gun stopped firing. In the faded light, Caden saw one of the Giants was down. Two lions pinned him down as his legs kicked wildly. All Caden could see was the kicking tremble, and finally, the legs lay still. The lions continued shredding their prey.

The second Giant backed into a corner and fired at anything that moved. It didn't matter. The lions were as swift as Shades. The male lion skirted low on all fours beneath the gun barrel and leapt, landing on the Giant's chest and face. There was screaming. The gunfire stopped. Caden gasped and turned away as the second pair of lions ripped and tore. A steady stream of dark liquid trickled down the drain.

"Just breathe," he heard Luca whisper in English. "They are the soldiers of the future, as are you. It is my wish that Refiners and these soldiers will fight side by side."

"What?" Caden sputtered. "With *them*?"

Luca nodded and gave Caden a gentle smile. "Trust me, Alex. Our enemies must feel my wrath."

We're all dead. A cold numbness spread over Caden, and he felt like he was falling into himself. He blinked slowly, noise getting muffled as his head felt heavy. *All of us, consumed under fangs and claws. There will be no escape nor salvation. I have given allegiance to the weaker side. There is no future with God.* Caden's eyes narrowed. What was brushing his cheek? As though in a daze, Caden slowly glanced beside him, rubbing his cheek.

Standing shoulder to shoulder was a Shade. It towered over him, its white fur out of place in the shadowed and bloody room. It casually stood with bald, clawed hands behind its back as its long tail circled around Caden. It slowly turned its head and regarded Caden, half its face bitten away. Caden stared up at Doeg without moving. He thought of stepping back, but what was the point? He was completely surrounded by enemies at all times. What's one more Shade?

"I've orchestrated a little game for you," Doeg said, its audible voice hushed to a rasping whisper. "You aren't utterly surrounded by foes yet. When you are, we shall play who-will-break-Caden-first. Catchy, isn't it?"

Caden couldn't answer as he faced the thick glass. The lion Freaks were finally done destroying their prey. They were walking about the room on all fours. Caden briefly glanced at one of the Giants. He didn't have a chest anymore. Or face. Caden flinched and turned away. He felt Doeg stoop closer, the Shade's whiskers brushing his hair. "In time, that will be your beloved Lil El." Caden didn't respond, but his heart leapt into his throat. "How sad." Caden couldn't feel a thing. No emotion. His senses even were having trouble feeling. He was slipping away-

No. He lifted his chin and made fists. *I can't hide from this.*

"There is wisdom in hiding."

Stop being a coward!

"You are being realistic."

If I die, I die for God! If I live, that'll be a miracle, so either way, I win. I win! Do you hear me, Doeg, I win! Not you! Caden stepped away from Doeg, and because there was limited room, he moved closer to the glass and the lions. Caden put his hands in his pockets and took a deep breath. *We win. This isn't over. I have an angel with more power than these guys on my side. And he has a lion head too!* His eyes narrowed as a muscle in his jaw moved. *We win.*

His thoughts stilled as he glanced at the dead Giants. A Shade and Viper were now pacing the room beyond. They looked irritated. Why were they there? *They were in the Giants,* Caden thought. He remembered his conversation with Noam back in the Sinai Desert. He had said the battle wasn't over when he killed the Giants. *The Demons aren't attacking because these Freaks are on their team.* He stared at the Demons, still unsure as to the relationship between Giants and Demons. He lifted his chin and his hatred for Giants grew.

Caden sharply inhaled and lifted his chin. The lions were approaching the glass. He leaned back, his mouth dropping open, and realized how large they truly were. Most were at least a head taller than a man. Some limped as they came, and the male's ear was now missing the tip. Every one of them were washed in red. Their golden eyes stared at the mirror with unnatural, human intelligence that sent shivers down Caden's spine.

We win, he told himself again and cursed.

Each lion bowed, their heads, longer than Caden's forearm, dipping low. Their mouths opened, and as one, they said, "Long live the king!" Isaac laughed. Some of the bodyguards moved back. The woman gave a little squeaky cry.

Caden didn't move, the hair on the back of his neck standing on end. *Freaks that are talking animals too. What else can they do?*

Luca glanced around, smiling. "Behold, the Sovereign Lion has become flesh and lives among us. The people will see their glory, which reflects my own. This is the future.

We will make our enemies feast on their own flesh and get drunk on their own blood as with wine. Then all the world will know that I am the king, the savior, the mighty one of the New Kingdom." Isaac led the room in a loud applause with shouted encouragement and praises to the king and the New Kingdom.

Caden alone did nothing. A steadily growing anger filled his chest, heating his blood, and narrowing his eyes. *Do You see this, God? You've got to get us out of this one.* He stared at the male lion's watching eyes. It was far too similar to the Sovereign Lion. The same golden eyes. The same unwavering stare. The same arrogant confidence that, someday, Caden was going to kneel. Caden lifted his chin and tightly crossed his arms. *Never,* he thought and heard Doeg laugh.

———

"CONSIDER IT PURE JOY, *my brothers and sisters, when you face trials of many kinds."* Caden frowned as he stopped reading and glared at the little Bible. He lay in bed, trying to find some reason to keep trusting in God after what he'd just seen.

Once telling Luca what he thought of the lions, how impressive and terrifying they are, and that their enemies didn't stand a chance, he had showered. It was a very long shower. He realized he was trying to wash all that blood and fear off him and quickly got out, knowing that was ridiculous.

He hardly spoke to Dasha, who detailed how she'd received word from Under Fire. The university nearly had fifty-thousand students come through their gate. Students were starting to travel abroad on their own, by whatever means they could, so the news of Yeshua's return was beginning to spread. BiggieFishie was helping get the word around too, which Ellie and Ophir were tackling well.

They also caught the rabbi spy Luca had sent. He became a Christian and was martyred three months ago, as Caden expected. There had been other spies too, but most became Christians. Dasha had found that amusing, but Caden was hardly listening. She asked if he was alright, and he nodded, grabbed the Bible, and plopped down on the bed.

Pure joy? Caden thought, rereading the verse again just to make sure he didn't miss anything. He hadn't and couldn't withhold a few curses. *How's that supposed to happen?*

"Because you know that testing your faith produces perseverance." the Bible continued.

What if I don't want perseverance? This is some churchy BS. What does this James guy know anyways? Caden cursed and shook his head, discouraged he had just read the first sentence in the Book of James and was already pissed. He forced himself to keep reading and was doing okey until he reached verse twelve. It said something about blessings for people who persevere under trial because God will give them life in the end.

Yeah, but what if we don't survive the trial? How can You give us life when we're already dead? Maybe, back to life, like Yeshua, or... is it a different life I don't know about? What does this even mean? Caden growled through gritted teeth and nearly chucked the Bible against the wall. He stopped at the last second and tossed it across the bed.

Dasha, who had been painting her nails, stopped, and stared at him. "You're not alright." His answer was a bit too colorful and harsh. She glared at him as her left brow rose higher than the right. "Is that so?"

Caden cursed again and ran fingers through his hair as he looked away. "Sorry. It's... today's been rough."

"No kidding."

Caden crossed his arms and dipped his head as he sealed his mouth shut. *She's not the enemy,* he thought. *Don't put her in your crosshairs. Just ignore her. Keep it together!* To his chagrin, Dasha put away the nail polish and sat down on the bed. He tried not to glare at her as his crossed arms drew tighter. *What's she doing? Why do women have to be so nosy? Just leave me alone!* Humming softly to herself, Dasha grabbed the Bible and flipped through the pages. *Keep it all inside,* Caden thought as he fixedly stared at the wall. The wall didn't care if he glared at it.

Caden's throat bobbed, and it nearly felt that bits of him were crumbling and falling off. He couldn't do this. He needed to warn Under Fire about the lions. They didn't stand a chance against them! Asher would be eaten alive, Ophir ripped to shreds, and Ellie-

Caden closed his eyes tight, his thoughts spinning as the internal screaming started up again. It grew louder as dread split through his thoughts and painfully tightened his chest.

The radio sprung to life. Caden glanced at Dasha as she turned the small radio up in volume a bit too loud and rejoined him. She cleared her throat, grabbed the Bible, and flipped to a random page. "Now faith is confidence in what we hope for". Caden's brows rose in surprise. "And assurance about what we do not see." Caden turned away with a shake of his head. He already tried that. All the Bible had to say was 'be better', 'why aren't you holy', and 'praise Yahweh while the world stomps on your neck'. So very encouraging.

"This is what the ancients were commended for." Dasha settled into her seat and drew the small book closer. She dove into Hebrews eleven, and, very slowly, Caden actually felt himself unwind as she spoke. Either it was her calm, feminine voice or the words themselves, he didn't know. Whatever it was, he found his thoughts gradually stopped panicking. He started listening, and his tightly bunched shoulders loosened.

The chapter listed the heroes of the Bible and how each used faith to accomplish what God had for them. He closed his eyes and laid his chin on his chest, trying to find some meaning in the old script. *Please, God,* he prayed. *I know You're not speaking to us right now, but please... I need something. I've got nothing left. I'm so weak. You've got to do something!* Caden let out a sigh as his arms slowly uncrossed and lay at his sides. He waited and tried to hold himself in one piece.

"Through faith," Dasha continued, "these heroes conquered kingdoms, administered justice, and gained what was promised; who shut the mouths of lions," Caden's eyes opened as he faced Dasha, "quenched the fury of the flames and escaped the edge of the sword; whose weakness was turned to strength; and who became powerful in battle and routed foreign armies."

Caden kept staring at Dasha as she read on. He didn't hear what came next. *Shut the mouths of lions,* he thought. Caden ran a hand over his face as he turned away. He looked down and huffed a tired chuckle. *This isn't over, is it?* He smiled and glanced at Dasha, grateful for her nearness and, most of all, not asking questions. He leaned back against the pillows and listened again as she continued reading into chapter twelve. In a few minutes, Caden was fast asleep.

TWENTY-TWO
BLASPHEMER

CADEN STARED down at his phone, not paying attention to the random pictures and useless text of people he hardly knew. Though it was morning and the sun was hardly up, sweat collected on his brow. He straightened as he sat by the coffee table in Dasha and his room and started typing a new post. He erased it and rewrote it, only to erase it again. This was important. Very important.

He didn't acknowledge Dasha as she sat beside him and passed him a cup of tea. She sat back, a cup nestled in her lap. He could feel her watching him. She was always watching. She flicked her hair back and set her feet on the table. "Alex?"

"Not my name."

Dasha glared at him. "Then tell me your name."

Caden didn't answer as he ran his fingers through his hair and erased the post again. "Not now, Dasha."

Dasha sighed and continued to stare at him, waiting. "Alright." She set down her cup with force and grabbed the phone from his hands.

"Hey!"

"Sush!" She said more in Russian as Caden reached for the phone.

"Stop it. I've got to do this! Luca's coming soon. We've got to be at HQ in an hour!"

Dasha waved a hand at him and sat back. "You over-think things. Everything actually. Tell me what you want to say, and I'll write it."

"Dasha-"

"Let me help you, Sammy."

"I need to send a message to Under Fire. They've got to evacuate, but it has to be written right!"

Dasha scoffed as she reached for her tea. "They just look at your emojis."

"Luca's reading my posts." Dasha slowly nodded as she took a sip. "He asked me to post something that hints he'll show the future's soldiers. He saw how many people are following me." Caden sighed as he sat back. "Freaks me out that he even knows about my page."

Dasha shrugged. "Yeah, you do have lots of followers. A few million. Surprised that many have access to the internet."

Caden shot her a look. "Is that all you can think of? *Luca* reads my posts. I knew he would eventually-"

"Really? He has the entire time!"

"-but I thought it would be later. I must warn Under Fire *and* do what he asks at the same time. It's like deliv-ering a message that'll stab the sender in the back."

"Feel guilty, Darrick?"

"Do I look guilty? And stop trying to guess my name."

"Why, is it a weird one?" Caden fell quiet, and Dasha smiled. "Maverick. Francis. Theodore?"

"He'll see I've turned on him," Caden muttered. His throat moved as he looked down. "Then it's off to the chopping block for me."

"Nope," Dasha said as she kept scrolling on the phone. "You'll see Rapham first."

"I really should've punched you when we first met."

"Yes, yes, regrettable. Okey, tell me what's happening today, so I know what to post."

"The Prime Minister's coming to tour HQ and where Kingdom's Peace volunteers are processed, and why there are so many steps to join."

"Yeah, that is a bit weird."

"Luca's getting paranoid."

"He should be. He's got a rat living right under his roof."

Caden glanced at the door and leaned closer. "Please," he hissed, "say that a bit louder. I don't think the Sentinels heard you!"

"Are you part of the tour?"

"Luca wants to show off the new Refiner recruits."

"Cool."

"Not cool."

"Hum."

"I hate the uniform."

Dasha shrugged. "You do look nice in it."

Caden stared at her. "When have you seen me in uniform?"

"Please," she said, flashing him a wide grin. "I'm the crazy Russian. I know many, many things, Phillip."

He tried to hide his smile. "He's hoping to boost morale and show people how powerful the New Kingdom is when all allies stand together, or some garbage like that."

"Nice, nice, got it." Dasha mumbled as her thumbs worked across the keypad. Caden frowned and reached for the phone, to which she lifted a shoulder and turned away. "Say cheese." she said and held up the phone.

"What, now?"

Dasha chuckled as she took the picture. "Anything else?"

"You're insufferable-"

"Incorrect answer. Posting-!"

"Smiley face! Two of them. The one with the mouth open and eyes shut and the other with the eyes and mouth shut. That too."

"Why?"

"That's the code for Under Fire," Caden said, his voice lowering. "They need to evacuate." A muscle in his jaw flexed, thinking of everything he loved under Luca's wrath, both bullets and fangs.

Dasha lifted her chin, seriousness overtaking her playful attitude, and she quickly did as instructed. "Done." she said and handed back the phone. The two said nothing as Dasha enjoyed her tea and Caden stared out the window. He didn't want to go. It was peaceful here. Quiet. And he wasn't alone.

"What's the new soldier?"

Caden glanced at her as he stood. "Freaks," he said. "They're lions that stand up like men. And they talk."

Dasha's brows rose as she finished the tea. "That's swell."

"Yep." With a curse, Caden ran a hand over his face and marched across the room to his shoes.

"Hey," Dasha called, lowering her feet to the floor. "We should, I don't know... let's pray before you go or something."

Caden glanced at her as he adjusted his shoes. "You? Praying? You unbelieving pagan-"

"Shut up, Victor."

Caden quickly walked back over and sat down beside her. "Good idea." He held out his hands and she glared at him.

"Don't touch me."

"Just hold my hands."

"Why?"

Caden paused. "I don't know really. Christians did it all the time before the World's Crash; I remember in church. It's just what they did."

"If you don't know why, then don't do it."

"Just hold my hands."

"We're not dancing-"

"Dasha!" She huffed and gripped his hands a bit too tight. "Now close your eyes."

"This is getting creepy."

"I have to go!"

"Forget about praying! Who's listening anyways?"

Caden rolled his eyes, glanced at the clock, and cursed. He cleared his throat and closed his eyes. "Dear Yeshua." He tried to think of something churchy to say, but also didn't want to pray some formula, unpersonal chant. There was too much on the line for that nonsense. "We suck." Dasha clicked her tongue. "But You don't. We're freaking out, but You're not. We don't know what's coming, but You do. How lucky for You. Sometimes, I envy that, but," he shook his head, "but I guess I'm not ready to know. So... just, just keep us levelheaded. Keep us alive. And, most of all, keep us thinking of You. But, positive thoughts and not cussing You out or being pissed and stuff like that. Something good and, well... Godly, I guess."

Caden sniffed and found himself focusing on the smaller, callus hands he was holding. Her grip had loosened, and it felt like they were resting, hand in hand. "And," he stammered. "And thank you for this crazy Russian." He smiled. "I just, yeah... thanks. Amen."

He opened his eyes and found her staring at him with those vibrant blue eyes like a clear morning sky. She was still holding his hands and seemed closer than before.

Caden looked from her eyes to her lips. They were slightly parted and rosy as ever. He looked back into those eyes and realized he was still smiling. He could've sworn she started to smile, but Dasha abruptly stood and walked across the room. Caden blinked, his smile falling as his hands rigidly stayed where she'd left them.

"Don't die." she said over her shoulder as she walked to the bathroom.

"Yep," he muttered, standing. "You too." She didn't answer as she slammed the door. Caden shook his head as he stared after her. "Crazy Russian." he mumbled.

CADEN RIGIDLY STOOD beside Moshe and tried not to stare directly into the cameras. They've been told a dozen times, he thought he'd remember. They stood in the entranceway of KUS Headquarters. The entire place was decked out in more Israeli flags altered with the Sovereign Lion than Caden has seen before. More than needed Sentinels stood guard, their white armored uniforms clean, and weapons sparkled. Each kept a firm, hard look on their face, as though ready to fight and die for their king at any second.

At the center was Luca, dressed in his white military best. It looked different from everyone else's, with golden tassels, red cuffs, and a sword. Caden stared at the outfit, wondering if he even earned the metals on his chest. *Probably,* he thought. *Wonder what he did.*

Beside him was Isaac, the Prime Minister, and a large gathering from both parties, all dressing their best or in uniform. Caden couldn't help but notice Hugh Wiltshire standing on Luca's right, always pleasantly smiling, but very oddly close to the king. The Fiends never strayed far from Hugh, nearly enshrouding him in darkness, and, often, Caden lost sight of his face. He eyed the Refiner recruits around him, seeing their puffed chests and forced, firm expressions. They so wanted to be just as bad and cool as Rapham and the other Refiners. Everyone stood at attention to either side of Luca, Isaac, and Ahmed, the host conducting the tour.

They had led everyone several times through the complex, explaining where everyone was to stand and how to act and who would speak when. All the while, camera crews were following with lights that were too bright and puffy mikes on long booms. It was a bit over-whelming.

No, they're not the problem, Caden told himself as he got into position next to Moshe. A Shade landed a few feet from him, its claws grading across the floor as it braced the impact. Caden closed his eyes, and his body tensed to leap away, but he stopped himself. The Demon stood with a flick of its tail and strolled through the sea of faces. It nodded to a Viper who sat on a Sentinel's head, and another slithered up his pant leg.

Fiends circled overhead and nearly looked like they were dancing. Another Shade crouched low to stare into the camera and wave. A Wither laughed as it wrestled on a Sentinel-looking disguise. Three Vipers discussed who was easier to deceive, teenagers or the elderly. A Fiend's face shaped from a mass of darkness, and the eyes shone from a spiked, fanged face. Someone unknowingly walked through it, and it disintegrated, only to reappear deeper in the shadows. Two Shades leisurely chatted in a dark corner. A woman adjusted her scalp, revealing her Wither skin beneath for a moment.

Caden took in a slow breath, feeling his heart pounding against him. Yep, his uneasiness had nothing to do with the cameras. Though HQ was always crawling with Demons, they weren't ever this relaxed. He'd seen at least five smiling and even a Shade laughing merrily. Caden swallowed the hard lump in his throat as a Wither, dressed as a cameraman, walked by. *At least the lion Freaks aren't here,* Caden thought. *Yet.*

They were the grand finale of the tour. Everyone had been briefed on what they were and how to react when they stepped into the open. Caden envied them; they didn't know what was coming. *Raw Peace,* he told himself, imagining The Door and the security Yahweh had waiting for him. *We win. If I'm on the winning side, that is. I mean, can prayers defeat fangs and claws?*

Caden's eyes narrowed as he clenched his teeth. He heard the scrape of claws behind him and didn't bother looking to see what it was. He heard the swish of a long tail and felt hot breath on the back of his neck. "When will illumination finally strike, boy?" Doeg whispered. "I am the only god in your life."

You will suffer for eternity in Hell. Caden lifted his chin, knowing with one swipe, Doeg could slice him in two. His hand tingled, the long-ago scar still visible where Doeg slashed him.

"Hum, I could disembowel you. Here. Now."

Caden found himself smiling, regardless of his pounding heart. *You keep threatening, but you never do anything.*

Doeg fell quiet. "I don't see your angel pet-"

I will conquer kingdoms, administer justice, gain what was promised, and shut the mouths of lions, Caden thought, reciting the verses Dasha read to him the other night. *I will-*

"You will face death today." Doeg snapped its crushing jaws. Whiskers brushed Caden's neck, and saliva splattered the back of his head. Caden tried not to flinch away as he clenched his fists.

"You alright?" Moshe whispered.

Caden shot him a quick look and smoothed back his hair. "Sure."

"Just imagine everyone in their underwear. I've heard that helps."

Caden nodded absently and tried not to watch the Fiends spinning around each other overhead. "We're all gleeful," Doeg whispered. "Can you guess why?" Caden didn't bother answering as he lifted his chin. *"The king has come."*

Anger filled Caden's chest as his eyes darted to Luca. The king was making final adjustments to the script with Ahmed, hand on his shoulder, personably smiling as usual. *Shut the mouths of lions. You said I could do that, didn't You, God? Isn't that what the Bible said?*

"That's what righteous Christians can do."

Oh, shut up! That's the lamest comeback you've said yet!

"Are we ready?" Luca called as he turned to the producer.

Caden straightened, trying to rid his mind of Doeg and the Demon horde. He took in a breath and remembered he was about to be on live TV. Everyone would be able to see him. Luca bragged about being able to send it across the entire world, even into some of the Dark Lands like Iceland, Canada, and America-

Caden stiffened as his eyes widened. *Nathaniel could see this.* His breath quickened. *And Thomas Whitney-*

"Camera's ready!" the producer called.

They'll blow my cover. They'll send me to Rapham. To the lions. To the chopping block-

"And action!" Caden gritted his teeth, lifted his chin, and forced his face to stay impassive as the cameras' little, red lights blinked on. It was too late now. Out of the corner of his eye, he saw Doeg's mangled profile.

"As I said," the Demon whispered, saliva dripping from its fangs. "You shall face death today."

Caden's chest felt tight, and he heard Luca begin speaking, his voice echoing in the filled, yet quiet room. He started to hear his heartbeat in his ears as his shoulder tingled in that little place Bobby Rut had pinched him. This was it. There was nowhere to run and-

Oh, get over it! Caden told himself, his eyes narrowing. *God knows what He's doing! Shut up and trust Him!*

He glanced at the cameras, imagining Nathaniel on the other side. What would he do if he saw he failed and Caden was still alive? *Hope he chokes.* Caden lifted his chin and forced himself to breathe steadily. It was annoying how freaked out he got all the time. Life was freaky, but he was just sick of getting involved in all the fear. *God's not afraid,* he thought. *Neither should I be.*

"God is terrified," Doeg whispered in Caden's thoughts. *"That's why you're stuck here, and He's at ease on His luxurious, golden throne."*

Luca and Isaac talked back and forth, sharing about this new soldier that would lead the allies of the New Kingdom into victory. "To tell you the truth, I was inspired by the holy Scriptures," Luca said. Caden frowned, giving himself a reason to ignore Doeg. "In the ancient Book of Daniel, chapter seven. It speaks of lions with the wings of eagles who, after given the heart of a man, can stand on two feet and live and think as men. The context of the ancient text was artfully depicting nations coming together as conquerors. After the Day of Vanishing, we found winged lions, mostly in Tanzania, and shipped them here."

"So, do they still have wings, your majesty?" Ahmed asked.

"We found that, once recovered from the transplant, the wings were rejected by the body. They all fell off or, in some cases, seemed torn off."

"How very odd."

"Yes, I would've preferred flying soldiers. Think of the potential!" Caden did and imagined Under Fire getting dive-bombed by roaring, flying monsters. He withheld a shiver as Doeg and several Demons chuckled.

"Your majesty," Isaac said. "Didn't you mention flight is in your army's future?"

Oh no.

"Indeed," Luca said with a smile. Several Demons nudged one another with big nods and grins. "We have found many other animals who want to join us as allies. The common man calls them Freaks of Nature, which I find far too harsh a term for these beautiful creatures. They are survivors of a dying world, as are we. I like to call them Leovirs."

"Hum," Ahmed grunted. "Leovirs. I like that, your majesty. Is that Latin?"

Luca nodded. "It means man-lion. Werelion sounded too..." he waved a hand around, "unprofessional and laughable."

"Yes, I agree. What is your vision with these creatures?"

"It is my same vision for everyone. Peace." Caden ground his teeth. "Soon, man and beast will thrive in perfect unity. A wolf will come alongside a lamb, the cow and lion will graze together with their young nearby, and children can play among them. No one, man or beast, will injure or destroy in my royal New Kingdom. For there will be universal submission to my sovereignty."

Those gathered nodded and muttered their approval as Luca stood, proud and tall, looking each in the eye with a smile. The Demons let out whoops and cheers, much to Caden's surprise.

Hugh nodded passionately as he pressed his hands together and closed his eyes. "Let it be so." he sighed.

"Blasphemer!"

Caden's eyes widened as every muscle flexed to move. He knew that voice. Swift, forceful steps clicked across the great room as everyone turned, buzzing. The Demons' smiles fell as several cursed. Every Shades' nape bristled, the Vipers hissed and showed long, poisonous fangs, the Withers donned Sentinel skins, and the Fiends shot before Luca and Hugh, their spiked, smoky faces materializing.

Caden slowly turned and saw a very mad, very unwise Israeli storming their way. *No, Yohanan,* he thought. *They'll kill you!*

"Stop misquoting Scripture!" Yohanan bellowed over the muttering voices. "Haven't you read the end of Revelation? Add to Scripture, and you'll be cursed!"

"How did he get in?" Isaac demanded.

"That Scripture is in the context of Heaven." a new voice called.

Caden closed his eyes and dipped his head, his heart beginning to race again. *Raw Peace Raw Peace! Abba, get out of here!*

From the other side of the room, Elijah strolled forward. "It has nothing to do with you and your so-called kingdom."

Sentinels instantly formed a perimeter as the camera crew skirted back. "Keep rolling." the producer hissed as they moved far out of the way.

Luca glanced between the two and raised a hand, telling the Sentinels to stand down. They lowered their weapons, but none moved from around the king. The gathering hushed as Luca shook his head. "Gentlemen, what can I do for you?"

"Drop dead!" Yohanan snapped.

Isaac lurched forward, jabbing a finger. "Is that how you speak to your king, boy?"

"Him? My king?" Yohanan actually started laughing. "He is no king! He's a thief!" A few Sentinels raised their weapons again as Refiners and other allies gasped, their faces turning red with rage.

Many voiced their outrage:

"How dare you!"

"Kill him."

"Off with his head!"

"He's stolen the title of the *real* king!" Yohanan shouted. "King Yeshua sees! He will not be mocked!"

Luca grinned. "Yeshua. You know, He's been dead for thousands of years-"

"He died, yes!" Elijah bellowed, his voice carrying a bit like Han's. "But the grave cannot contain our King."

"He's coming back!" Yohanan shouted. "On a white horse, dressed in a robe dipped in blood! His eyes are like fire, and a sword comes out from His mouth, slaughtering all who oppose Him! All of you!" Yohanan shot out a finger as though it were a weapon. "On His robe is written King of Kings and Lord of Lords!"

Luca's smile grew as he chuckled. "Fiery eyes? Robe in blood, hum. That sounds like a very scary person. Oh, and this sword-mouthed king of yours, will he kill me?"

"No," Elijah said with sound finality. "You will live. And curse the day you were born."

"Hum," Luca sighed as he glanced between the two Witnesses. "Is that so?"

"The time to decide is now," Elijah said. His gaze bore into one person at a time. When he looked at Caden, their eyes met. It was a fraction of a second, but, finally, Caden didn't feel so terribly alone. "Time is short! Yeshua will come any day now. He has already gathered those who follow Him on the Day of Vanishing, but there is still a chance. He is gracious and slow to anger, abounding in love, thus giving you a second chance."

The Demons closest to Elijah fell over and writhed with cries as they crawled away from him. Caden blinked and realized Elijah must've been quoting Scripture. "He doesn't desire the death of the wicked," Elijah said, forcing other Demons to cower and cry out in pain, "but refuses to let them go unpunished."

"And, yet, *I'm* the villain!" Luca cried. "Though I accept all just as they are!"

"He will come without warning, like a thief in the night."

Luca scoffed. "I thought *I* was the thief. Does this make any sense to all of you?" He motioned to those listening, and they shook their heads. "Do you understand?" Luca pointed at the cameras and the untold numbers watching. "No! No one understands this blabber! This zeal for a dead God from a dead age. *This* is the new order, the new world, the New Kingdom. Your lies will not deceive true allies of the king."

"You are not a king!" Elijah shouted. A few Demons flinched as his words echoed around them. "You are the Antichrist, the blasphemer against Yahweh, His name, and His Heavenly home. Though you have been given authority and have been permitted to make war against Yahweh's people, you will not succeed." Isaac's face was bright red with rage as several Sentinels stood ready, fingers on the trigger.

"Well, this is all very touching," Luca said. "But we're in the middle of-"

"I wasn't finished." The room fell silent as Luca's amusement gave way to a dark stare. Elijah stared back, unmoved and unafraid. "You will be alive as you are thrown down into the fires of Hell. There, you will spend eternity in torment and the absence of Yahweh. You and your False Prophet."

Luca lifted his chin, his eyes narrowing. "I don't have a False Prophet, sir."

"It is the one filled with evil Spirits and wickedness

who guides others deeper into your lies and self-worship."
Elijah shifted and fixed his gaze on Hugh. The
Englishman straightened before he was covered by the
Fiends that swirled around him, their fanged mouths
glowing from liquid fire.

"If you gentlemen think your Spirits' see into the
future," Hugh said, stepping forward and closer to the
cameras. "Then here's a prophecy from the Heralds." He
closed his eyes, his hands clasped at his chest, and his face
disappeared in black smoke. "You two will die," Hugh
said, the Fiend's darkness clearing enough to see the man's
eyes. "Your bodies will lie in our streets for days. And all
the world will see you rot and decay."

Icy cold washed over Caden as he stared at Hugh.
Demons don't know the future! Do they? His throat bobbed.

The people's anger spilled over to relief. Luca spread
his arms and smiled. "This is the fate of all terrorists
against the New Kingdom-"

"Turn!" Yohanan shouted. "Haven't you heard us
before? Turn! All of you! Yeshua is coming! He will
gather the birds to feast on the flesh of the dead; the kings
and generals, the mighty, and all people, great or small!"

Luca spun, squarely facing Yohanan. "The only flesh
to be devoured is yours! Don't you realize?"

"We are not here for battle!" Elijah shouted. Yohanan
opened his mouth, but snapped it shut, fire in his eyes.
"We come to warn-"

"You're under the Sovereign Lion's Watch!" Luca
continued. "You are surrounded. Your God has betrayed
you by abandoning you into my den of lions."

Caden caught movement out of the corner of his eyes.
There was something lurking in a doorway. It was a big,
furry thing, and it stood upright like a man. Caden's heart
leapt into his chest as more Leovirs stepped from every
door and hallway, lips pulled back and tails lashing. A

woman screamed. The people flinched back. One of the cameras shattered as the cameraman fled.

Yohanan straightened, his eyes widening before his shoulder squared. Elijah slowly regarded each in turn, his expression unchanged. Caden looked to the Sentinels, their weapons raised again and trained on the two threats. The Leovirs circled the room's perimeter. Demons surrounded Luca and Hugh, every Shade's nape bristling, every Fiends' face shaped as liquid fire dripped from smoky fangs. The Vipers hissed, spraying poison. The Withers donned larger, dangerous forms.

It's forty to two, Caden realized numbly. He felt like a spectator, just someone on the outside instead of standing a few feet from the fire-breathers' target. This wasn't happening. It couldn't be happening. Without a word, Yohanan and Elijah took in deep breaths and opened their mouths. Embers drifted from their lips.

TWENTY-THREE
FIREFIGHT

THE ENTIRE ROOM sucked in a breath and held it. Someone with heels took a step back. Caden heard the Leovirs' heavy panting. There was a subtle crackling sound from the Witnesses. *Like a fire,* Caden realized, dread turning him cold. Elijah's mouth glowed like a furnace. Yohanan's chest expanded as he stepped forward. Caden didn't know who was the first to move. Maybe that woman with the heels ran first. Maybe one of the Leovirs was just getting too impatient. Regardless, everyone moved at once in a frenzied haze of chaos.

Roars echoed in the large room. Screams shot into the air. Guns opened fire. Luca shouted orders no one listened to. There was a sudden, raging wind. Caden had no time to look, but his back felt a wave of dangerously intense heat. He forced himself through the tangle of running bodies toward a door, preparing to leap through.

A Leovir stepped out. A male. His mane made him look twice as big. He stood on his hind legs and had to duck through the doorway. His golden eyes fixed on Caden. Caden stumbled to a stop just outside the doorway, heart in his throat. The beast wore white armored plates that covered his chest, thighs, and shoulders. His human-like hands flexed, and dark claws slid out into the open. Caden crouched low to the ground, bullets pinging around him as the room's temperature quickly rose. Screams of panic turned shrill with pain. He could smell burning plastic, metal, and meat.

I'm trapped, Caden thought. It was a vague thought, like someone else's opinion. Panic constricted his chest as he stared at the Leovir before him and sensed the chaos behind him. *I can't run. I can't fight.*

"Then you'll die." Doeg whispered.

Caden could feel fur brushing his cheek. *I'll stand firm.* Heart racing and panic trying to squeeze his throat, Caden slowly straightened. His feet squared as he lifted his chin. The Leovir stopped, his ears snapping in Caden's direction. One of the ears was docked by a recent wound.

Caden took in a breath and walked past the Leovir into the room. He didn't acknowledge the people shoving past him through the door. Something tugged on his shoulder, testing his armor, and sent a hole into the wall. He glanced down at the obvious dent in his shoulder's armor plate, but steadily kept going.

Why am I not panicking? He knew his internal screaming should be edging on hysteria by now, but he heard nothing. He should be shaking at least, but his steps were sound and unwavering. Though contrary to all he'd ever known, it felt natural to stroll through the chaos.

Why wouldn't he? Han was there, somewhere, protecting him, and Yahweh had said Caden was immortal until the moment he was to die. If that was now, then he would die. If it's later, then he could just keep on strolling. But that wasn't quite it. No logical reason made sense. Caden knew the logical thing to do when faced with

Leovirs, a firefight, and two fire-breathers was to scream in panic and flee. So, what was it?

Raw Peace, Caden thought, his chest puffing. *This is real Raw Peace.* It wasn't a feeling. It wasn't a sense of love or belonging. It was fighting the chaos and terror the world brings with calm, collected silence. For the first time, Caden truly felt like peace was his armor, shielding him as firmly as his physical armor. Caden couldn't withhold a smile.

Once in the room, he stopped. *This isn't what soldiers do.* He blinked, thinking, realizing what had to be done. He walked back out the door, back into the chaos. The headquarters of the King's United Society was in flames. The thunderous crack of gunfire rose from the center of the room, but there were far less Sentinels than before. Human-shaped torches rolled on the ground or lay motionless.

Through the columns of thick, black smoke, Caden could just make out Luca. He had grabbed a gun and knelt, firing at Elijah. Elijah himself Caden couldn't see. Instead, a roaring, rushing orange and yellow fire streamed from where Elijah had stood. Every minute, the stream would stop, and Elijah would be visible. He stood as he had before, legs firmly planted, hands at his sides, face chiseled from stone and unreadable.

From Caden's distance, he saw his clothes were red about his shoulder and one of his legs. *He's wounded.* Elijah's barrel chest swelled as he sucked in a breath to let loose another flaming torrent, hiding him completely. *He's armed with the Raw Peace too.* Caden stared at the inferno gushing onto the Sentinels and the few too slow to run. His brow slicked with sweat as his cheeks stung with heat. *There's the Akal Esh, Yahweh's Consuming Fire. The danger of His Raw Peace.*

As he watched, something on the ground caught his

eye. It was a writhing mess of flames and white fur. Caden blinked, recognizing the Shade. It caterwauled horribly as it burned. Caden's mouth dropped open as he realized more Demons suffered in the flames. Vipers slithered low, trying to avoid the fire over their heads, but he could tell the heat was cooking them. Withers' overlaying skin was peeling off, showing their shrunken forms beneath. Shades cried like dying cats as they fled.

Fiends, their entire bodies formed, spewed liquid fire toward Yohanan and Elijah. Their fire was a deep orange like the embers of a dying bonfire. Though they were the only Demons to get closer to the Witnesses, once their flaming flow touched the *Akal Esh*, they were consumed and overcome by Yahweh's pure, fiery wrath.

The Leovirs, much to Caden's surprise, had held back. He thought they'd plunge headfirst into the flames, forsaking their safety to serve the king. Apparently, their new human heart gave them a more human-like character than Luca had bargained for.

Caden's eyes narrowed as he shielded his mouth against the smoke filling the room. *They're not running though,* he realized, his hair standing on end. *They're grouping together.* He watched as they lowered and slowly stalked on all fours. He remembered videos about African lions and how they took their time catching their prey. They worked as a unit and synchronized attacks. He looked to Elijah and Yohanan. Leovirs were steadily stalking behind them. Caden lifted his chin as a cold thrill rushed through him. *They can't fire-breathe behind them. And they don't notice the lions!*

Heart quickening, Caden looked down, thinking fast. He had to help them, but he still couldn't blow his cover. A bullet rocketed through the wall beside him, throwing drywall in his face. Caden flinched back and knelt, making himself a smaller target. *What would gain me favor with Luca and draw attention to behind Yohanan?*

His brother-in-law was the closest Witness. Beside Yohanan lay one of the camera crew. His leg had been shot, and he was beating his chest as flames burned his clothes. An idea struck Caden. It was a very bad idea, but it seemed most of Yahweh's ideas appeared bad in the moment. With a hissed curse, Caden's stomach lurched, knowing he was going to obey regardless.

"That was your idea," Doeg whispered in Caden's thoughts. *"Not the voice of Yahweh. Why follow your own leadings?"*

Caden didn't bother answering. He didn't have time. He rushed back through the doorway, knowing it was a conference room and a jug of water lay on the far counter. He shoved through the screaming, cowering people and grabbed a decorative neck wrap from a woman. She didn't seem to notice him as she wailed and held her shot leg. Caden plunged the wrap into the water and tied it around his mouth and nose as he ran through the door.

Someone bumped his shoulders as they kept in step. He glanced and found Moshe beside him. "I'm helping!" Moshe cried as he reached for a discarded weapon.

Caden jerked him upright. "Wounded!" He yelled and pointed to the cameraman behind Yohanan. Moshe's eyes flickered with panic, realizing Caden was going to step into the line of fire. Caden didn't wait.

Crouched low, Caden ran towards Yohanan. It went against everything his body was telling him to do. He wondered if this was what firemen felt like while jumping into a burning house instead of racing away. Heat stung Caden's face. He smelt his hair burning. The air was thick, hot, and deadly. Sweat dripped from his nose.

Yohanan's fire blast stopped suddenly, and the Witness sucked in a breath. As he did, he noticed Caden. He pivoted and aimed his gaping mouth directly at him. Caden looked up, seeing the rage and determination in Yohanan's eyes. Deep into Yohanan's throat glowed with a flickering orange.

With a gasp, Caden ripped down the wrap covering his mouth and nose as he threw himself to the floor. The rushing fire sounded like a monster screaming over his head. Caden's back and legs stung with intense heat. He let out a cry, drawing himself into a ball as he reached the wounded cameraman.

Yohanan's flaming breath stopped abruptly. Caden gasped and hoped he wasn't on fire, but realized he was. His leg felt stuck in an oven. Hands smacked his shin and foot, snuffing out the flames with force. Caden raised his head, glancing at Moshe, his face red hot and shiny with sweat. He turned back to Yohanan. The Witness stared down at him and blinked. *It's me, you idiot!*

Concern broke through Yohanan's fierce stare. Pointedly, Caden looked behind Yohanan. The Leovirs were close. Too close. He grabbed the cameraman and yanked him into his arms. Out of the corner of his eye, Caden saw Yohanan face the Leovirs. A Leovirness leapt, clawed paws extended and fanged mouth gaping in a roar. Yohanan threw himself out of the way and rolled to his feet. The Leovirness landed, her tail smacking Caden's back. He coughed, the blow like a punch.

Caden forced himself to his feet, his leg throbbing with searing pain. He yelled through gritted teeth and hooked under the wounded man's arms. Moshe grabbed his legs. He saw the glow of fire reflected in Moshe's terrified, wide eyes. The heat struck his back, nearly sending him off his feet.

"Move!" he screamed to Moshe as they dragged the wounded man. Ignoring the cameraman's cries of pain, they hauled him to the room everyone fled to. Once inside,

Caden grabbed another Refiner recruit who wasn't screaming in panic. "You! Get this guy out the window!"

"How? I don't-"

"Break the window! Throw him out! We'll get more! Got it?" The recruit stared at Caden, mouth slack and face pale. Caden grabbed his shoulders. "Got it, Refiner!" The young man's mouth closed and he nodded once.

Caden and Moshe raced out to get more wounded. Once entering the room, Caden reeled from the thick, oppressive heat, choking smoke, and stench of burnt meat. Yohanan was now in a corner, sending fiery blasts at the remaining shooters and the circling Leovirs. A few of the monsters were consumed in flames and lashed about, trying to free themselves.

Mouth covered with the damp neck wrap, Caden squinted in the smoky haze. "There!" Moshe cried, and the two grabbed a Sentinel who wasn't moving. Every time they ran back into the room, half of Caden's brain questioned his sanity. Maybe that was Doeg. It didn't really matter, sometimes, his own doubts and Doeg's lies all sounded the same. He ignored them both and found more wounded to haul to safety.

He kept an eye on Yohanan and Elijah if they needed his help again. Yohanan was doing fine. Though in a corner, he wasn't cowering from the Leovirs like a normal man would. He actually seemed to be having fun aiming at the Leovirs and cooking them, one at a time. Elijah had had enough sense to watch his back. He kept his head on a swivel, seeing any who tried to creep behind him.

As Caden turned to focus on another wounded, something caught his eye. He looked above Elijah and saw one of the second-floor windows, overlooking the vast entry room, had been shattered from the inside out. Standing in the gap was a Leovir, tail lashing and hind legs bunched, ready to pounce at the right time. Dread choked Caden

as he turned to Elijah, seeing he was completely oblivious. Caden didn't have a plan; there was no time to
make one.

"You get this one!" he bellowed to Moshe and charged
through the madness.

He circled the charred remains at the center of the
room and drew closer to Elijah. He literally felt the bullets'
forcing the air this way and that as they flew by but kept
going. If they hit him, he'd be dead, and that was that. No
point focusing on it; worry wasn't known to be
bulletproof.

Caden's eyes darted around, trying to find someone
wounded close to Elijah. There were only bodies. At last,
he noticed one survivor needing help. His pace faltered a
step or two. *I can't save a Leovir,* Caden thought, and his
stomach turned inside out. The beast staggered against the
wall and leaned on a huge flagpole, making the Israeli flag
quiver overhead.

With a curse, Caden lengthened his strides and surged
toward him. The lion's tail smoked as fire licked its tip.
Caden yanked the wrap off his face and clamped it around
the lion's tail. Vaguely, from the depths of his mind, he
remembered cats hated their tails touched. He saw movement and dropped. A clawed paw shot over his head,
barely missing him.

Caden reeled back and raised a hand. "You were on
fire!" The Leovir's snarling lips relaxed as he stared down
at Caden, golden eyes narrowed. *You again,* Caden
thought, seeing his clipped ear. Caden shot a brief glance
at the Leovir crouching overhead and stood. "Come on.
Lean on me and-no wait. I'm too small-"

The Leovir lay a humanoid hand on his shoulder.
Caden's legs nearly buckled under the weight. The Leovir
steadied himself while holding onto the flagpole. It
swayed, also unsteady. Caden stared up at the waving flag,

seeing it was directly beneath the hidden Leovir. He blinked, another hair-brained idea questioning his sanity.

"I said I'm too small!" Caden cried and tried to fall convincingly. As he fell back, he grabbed the Leovir's hand and mane. The lion grunted a gruff moan as his wounded leg couldn't hold him. He fell, nearly crushing Caden. Caden felt every bone strain under the weight, and he would've screamed if the wind hadn't been knocked out of him.

He tried to breathe but got a mouthful of mane. He coughed and sputtered, dragging himself out from under the beast just in time to see the flagpole drop. The Israeli flag fluttered directly toward Elijah. He saw the movement, turned, and looked up. His body tensed, finally seeing the Leovir crouching overhead.

There was a roar as fangs and claws leapt. Fire travels faster than lions. The leaping lion was engulfed in fire in midair. Its roar turned to a shrill caterwaul. Elijah took one step to the side, and the Leovir crashed to the floor and rolled against the wall, yowling as the flames claimed him.

Caden nearly leapt into the air with a cry of victory, but his burnt leg throbbed, and he was seeing flashes of light. Had he hit his head? The Leovir beside him staggered upright, and Caden craned back his neck to look at him. "You alright?"

"Useless human cub." the Leovir snarled in Hebrew. Caden drew back with hands raised. With a huffed growl, the Leovir took a heavy, limping step again.

"We can go in here," Caden said, pointing to a broken-down doorway. "We could get you out-"

The Leovir's lips pulled back, revealing fangs longer than Caden's fingers. The beast lowered to Caden's level and growled hot breath across Caden's face. Caden froze, his face washing of color. He didn't move. "I did not request your help, useless cub."

Caden sucked in a shaky breath and swallowed hard. "I... I don't speak that." The Leovir's eyes narrowed suspiciously.

The crack of gunfire stopped. The roar of fire continued on a moment longer, but abruptly ended. Both Leovir and Caden turned and looked across the room. The few Sentinels and Leovirs standing had raised their arms in surrender. Yohanan and Elijah, still on either side of the room, panted as they faced their enemies. Their bodies were drenched in sweat, and both had been shot more than once.

But nowhere fatal, Caden realized with shock.

One cameraman was left, and he manned his camera as steadily as he could. He panned from Yohanan to Elijah. Without a word, Elijah and Yohanan limped toward HQ's entrance.

"We are not here to fight," Elijah bellowed suddenly, his voice echoing in the deathly stillness. "We are here to warn you. All of you!" They stopped and stared directly into the camera. The poor cameraman started to shake. "King Yeshua-"

"-the *real* King!" Yohanan cut in.

"He's coming," Elijah continued. "He will come at any time. No one knows the specific hour or day, but He will come. He is coming to save those who are eagerly waiting for Him."

"Everyone will see His coming," Yohanan said. "Those who wounded Him and every people of the earth will wail in terror. He will repay everyone for what they've done. The evil and the good! That means you!"

"This is a taste of King Yeshua's wrath!" Elijah called, sweeping his arm at the destruction behind them. "Turn.

Time is short. All King Yeshua needs is your allegiance. Follow *His* new kingdom, not this kingdom of darkness."

"Let Him be your King," Yohanan said, stepping closer to the camera, "and live."

"Be ready," Elijah said, his voice firm with finality. "He is coming, regardless if you believe in Him or not."

The two Witnesses stepped back and turned to one another. Yohanan smiled and clapped Elijah on the shoulder. "I need a doctor." he muttered, and Elijah nodded, slowly limping to the door. As they walked through the now blackened, broken doors, Elijah glanced behind him. He seemed saddened at the destruction and death. His eyes fell on Caden. Though saddened, there was power in that gaze. A power Caden also held.

We win, Caden thought as Elijah and Yohanan strolled through their enemy's headquarters, now on fire, and walked away.

─────

CADEN IGNORED Dr. Ricci's orders to stay off his leg as he limped through headquarters. It was night, HQ's fires had finally been put out, but the smoke still stung the air. As did the smell of blood. Mere minutes after Elijah and Yohanan left, Luca stepped from a room, sooty with a torn shoulder and bleeding brow. He began shouting orders, orders Caden didn't hear. He was beyond relieved his Abba and brother-in-law weren't dead. How were they not dead?

He was ordered to report to Dr. Ricci and wait his turn as dozens of wounded were looked at. All the while, Sentinels, Refiners, and Leovirs raced about. Caden assumed they were containing the fire but was gravely mistaken.

"What, no." Moshe muttered as he also waited for Dr.

Ricci. He held his arm, which was dislocated at the shoulder, as blood seeped from a gash on his brow. "They're attacking."

Caden's eyes narrowed. "Attacking who?"

"The terrorists."

A hard lump formed in Caden's throat. "Which ones?"

"What do you mean which ones? The terrorists at Under Fire!" Caden had fell silent, unable to feel a thing besides screaming, horrible helplessness.

That helplessness didn't lift from his shoulders as he walked through headquarters. He had pretended to help clear the destruction and aid the wounded, but he was waiting. Waiting to know if his sister's head would roll through the courtyard. What if Under Fire didn't receive his warning for them to evacuate? Should he have posted two messages? Maybe if he went in person, they would've moved faster? He could've done something better. He failed them. They were all dead, by bullets, fangs, or the ax, they were all dead.

Throughout the day, the blast of distant gunfire had echoed throughout the city. Missiles from military helicopters tore down buildings. If he listened hard enough, Caden could hear screams. It was torture. *Raw Peace,* Caden thought. *Where did all the Peace go?* The overwhelming peace that had armored him during the firefight was gone. Did Yahweh think he failed and didn't deserve it anymore?

The hours past. As dusk fell, Humvees arrived, the back stuffed with people. It didn't take long for Caden to realize the people were prisoners. Floodlights washed the courtyard with brilliant light as more chopping blocks were set up. Sentinels already stood waiting with heavy axes. The helplessness consumed Caden as people—men, women, and even young teens—were dragged up HQ's steps and to the courtyard. Most were already tied and wounded in some way.

I failed, Caden thought. *They didn't evacuate.* He wanted to sag to the floor and sit, staring into nothing. He backed against the wall and watched the line of his people, his Christian family, be led to die.

Through the sea of terrified faces, one stood out. It was a young man, a bit older than Caden. He wasn't cooperating, even though his arm was obviously broken. Caden's heart leapt into his throat. It was Asher. Rage swept over Caden, turning his blood hot. He moved without thinking. He stepped in front of the Sentinel dragging Asher and he stopped them. "What do you think you're doing?"

The Sentinel stared down at him and quickly noticed his Refiner's uniform. "Leading prisoners to execution, sir."

"Not this one! Take this one away. Put him in the lower levels!" Asher stared at Caden, his eyes bugging from his head. Caden ignored him, his heart beating with force. Either from terror or rage, he didn't know.

"Sir," the Sentinel said. "Those aren't my orders-"

"What is your name?"

The Sentinel stiffened. "Um-"

"Name and rank!"

"Junior Refiner!" Caden's head snapped around, and he hid his rising terror behind a piercing glare. Rapham was walking his way. He was holding a heavy ax. "Trying to usurp authority? You do not outrank a Sentinel!"

Caden gritted his teeth and faced Rapham. "I know this one. I've seen him." Rapham's brows rose. *He's an interrogator, he'll know when I lie!* "He's always at the Temple Mount with other terrorists. He's always close with that Elijah guy. Don't you recognize him? They both are all over TV!" Rapham lifted his chin and glanced at Asher.

"He's lying," Asher slurred, obviously exhausted. "I've never-"

Caden didn't realize he backhanded Asher until he felt his hand throbbing from the blow. Asher would've fallen over if the Sentinel didn't already have a hand on him. "You will speak when spoken to!" Caden hissed through gritted teeth. Asher gaped at Caden, blood dripping from his mouth.

"Take him down," Rapham said quietly. "I will deal with him."

Goosebumps dotted Caden's arms. "Let me." he blurted out.

Rapham laughed. "You? You know nothing of inter-rogation."

"Then teach me-"

Rapham stepped closer to Caden. "His majesty may favor you, but I," he adjusted his hold of the ax, "I do not."

Caden held his gaze a moment, his heart quickening, frantic to save Asher from Rapham's brutality. He could say nothing and turned away. "You're right," he said, numb and cold and feeling dead inside. "After all, you always know when someone lies."

Don't lie, Asher. Be as gentle as a dove and shrewd as a serpent!

Rapham nodded his head to the Sentinel who dragged Asher from the line of prisoners. Caden watched them go out of the corner of his eye. He wanted to grab a gun and start shooting. He wanted to save his brother. He could do nothing. Rapham scoffed and headed for the courtyard. Caden stiffly stood, not knowing what to do, trying to understand the horrible and ever-changing circumstances. It was all too much too soon. He couldn't keep up-

A hand lay across his shoulders. He flinched back and found Luca's charming smile. "I heard you were wounded, Alex," Luca said. "Should you be on that leg?"

I should kill you. Caden glanced down at his foot, trying to hide the murderous rage in his eyes.

"Look at this!" Luca said, sweeping his arm. "They tried to hide from me, but I will not be mocked."

Caden blinked. *They did evacuate.* He lifted his chin, feeling a great weight lift from his shoulders.

"We routed several directions and hunted them down. We were given a generous tip from one of Mr. Elijah Mizrahi's own family members. He said he wanted to spare the rest of his family, that their so-called King Yeshua had failed him."

Caden glanced at him, realizing he was speaking of Elezaro. He blinked slowly as his thoughts spun. *He betrayed his own family,* he thought. *Everything we've all been working for!*

Luca took in a deep breath of the sweat, smoke, and blood and sighed. "It's a good day. I heard what you did during the attack." Caden dared not to look at Luca, his skin crawling. "You risked yourself, running into the line of fire to save the wounded. The other allies mentioned you. Benaiah especially."

Caden's brow furrowed. "Who?"

"The wounded Leovir you helped steady." Luca clapped him on the back. "Very honorable. I'm proud of you." Caden looked down again. All he wanted to do was beat the pleased smile off Luca's face.

"Oh!" Luca exclaimed. "Here comes the Refiner lieutenant I keep referring to." Luca whistled, and a man who had just come from the courtyard headed their way. Luca clicked his tongue. "He's so inspiring. You two must meet, he serves with such an intensity, even with his physical limitations."

Caden turned and stared at the Refiner approaching. He held an executioner's ax in one hand, and his white Refiner's uniform was soiled with blood. He limped forward, one leg very stiff, as he heavily leaned on a cane. All breath left Caden as he stepped back. The internal screaming peeked, fading to empty white noise.

Grant Yarrow shuffled close and stopped short, staring at Caden. His head tilted to one side, and he smiled. "Fancy seeing you here, Max."

TWENTY-FOUR

POETIC IRONY

CADEN STOOD at attention and stared at Luca. He was sure it was an intense stare, for everyone knew his very life was in the king's hands. No, he was the Antichrist, the one who had just martyred dozens of Caden's people. *I'm dead*, Caden thought. He still felt nothing. He figured he should feel something. Terror. Panic. Dread of his impending doom. There was nothing. It was as though his soul had been sucked out, and he was just an empty, hollow shell.

He stood in Luca's inner office, Sentinels were on his right and left. He knew they were there to handcuff him at Luca's word. Across the room was Grant, he too had a Sentinel on either side. Caden's hair stood on end, for he knew, behind them and out of sight, was Buck. Grant's lumbering henchmen was apparently his second and followed him wherever he went. Luca obviously respected Grant and honored his request for Buck to join the meeting.

Before them was Luca at his desk. He stiffly sat, his fingers laced together, as he gave Grant his full attention. In the shadows to Luca's right was Hugh. He rigidly stood, silent as ever, observing over his glasses as the Fiends' ember eyes glowed in the dark haze they cast. Though it wasn't said, Caden and Grant were in a mini version of court. A verdict would be reached, and punishment inflicted. Caden kept staring at Luca, feeling very, very far away from himself.

"This boy is a con artist," Grant had been saying. "I know you believe him to be Alex Whitney, your majesty, but Alex is dead. He was killed a year and a half ago."

"How did he die?" Luca asked.

"I heard he was fleeing from his kidnappers. A Herald found him wanting and administered justice."

Caden shook his head. "I'm standing right in front of you, your majesty." Luca cast Caden a glance and returned his attention to Grant. Caden's throat felt like it was closing in on itself.

"This boy heard about Alex's death and his family," Grant continued. "He saw his chance and conned his way into House Whitney's graces, gaining a flight from America to here."

"That's not true," Caden said. He was shocked, his voice was steady. "I was brought here against my will. By you!"

"Please control yourself." Luca said, raising a hand.

Caden looked down as his fists clenched. "How can I be calm? These men kidnapped me. They threatened to kill me. To torture me." Caden's shoulder tingled as he remembered Buck's firm grip digging in. The helplessness he felt so long ago closed in around him. Here he was, surrounded by Grant and his wolves again, fearing for his freedom and life.

He wanted to make me a slave, Caden remembered. *Will he still try and do that again?*

Anything was possible. He remembered the casual way Grant tried on Don's coat as the poor man died under his dog's fangs. His screaming resembled the cries of the martyrs in the courtyard.

Grant laughed at Caden's accusation. "Come now, Max. We both know the truth."

"So, you two have met?" Luca asked, pointing to each.

"In America. He possesses unique abilities. Well, unique at the time. Now, I see it is becoming commonplace among the elite Refiners." Luca glanced at Caden as Caden tried to maintain a confused expression. Deep down, his heart began to race as his hands suddenly felt colder. "He sees Heralds." Luca's brows rose. "He did in America. I suspect he does still."

Luca sat back and turned narrowed eyes onto Caden. "Is this true?"

Caden shook his head. "I want to see them. I've reached out to them as Ally Hugh suggested, but nothing yet. Is that normal?" He glanced at Hugh and pointedly ignored the Fiends circling him. One of the Fiends shaped into its horned, fanged face. Caden could see liquid fire pooling in its mouth. He continued staring at Hugh as his fists tightened until the nails dug into his palms.

Hugh took in a slow breath and pressed his hands together, laying them against his bottom lip. "The young man is touched by Heralds, there is no doubt."

Grant nodded as he shot a hand at Caden. "As I said-"

"Excuse me, Ally Yarrow," Hugh said, slightly raising his voice. "This does not mean he specifically sees them. It only implies *they* know *him*."

Grant shrugged as he lifted his chin, his fingers rapping on the top of his cane. Caden eyed the fidgeted movement, knowing the circular end, which hid a narrow blade, was weighed perfectly to shatter bone. "Their hand is on him," Grant said. "Proves my point enough."

"The Heralds' hand is on you too, Ally Yarrow." Hugh

raised his thin brows as he looked Grant in the eye. Grant simply smiled and shook his head.

"Young man," Luca said, turning in his seat and facing Caden.

No one's calling me Alex, Caden realized.

"Tell me your side."

"I was kidnapped. By a crew led by Grant Yarrow and Buck. Buck put a gun to my back, and he walked me to their crew. They-" Caden's calm voice finally cracked, and he stopped, turning away. Grant watched him with a cool smile. "They wanted to make me a slave and steal a fortune from my family in ransom."

"Why didn't you tell me this in your report submitted months ago?" Luca asked. Grant's fingers rapped the metal ball, his smile growing.

"Grant-"

"Lieutenant Refiner Yarrow."

Caden withheld a curse and forced himself to comply. "Lieutenant Refiner Yarrow isn't the first to think I see Heralds. Those who suspect that never treat me well. I didn't want you to see me like the others did."

"And what way is that?"

"Like a pet to come when called."

Luca nodded slowly. "But you never mentioned Lieutenant Refiner Yarrow."

Caden looked down, the coldness in his hands spreading up his arms. "I..." he stammered. "I was afraid. He-"

Caden cut short. *Oh, God, don't let them take me!*

Grant's belting laugh startled Caden. "You can see, your majesty! A con artist! Tell me, Max, where did you study? Was your father a hustler or thief? Or did you learn at a young age to con what you wanted out of others?"

"He threatened to break me!" Caden cried. He

couldn't hide the growing fear in his voice. "He said if I did his every wish, he'd only break half my bones! He was going to kill me! Everyone knows hostages don't survive! You tell me! Do you think these guys, if they took a hostage, would they let them live?"

Luca stared at Caden, deep in thought yet unreadable. "Lieutenant Refiner Yarrow," he said, facing Grant. "Why do you keep calling him Max?"

"He introduced himself as such in America."

"Why do you want to break his bones?"

Grant lifted his chin, his smile twitching, as he tapped his crippled ankle with his cane. "Recompense."

"I did not do that!" *Don't say that!* Caden thought as he cursed.

Grant glanced at him. "Who did, Max?"

"That was a friend, trying to rescue me."

"Alex Whitney was said to have no friends-"

"They did save me."

"So, I *didn't* drag you to the Middle East?"

"My friends rescued me *here* after we arrived!"

"Why would I want to bring you here, Max? Why not stay in America?"

"It's a Dark Land. There isn't wealth and power in a Dark Land, something you apparently can't live without!"

"Transferring money across the world was difficult before the World's Crash. It is near impossible now. See? Your lies are unraveling-"

Caden scoffed as he finally found the courage to face Grant. He nearly flinched back and turned away but told himself to stand firm. "You knew James West would get caught. He was a weak man, he would rat you out to my uncle. You had to get somewhere far away. But what do I know? I can't guess the motives of kidnappers and murderers!"

Grant squarely faced Caden as his smile spread, showing white teeth. "I never kidnapped you-"

"Lies!" Caden cried, stepping closer to Grant.

"But I now am a cripple because of you."

"No!" Caden stepped closer again, his fists at his side. "Lies again-!"

A thick, beefy hand dug into his shoulder, easily dragging him back. Caden didn't even have to look to see who it was. "Get off, Buck!" He pulled, but Buck had already twisted his arm behind him again. Caden yelled through gritted teeth; he wouldn't endure this again.

Luca held up a finger, and Buck stepped back. Caden, gasping and shaken, nearly fell to the floor. He steadied himself with a curse and glanced back at Buck. The huge man stared back at him with indifference. "You knew his hold." Luca muttered thoughtfully.

Caden took in a breath to regather himself and stepped toward the desk. "I said they kidnapped me. I know their brutality! What have I done for you to doubt me? Please! Listen to me! Your majesty, this man is a murderer and a kidnapper." He shot a finger at Grant. "He's a ruthless, heartless man who has no value for human life! I've watched him let his dogs tear one of his men apart without batting an eye! There is no mercy in him. The only concern he has is for himself. He thrives on the suffering of others. He discredits everything your New Kingdom represents. He discredits *you*!"

The room was silent. Caden felt his stomach drop as he snapped his mouth shut. He glanced down, his chest heaving with every breath, as his nails kept digging into his fists. He felt the eyes of everyone present heavy on his shoulders. The tap of Grant's fingers against the metal ball filled the room.

"Your majesty," Grant calmly said. "I wonder, how was Under Fire evacuated before the attack even launched?"

Luca stared down at his desk without a word. "They knew." Caden straightened, his hair standing on end. "They knew in advance." Caden's heart slammed into his chest as Grant shook his head. "Your majesty, you have a little, sneaky rat."

Caden turned to Luca. The king was studying him, his eyes slightly narrowed as his lips pressed to a thin line. The cold nothingness spread, filling Caden's chest with dread. He raised his hands as he struggled to find words. "Your majesty-"

Luca stood. "You two will return to your quarters and stay until I've made my decision." Caden opened his mouth to speak, but Luca arched a brow, silencing him. Caden felt Grant's eyes on him as he was escorted by the two Sentinels. The coldness had reached his legs, and he hardly felt the steps needed to reach his room. Once inside, and finally alone, he heard the door lock. He stood in the center of the room and stared, his arms limp at his sides. He couldn't move.

"What are you doing?" He jumped with a curse, finding Dasha coming from the bathroom.

She's in danger here, Caden thought as he straightened, the sight of her strengthening him, giving him a purpose beyond himself. He rushed to her side, grabbed her wrist, and pulled her close. "We're locked in."

"I heard the key. What-?"

"Quiet and do as I say. No! No arguing! You must leave. Now."

Dasha stared up at him, her eyes narrowing. "They're on to me."

"Well, we can't run. That will prove your cover's blown-"

Caden grabbed both her arms and looked her in the eyes. "An old enemy's back. He wants my head. If he knows you're with me, he'll want yours too. If Luca believes his lies, then I..." Caden stopped short, and he cleared his throat.

"Then you're dead." Dasha whispered.

"Very. Very dead. Forget packing."

She stared at him, studying the near manic look in his wide eyes. "You think this is best?"

Caden stiffened, realizing she was fully trusting his judgment. "Yes." She blinked and nodded. "Go out the window." Caden glanced out, remembering they were several stories up.

"I can manage," she said, knowing his concern. "I'll say I got stuck shopping when the Refiners attacked the city."

"Dasha, you're not coming back-'

"And I'll stay with friends on the south side."

"Dasha-"

"That's our story." She fixed him with a fierce look.

He sighed a curse and shook his head. "Take the Bible," he whispered. "I've memorized enough, and they'll find it." Dasha nodded as she rushed to the air vent and opened it, removing the small, precious book. She tucked it into her belt and walked toward the window while putting up her hair. He watched her go. There was a physical pain in his chest, like part of him was leaving too.

Dasha opened the window but stopped. Without a word, she turned around and quickly walked back to him. She was hugging him before he realized it. He tightly wrapped his arms around her. "Find me." she whispered. He closed his eyes, not knowing what to say. "Sammy!" she snapped. "Find me!"

"Alright! I'll find you!" They kept hugging. With gritted teeth, Caden took a breath. "Caden," he whispered. "My name is Caden Johnson."

Dasha drew back, shaking her head. "Don't tell me that-"

"If I'm to die, someone should know my name."

Dasha sighed as she stared up at him, her vivid blue eyes searching his. "I like Sammy." Caden laughed suddenly, and she grinned. "I'll tell you who I am." Caden's brows rose. "When we see one another again." He sighed heavily and shook his head. A saddened seriousness overcame her, and Caden's brow furrowed. "Always protecting me." she whispered, shaking her head in bewilderment. With a grunt, Dasha drew back and walked to the window again. "We win." she said over her shoulder.

Caden straightened. "What's this? I've swayed you to my religious suicide mission?"

Dasha didn't answer as she stood on the table and stepped out of the window and onto the sill. The wind caught her hair as the fading light shone behind her. She didn't respond as she gave him one last look. It was sad and tender, one full of longing. It struck Caden's heart, feeling he was losing his helper and teammate. Without a word, Dasha started climbing down and was out of sight.

Caden wanted to watch her progress and make sure she reached the bottom safely but forced himself to shut the window. He'd draw attention to her; it was the last thing he wanted. *I'll find you,* he thought, wrapping his arms around himself. *I know I'll find you.* He remembered seeing his older self and older Dasha, their armor advanced and futuristic-like, as they beat Demons together. It seemed too otherworldly and unreal. Maybe because it wasn't real. He had been trudging through the Sinai Desert beforehand, the sun had scrambled his thoughts. Mirages were common in the wastelands-

Caden hissed a curse as he glared at the ceiling. Doeg flashed him a crooked, fanged grin. Caden straightened as he roughly scrubbed his face with his hands. Muttering under his breath, he crossed his arms and began pacing the room. He heard Doeg softly drop to the floor. His eyes

closed briefly as he recalled a line of Scripture to focus on.
These heroes of faith conquered kingdoms, administered justice-

"You understand those are ravings of an unknown
author."

-and gained what was promised; who shut the mouths of lions-

"You misquoted that line."

*-quenched the fury of the flames and escaped the edge of the
sword;-*

"Scripture misquoted is blasphemy. Did you not hear
Yohanan?"

*-whose weakness were turned into strength; and who became
powerful in battle-*

"Where is your power, oh hero of faith?"

Caden gritted his teeth. "The fact that I can pace in
circles around you without panicking is proof enough."

"You are bound for failure. Everyone knows."

"You are bound for Hell."

Doeg's ear flicked as its icy eyes narrowed. "My
assault on your mind is lacking."

Caden scoffed. "You think?"

"I've decided to change tactics."

"What? Attack my Spirit now? I know enough Scripture to disarm you."

Doeg's tail flicked as its head cocked to one side. "No,
I believe it's your flesh's turn to suffer."

Caden cast the Demon a hostile look. The Spirit
grinned without another word. Caden opened his mouth
but shut it quickly. "Why do I even talk to you?" he hissed
and refocused on the verse. Where was he? Something
about battles and power?

He's distracted me from the truth, Caden realized. He
continued pacing and muttering Scripture. His singed leg
began to throb with dull pain, but it helped Caden focus.
Doeg held its tongue, which made Caden uneasy. The

Demon kept watching as though it was waiting. *Why don't these verses hurt him?* Caden thought with frustration.

Doeg stiffened suddenly, its ears leaping upright as it stared toward the door. Caden's pacing stopped. The Demon's face split with a smile as it settled on the floor and leaned forward. Caden's breath caught in his throat; it was the same look Doeg gave when Trace was shot to bits.

Raw Peace, Caden thought as the door unlocked. *Please, God. Save me.* Hands grabbed him. A swift kick to the back of his knees sent him to the ground. A heel shoved him down. Caden curled into a ball and ducked his chin as boots kicked against him on all sides. He tried not to yell. He couldn't help it. They backed away enough to jerk him to his feet.

"Move!" They were Sentinels. Three of them.

Caden tried to breathe as they tied his hands. He watched blood drip from his face onto the carpet. *Raw Peace,* Caden thought. It was all he could muster as they put a bag over his head and dragged him out.

———

CADEN WAS FINALLY ALONE. Well, he wasn't sure, the bag was still on his head, but he couldn't hear anyone. After a quick car ride, a flight of stairs to an elevator going down, Caden knew exactly where he was. The pungent smoke and blood smell gave it away. He was in the KUS Headquarters. Once leaving the elevators, Caden recognized the cold, earthy smell from his introduction to Leovirs. They were in the lower levels. The classified zone. The place no one could hear screaming.

Caden's breath quickened, but his chest couldn't fully expand because a leather strap sinched around him. That made him panic more. Leather straps looped around his wrists and ankles too, keeping him stiffly sitting in a metal chair. Caden squeezed his eyes tight as sweat trickled down his brow. He tried to think rationally, to assess if anything was broken from the Sentinel's beating, and to see how much strength was in his reserves.

All he could think of was what he had done. He wasn't alone in the lower levels; Asher was there too. Somewhere, trapped in a dark cell or strapped to a chair, he too panicked alone. And what of Ellie? Had he missed her among the constant stream of faces awaiting execution? Was she just another tally on an ever-growing list? Caden misjudged Yohanan's character. He couldn't keep Lil El alive! Elijah would be long gone, fleeing the country. Caden wouldn't see his Abba ever again. He had abandoned him. And Dasha. Sentinels guarded the perimeter of Luca's home. She would've been spotted. Were women prisoners given similar treatment down here, or was it worse?

With a groan, Caden tested his bonds, knowing full well they wouldn't budge. His breath raked through his throat. When was his last drink of water? What time was it? He usually was in bed right about now. Caden gritted his teeth, knowing this was no way to begin things. *I have to stay calm. I have to be at peace. But where is it? Where'd all the Peace go!*

The bag ripped from his face. Caden reeled back as brilliant light struck him. He blinked, squinting, seeing nothing. What was that? Water. He could hear water sloshing about. "I just wanted to make you my slave." Caden sucked in heavy breaths as his eyes darted around. "But not now." His hands fisted as he heaved against the leather straps. Again, they didn't move. "You've mocked me before the king." Caden closed his eyes as he forced himself to sit still. Each heartbeat thudded in his ears. Each breath shook him. "Now," the scraping sound of halting footsteps approached. A dark figure cut through the bright light. A tall man with a cane. Caden raised his chin and stared into nothing. "Now, I want you to curse the day you were born."

Caden didn't answer as his eyes slowly adjusted. Another figure stepped into the light, casting hefty shadows. He was carrying a pail and rag. Caden glanced between Grant and Buck. So, Luca had believed them. Who did he suspect Caden to be now, the rat or simply a con artist? Caden blinked the sweat from his eyes and focused on slowing his breathing.

Listen to their questions, he thought. *That'll tell you what they think.* Grant raised his cane. All Caden's thoughts halted. Grant shuffled forward and lay the weighted ball on Caden's chest. *Ask a question,* Caden internally demanded. *Ask me something!*

With a shove, Grant sent Caden's chair back. Caden braced for the fall, but found himself stopping at an angle, propped against a table or bench. Beneath him was a drain. Buck walked to one side, humming softly to himself, as Grant came to the other. Caden couldn't stop himself from squirming. The more he fought, the more he saw how trapped he was, and the more franticly he struggled.

Grant stared down and grinned in amusement. "Max?"

"Get away from me!"

"Answer me this."

"Don't touch me-"

"How long can you hold your breath?"

Caden shook his head as Buck dunked the rag into the pail of water. "What are you talking about? I thought you were into breaking bones."

"Oh," Grant sighed. "I do. Especially for you, Max-"

"My name is Alex!"

Grant chuckled. "Do not be hasty, Max. Your bones will shatter in time, yet we cannot leap to the climax. For now, I want to get to know you. The *real* you." He gently smoothed back Caden's hair from his eyes. Caden flinched away with a curse. "Who will we find after the screaming and writhing has stopped and you finally realize no one is listening to your pleas?"

With hissed curses, Caden looked up. Beyond his two tormentors, he saw a flag of the Sovereign Lion. It stared down at him with unwaveringly realistic eyes. Far too realistic. Caden blinked, realizing it was a Leovir watching from the railing of an upper level.

Benaiah. Their eyes met, the Leovir's clipped ear swiveling. Caden could only breathe, his mind blank, as panic sapped his strength. He was going to die under a *real* Sovereign Lion's Watch. The poetic irony was sickening. All thoughts cut short as Buck slapped the wet rag over Caden's mouth and nose. Caden gasped, only to feel water pouring down his throat.

The water filled his nose, and his mouth gaped, trying to gasp in air. All that met him was water. He tried to turn his head, but Buck held a fistful of his hair, making it impossible to move. Pain inflamed his throat and lungs. Panic took over. He didn't realize his body convulsed, violently straining against the leather straps that held him down.

Caden coughed, the water bubbling from beneath the rag as he lost precious air. There was nothing in his world at that moment but the agony and relentless water. He wanted to scream. He was dying. He could feel it. His eyes bulged as he stared up at the now blurry Leovir. His thrashing slowed as his chest heaved to no avail. Caden's limbs fell still. His eyes rolled back in his head. Everything plummeted into darkness.

IF YOU LIKE THIS, YOU MAY ALSO ENJOY:
REVELATIONS
BY TERRY JAMES

Tyce Greyson, a TV journalist and reporter, visits the Wailing Wall at the Temple Mount in Jerusalem. He is confronted by a Jewish cleric while he is photographing the area for a story he will be doing for a magazine. The Rabbi says to him: "Israel is the sign of the end." A blind writer in the genre of Bible prophecy is later interviewed for a book in his study by Greyson, who is a television reporter for a nearby TV station. The writer tells the story of the interview and the young reporter informs him that he is now interested in Bible prophecy. Greyson tells the writer he intends to go to Patmos in the Aegean to visit the cave of the Apocalypse where John was given the Revelation. Greyson is given a new job as an anchor for a local station in New York City. While doing broadcasts, Greyson has episodes, that bring on visions. While on air, he makes predictions that come true. He becomes well-known as excerpts of his "prophecies" go viral. Greyson must fulfill the destiny appointed to him as one who is of Jewish parents. The blind writer wraps up the story in a twist that confirms it is all part of human history's consummation. It is a story that both he and Tyce Greyson know must be told.

AVAILABLE NOW

ABOUT TERRY JAMES

Terry James is an author, general editor, and co-author of more than 40 books on Bible prophecy and geopolitics—hundreds of thousands of which have been sold worldwide. He has also written fiction and nonfiction books on a number of other topics. His most recent releases are *The Disappearing: Future Events That Will Rock the World* and *Lawless: End Times War Against the Spirit of Antichrist*, a compilation by top authors, speakers, and broadcasters on issues facing this generation. His most recently released novel, *Michael: Last Days Lightning*, achieved number one in Christian fiction on Amazon.

Terry is a frequent lecturer on the study of end-time phenomena and interviews often with national and international media on topics involving world issues and events as they might relate to Bible prophecy. He is partner with website founder Todd Strandberg and general editor of www.raptureready.com—rated the number one Bible prophecy website with more than 250,000 unique visitors and 3 million hits per month.

Terry speaks often at prophecy conferences and has appeared on national secular programs such as *The Nostradamus Effect*. He is a member of the Pre-Trib Research Center, founded by Dr. Tim LaHaye. Currently, he lives with his wife Margaret near Little Rock, Arkansas.

ABOUT HEATHER RENAE

Heather Renae's ministry is writing sci-fi and fantasy for Jesus. She's inspired by her walk with the Master and her mountainous home in Eastern Oregon. When she's not writing, she's hiking, enjoying friends and family, and chasing after her two kiddos—lovingly nicknamed her scallywags. To see what she's up to, follow her on Facebook at Heather Renae.